THE
DARK

SHARON BOLTON

ORION

An Orion paperback
First published in Great Britain in 2022 by Orion Fiction
an imprint of The Orion Publishing Group Ltd
Carmelite House, 50 Victoria Embankment
London EC4Y 0DZ

An Hachette UK Company

1 3 5 7 9 10 8 6 4 2

Copyright © Sharon Bolton 2022

A CIP catalogue record for this book is
available from the British Library.

ISBN (Mass Market Paperback) 978 1 4091 9836 9
ISBN (eBook) 978 1 4091 9837 6
ISBN (Audio) 978 1 4091 9851 2

Typeset by Input Data Services Ltd, Somerset

Printed and bound in Great Britain by Clays Ltd, Elcograf S.p.A.

For Belinda, who is my BFF, and for Simon, who was hers

A Letter to My Readers

Welcome, dear reader, and thank you for choosing *The Dark* from the millions of books on sale today. I'm honoured, not to mention pleased as punch.

As all good authors should, I write the sort of books that I love to read myself: tense and twisty tales of dark deeds, peopled by characters who are compelling but deeply flawed; stories full of passion and intrigue, when lives are frequently on the line and the narrative flows at breakneck pace. I write in the Gothic tradition that I love, packing my books with chills, thrills and tons of creepy atmosphere.

Given this, you might imagine I live alone in a ruined Scottish castle, scribbling through the night in candlelit rooms, wandering the windswept hills by day in pursuit of the muse.

Nothing so glam, I'm afraid. In reality, I'm a middle-aged mum in the home counties (although the famous *Midsomer Murders* is filmed in our village, so there may be something in the water after all), I live with my lurcher dog Lupe, my husband, and, occasionally, our university-aged son. My passions, apart from family and stories, are wild swimming and sailing, and I enjoy nothing more than a cosy dinner with friends and lashings of cold white wine.

If you're new to the Lacey Flint stories, I hope you love her as much as I do, and if you'd like to stay in touch in-between books then please sign up to my newsletter, or find me on Facebook, Twitter and Instagram.

www.sharonbolton.com
🐦 : @Author.SJBolton

📘 : @SharonJBoltonCrime

📷 : @sharonjbolton

And now, it's time. Take a deep breath, tread carefully, but most of all, enjoy your walk on the dark side.

Prologue

A few hours after midnight, two young women sat in a car close to the edge of a cliff; one of them was dead, the other merely felt that way. The spot they'd arrived at, leaving the road to drive the final yards over rough heathland, was the highest of Britain's chalk cliffs. It was also one of the most notorious suicide spots in the world, with cautious estimates giving it responsibility for a little short of five hundred deaths since the early 1960s.

The woman whose heart was, technically, still beating, wondered if two more might be enough to make the nice, round half-millennial. She switched off the ignition, let the sounds of the engine cooling fade into the night, and opened the door to say goodbye to the world.

Held tight by her seatbelt, her companion's eyes were closed, but as air flooded into the car, her hair blew across her face, giving it, for a second, the illusion of life continuing.

A cruel trick. The woman clinging to life – for a few minutes more – closed the car door and saw, with relief, the interior slip into darkness. Driving the eighty miles from south London, with nothing but her own thoughts and the recriminations of a corpse beside her, had been harder than she'd expected. Leaving the car, she stepped towards the black void that she knew was the cliff edge.

The night was cool for September, a light breeze blowing in from the west. Coming almost directly from the Isle of Wight, it brought with it hints of the previous day's fish catch, early autumn fires, ripe fruit falling from overladen trees. Then again, she'd always had an active imagination; the smell might be nothing more than the salt stench of the beach, a hundred and sixty metres below.

It would be a grim beach. It had embraced too many broken and battered bodies, absorbed too much blood of the dying, to be anything other. It was too late now, far too late, but there had to be better, sweeter places to die.

As the young woman's eyes grew used to the darkness, she could see the silver-white line of the chalk cliffs stretching west, and the flicker of the lighthouse in the bay. The moon was a little over half full, misshapen, oddly unsatisfying in its incompleteness, but bright as a polished coin, gently illuminating the clouds. The stars were tiny, flickering, like fairy lights about to run out of battery, the ocean endless blackness, a vast solid sheen that gleamed as though its dark light were coming from its depths. It was a silent ocean, robbed of voice; the waves neither crashing nor grumbling, let alone thundering, against rocks.

The pain of too much loss weighed the young woman down as she approached the cliff edge, expanding in her chest like rising dough, filling all the available space, so that even breathing was becoming hard. At the same time, the wind stung her eyes, forcing tears she'd been unable to shed until now. Tears were for bearable pain, for lighter sorrows; this pain couldn't possibly be released by tiny drops of water. It would burst forth when it came, exploding her skin, flesh and bones apart like shrapnel. It would get some help, of course, from the rocks below.

At least then, it would end.

When the figure emerged from the darkness, she thought her dead friend, grown impatient, had summoned the unnatural strength to walk herself to her grave. Her cry of alarm broke upon the wind.

Not her friend, a stranger, but one drawn with the same grim purpose.

'You can't stop me.' The boy was tense, quivering, like a runner on the brink of the race of his life. He, too, was feet from the edge. Were he to sprint forward, the momentum would take him over.

'OK,' she said.

He was about her age, late teens, although it was hard to tell in the meagre light. Shorter than she, he was thin at the shoulder, thicker around the waist, and he was panting, as though the walk here – there had been no other vehicles in the car park – had been hard work. Or maybe he'd been crying; his face was blotchy, streaked with mud in the half light. He must have been sitting close to the edge, half hidden among the grass, must have jumped to his feet at her approach.

'It's my choice,' he said, still poised to sprint. 'My life.'

'Fair enough.'

His clothes, damp from recent rain, smelled fresh and looked clean. They were newish, his trainers weren't cheap, and his dark hair had been well cut, not too long ago.

'You're one of them, aren't you?' He looked frantically around, as though others – her fictional co-conspirators – might be sneaking up on him. 'The people who try to stop us.'

She sighed. 'I'm not going to stop you.'

'This forum I'm in, it warned me there'd be people like you. It said to come between two and six in the morning, that I'd be least likely to come across someone then.'

His breath was ragged, his voice catching. She felt a moment of deep annoyance, that her final moments weren't to be peaceful;

that her thoughts would be dragged from her by this needy teen-ager who probably hadn't faced a real trouble in his short, spoiled life.

But that was unkind, and she didn't want to be unkind, not in the last minutes of her life.

'Your mate, in the car.' He was pointing back, as though she might have forgotten where it was. 'Is she phoning this in? Is she calling for, what do you call it, backup?'

The laugh, short and bitter though it was, surprised her; laughing felt like something she'd closed a final door upon. She said, 'I doubt it.'

He took a step closer to the cliff. 'Don't come near me,' he called, shrill as a startled old lady.

'Not planning to.'

She didn't want to be unkind, but this was getting tiresome, and besides, sooner or later, someone else would come along: a patrol car, the Samaritans, an insomniac do-gooder. She didn't have forever.

'It's a big clifftop. I won't get in your way if you don't get in mine.'

Stepping closer to the edge she looked down. She'd never been afraid of heights, but a wave of nausea swept over her; for a moment, it seemed that the ground beneath her feet was moving. Chalk was far from stable, its cliffs crumbled all the time. She bounced; nothing gave, and she felt a stab of disappointment. How much easier it would have been, to have the moment taken from her.

'You serious?' the boy said.

Possibly more than he. She wondered how long he'd been here, pondering his woes, kidding himself he was going to jump.

'You're not from the, what do you call it, the coastguard, or those Samaritan people?'

'I'm here to go over the edge, same as you.'

'You're lying, it's a trick, some reverse psychology bollocks. Make me think you don't care, so that I start to.'

'Is it working?'

'No!'

'Damn,' she muttered. 'I'm losing my touch.'

Silence, then, 'I'm Nick.'

He sounded, hesitant, unsure of his own name. She said, 'I didn't ask.'

'I left a note, for my mum and dad.'

'I'm sure that will make all the difference.'

A moment of just wind and, yes, now she could hear the waves below.

'Are you for real?' he said. 'You're actually going to jump?'

'Technically, I'm going to drive. Put my foot down and soar into oblivion, like Thelma and Louise over the Grand Canyon.'

'What?' he'd missed the pop culture reference.

'Doesn't matter. So long, Nick. Have a good death.'

'Wait!' He called out to her before she'd walked half the distance to the car. She turned and knew that that, in itself, should be telling her something: she could still be called back.

'It will be instant, won't it? Death, I mean. I won't know anything about it?'

Sighing, she joined him once more on the cliff edge.

'Instant deaths aren't that common,' she said. 'Decapitation will probably do it. An explosion, maybe. Otherwise, it takes time for the body to shut down. So no, it won't be instant. Quick, but not instant.'

'How quick?'

She pretended to think about it, although she'd thought of little else on the drive down here. 'Seconds, if you're lucky. Your bones will break on the rocks. Parts of your skull will go into your brain and there'll be no coming back from that, a couple of your rib bones might go into your heart, and it'll bleed out. Your lungs might get ripped apart too, again by your own bones, making it impossible to breath.'

She saw him shudder.

'If you're not lucky, your essential organs won't be too badly damaged. You'll be stuck on the beach for hours, probably paralysed, in a shed load of pain, waiting to bleed out, or for your heart to give up. Still, what do I know? It's not like I've done this before.'

'You are one of them, them councillor types. You're trying to frighten me out of it.'

Enough. She took a half step towards him. 'Do you want a push?'

His eyes opened wide in alarm. 'What?'

'I'll push you, if you want. Say the word.'

He backed away, hands warding her off. 'Stay away from me.'

'Your call.' She needed to get to the car, to get it over with, but something held her back.

'The impact won't be the worst,' she said. 'The worst will be the moment you jump, when you're in free fall. You'll regret it then, will give anything to be back up on solid ground, even with all the pain you're going through, but it will be too late.'

'If you think that, why are you doing it?' he glanced back at the car. 'Is it some sort of suicide pact, you and that other girl?'

A fresh wave of pain. 'She's already dead. She died a few hours ago. Drug overdose.'

'Was she, what, your girlfriend?'

'No. Just the only friend I had left.'

'I'm sorry.'

He looked it too. 'Thank you.'

Seconds ticked by.

'So, why are you here?' the young woman asked.

He didn't reply.

'Girlfriend break up with you?'

'I've never had a girlfriend.' His voice was ugly with resentment. 'Girls don't date guys who look like me.'

Curious, in spite of herself, she took another look at him, really looking this time. He was short, and the weight around his girth would sit better on his shoulders and upper arms, but there was nothing a decent diet and a few months of exercise wouldn't put right. His nose was a little hooked and his eyes rather deep set, giving him a hawklike look, but his hair was a glossy dark brown and his lips full and well-shaped. His worst feature was bad acne, covering the lower part of his face, and breaking out on his cheeks and forehead, but time and the right medication would sort that out. No scars, no disfiguring birthmarks. She opened her mouth to utter some platitude about his looks and decided she couldn't be bothered.

'Would you?' he asked, reluctant to let it go.

'You hitting on me?'

'Girls who look like you aren't interested in boys like me,' he went on. 'Even the ugly girls go after the good-looking ones. Guys like me don't stand a chance.'

He wanted her to argue, to tell him he was wrong, that plenty of girls would find him attractive. Half of her wanted to, if only so he would leave her in peace, but she was so very weary. More than anything, she wanted to sleep. The problem with sleep, though, was that it always came to an end. When you slept, you woke. From the kind of sleep she had in mind there was no waking up.

'You wouldn't, would you? You wouldn't go out with me?'

'No,' she said truthfully. 'Do you want to come with us?'

'What?'

'I'm getting in the car now. I'm going to drive over the edge. I don't think you'll ever have the courage to do it by yourself, but if you get in the back seat I'll take you with us.'

She was on her way back to the car and this time, she wasn't stopping. She called over her shoulder. 'Last chance. Just don't get in our way, because I won't stop.'

'I'm coming.' He caught up as she reached the car.

'Sure?' she said.

He looked on the verge of being sick, but he nodded.

She opened the car door. 'That side,' she told him. 'I don't want you grabbing hold of me when we go over.'

'Nice car,' he said, as he got in behind the front passenger seat.

'Stolen.'

She locked the doors and turned on the engine; tested the accelerator, although she already knew the car drove perfectly. Her hand was on the brake, ready to release it.

'Shit!' He'd touched the woman in the front passenger seat. 'She's really dead. This is sick. She's actually dead.'

'You thought I was lying to you?'

He was pulling at the car door, unable to deactivate the child lock in the back seats. 'I thought it was a trick, that the two of you were part of that coastguard service, that you'd drive me back down to Eastbourne.'

'Bad call.' Releasing the handbrake she held the car on the clutch. A fraction of movement in her left foot and it would shoot forward. She'd already seen that the ground ahead sloped down.

'Let me out!'

Oh, for God's sake.

He started banging on the car window, screaming. 'Help, let me out! Help!'

Well, she wasn't going to die with that racket going on. Besides, any second now, he'd realise he could wrap his hands around her throat and they'd be going nowhere.

She released the door lock. In a split second the boy was out of the car, running towards the cliff path. She watched until he vanished, until all, once more, was silent and still on the clifftop.

'Where were we?' she asked her dead companion.

The woman beside her had no answer to give.

'Ready to face the enemy?'

Still no answer; and so she sat, waiting for the pain to wash over her again, to give her the reason she needed to press one foot down and lift the other.

It didn't come.

She thought about the boy, racing back towards Eastbourne, cursing his bad luck at running into a psycho seconds before he ended everything. She'd saved a life tonight.

Damn it, it felt good.

'I wish I could have saved you,' she said to the woman beside her.

'How about I save you instead?' replied her dead friend.

And then, for no reason she could think of, she turned to the back seat, where the boy had been sitting minutes earlier. On the pale grey leather lay the bundle of documents she'd brought from the south London squat where the two of them had been living. No passports or driving licences, neither girl had ever applied for either; no birth certificates, because they'd been lost in officialdom years earlier. A card with a national insurance number, a library ticket, a student ID card. Very little to show for two teenage lives. One of which was most definitely over.

The question was: which one?

Entirely unexpectedly, from complete despair, a chance had arisen, and facing her now the possibility of a new start. A leaving behind of the pain and the loss and the hopelessness. She would be a fool not to take it.

She had never been a fool.

Switching off the engine, she acted quickly, removing from the car any paperwork that might identify its last occupants and wiping clean the steering wheel and all the internal surfaces she could reach. Releasing her friend's seat belt, she slid her hands beneath the dead woman's body and pulled her across the middle of the car and into the driver's seat. Then she put the car into neutral and released the handbrake. For a second it didn't move, and so she gripped the edge of the open window, braced her feet against the rocky ground and pushed.

Movement.

She pushed again and the car rolled forward. With one last look at her dead friend, she ran round to the back of the vehicle where she could put more muscle into the task. She pushed hard, the bumpy ground giving her feet purchase. The car picked up speed, veered a little to the left, and found a steeper slope. It rolled on, and she no longer needed to push.

She stood back and watched as the car gathered pace, until the front tyres reached the edge. For a split second it paused, and she thought perhaps it wouldn't work, but then the front of the vehicle dipped, a scraping of metal over rock pierced the silence, and the car upended, presenting its undercarriage to the night. A second later it was gone.

It seemed to take a very long time before the crash sounded. She didn't look; she had no need to see the devastation below. Instead, she left the heathland and began the long walk back to London.

After a year or so, she applied, successfully, to join the Metropolitan Police.

Part One

1

Twelve years later, more or less to the day

Since she'd joined the Metropolitan Police's marine unit, constable (soon-to-be-sergeant, fingers crossed) Lacey Flint had grown used to being surprised by the river. Huge and magnificent, at times both heartbreakingly beautiful and quietly terrifying, it had become a constant presence in her life. The smell of it never left her, nor did the sound. Its endless beat formed the rhythm of her life now; she lived on it, worked on it, played on it. She loved it with a passion shown to very few things in her life, and practically no people. Almost none. There was one, far away, whom she always had loved and always would, and another. *The other.*

But the Thames, though, the Thames was like home, nurturing, comforting, safe; at the same time a wild country of infinite adventures.

She knew it would never be her friend. No one with a brain took the Thames for granted, especially the stretch that flowed through London, the tidal part, the dangerous part. In little over a year with the marine unit, Lacey Flint had found dead women wrapped in shrouds and half-drowned living ones, fleeing dangers unspeakable in far-off lands. She'd found Iron-Age weapons, bones of prehistoric animals and messages in bottles that turned out to be suicide notes. She'd fished out smugglers' hoards and drunken pirates celebrating stag parties. She'd even encountered a mermaid.

She felt, at times, as though she'd seen everything the river could throw at her; and so the inflatable unicorn, lying grubby and forlorn on the foreshore, didn't alarm her. It should have done, but even Lacey Flint could make the wrong call on occasion.

September: the best time of year, full of golden light and silvery mist, when the river calms for a while, as most of the troublesome tourists go home and the drinkers perch less frequently on its walls. Lacey loved September; after all she'd been born in the month. Well, sort of.

She'd left her home, a vintage sailing yacht moored permanently in Deptford Creek, a little over forty minutes ago on her way, not to work, because her shift wasn't due to start till afternoon, but to a social event. For the longest time, Lacey Flint had eschewed friends, because friends had a habit of being curious, asking questions, unearthing secrets that should never see the light of day. But she'd learned, occasionally to her cost, more often to her benefit, that no matter how well you hid yourself from life, life – pesky business that it was – had a way of tracking you down. And so now she had friends, and two of them had arranged to meet her, for a late breakfast, at a sweet little place (their words, not hers) off Tower Bridge. It wouldn't usually take forty minutes to get from Deptford Creek to Tower Bridge, even with London traffic, but Lacey Flint was travelling by river.

Of course she was.

Her white, one-woman kayak flew across the water, even with a strong tide against her. Heading out for nearly three hours now the river was reaching peak flow, something around four knots, taking everything without sufficient power out with it, to the estuary, and ultimately the North Sea.

She kept close to the north bank, because keeping right, or starboard, was a Port of London Authority rule, and staying in the shallows kept her out of the fiercer reaches of the tidal flow. The dredgers, barges and catamarans in the central channel couldn't be relied upon to spot a lonely kayak, or to avoid it if they did see it; it really was better to keep to the edges when out on the river.

Lacey knew the river well, and since moving to Deptford Creek, she'd become exceptionally strong, kayaking most days, even swimming, although swimming in the tidal Thames was a by-law offence and, according to her boss, Superintendent David Cook, punishable by immediate dismissal if she was caught doing it again, and he meant it this time, Lacey. Going back, after breakfast, would be a doddle. The tide would be on her side and she'd zip along, using the paddle only for steerage.

Five minutes before the time she'd arranged to meet her friends, she approached St Katharine Docks. A stone's throw up-river, Tower Bridge soared high and pretentious in its Victorian grandeur, and there seemed to be two people among the numerous pedestrians on it who were watching her.

Actually, there were three, but she only saw two.

One of the two, the taller, waved and Lacey risked missing a stroke to waddle the paddle back. The smaller, darker-haired woman kept her arms wrapped around her chest; a chest that seemed bigger, lumpier than usual.

But then Lacey's attention was dragged from her friends by something incongruous near the pier ahead. A pool inflatable sat on the narrow strip of foreshore between the river wall and the water. The kind of floating toy that children played with in swimming pools, it was white, with rainbow markings, about a metre and a half tall at its head by about the same distance long and, at the very back of her mind she heard the faintest whisper: that a pool inflatable had no business on one of the most dangerous rivers in the world.

2

Helen spotted Lacey first, naturally, because Helen had never lost
her police officer's instinct to look around at all times, take stock,
spot the trouble, before the trouble itself even knew it was brewing. Dana had been able to do that once.

Crossing the bridge made Dana nervous these days, because
what if it started moving while she was still trying to make her
way to the other side and she couldn't get off? It had never happened to her knowledge, not in over a hundred years, but still.

Helen, oblivious to the possibility of a bridge-related disaster,
was looking downriver.

'The woman's nuts,' Helen said, meaning Lacey of course,
in a white boat that looked as though a determined wash might
overturn it.

Dana didn't argue. She'd concluded some time back that Lacey
Flint was nuts. Since the night they'd met, almost exactly two
years ago, when Lacey, covered in a dying woman's blood, had
shown remarkable presence of mind at an especially gruesome
crime scene, Dana had lost count of the number of times she'd
been horrified by the younger woman's recklessness. On the
other hand, she was one of the bravest people Dana knew, and
her instincts verged on brilliant.

Inigo squirmed against Dana's chest and her hand went automatically to his head to soothe him. She loved carrying him in the

papoose, strapped snugly against her body; it was the closest she could get to having him safely back inside her again, where no one could touch him, or hurt him, or take him from her.

Dana hadn't told anyone, not even Helen, that she'd never really known fear until her son was born, but that now it consumed her life: fear of an unusual cry or whimper, fear of too long a stillness in the night, of a temperature, a rash, of taking her eyes off him for the split second it took for him to vanish. The only time she felt safe was when the three of them were tucked up in the bedroom, Inigo in the crib by her side of the bed, and no, he might be nearly six months old, but he wasn't ready for his own room yet. Dana's world had become full of fear and yet, in a matter of days, she'd be leaving him, for hours at a time, in the Southwark nursery they'd just visited on the south bank, so that she could return to work.

Dana Tulloch was a detective inspector with the Metropolitan Police; or at least, she had been, until she became a mother.

She felt relief flooding through her as they left the bridge and walked the short distance to their rendezvous point. The café, also a busy delicatessen, was Sicilian, and the owner, who didn't normally allow tables to be reserved, always made an exception in the case of two senior police officers. Busy packing truffle oil and dried mushrooms into a paper bag for a waiting customer, he greeted Dana and Helen with a tight-lipped smile and indicated a table by the far wall.

Back aching, Dana released Inigo from the papoose, sitting him on her lap. Her arms would remain pinned to her side for the remainder of their visit to stop him tumbling, but Ini was an active, impatient baby, who hated being still, even worse, restrained.

'Here she comes,' said Helen and Dana turned to see a slim, fair-haired young woman in sports clothes in the street outside.

It was the first time the two of them had seen Lacey since June, when she'd been co-opted, by their mutual friend, Mark Joesbury, into a tricky undercover operation in the North West. Technically, the op had been a success, and some very dangerous men were awaiting trial. On the other hand, a young woman had died. No decent officer got over something like that easily; Mark hadn't and it was unlikely Lacey had either.

The doorbell sounded, and Lacey pulled her face into a smile that, to Dana's eyes, looked forced. She'd certainly taken some persuading to meet them this morning.

'Good lord, he's huge.' Lacey's eyes stayed on the baby as she kissed Helen and smiled at Dana. 'How was the nursery?'

'At least two degrees too warm, and they need some soft furnishings to soak up the noise,' Dana replied. 'There are big kids running around near the babies' cots and I'm not convinced the food they serve is as organic as they claim.'

'Absolutely fine,' Helen said. 'Lovely staff and very happy kids. It's the best rated in south London and he starts on Monday morning. Looking forward to it, aren't you Rug-Rat?'

Helen pulled a freakishly distorted face at Inigo, who squealed and flapped his hands in the air.

'Babies need social interaction,' Helen added. 'So do their mothers. Failing that, they need to get back to work.'

'He's so happy,' Lacey was still smiling at Inigo. 'I don't think I've heard him cry yet.'

'That's because Dana never puts him down,' Helen said. 'Ask her if you can hold him. Go on, give it a try. She'll find some excuse not to let you.'

'Of course, Lacey can hold Ini,' Dana snapped. 'But she's just kayaked from Deptford and she probably wants to get her breath back.'

Lacey took her seat.

'Feels like ages,' Helen began. 'We haven't seen you since you got back from Cumbria.'

Let it never be said that Helen didn't tackle difficult subjects head on.

'Glad to be back on the river?' Helen pressed on. 'Or has Cumbria changed your mind about staying in uniform?'

Eighteen months ago, on the brink of leaving the police for good, Lacey had requested redeployment, a move normally forced upon officers who'd fallen from favour. Lacey, on the contrary, had turned her back on a promising career in CID and returned to uniform service as part of the marine unit.

'There's a lot to be said for the quiet life.' Lacey smiled, to show she was half joking. The Thames was one of the busiest urban waterways in the world, a well-used route for both people and drug smuggling. And it had a high body count.

'Dana has something to ask you,' Helen said.

Damn it. She'd wanted to wait.

'What?' Lacey looked curious, just a tiny bit wary.

She'd planned to sound out how Lacey was feeling, maybe even put the conversation off for another day.

'You know Neil's been acting DI while I've been on maternity leave?' Dana began.

Neil Anderson was Dana's deputy in Lewisham's Major Incident Team, an officer Lacey had worked with several times.

'His promotion is likely to be confirmed in the next few weeks and he'll soon move on,' Dana continued. 'The team will be rejigged and there'll be a vacancy. I've sounded out the powers that be, and if you were interested in moving back to CID, your application would be looked on favourably.'

Lacey's eyes were clouding over. Well, she couldn't say she hadn't been warned. Helen, Mark, even Dave Cook, Lacey's boss at the marine unit, had all told her that Lacey was fine where she was, thank you very much. Intent on protecting a young woman they all cared about, they'd argued that Lacey had been involved in too many dangerous and difficult cases, had faced more death and darkness in her fledgling career than most coppers saw their entire service.

Dana couldn't argue, but the waste of talent drove her nuts. Lacey had the makings of a great detective.

'I can think about it,' Lacey said, her eyes on the table. 'Thank you.'

Ignoring the told-you-so look on Helen's face, Dana said, 'There was one thing, though—'

The food arrived before Dana could finish. Oatmeal with berries for her, a croissant for Lacey, and an extravagant plate of poached eggs, hollandaise sauce and pancetta on ciabatta bread for Helen, who never seemed to gain an ounce, no matter what she ate. Inigo, who'd been showing an interest in real food recently, reached for his mother's bowl. Propping him on one arm, Dana tried it. Far too hot, and probably salted. She'd palm him off with a raspberry.

'Dating anyone?' Helen asked Lacey, which was another topic best avoided in Dana's mind. Lacey's *on-off, will-they-won't-they* relationship with Mark Joesbury seemed to have stalled completely.

'What about that colleague of yours, you know the one who climbs like a monkey. What do they call him? Batman?'

Mark was keeping tight-lipped about it too. That said, Mark was avoiding Dana and Helen almost as much as Lacey had been, probably trying to avoid exactly these questions.

'Spider-Man,' Lacey answered. 'AKA Finn Turner. And no, he's too much of a player for my taste.'

'Seen anything of the new boss of SCD10?'

Helen meant Mark, recently promoted on the back of the Cumbria case. Honestly, did the woman know the meaning of the word 'tact'?

Out on the foreshore, fewer than two hundred metres away, a man was blowing more air into the plastic pool inflatable.

3

'There was something you wanted to ask me,' Lacey reminded Dana, as they got up to leave.

Bill paid, baby paraphernalia gathered into Helen's backpack, Inigo safely in his papoose, the three women said their goodbyes to the café owner and stepped out onto the embankment. The day had grown brighter, clouds clearing to leave a cornflower blue sky, but a fresher breeze was coming off the water.

'We can do it some other time,' Dana replied. The others had been right, Lacey wasn't ready for a return to CID. Her refusal to talk about Cumbria, her evasive replies when questioned about Mark, her reluctance to talk about herself on any level, all led to the same conclusion: Lacey wasn't ready.

'No, you can't,' Helen argued. 'Get it over with, or this will drag on.'

Dana gave a very audible sigh. 'It's just – people really are very keen to get you back into CID, Lacey, they know what an asset you'd be, but . . .'

Damn Helen, this really wasn't the time.

'. . . there is some – I won't say concern exactly, just a bit of – well, you could call it disquiet – and the extent to which you can put minds at rest – it could smooth things over very helpfully.'

Helen breathed out loudly through her nose.

'Spit it out,' Lacey said, her face a picture of patient amusement.

'Questions are being asked about your monthly visits to Durham prison,' Dana said in a rush. 'I understand you and Victoria Llewelyn have a history, and everyone knows you were instrumental in her arrest, and there's no question that you've acted improperly at any time, the hearing made that clear. It's just . . .'

'It doesn't look good.' Lacey's face had closed down. Not meeting Dana's eyes, she pulled out her phone. 'Look, I've got to go. I'm going to miss the tide. Let's do this some other time. Good to see you both.'

And that was that. A quick kiss on both their cheeks, a lingering one on the top of Inigo's head, and Lacey had left them, striding off towards Tower Bridge Quay.

'Told you so,' said Helen.

4

Out of sight of Dana and Helen, Lacey allowed her footsteps to slow. She'd always known this would happen; she'd been lucky, in a way, not to have faced it before now. Her regular visits to one of the most notorious serial killers the UK had ever known had been bound, sooner or later, to become an issue.

More questions would come, Lacey knew, from people who were not her friends, until her situation became abundantly clear. Either she ceased her monthly visits to Durham prison, or she waved goodbye to any chance of promotion. Even her job might be at stake.

A passenger ferry was pulling away from the pier, creating a sparkling silver fan in its wake, as Lacey made her way towards the water. Ahead on the ramp, two gulls fought over the remains of a mitten crab, and a gold foil balloon, wishing someone a happy 21st birthday, struggled to be free from where it had snagged on the bridge. Lacey, lost in thought, saw none of it.

Nearly two years after her arrest, few long-term prisoners attracted a fraction of the public and media interest as did the woman known to the world as Victoria Llewellyn. Partly, her notoriety could be explained by the fact that she was young and beautiful; equally by the considerable public sympathy her case had generated.

Because, aged just sixteen, Victoria and her fourteen-year-old sister Cathy had been gang-raped in a Cardiff park by five English public school boys. The boys' parents had thrown all their wealth and influence at the allegation, ensuring no charges were ever brought.

The lives of the two sisters – dysfunctional to begin with – had fallen apart. The story the world believed was that the younger, Cathy, had gone completely off the rails – running away from home, living rough on the streets of London, only to meet a tragic death in a riverboat accident some years later. Then, learning of her sister's death, Victoria had embarked on a brutal plan of revenge. Determined to destroy the boys who'd raped her, to ruin their lives as her own had been, she'd focused her fury on their mothers. One by one, horribly and publicly, she'd abducted and murdered the four middle-aged women. With every intention of claiming one last victim, she'd been tracked down and arrested – by Lacey.

The world – or at least the part of it that was the Metropolitan police – believed that Lacey Flint and Victoria Llewellyn were old friends, that they'd met and grown close when Victoria had been searching for her sister, and when Lacey too had been living on the streets. They believed that a long-standing loyalty drove her monthly visits to Durham.

What the world believed wasn't true, of course; the real truth was a secret that could never see the light of day. Lacey could never tell the world who the woman in Durham prison really was; any more than she could cut her out of her life.

It was lucky, then, that she had no intention of returning to CID, that she could cheerfully live out her days with the Met being nothing more than a humble river constable. She could even leave the police if she had to. Because the woman known – mistakenly – to the world as Victoria Llewellyn was as essential to Lacey as breathing.

5

'OK,' Helen said in that drawn-out, nervous tone people use when what they really mean is that something is very far from OK.

The two women were a third of the way up Tower Bridge steps and, for some reason, Helen had glanced down, possibly to watch Lacey paddle away.

'What?' Instinctively, Dana's hands wrapped around Inigo's papoose.

Helen didn't reply, and so Dana followed her line of sight. Down on the embankment two people pushing prams, a man and a woman, had stopped to chat. And two other men, with scarves around their faces, were approaching them fast. As they reached the woman's pram, and one of them leaned into it, Helen started to run back down the steps.

From her vantage point Dana watched, in horror, as one man scooped the woman's baby – a girl, dressed in pink – out of her pram and ran with her towards Tower Bridge Quay.

A baby was being abducted right before their eyes.

Reaching the bottom of the steps Helen set off at a sprint, but the second man had followed the first and both of them were thundering down the pier's access ramp. Passers-by who'd witnessed the incident were yelling, one set off after the two men. The mother began to scream. The man she'd been chatting with, who also had a pram, started yelling that they needed help, could they get some help, and was anyone calling the police.

Dana could think of nothing but the child in her arms. Keeping him safe, that was her job now. Her only job.

'Dana!' Helen was yelling back at her. 'Call it in!'

As Helen disappeared down the ramp, Dana struggled to get her phone from her pocket. All the numbers she'd carried in her head for years – she'd always had such a good memory for numbers – had deserted her, so she pressed the nine key three times and hoped it still worked.

The bereft mother, hysterical now, was leaning over the embankment wall, screaming at the people below; people Dana couldn't see, but who must include the two abductors, several innocent bystanders, Helen who'd run straight into danger without thinking because that's what she did, and Lacey Flint, of course, who'd be down on the foreshore by now, and who attracted trouble like purple flowers drew the bees.

Dana's emergency call was answered and she found the words she needed.

'Abduction in process on the north embankment, a few yards south of Tower Bridge. Young infant snatched from its mother. Heading down Tower Bridge Quay to the river. Urgent assistance needed.'

She could speak, but she couldn't move. In the old days she'd have been right behind Helen.

'Dana Tulloch, detective inspector with Lewisham MIT, off duty.'

Picking up on her distress Inigo started to whimper.

'Two males, white I think, faces covered. They must still be on the pier, unless they've got onto the water somehow. I can't quite see.'

If she got closer, she'd have a better view.

'You need to alert the marine unit; they must be planning to escape via the river.'

Still, she felt herself frozen on the spot, not knowing whether to stay put, where she and her baby were safe, or get into the thick of it, secure the scene, comfort the howling mother, do her job?

And then the decision was taken from her, because the other male in the grim tableau, the dad who'd been left behind, lifted his own pram and hurled it over the embankment wall. It vanished, plummeting to the river far below.

6

Detective Chief Inspector Mark Joesbury was at his desk, which always put him in a bad mood. Regularly and frequently he told himself he'd been promoted to the level of his incompetence and so dark was his mood these days that he genuinely believed it. In his younger days, in junior roles, he'd excelled. In uniform he'd found a rapport with the communities he policed that brought an inflow of information most coppers could only dream of. Promoted rapidly to detective his solve rate had been unparalleled, and his potential for undercover work spotted. As a covert operative in the Met's SCD10 his unconventional approach had brought him to the brink of dismissal more than once, but he'd always got the job done. He'd led some of the most dangerous and high-profile operations in the country, culminating in saving the lives of the family of the president of the United States. His bosses had tried to move him then, arguing that he was on the verge of having a public profile, the kiss of death to an undercover operator, but he'd argued for one last job. One last job, in which he'd nearly lost the woman he loved (not for the first time) and had killed a man. For the first time.

And that was that. A desk job for DCI Joesbury. From now on, he'd be the one planning the ops, sending the Young Turks into the field, putting other men and women at risk. From now on, all the blood would be on his hands, because the buck stopped with him.

And he really wasn't very good at it.

'Sir.'

One of his new team was leaning into his office. A graduate of Cambridge University's computer science programme, a specialist in online finance and fraud, twenty-eight-year-old Theo Cox had worked in the city for a while, before joining the Met as a civilian consultant. His first job, after training, had been an assignment to Joesbury's team.

Theo dressed well for a copper, and Joesbury had a feeling his suit that morning was a silk mix, if not pure silk, and almost certainly made to measure. He invariably wore shirts and ties in bright shades of blue or lilac to bring out the colour of his long, deep-set eyes. His hair was Scandinavian blond, perfectly cut.

Grateful for the interruption, Joesbury closed the report he'd been scanning. 'Theo, what can I do for you?'

With the unshakeable self-confidence of the public school, top university background, Theo was already in the room. 'You said we had to let you know immediately if anything out of the ordinary happened around Tower Bridge?'

Theo was monitoring 'noise', online activity in and around the capital, watching for the errant flow, the tic, the beginning of a pattern, anything that might indicate a problem brewing.

'What've you got?'

The boy's hands were empty; it was like this lot had never heard of paperwork. 'Came in seconds ago. The system flagged it up. I've sent it to you.'

Joesbury opened his inbox. A few lines of text, an internet alert.

Theo barely gave him a chance to take it in. 'Abduction of an infant on the embankment south of Tower Bridge. Off-duty police officer in attendance. Uniform on their way.'

'Dana,' Joesbury said, seeing the name of his best friend and godmother to his son on the screen. He glanced up. 'It's ongoing?'

Theo gave a sharp, excited nod. 'Looks that way.'

Tower Bridge was a little over a mile down the embankment from Scotland Yard.

Joesbury was on his feet. 'Get your coat.'

7

The Thames has an impressive tidal reach, boasting a range of up to seven metres between some high and low tides. While not remarkable in absolute terms (the Severn, with fifteen metres, might sneer) seven metres means a river that runs high against the embankment walls at the start of the day can reveal sizeable areas of foreshore six hours later.

When Lacey Flint got back to Tower Bridge Quay on that mid-September morning, the tide had been going out for three hours and a narrow strip of grey beach had appeared, spattered with dirty rocks and damp rubbish. The river wall, festooned with ancient mooring chains, stretched fifteen metres high, its upper parts a dirt-blackened stone, its lower reaches dripping with emerald weed.

Lacey made for the inside of the pier where she'd left her kayak. The pier owners were relaxed about her mooring up. Most people who work on the river prefer to stay on the right side of the marine unit and Lacey, in her time with the division, had become popular with the law-abiding members of the river community. Less so with the less than.

The pool inflatable she'd noticed earlier was still there, a few yards further down the foreshore, held now on a thin stretch of rope by a man in dark running clothes. Lacey's first instinct was relief that it wasn't in the hands of kids, a feeling that lasted less than a second.

She'd barely settled herself in the kayak when a commotion broke out on the embankment above her head. Screams rang through the routine hum of London and a woman – Lacey thought she recognised Helen's voice – was shouting. A car horn sounded. Footsteps running. The suspended walkway that led from embankment to pier, designed for careful slow passage, began to bounce and judder as heavy footsteps ran down it. Two men were heading her way.

Responding instinctively, Lacey scrambled out of the kayak and pulled out her phone as the first runner, his face half covered by a scarf, made eye contact and checked his speed. Light eyes. A white male. Young, thin. Clutching something to his chest.

A third man appeared on the walkway, older, dark-skinned, in workman's clothes, giving chase.

'Stop them!' he yelled as he set off down.

The first two men picked up speed, then Helen, too, appeared. The first man reached the pier and, for the love of God, that was a baby in his arms. He leaped over the pier's railing, landed on the foreshore and raced past her.

'Lacey, it's a baby!' yelled Helen, unnecessarily. The baby, aware on some level that its safe, orderly world had been turned upside down, was yelling its head off.

Lacey gave chase, knowing her chances were slim. She had neither uniform nor warrant card, no radio for instant access to Wapping Control, no colleagues to back her up. She was just a girl, facing three blokes, intent on something unspeakable. As she left the pier she sank into grey mud, and could only watch in horror as the three men lowered the baby onto the inflatable and pushed it out across the water.

She'd known there was something wrong about that inflatable. Why hadn't she acted earlier?

Then the three men were coming at her, like the front row in a rugby team. The first struck out with his right fist; the blow caught the side of her head and knocked her off balance. The second yelled something she didn't catch. She almost fell, taking several drunken paces to get her balance back as the men's squelching footsteps receded.

She didn't so much as turn to watch them flee. The baby.

Lacey ran to the water's edge – the inflatable's line, there was a chance she could catch it – but the greedy river had claimed its latest sacrifice and the toy, a unicorn she saw now, white with rainbow markings, was nearly twenty metres downriver.

A hand touched her shoulder. 'How deep?' Helen said. 'Can I wade out?'

Lacey spun away. 'No chance. Get on to Wapping. They've got minutes to cut it off.'

Minutes at most. The outgoing tide typically travelled at four knots and Wapping police station, where the marine unit were based, wasn't far downriver. As Lacey climbed once more over the pier's railing she saw that the fourth man, Asian, in work clothes, was running along the foreshore after the three men, but he was older, slower and they had a head start. She heard Helen on the phone, giving her name and police rank, demanding to be put through to Wapping station and knew she had to leave all that behind. The river, the baby – that was all she could think about now.

Police officers are trained to see, to notice, and the marine unit officers could not be on the river without constantly taking in their surroundings. Lacey Flint was no different; if anything, she was better at it than most. There had been a Targa, one of the boats the unit used to patrol the river, tied up at the pier at Wapping police station as she'd paddled past earlier, and two high-speed rigid-inflatable-boats, or RIBs. Her colleagues could be on the river in minutes.

'I can catch it,' she yelled back at Helen as she jumped into her kayak. 'Get the river cleared of traffic. And get the guys at Wapping out on the—'

As the tide took her, she saw Helen turn and gasp. A baby's pram had appeared, balanced on top of the embankment wall. It hovered and then fell, landing heavily on the sand fifteen metres below.

8

At the foot of Tower Bridge steps a crowd had gathered. Somewhere in the distance, a siren was drawing closer.

The man who'd thrown the pram was on the other side of the busy road, heading north towards the city, and Dana had to let him go. Another man, in a suit, carrying a copy of the *Financial Times*, broke away from the group and made for the pier. With one hand firmly on Inigo's head, Dana ran towards him.

'Sir.'

He turned at the head of the ramp.

'Sir, I'm an off-duty police officer. Uniformed police are on their way. Until they arrive can you please stay here and stop anyone going down to the river?'

The man gestured towards the water. 'He threw a baby.' He swallowed. 'That pram he threw – there was a baby in it. He threw a baby over the wall.'

'I know that, sir. My colleague is down there, and I'm going myself. It's a crime scene now and we need to secure it. Can you help us, please? For a few minutes?'

He looked uncertain, then relieved. He nodded his agreement and so she slipped past him. Still holding tight to Inigo's head, Dana ran down the ramp.

Three people came into view. Helen, talking into the phone, her eyes fixed on the upturned buggy; her partner, the bravest human she knew, fazed by nothing, looked about to be sick. The man who'd chased the abductors was leaning against the pier rail, out of breath. He too was staring in horror at the pram, half hidden by mud. 'Babies,' he muttered as Dana drew close. 'Who does this to babies?' And Lacey, back in her kayak, paddling furiously away from the pier. No sign of the first baby, or the two men who'd abducted it.

'Yes, Constable Lacey Flint is in pursuit,' Helen was saying. 'She's in a kayak. She's about . . .' Dana watched Helen drag her eyes towards the river '. . . about fifty metres downstream of Tower Bridge. I can't see the inflatable. Yes, white, about a metre and a half at its tallest point, with rainbow markings. A unicorn. We need teams out on the river. Now.'

As Dana put her hand on her partner's shoulder Helen actually jumped, relaxing only when she saw who'd approached. Disconnecting the call, her eyes went quickly to Inigo.

'He's fine,' Dana said. 'What's happening?'

'Three men, one waiting down here for the other two. Baby on the river, in a very flimsy-looking inflatable, Lacey in hot pursuit. And then that happened.'

Helen indicated, with a terse nod of her head, the upturned pram.

Lacey was already out of sight. She was brave too, super-fit, more than capable, but how could a baby survive out on the river? And in the meantime, another tragedy, metres away.

'We need to look,' Dana said.

'I know.'

Neither woman moved. Helen said, 'I don't think I can.'

Dana unclipped the papoose. 'Take Ini,' she said.

Dana's body felt cold as she handed over her son and, as she stepped forward, towards what she instinctively knew would be the worst thing she'd ever seen, she felt as though something essential inside her had gone; as though if she looked back at Helen, their son would have vanished. As her feet sank into the mud, she found herself doubting she'd ever been a mother.

This was her job though; she had to get herself over there.

The mud was deep, already Dana's shoes were filthy, and that had to be a good thing. The landing would have been soft. But the fall was over fifteen metres. Even strapped in, the baby couldn't have escaped serious injury. If anything, the straps would have made matters worse, fixing the tiny body in place as the jolt of landing shook it apart. The poor little thing would have stood a better chance if it hadn't been strapped in. As it was, the most likely result, Dana knew, was that the infant's neck had broken.

What kind of father threw his infant child to an almost certain death? No kind of father, she realised. The baby she was about to see had also been abducted, in order to be murdered. Two dead babies, because the one on the river couldn't survive. How could such a pretty day have gone so badly wrong?

The pram, when she reached it, was one she recognised, a Silver Cross Pioneer in Eton Grey. It retailed at nearly nine hundred pounds and had been on their shortlist of six.

Oh, for God's sake, Dana, I cannot look at another pram, will you make a decision?

It was upside down, the grey fabric roof largely hidden in the mud, its wheels still spinning.

Dana wasn't sure she could do this either. A murdered baby, it was unthinkable. And yet, if it had to be done, it should be done by a mother.

The thought gave Dana a courage, of sorts, and taking hold of the aluminium framework she pulled. The foreshore pulled back. She sensed a presence at her side and realised Helen, with Inigo strapped to her own chest now, had approached.

From beneath the fabric came the sound of a baby: a splutter, a wail, then a high-pitched cry. Both women looked at their own child – fast asleep.

'It's alive, for God's sake, Helen, get it out, it's alive.'

They reached out together, grasped the pram and pulled. This time, their combined strength drew it from the mud and set it upright.

The baby inside, still strapped in, dressed in a blue-and-white striped suit, with a blue cap, seemed entirely unblemished, other than a spattering of mud across its – his – face. The crying continued, and yet the face the two women stared down at was motionless. He – it – was entirely lifeless, and yet, not dead. Not a baby at all, but a life-like baby doll with an internal sound mechanism.

9

The unicorn had a head start but Lacey's kayak was designed to move swiftly through water. Considerably more aerodynamic than a circular float, it would catch up quickly, all other things being equal.

All other things, though, were not equal. The unicorn had been swept out towards the faster flow of the central channel, where it would be dangerous for Lacey to follow. A fast-moving refuge barge would not be looking out for tiny craft in its path. One of the passenger ferries could mow them both down.

The distance to Wapping from Tower Bridge was a little over a mile and the tide would cover a mile in minutes. Technically, there was time for the marine unit to intercept the child, but only if her colleagues were able to get immediately out on the river. Sometimes that couldn't happen: keys mislaid, boats needing re-fuelling, the right officer temporarily out of the building. Helen's phone call would have alerted the Port of London authority, which technically had responsibility for safety on the river, but their lifeboat stations weren't close enough.

A rouge wave washed over the kayak. Open-mouthed from the effort of paddling, she registered the gritty, oily taste of Thames water as the inflatable – closer now, maybe fifty metres away – bounced on a similar wave. Children's inflatables were designed for swimming pools not fast urban rivers. The gentlest of waves, the tiniest of washes from a passing boat would tip it and the baby would sink like a stone.

The unicorn didn't tip, but it was spinning on the current. Its circular shape couldn't hold a course in the water and the lack of keel was sending it in different directions each time the wind caught it. Forty metres away, but the wind was taking it back towards the north bank. There'd be less river traffic closer to the shore, but conversely, more obstacles that could overturn it.

'Get to the side!'

Without her registering its presence, a motorboat had approached Lacey from behind. Glancing back, she saw the vessel's skipper yelling at her. 'Get out of the channel!'

There were four people on board, one of whom seemed to be filming her on a video camera.

'Move to starboard,' she called back. 'Stay away from that inflatable.'

Twenty metres now between her and the baby, and they were skimming past the houseboats of the Hermitage riverboat community. Residents were running the length of the boats, keeping pace with the inflatable.

'Baby!' one of them yelled at her. 'There's a baby.'

The motorboat, its crew having grasped something of what was going on, was keeping pace with her, and that was a good thing. Far more visible than she, its presence would protect her flank.

The riverboats fell behind. Ten metres, and she could hear the baby screaming, could see its hands, raised in the air like tiny flags.

'Stay behind me,' she yelled to the skipper of the motorboat. 'Try and protect me from wash.'

'Will do.'

Ahead on the river, a blockade. The marine unit's Targa and both RIBs were out, holding their position on the tide. Officers standing upright on all three craft held binoculars to their eyes. A loud horn sounded. They'd seen her.

Seven metres. Six. And the flimsiness of the inflatable toy was actually saving it from disaster. It bounced on the lightest wave. Were anything to impede it, stop its progress over the water, it would tip and be submerged in a split second.

It was seconds away from striking the stationary vessels ahead.

It could not be allowed to tip; she had to get to it first. Lacey put her head down and paddled harder, making the tiny adjustments that would keep her on the inflatable's tail.

Five metres, four. She whisked the paddle out of the water.

Three metres, two, one. Her kayak was alongside the inflatable. She could see the baby, terrifyingly still now. She leaned out and grasped its sodden Babygro. A wave washed over the bow of the kayak and she held her breath; the bow reappeared and the kayak found its balance. She heaved and felt the weight of the baby. A heart-stopping moment of knowing this was where it could, finally and devastatingly, go wrong. The Babygro held. The infant's eyes opened wide with surprise and then it was tight against Lacey's chest: warm, solid, alive.

10

Joesbury left his bike – a Ducati Panigale V4R in pillar-box red that he knew in his heart made him look like a middle-aged dick – in the charge of a uniformed constable, showed his warrant card to the officer securing the scene and led the way down towards the foreshore. Theo's face was wax pale, and the gleam of sweat on his temples wasn't about to be wiped into oblivion. Across his forehead was a reddened pressure mark of a too tight helmet. His hair, which had been perfect minutes before, was flattened against his head.

'Not ridden pillion before?' Joesbury asked, as he caught sight of Dana and Helen on the beach, standing with a uniformed police officer.

'Many times, sir. Many times.'

Deciding it wasn't a conversation he wanted to pursue, Joesbury strode down the last few metres of the pier. 'Going to get your shoes dirty,' he snapped, as he stepped onto the foreshore.

The kid's Church's loafers, that retailed upwards of six hundred quid, would be ruined and Joesbury knew he really had to stop being a twat. He probably had driven too fast on the way over.

'You three OK?' he asked, his eyes bouncing from Dana, to Helen, to the patch of dark hair strapped against Helen's torso. 'Piers Morgan says real men don't wear papooses,' he added, because being a twat was something he really couldn't help these days.

'Piers Morgan can kiss my arse,' Helen replied. 'As can you.'

Fair play, he'd asked for that. He introduced himself to the uniformed constable before turning back to Dana.

'Who's in charge?' he asked.

'Gayle for the moment.' Dana indicated a blonde officer in her thirties who was fastening police tape around the pram. 'Neil eventually, but he's on another job. He's on his way.'

Joesbury knew both Gayle Mizon, a detective constable and Neil Anderson, acting detective inspector, based like Dana at Lewisham.

'Which way did the perps go?' he asked and then, when the direction had been pointed out by Helen, 'Heading for the Tower of London steps would be my guess. Two hundred metres upriver. Did anyone pursue?'

'There wasn't anyone.' From Helen's tone she was still narked with him. 'Dana and I were focused on the baby. Babies, as we thought at the time.'

Joesbury nodded, absently. He'd been briefed on arrival that the baby in the pram had turned out to be a hoax; there was still no word on the one on the river.

'Any chance the other baby wasn't real?' Theo asked.

'I heard it screaming,' Helen replied. 'And I've heard my fair share of infant screams the last six months, so I'm going with real.'

'That one screamed too.' Dana glanced back towards the pram in the mud.

Theo was looking up and down the river. 'Two hundred metres is a long way to run on this mud,' he said.

'Escaping by boat would have been riskier,' Joesbury replied. 'Three blokes on foot can hide themselves in London a whole lot easier than a boat can on the river. And the marine unit RIBs are bloody fast.'

'And not far away,' Helen agreed. 'I'd say these guys knew what they were doing. And we're looking for four. The dad who tossed his pram was involved.'

'Description?'

'White males, fairly young from the way they moved and the speed they ran. Twenties, early thirties at most. Three had scarves around their lower faces.'

Joesbury knew he didn't look impressed, but for the love of God, these two were senior officers, was that really all they could give him?

'We were focusing on the babies,' Dana said. 'It all happened very quickly and yes, we let ourselves be taken by surprise.'

'Don't apologise to him,' Helen snapped. 'We don't even know why he's—'

Helen's phone was ringing and she turned away to answer it. She listened, for several long seconds and then drew in a sharp breath.

'The baby's safe,' she said when she ended the call, and Joesbury saw that her hands were shaking. 'Lacey got to the float and managed to grab the kid. They're both on their way to the Royal London. The baby's very cold but, well, we'll have to wait and see. At least it's out of the water.'

Dana's eyes were gleaming.

'Lacey?' Joesbury queried. 'As in . . .?'

Neither woman seemed to want to look at him. 'We met her for breakfast,' Dana said, after what felt like an age.

'She was on the pier when it all kicked off,' Helen added. 'She came by canoe.'

'I guess we should be grateful she didn't swim,' Joesbury replied.

'Are you talking about Lacey Flint?' the uniformed constable was looking from one detective to the next. He caught the look on Joesbury's face and stopped.

'I mean,' he went on, 'isn't she the one who—'

'Whatever you're about to add, the answer is probably yes,' Helen told him, before turning to Theo. 'And since DCI Joesbury is not about to introduce us, I'm Helen Rowley and this is DI Dana Tulloch. Welcome to the crime scene, potentially one of the worst of any of our careers, although as things seem to be turning out—'

Dana reached out and stroked a hand down her wife's arm. 'Mark?' she said. 'Why are you here?'

11

The man who, a couple of hours earlier, had seen his carefully laid plans go seriously awry was trying to be calm, telling himself it really hadn't been that bad.

The four operatives had all made it safely back to their respective bases, possibly even without being picked up on any surveillance equipment. Not that it would matter if they had; they'd served their purpose and wouldn't be used again.

The incident had already been picked up by the media. It had featured, in vague terms, on a 'breaking news' bulletin – *'reports are coming in of a serious incident on Tower Bridge in London. Emergency services are at the scene and people are being advised to avoid the area.'* The main lunchtime programmes had gone into more detail and a press conference was scheduled for four o'clock.

It would have been the perfect start, had it not been for that bitch on the foreshore. He'd expected there to be witnesses, maybe even have-a-go-heroes in the way; he'd never dreamed some mad cow would go after the kid on the water, would actually save it.

The mewling little shit-machine should have been crab food by now.

His hands were clenched, his nails, grown too long again, were digging into his palms. Knowing he had to make the best of it, he pulled up Rage, a dark web site he'd launched a few weeks earlier.

The footage taken from Tower Bridge of the inflatable spinning out across the water had already been posted by one of his associates, edited so that the bitch in the kayak didn't appear. He needed the focus to be on the magnificent gesture, not the lucky intervention.

Well done, brothers, he wrote beneath the post. *What a wonderful, glorious start.*

12

Fretful after the morning's excitement, Inigo took longer than usual to feed and was disinclined to fall into his usual milk-drunk slumber. In the corner of the room – used for interviewing children and vulnerable people – was a TV set. Knowing that background noise often soothed her son, Dana flicked the remote and the familiar face of the host of the daytime show, *Loose Women*, filled the screen.

'Let's have a look at what's got everyone talking this morning,' she was saying, as the picture changed to show a recording of *Question Time*, the BBC's news and current affairs show, screened the night before. One of the guests, a British actor named Fergus Lord was speaking. 'I'm not saying Emma isn't an exceptional actress,' he was saying.

'Actor,' the left-wing, female politician to his left corrected him.

Lord gave her a sideways look. 'Whatever. I'm saying that when the two of us were contracted to work on *The Turnaround*, I was the bigger star.'

The camera cut to the *Question Time* studio audience, to faces displaying disdain, disbelief, mockery.

'I had more TV credits to my name, she was relatively unknown,' Lord went on, either not realising, or not caring that he was losing the sympathy of the onlookers. 'I was considered the bankable talent, of course I was going to be paid more.'

The clip ended, the shot on screen was once again the *Loose Women* studio and the camera panned back to show Lord behind the large, curved desk, flanked by the host and three other women, all regular contributors to the show.

'So, your comments on *Question Time* have caused a bit of a furore,' the host began. 'Do you want to apologise?'

Fergus Lord was around thirty years old, an actor who'd found fame in his late teens on a popular daytime programme about an elite public school, and who'd played to his niche ever since with a succession of loveable posh-boy roles. He was also a stand-up comedian whose political views leaned to the right. Notwithstanding that – maybe because of it – he'd enjoyed a surprising success on the northern working-class club circuit. Unapologetic about his privileged background, he spoke unashamedly and directly about issues that impacted the working man.

'Absolutely not,' he replied, in his distinctive public-school voice. 'I said nothing offensive or unreasonable.'

'Emma Winter was in more scenes than you, and had – I think someone worked out – twenty per cent more lines, and yet she was paid fifty thousand pounds less for the series?'

Lord gave a heavy sigh. 'She was paid the amount her agents were able to negotiate, as was I. It had nothing to do with sexual discrimination or the so-called gender pay gap. It's commercial reality.'

'So-called gender pay gap?' a second panellist interrupted. 'You don't think it's real then?'

Lord's easy shrug gave the impression the question bored him. 'I'm sure you can quote statistics at me. My point is there are reasons why women don't always earn the same as men, that have nothing to do with discrimination.'

Another panellist said, 'Don't you believe in equal work for equal pay?'

'I believe in equal pay for equal value,' Lord replied. 'When the female talent has the same box office appeal as the male, then the pay will equal itself out. It will have to. Until then, work harder, ladies. Earn the big bucks you think should be yours by right.'

As jeers rang out from the (mainly) female audience, the door to the interview room was pushed inwards and one of Dana's colleagues, Detective Constable Gayle Mizon, stood in the doorway.

'Lacey's back from the hospital,' she told Dana.

Gathering her stuff together – infants needed so much kit – Dana balanced baby on one shoulder, bag on the other and left the interview room. The TV had done the trick though; Inigo was fast asleep.

On the stairs, she and Gayle met Lacey. 'Is he OK?' she asked quietly, glancing down at the baby.

'Doesn't like his routine being upset,' Dana whispered back, conscious of how uncomfortable she felt in this place, where once she'd been entirely at home. Inigo had changed everything. 'Are you?' she asked, as they reached the top of the stairs.

The other woman forced a cold smile. 'Day's work for me.'

Beyond the opaque glass of the incident room door they could see vague shapes, hear muffled voices.

'Welcome home, boss,' Gayle said, with a humourless smile. She opened the door and led the way inside.

Around a dozen people were already settled in the room, including Neil Anderson and Pete Stenning who, together with Gayle, formed the nucleus of Lewisham's Major Investigation Team. They were Dana's squad, her people, and she'd never been less pleased to see them. Also present was Superintendent David Cook, head of the marine unit.

'Who invited you, David?' Dana said as she and Lacey took seats and Gayle leaned over the tech equipment.

'I did,' Cook replied. 'It happened on the river.'

Cook was notoriously territorial about his patch.

'First things first.' Neil got to his feet. 'The baby snatched from its mother this morning at the foot of Tower Bridge is doing well and is expected to make a full recovery, thanks to the prompt action and great courage shown by Constable Flint. Well done, Lacey.'

A flutter of applause broke out. Neil said, 'Lacey, are you OK?'

'Fine and dandy, thank you, Sarge.' Lacey's forced smile sent a different message. 'I mean, sir.'

'Sarge will do.' Neil cleared his throat. 'Less encouragingly, the four men involved in the abduction vanished. We know they left the foreshore by the Tower Millennium Pier and ran along Lower Thames Street. After that, we think they split up. We're running the facial recognition software, but it may take some time. Any thoughts, Mr C?'

'That would be the first exit point they came to,' Cook replied. 'No one runs along the foreshore for any distance. There are mud patches you can drown in, and even at low tide a lot of it is under water. My guess is they scoped it out previously. Check footage for low tide going back a couple of weeks. There are a lot of cameras on that stretch of the embankment, the tower's always a hot target. You might spot them again, without half their faces covered.'

'On it,' Pete said, making a note.

'We've interviewed all witnesses at the scene,' Neil went on, 'although we may need to speak to some of them again. We're also appealing for more: people in cars, on passing buses, that sort of thing, and we'll have a presence at the bridge for a couple of days.'

It was standard procedure. Placards would detail the time and date of the incident and carry a contact telephone number; a uniformed constable would be on site to talk to passers-by.

Neil said, 'We think it was planned to minimise the risk of the four men involved being identified, or even chased. The two attackers had their faces covered. All attention was on them, so nobody paid any mind to the dad who was assumed to be an innocent bystander. The pram over the wall was a master stroke. Once that happened, everyone on the embankment was looking down to see what happened to the baby they thought was in it, and the people on the foreshore focused their attention first, on the baby in the water, and second, the baby they thought was in the pram.'

'The fake baby wasn't a doll,' Gayle added. 'It's quite a sophisticated piece of equipment used as a learning aid for people giving childcare classes. It's called an Infant Simulator. They're not readily available so we may be able to track its purchase down.'

'The thing's frigging spooky,' Pete said. 'I had to take it down to evidence. It started crying as I left it. I'm not lying, it was hard to walk away.'

Neil glanced at Dana. 'Without the plummeting pram, Helen would probably have given chase.'

Dana said, 'She'd have caught them too, or one of them at least. Helen's a very good runner.'

'Not surprisingly,' Neil went on, 'our best information came from the three of you. Helen spoke to us at length before she went, as did Lacey while she was still at the hospital. We've fed in your thoughts too, ma'am.'

After a few taps on Gayle's laptop, four photo-fit pictures appeared on the screen behind Neil. The team had done well to get them produced so quickly but they were still vague. All four men looked more or less the same: white, any age between twenty and thirty-five, hair a dull brown, nondescript eyes, no distinguishing features. The two men who'd snatched the baby had scarves around the lower part of their faces. The third, who must have been the one on the beach because he appeared in the best detail, had curly dark hair and thick eyebrows. The one who'd pretended to be the dad wore a tight-fitting woollen cap over his hair.

'Ladies, anything to add?' Neil's eyes flicked from Dana to Lacey. Feeling yet another stab of guilt that she'd taken so little part in the events of that morning, Dana shook her head.

Lacey spoke. 'They moved like young men, but not particularly fit young men. When the two who'd grabbed the baby reached the beach, they were both breathing heavily. And they ran badly, clumsily. Not natural fighters either. One of them hit me, but if he'd known what he was doing, he'd have sent me flying.'

Dana asked, 'Who's spoken to the parents?'

Gayle looked up from her laptop. 'That was me. Mr Liam Brown and a Ms Jessica Standish, not married, but been together for six years, co-own a house, seem a settled couple. Comfortable financially but a long way from rich, so kidnap and ransom seems a non-starter. Both work full-time, which is why Ms Standish and Baby Amelia were on the way to the nursery at Southwark.'

The same nursery Inigo was due to start at on Monday; if she ever let him leave her sight again.

'We need to talk to them again,' Gayle went on. 'I've arranged to go round to their house later this afternoon, but they insist they had no idea who any of the four men were, and they can't imagine why anyone would want to hurt their child.'

'We don't take that on face value,' Dana said. 'Talk to their neighbours, their work colleagues, staff at the nursery. See if anyone noticed anything out of the ordinary. If they'll give us access to their computers we can run through their finances, see if they owe anyone money. Anything suspicious, anything at all, and I want us applying for warrants.'

'One thing we need to focus on,' Neil said, 'is that the boss has agreed to a press conference at four o'clock. He wants you to go up and see him, ma'am, so be prepared to be on the platform.'

Dana wondered if there was any point mentioning that she was, strictly, still on maternity leave.

'We can run through what happened, outline how the investigation will run, appeal for information,' Neil went on. 'But we have to be prepared for the big question.'

He paused.

'Why.' Dana said.

Neil nodded. 'Exactly. Why would four men conspire to abduct a baby and set it afloat on the Thames?'

Silence in the room for several seconds, then Lacey said, 'Publicity.'

All eyes turned to her.

'Publicity for what?' Neil asked.

Lacey shrugged. 'No idea. But if the parents are telling the truth and it was nothing to do with them, then it was done to attract attention. That's what I was thinking, all the time I was trying to catch up with the inflatable. This is a stunt.'

'I think Lacey's right,' Pete said. 'I think we're going to see it on news channels the world over tonight. An inflatable unicorn, floating down one of the most famous rivers on the planet, with a live baby on board? That's an image that will stay in people's heads for a long time.'

'They won't have any decent footage, though, will they?' Dana asked. 'Just stuff shot some distance away from the banks. That has to be a relief.'

'Unfortunately, they have,' Gayle admitted. 'The boat that assisted Lacey this morning had a group of river surveyors on board. They had video cameras and got quite a lot of close-up stuff. It's already out there.'

'Are you telling me I'm going to see Lacey and her kayak on the evening news?' Cook's colour was rising. In his eyes, kayaking was a step up from swimming – for one thing it was legal – but he still didn't like it.

'Let's hope not,' Neil said. 'We slapped an injunction on them and made them remove any shots of Lacey herself, but we can't guarantee something didn't leak out. And if the news media have an image, they'll use it.'

Dana glanced at Lacey. She'd gone even paler than usual. For as long as she'd known her, Lacey had avoided publicity of any kind. For the first time, Dana began to wonder if there might be a reason behind that.

'Well, that will put paid to her undercover career.' Cook didn't approve of Lacey's frequent secondments to the covert operations unit. 'But I've got an even bigger question I want answering.'

'What's that?' Dana asked.

Cook said, 'I want to know what Mark Joesbury and his boy wonder were doing on the foreshore this morning.'

'I think we all want to know that,' Dana agreed.

Lacey took a long, careful look around the room. 'Mark was there?' she said.

'He was,' Dana replied. 'And he arrived far too quickly for it to be coincidence. Somehow, he and his team knew it was happening. They know something we don't.'

13

'So, they threw you out too.' Helen put the tray down and off-loaded coffee, Coke zero, a chicken sandwich and a blueberry muffin.

'I'd told them everything I know.' Lacey was holding a sleeping Inigo, surprised at how heavy he felt in her arms given how small he still was. 'Besides, they wanted to talk about Mark.'

'So do I. What was he doing there?'

Lacey kept her eyes on the baby. 'No idea. I was long gone before he arrived. Not that he'd have told me anything anyway.'

The baby Lacey had snatched from the river that morning had been lighter than Inigo, but still a substantial burden to lift with one outstretched arm. She shivered, remembering her dread of the Babygro ripping apart, of the child slipping from her hand.

'Sure you're OK?' Helen was watching her closely.

Even as she nodded, Lacey knew she was a long way from OK. All she asked for was a quiet life, well as quiet as it ever got with the police, to patrol the river, maintain order, keep people safe.

She could say none of that to Helen, and so instead focused her attention on Inigo. As though aware of her staring, Inigo's eyes opened. Such deep blue eyes, with long dark lashes, looking at Lacey in wonder. Silky dark hair but pale skin. He was fairer than his mother. Lacey had never asked about Inigo's father, it would have seemed impertinent somehow. His parents were Dana and Helen.

Helen said, 'So, a bizarre, attention-seeking stunt that could have had disastrous consequences takes place in a high-profile location and purely by coincidence the new boss of SCD10 appears on the scene. What does that suggest to you?'

'It wasn't random,' Lacey said. 'It was part of something big. Mark and his team were expecting it.'

Helen snapped open her Coke. 'My thoughts exactly. And another thing, one of those blokes on the foreshore, the one with the blue scarf round his face. He shouted something at us. Did you catch it?'

Lacey shook her head. The river had been noisy: wind, boat traffic, vehicles on the bridge.

Helen said, 'He called me a fucking foid.'

'A what?'

'And then he said it again. Fuck off, foid.'

Inigo gave a heavy sigh as his eyes closed again. 'What's a foid?' Lacey asked.

'Good question. So, while you were getting checked out at the Royal London, I looked it up. Turns out FOID can be a firearm owner's ID card in Illinois, a Form of Identification Document, or a class of mineral found in igneous rocks.'

'I'm glad we've cleared it up.'

Helen took a swig from the Coke can. 'So, I dug a bit deeper, and learned that it's also short for femoid, or female humanoid. A term used to describe women, suggesting they're less than fully human.'

'Used by who?'

Helen said, 'Men who hate women. Turns out there's a lot of them.'

'It was a baby they tried to kill, not a woman.'

As Helen glanced down at Inigo, her face seemed to contract, as though she'd experienced a sudden, sharp pain. 'And what's the very worst thing you can do to a woman?'

Looking at Helen's face, it wasn't hard to guess. 'Hurt her baby,' Lacey said.

'Anything happens to this little tyke, it will kill Dana. That's not a figure of speech, she'll actually die.'

Not only Dana, Lacey thought. She said, 'And Mark is involved somehow?'

Helen leaned towards her across the table. 'That's what I think. So, of the two of us, who's best placed to get the lowdown from Mark Joesbury?'

No, she wasn't doing that. 'Why don't you ask Dana?'

'She'll tell me nothing. Tight as a Dachshund's arse, that one. Come on, what's the story with you two?'

How could she possibly answer that when she didn't know herself?

'We've both been busy,' Lacey said, checking her phone. The boss had offered her a lift back to Wapping and her shift was due to start in less than an hour.

'He's found time to start dating that woman from the BBC.'

Having dropped the bombshell, Helen proceeded to noisily unwrap her sandwich. 'They had a weekend in Somerset last month.'

Lacey kept her eyes on the baby. 'He's seeing someone?'

'No, I wanted to see how you'd react,' Helen replied. 'And you'd better give me Ini before you pick up your coffee or Dana will slaughter us both. Be sure to tell her I drank Coke if she asks.'

The baby was handed from one woman to the other. The movement woke him up, and he beamed into Helen's face.

'So, is he seeing someone or not?' Lacey asked, because she couldn't help herself.

'Not,' Helen said. 'We wish he were, because he's a pain in the arse. No, scratch that. A male menopausal cliché is what he is. Have you seen that bike he's riding around on? He'll kill himself before the year's out. Or someone else.'

'He's not enjoying the desk job?'

Helen snorted. 'The irony is he'd be bloody good at it,' she said. 'He knows the work better than anyone. He's got a very organised brain. His crew love him. He's just miserable, and he's making everyone around him miserable. Seriously, Lacey, can't you take one for the team?'

Helen could always make her laugh.

'It can't be that bad,' Lacey objected, knowing it totally was that bad, for her anyway. Every night, desperate to get to sleep, he was in her head; every morning, the first thing she thought about when she woke. There were times when her body was wracked with phantom pain, she wanted him that much.

'You still OK for Sunday?' Helen asked. 'Because Mark will be there. For some reason Dana insisted on making him godfather. I mean, the woman hasn't believed in God her entire life. She's been a secular Hindu since she was ten.'

Inigo's christening. Helen and Dana, such unconventional women, had become totally conventional in the rearing of their son.

'Of course,' Lacey said. 'I'm looking forward to it.'

She was dreading it. Church, followed by several hours of small talk, trying to avoid being anywhere near Joesbury; at the same time constantly aware of his presence.

The two women were silent for a moment. Puzzled by the quiet, Inigo started squeaking, waving his arms around as though to attract attention. Helen leaned forward and blew bubbles against his nose, making him squeal with delight.

'Don't tell anyone you saw me doing that,' she said. 'I pretend I hate the brat.'

An alert on her phone told Lacey that Mr Cook had finished his meeting. Knowing he wouldn't want to be kept waiting, she said goodbye and hurried out, looking back when she reached the doorway. Helen, totally engrossed in her son now, was staring, transfixed, into the infant's eyes and in that instant, Lacey saw directly into the other woman's heart. Helen was hiding a love that threatened to consume her.

Tell me about it, she thought.

14

Mark Joesbury kept a suit at work, plus a clean shirt, decent shoes and a tie, which was lucky, because not long after he'd got back to Scotland Yard he'd been told to be at the front door in ten minutes. He was going out again – this time with the commissioner. The drive to Marsham Street took no time at all.

'How long do you think we've got?' his boss asked, as the two of them were checked through security. 'Before—'

'Shit hits the fan?' Joesbury suggested.

'I was going to say before the cat's out of the bag.'

'Anybody's guess, but not long,' Joesbury said. 'The dark web's full of it. The video footage is all over the surface web too. We've been trying to get the pictures of the off-duty constable taken down but we're pissing in the wind.'

'Marine unit officer, wasn't it?'

'That's right. On scene when it happened.'

'Lucky.'

Their destination was a large, glass-fronted room on the first floor. The male assistant at the desk greeted the commissioner by name. 'She'll see you straight away,' he said. 'Go right in. Can I get you coffee?'

'Mind your language,' the commissioner muttered as she preceded Joesbury into the room. 'Good morning, Home Secretary.'

Alison Brabin, holder of one of the UK's four great offices of state, was disturbingly sexy in the flesh. Her figure was substantial, verging on plump, but everything was in the right place and perfectly proportioned. Her lilac suit could have been described as tight, if you wanted to be unkind, but few people in her presence, men anyway, felt inclined to be so. Her hair was blonde, shoulder-length, purposefully untidy and her make-up colourful. She looked like an actress from a soap opera; she was a corporate lawyer by training, with a razor-sharp brain, and when she stood in for the PM at prime minister's questions, the leader of the opposition had been known to order a strong pre-lunch drink immediately afterwards.

She wasted no time. 'Commissioner, what's the likelihood of this morning's incident being an isolated attack?'

'Practically zero.' The commissioner didn't either.

'So, it's begun,' Brabin said. She'd yet to look at Joesbury.

'How up to speed are you, ma'am?' the commissioner asked.

'Let's sit down.' She walked towards a conference table at the far side of the room. The trail of perfume she left in her wake was light, floral, with a hint of oranges; the same that Lacey wore.

Pulling out a chair, Brabin said, 'I've been kept informed of discussions at JTAC. Come on, both of you, I don't have all day.'

JTAC or Joint Terrorism Analysis Centre was a multi-agency task force operating under the auspices of MI5 to monitor terrorism threat in the United Kingdom.

'I'm told you're our best shot at catching these people,' Brabin said to Joesbury when the three of them were seated. 'So, I wanted to get my brief from you. Assume I know nothing, but please be economical with my time.'

'We believe the attack this morning was carried out by a group that call themselves MenMatter. They're self-described incels,'

Joesbury began. 'That's short for Involuntary Celibates; to put it succinctly, men who can't get laid.'

A subtle reaction from the woman opposite: her eyes narrowed as she leaned a fraction away from the table, away from him.

'These are men, mainly young, predominantly white, who believe they're entitled to a loving, sexual relationship with an attractive female,' he went on. 'They think it's their God-given right.'

The home secretary's eyes didn't leave his.

Joesbury said, 'They believe their lack of success is nothing to do with their own behaviour, but down to society placing too great an emphasis on superficialities, predominantly looks, but also material success. In their eyes, even the ordinary women aspire to the best-looking, most successful men, the alpha males, leaving the average and the ugly unable to form meaningful connections of any kind.'

'And these losers are terrorists now?' Brabin asked. 'They can put on a pair of trousers and drag themselves away from *Grand Theft Auto* for long enough to organise something?'

'Most, probably not,' Joesbury replied. 'It only needs a few.'

'This might give you a better idea of what we could be facing.' The commissioner slid a typed report across the table. 'May 2014, Isla Vista, California, a man called Elliot Rodger killed six and injured fourteen, by shooting, stabbing and vehicle ramming. He exchanged fire with the police before turning his gun on himself.'

'Beforehand, he posted a video on YouTube,' Joesbury added. 'He claimed he wanted to punish women for rejecting him and sexually active men because he envied them.'

'Rodger's become known in the incel community as The Supreme Gentleman,' the commissioner said. 'A sort of patron saint.'

Joesbury said, 'Three attacks in Canada, including ten people killed by a van, another nine in a classroom in Oregon. More recently, nine people killed in Germany by a bloke called Tobias Rathjen. Like Rodger he published a manifesto in which he referred to an inability to form a successful relationship.'

The commissioner said. 'We think this morning was the start, and that it's going to escalate quickly.'

Brabin said, 'And you know this because you have a team monitoring the dark web, where most of this stuff gets posted?'

'We've been keeping a watching brief for some time,' the commissioner jumped in. 'As have our colleagues in the National Crime Agency, the security services and GCHQ.'

Joesbury said, 'I've got four officers with computer science degrees, including one woman pretending to be a bloke, trying to infiltrate this community. Two of them are Cambridge graduates, one's from Imperial, the woman's from LSE. As well as monitoring what's going on, they each have several online fake identities. They're pretending to be the people they're hunting. Its classic covert work, only in the cyber world.'

The home secretary nodded to show that she was following.

'What works in our favour,' Joesbury went on, 'is that terrorist groups want to be noticed. They need the world and their own toxic community to know that something is coming.'

The commissioner added, 'These guys talk about a Day of Retribution, when those who've made their lives miserable will get what's coming to them. We've been seeing increasing references to it.'

'It's a delicate balancing act,' Joesbury said. 'They want to get their communities excited, wound up about what's coming, without giving too much away.'

Brabin said, 'Why babies? Why was the first attack on babies? How does that fit with their woman-hating agenda?'

'We think it's about attention,' Joesbury said. 'Terrorists want to shock, to have everyone talking about them. An attack going unnoticed would be the worst kind of failure. Well, what would cause more outrage than an attack on a baby?'

'Killing a puppy?' Brabin suggested.

Joesbury let his lips relax into a half smile. 'I stand corrected.'

The commissioner cleared her throat. 'What we need to decide,' she said, 'is whether we go public today on our belief that this morning's incident was the work of terrorists and the start of a planned campaign, or whether we downplay it, for now, as an isolated incident. Ultimately, ma'am, that's your call.'

'The current view of JTAC is that we keep the lid on it,' Joesbury said. 'Once we admit we're talking terrorism people will panic. They'll want to know what we're doing, who we're targeting, why we don't know more than we do. The media will be on our backs non-stop.'

'On the other hand, if we don't and there's another attack, we'll be blamed for not warning people,' the commissioner said.

'We can't warn people when we have no idea what's coming next, or when, or where,' Joesbury said. 'And God help us if we admit that publicly.'

For a moment, nobody spoke.

'We can warn nurseries in the city,' Brabin said. 'Get them to tighten up their security. And get extra presence on the approaches at drop-off and pick-up time.'

'We can,' Joesbury agreed. 'But I think that's locking the stable door when the horse is stealing apples in the next village. I don't think they'll target babies again. For one thing, most people draw the line at hurting babies, even sexually frustrated men, and for another, it confuses the message. It's women they hate, young women who are sexually active, just not with them.'

'But they don't only target women,' the commissioner argued. 'All the high-profile attacks we've seen in Europe and North America have killed and injured men as much as women. They hate men too, the successful ones anyway.'

'So, young, attractive, sexually active people,' Brabin said, getting to her feet. 'Lucky there aren't many of those in London.'

15

'We're talking every bar and restaurant, every nightclub, gym, spa and health club in London being possible targets,' Joesbury told the group. On his way back to Scotland Yard, he'd contacted both Dana and David Cook, asking them to join his own team for a debrief. The commissioner had asked if he wanted to include Lacey and Helen, given that they'd been at the scene, and were serving officers. He'd probably been a bit over-aggressive in his snapped response. No, he didn't want either of them anywhere near the investigation.

He wondered now whether it was because of Lacey that he'd been giving Helen such a hard time the past few months. The two of them, physically, were similar: slim, athletic, fair-haired, with classically beautiful features. They were both perfect examples of 'Staceys', the nickname incels gave to the most desirable, least attainable women. Having that morning's operation thwarted by two 'Staceys' would be a bitter blow for the MenMatter move-ment to swallow. He could use that, he knew, push both Helen and Lacey centre stage, provoke a reaction from the incels. Except he was never willingly working with Lacey again; he simply couldn't think straight when she was around.

And so the meeting was him, Dave and Dana, and his young team, on which so much depended: Theo Cox; Archie Leech, an Imperial graduate; Georgie Lock, a woman of mixed British and

Hong Kong Chinese heritage who'd studied computer science and psychology at the London School of Economics; Warwick Bowman, like Theo, a Cambridge graduate but with a master's in law. Four kids, all of them brilliant.

Joesbury went on, 'Not to mention cinemas, theatres, parks on a nice day, Sunday morning rugby matches with the wives and girlfriends cheering on the Chads.'

Georgie turned to Dana, '"Chads", like "Staceys" is part of the incel lexicon. Chads are the attractive, sexually successful, alpha males.'

'Like us.' Archie grinned at Theo and Warwick. 'We're poster boys for the Chads. I'm sure you were too in your day, sir.'

Joesbury didn't react; he'd heard it all before. And the three young men were, as Archie had pointed out, all of a physical type: tall and athletic, fair-haired, good-looking.

'The home secretary doesn't want us going public for the time being,' he continued. 'She thinks the country isn't ready to face a brand-new terrorist threat, one that potentially threatens half the UK population.'

'We might have no bloody choice,' Cook grumbled. 'We're about to enter the run-up to Christmas. A lot of festive merry-making takes place on the water. Making sure it happens safely is my responsibility.'

'She thinks, and I agree with her, that once it's all out in the open, the people behind MenMatter will become more cautious,' Joesbury said. 'The chances of infiltration will be reduced. We've got a window, and we need to make the most of it.'

'Do you have any idea who these people are?' Cook asked.

Warwick, the only male member of Joesbury's team not naturally blond, but who'd bleached his hair silver to fit in, tapped a few keys on his laptop and turned it to face Dana and Cook. The screen showed four internet handles – MadHatter,

Joker, BlackPill88 and AryanBoy – along with distinctive, colour-ful avatars.

'These are the guys we're interested in,' Warwick said. 'They're all prolific posters – Reddit, 4Chan, YouTube, Twitter – they pop up again and again. Even more so on the dark web. They're all subtle, they avoid the worst of the language and abuse, but they're definitely groomers. They're constantly suggesting other sites, other discussion groups, luring the newbies in.'

'Do we know anything about them at all?' Dana asked. 'In real life I mean.'

Warwick shook his head. 'Not much. They all use Tor brows-ers so we've no way of tracing their IP addresses, but from the oc-casional reference to life in London we think they're city-based.'

'Tor browsers?' Cook queried.

'The dark web is the part of the internet that can't be accessed by normal search engines,' Theo explained. 'To get onto it, you need a software browser called Tor, which keeps all your searches anonymous.'

'On you go, Warwick,' Joesbury said, when Cook had nodded that he understood.

Warwick said, 'So, the four guys at the centre. If we look at them one by one . . .'

The laptop screen changed to focus on the first of the avatars, MadHatter, a white-faced man with a shock of red hair, yellow eyes and an outlandish, ribboned hat.

'The picture is the actor Johnny Depp, in the film *Alice in Won-derland*,' Warwick said. 'We're pretty confident the man behind the handle isn't him, though. MadHatter, we think, works a nine-to-five job, because his posts typically appear after seven o'clock in the evening and run into the small hours, but not all night.'

The screen changed to show a second picture, actor Joaquin Phoenix in his Joker makeup.

'Joker doesn't appear to have a regular job,' Warwick said. 'He might work, but if he does, it will be from home. He often posts in the small hours and at odd intervals through the day.'

Dana asked, 'He can't be using a work computer?'

'If he does that, we'll find him,' Theo said. 'Company tech won't have the same safeguards built in that these guys have at home.'

'They won't risk using work computers,' Archie said. 'Their IT department would pick up any dodgy stuff.'

'Next up is BlackPill88,' Warwick went on, as the screen changed to show a shadowy figure behind streams of vertical green lines. 'Another movie reference. This is a shot from *The Matrix*. Early in the film, the character Neo is given a choice. He takes the blue pill and returns to the safe but false world he's grown used to, or the red pill, and sees the uncomfortable truth about what life has become.'

'We see a lot of references to blue, red and black pills on incel sites,' Georgie added. 'Taking the red pill refers to the moment when the veil falls away and a man can see the world for what it really is: a complex system of structures, laws and beliefs that are designed to favour women.'

'How the hell do they come to that conclusion?' Dana asked.

'Men fight on the front line,' Theo told her. 'They do the worst, the dirtiest manual jobs, have the highest suicide rates, are more likely to die violent deaths, suffer the most financially in divorce, lose their children, are tricked into bringing up other men's children, and so on.'

Georgie said, 'When you take the red pill, you realise how hopelessly skewed the world is against the entire male sex. Supposedly. The black pill refers to an incel who has given up, who's contemplating suicide.'

'BlackPill88, like Joker, could be unemployed or self-employed, judging by the timing of his posts,' Warwick said. 'And then we have AryanBoy,' he went on, as a swastika filled the screen. 'We think he's the boss. All of them are educated, although BlackPill's spelling falls apart from time to time. AryanBoy, though, is smart and wants everyone to know it. He likes to drop in references to traditional philosophy and the classics. He's a bit of a show-off.'

'Do they know each other? In real life, I mean?' Dana asked.

'Hard to say,' Warwick replied. 'They may never have met but if they're planning the attacks together, they'll have a way of communicating that's away from the web.'

'Have any of them reacted to this morning's events?' Cook asked.

Joesbury couldn't help a sigh. 'Oh, God yes. They are having the time of their lives.'

16

History has changed, the latest post on the Rage website read. *The battle has begun.*

The author sat back and admired his work. The pictures taken by zoom lens that morning had turned out well.

The course of history has been changed, would have sounded better, but probably too late to faff about with it now. Since his first post about the attack, nearly four hours ago, the site had gone into orbit. Two thousand comments already and they were coming in all the time. Nearly four hundred active users at that moment. All over the UK, Europe and – yes, they were getting posts from North America now, their US cousins had woken up – men were celebrating the first strike in a war that he'd promised would change the world. Pretty soon Australia, New Zealand and the Far East would be online too.

Great news to wake up to. Well done lads.

Fucking brilliant.

So glad someone's finally doing something.

Amidst the jubilation, one or two dissenting voices had appeared, questioning why their first target had been an infant. Dissent wasn't helpful at this early stage. He decided to add another post.

The foids' biological urge to reproduce, to bring babies into the world, lies at the core of the structural unfairness we suffer. This strongest, basest of urges drives them into the promiscuous behaviour we see around us. When the Staceys copulate with the Chads they're giving in to this disgusting urge with no idea of what's driving them. Foids, remember, don't have the intellectual capacity to understand their own behaviour. An urge tells them to fuck, and so they fuck, with the biggest, strongest, best-looking Chads they can get. That same instinct, manifesting in a need to make strong, good-looking babies, further pushes them towards the alpha male. Only when they're knocked up, when they realise the Chad won't be there for them, do they turn to the beta cucks to bring up their little bastards. A baby might look small, innocuous, but brothers, so does a bullet.

Nice. In fact, some of his best work. One last sentence should do it.

Waste no tears on the infant that was sacrificed this morning. It was a girl.

OK, strictly speaking the brat had survived, but it was a good line to close on.

17

Lacey Flint owned very little stuff. Buying a 1950s sailing yacht moored permanently, albeit illegally, at Deptford Creek's Theatre Arm marina, had been entirely out of character, and eighteen months later, she was still reeling from the enormity of the change it represented. In compensation, perhaps, for this huge thing she now owned, she'd kept other possessions to a minimum, throwing out much of what little she'd had, buying nothing that wasn't necessary and unavoidable. From time to time she comforted herself with the notion that, should she need to, she could weigh anchor and sail away with all her worldly goods.

Of course, she'd have to learn to sail first.

The boat rocked as someone stepped on board. 'Lace!' a voice called, sounding nervous and pissed off at the same time.

'I'm below.' Lacey closed the laptop as a pair of trainers appeared on the cabin steps.

'There are no lights in this place,' a voice complained. 'I nearly went in twice. I mean what the fuck?'

'Told you to bring a torch,' Lacey muttered.

Emma Boston was a freelance journalist. The two women had met two years earlier when both had become embroiled in the gruesome murders perpetrated by Lacey's old friend, Victoria Llewelyn. Initially deeply suspicious, each had learned to trust the other and they'd worked together several times, usually when

Lacey felt an issue needed to see the light of day. Sometime over the last two years, Emma, like Dana and Helen, had become a friend.

In her mid-twenties, a little younger than Lacey, Emma had been disfigured in a fire at some point in her history and the right side of her face, especially around her lower jaw and neck, was badly scarred. In the time she'd known her though, Lacey had noticed improvements in Emma's appearance, thanks, probably, to Emma's elevated standing as a journalist. Her friend had had several investigative pieces accepted by major print outlets and had won a prestigious award.

'I can't stay late,' Emma told her, as Lacey bent to take food out of the oven. 'I've got a meeting with the *New Statesman* at ten. Was it you on the river this morning?'

Lacey didn't look up. 'Don't know what you're talking about.'

'Off the record? Seriously.'

'Right place at the right time,' Lacey said. 'I got lucky. So, can you help, or are we just doing girls' night?'

Emma laughed. 'The Manosphere? That's what you want to know about?'

'I'd never heard of it before today.'

Before her shift, though, she'd had time to google the term *female humanoid*, and had felt like she'd fallen down a very dark rabbit hole.

She opened cartons, put serving spoons in place, and the smell of ginger, chilli and garlic filled the cabin.

'I guess you could say it's like a connected mass of individual cells,' Emma said. 'All of which operate online, each with their own unique identity, goals and lexicons, but having a lot in common.'

Grabbing pen and paper that lay ready on the table, Emma drew a rough honeycomb of hexagonal shapes.

'Incels.' She wrote the word in a cell. 'Probably the nastiest of the bunch. Then you have Pick-up Artists, MGTOW, or Men Going Their Own Way.'

As she named each group, Emma wrote the name down in a cell of the honeycomb.

'Men's Rights Activists, White Supremacists, Homophobes. There are others. Basically, men with a grievance, often minor, sometimes imagined, who get together in online spaces and are radicalised. Have you heard of the alt-right pipeline?'

'I'm guessing it's nothing to do with the Thames sewerage project.'

'It's a way of targeting young, white men with a grievance, offering them scapegoats – ethnic minorities and women, typically, homosexuals occasionally – and then gathering them together in communities where their views can be validated. They start to feel better, so seek further validation. It's a vicious spiral, going ever downwards.'

'And it's a pipeline because . . .'

'It has entry points, that seem anodyne and entirely mainstream. People like Jordan Peterson, the Canadian professor, and Ben Shapiro, the American conservative social commentator. Steven Crowder is another one. For the most part, their views aren't unreasonable, but when men watch their channels, the algorithms kick in, and the content suggested starts to get a bit more radical. It's subtle, so users don't realise the tone has changed, that they're being sucked into the pipeline.'

Lacey stayed silent; this felt like something Emma needed to get off her chest.

'Here in the UK you've got, let me think, Fergus Lord, that actor on *Question Time* last night. He's been ranting on Twitter for ages about men's rights, fathers' rights, and so on. So, you've got these charismatic, intelligent commentators posting on social media channels that everybody has access to. Over time, they get drawn into more disturbing and violent discussions. And not all of these are taking place on Facebook and YouTube.'

'Sites like 4Chan, Reddit?' Lacey said. 'And then the dark web? I gave myself a bit of a crash course this afternoon.'

Emma put her fork down and sighed. 'Lacey, if you were on any of these channels, you'd see the abuse that gets hurled at women simply for the crime of existing, having a voice and opinions.'

A wave rocked the boat, swaying the wine in the women's glasses.

'Every time I write an article, or share a piece, it comes pouring in,' Emma continued. 'If the content touches upon feminism or women's issues, it magnifies a hundredfold. And it doesn't matter how many times I tell myself to ignore it, it gets through. There's not a day goes by when I'm not told I'm too ugly to be alive.'

Emma drank and swallowed hard.

'I need more of an online presence, don't I?' Lacey said, quietly. 'I should know what's out there.'

Emma sniffed. 'You can't progress through the police if you're not internet savvy. You'll be stuck on the river all your life.'

Lacey thought about it. 'Not necessarily a bad thing.'

'For some people, maybe not. For you . . .' She left the thought hanging.

Emma was right, Lacey realised. She'd thought she could be a police officer and hide from life's toxic underbelly. She'd been a fool.

'Can you help me?' Lacey asked. 'Get me started?'

'Give me your phone.' Emma held out her hand. 'And welcome to the dark side.'

18

It was close to midnight and Inigo was screaming; Dana was close to doing the same. Helen, in pyjamas, red-eyed from interrupted sleep, appeared in the kitchen doorway.

'Dana, no offence, but if I hear "The Wheels on the Bus" one more time I'm going to break something.'

Dana spun on her heels, the unexpected motion making Ini notch up the volume. 'Do you have a better suggestion?'

Helen yawned. 'Has he got a temperature?'

'No, I checked. He was fed an hour ago. He's dry. He's just being bloody difficult.'

You dare, she thought. You dare say it's me, that he's picking up on my stress.

Helen wasn't stupid. 'Let me take him out in the car,' she said.

'It doesn't work. He wakes up again the minute you take the seat out of the car.' Helen had never learned the knack of easing the car seat out of the vehicle, just one item on a long list of things Dana found irritating these days.

She handed over her son, whose screams only gained momentum; there were times when only she was good enough. 'I'll take him for a walk.'

In the hallway Dana pulled her waterproof coat from its hook and unbuttoned the outer covering on the pram. Helen followed, raising her voice to be heard. 'It's nearly midnight.'

'Tell your son that.'

Sighing, Helen lowered Inigo into his pram. 'Pass me my coat.'

Dana was pulling a hat over her hair, tucking Ini into his blankets. 'Go back to bed. I'll do it.'

Helen had to be up at five to catch a plane to Brussels. Even so, she stood in the doorway, blocking the exit. 'You can't go out on your own.'

'I'll stick to the High Street. There's always people around. I'll be fine.'

There had been plenty of people on the Thames embankment that morning, but wisely, Helen didn't remind her of that. 'It's pouring,' she said, instead.

'And you can help with that how, exactly?'

Helen pulled the clear plastic cover down over the pram. The baby, at least, would stay dry. 'You'll stick to the High Street?'

Dana nodded as she opened the door. The night had turned evil. The rain was heavy, bouncing off the road, creating puddles like black glass, and the trees in the street were reeling under the force of the wind. Strangely, it might actually help. Inigo loved storms. He'd been born into one, a miserably wet Monday morning. Months later, he loved watching leaves bounce in the wind, was often soothed by the sound of the rain beating against the windowpanes.

Helen said, 'Have you got your phone?'

Backing out, Dana eased the pram down the steps. 'I'll only be ten minutes.'

'Don't you dare move.' Helen returned in seconds, holding Dana's phone out. Dana tucked it into her inside pocket, pulled on gloves, and went out into the night. Within seconds, the street-lamps, the neon glow from the late-night shops, the rain-streaked colours of the night and the wind rocking the pram, had their usual mesmerising effect on the baby. Fewer than ten minutes and he'd be fast asleep.

She had a well-practised route that would take her along the main road for a few hundred metres and then north towards Albert Bridge, before turning right again and heading for home. She tugged her hat over her ears and kept her head down.

It was working. She watched her baby give a heavy sigh. His eyes, open for the moment, were glazing over. He blinked, his eyes closed and opened again but she could see the effort now behind that simple action.

The traffic, a gentle, constant hum in the background was helping too. London never slept, not really. From somewhere behind her a sound broke through the buzz of rain and car engines; a sort of tinkling clatter, of a glass bottle being thrown, but she didn't look back. At the corner she turned onto the A3220, the road that would shortly become Albert Bridge, and took the opportunity to glance into the street she was leaving.

A man in a baseball cap, about a hundred metres back, seemed to be looking directly at her.

At last, Inigo's eyes closed and stayed that way. He would sleep now until around six, but then the two of them would be alone until Helen got back the following evening.

Reaching the end of her own street, Dana turned again, and stopped. Two police cars were parked across the road, blue lights flickering. An arrest was taking place. As she watched, an officer approached a nearby door and banged on it. From another house, someone started yelling. She couldn't take Inigo past this; the noise would wake him.

She set off again, staying on the A3220. After several yards she glanced back, curious about the ongoing arrest, and saw, once more, the man in the baseball cap. Still behind her, the gap between them had narrowed and he was little more than twenty metres away.

Dana picked up her pace. The traffic was quieter now, with seconds of silence in between each passing vehicle. When she reached the road that circumnavigated Battersea Park, it would be quieter still. She felt unease growing and along with it a sense of annoyance, that her instinctive response to a lone male at night was to fear him. Annoyance at herself – most men posed no threat at all to women – but at him too. He could have crossed the road, walked on the other side, been the tiniest bit sensitive.

Embarrassed at how easily she'd been spooked, she made herself slow down; at the same time, pulling back her shoulders and standing a little more upright. She wanted to look back, but some instinct told her not to let him see her fear, because that would give him power. She felt against her jacket pocket to check her phone. Helen could be with her in minutes, but she'd have gone to bed, might even be asleep, and she had an important meeting the next day. And if she called her partner out of bed now, she'd never be allowed out of the house at night again without a fight.

Unable to stop herself, Dana picked up her pace again. They'd settled, eventually, on this particular pram because Helen could run with it; Dana could run too, admittedly not like Helen, but if she had to.

Almost without realising, she'd started glancing across the road into shop windows, into the windows of passing vehicles, to see if she could spot the man behind. When she could stand the suspense no longer, she looked back. He was fifteen metres away.

A white male. Around five eight, slim build, age between twenty and forty. He wore a dark jacket, the collar pulled up and the cap over his hair. He kept his eyes down, making it impossible to see his face. He bore an uncomfortable resemblance, in age, style of dress, manner, to the men abducting the baby that morning.

A black cab passed, heading for the bridge, leaving the road empty.

They were no more than a quarter of a mile from the river. No distance at all. Both Inigo and his pram could be over the side in seconds and there'd be nothing, nothing at all that she could do. The screaming woman from this morning could be her, seconds from now.

Dana picked up her pace again, almost running, but he was close enough now for her to be able to hear his footsteps.

How was this possible? How had they found her again so quickly? He wouldn't be alone, he would have his mates with him somewhere, none of the attackers from that morning had been picked up. They might have a vehicle, be planning to grab her child and speed off with him. How could she not have realised before how completely helpless mothers with babies were?

She glanced back again. The man had a phone held high in his hand, almost as though he were filming her.

Enough. She stopped and turned round.

He stopped too. She knew now, knew that she hadn't been imagining the threat. In that split second, they knew each other.

She could see the gleam of eyes leering from under the baseball cap. On the road, a car went past and then another, but if they even noticed her, had a sense of her distress, they didn't choose to get involved.

How had she let this happen?

Dana turned and ran, knowing the rough movement would wake Ini but that was the least of her problems now. She sped round the corner to find the Prince of Wales Drive as dark and empty as she'd expected. On one side, the park, rimmed by high trees and dense bushes; on the other, houses, all of them dark and still.

Phone Helen? The man would be upon her first. Phone 999? The same applied. She could yell for help, but the chances of a have-a-go-hero being awake and willing to have-a-go were not in her favour. The man was keeping pace. Not running, the way she was, but he didn't have to. He was dressed to move quickly, she wasn't. He wasn't encumbered with a baby. All he had to do was sprint for a few seconds and he'd be upon her.

Do something!

Dana stopped and turned. Panting, more frightened than she'd ever been before, she pulled her phone from her pocket, opened the camera app and took his picture. From little more than five metres away, the length of a large room, they stared at each other.

'How dare you!' Dana took every ounce of fear in her body and made it sound like fury.

He took a step back. 'You what?' His voice was low-pitched, muttered.

'How dare you follow me at this time of night? How dare you try to frighten me? I'm a serving police officer and I've just taken your photograph and sent it out on the Met's active network. Every single officer on duty in London right now will be looking at your face. Several armed teams will be on their way here. Facial recognition software will be searching the database and it will find out who you are.'

Only the photograph part was true, the rest bullshit. There hadn't been time for Dana to forward the man's picture anywhere and she doubted it would be clear enough to be useful. This was a stand-off now; about which of the two of them had the biggest cojones.

'If anything happens to me or my child, the world will know exactly who's responsible,' she said. 'Can you hear sirens?'

His eyes darted left and right.

'Keep listening. You will.'

He took a step back, and then another, his hands raised in surrender. 'I don't know what you're on about. I wasn't following you.'

'I want your name. And some ID.'

'Mad bitch.' The man turned on his heels and ran. In seconds, he'd rounded the corner and was out of sight.

Cojones question asked and answered. This time.

19

A little over three miles from where Dana lay awake, shivering, beside a sleeping Helen, whom she hadn't had the heart to disturb, Mark Joesbury had yet to even try to sleep. He was in his Pimlico flat, in the room that served as both office and bedroom for his son, surfing the Manosphere and despairing of his own sex.

A message pinged into his inbox. It was from Archie, who possibly practised the dark arts, because he never seemed to sleep.

Activity on the Rage site, the message read. *Active chat line, begun about 1800 hours, not long after the press conference aired. Something could be happening.*

Joebury opened his Tor browser and followed Archie's link. The thread he'd been monitoring had nearly a thousand comments, with some two hundred active users at that time. A post from AryanBoy had started it all.

Our day is at hand, it read. *Foot soldiers of the revolution, this is your call to arms. Strike back tonight. Carpe Diem. Take inspiration from our brother in Calgary.*

Below his opening paragraph, AryanBoy had copied a post from a different thread, from a user in Calgary, Canada.

I get a real buzz from following women in deserted car parks and parking garages. I get closer and closer until I can practically touch them. Gives me an erection seeing how nervous they get.

This is simple, effective and brilliant, AryanBoy's post went on. *Use your natural-born advantage to strike back. The foids fear us. They fear our strength, our superior physicality, they know we can harm them. Go out on the streets tonight, brothers, and put the fear of God into a foid. Follow one, get close, remind them who we are.*

'Jesus wept,' Joesbury muttered.

A stream of comments followed, more appearing in real time as Joesbury scanned down.

I'll do it, I'm going out now.

Brilliant idea, I'm in.

Let's do it, make the bitches wet themselves.

Then others, advising caution.

Don't get too close.

Cover your face, watch out for CCTV.

Above all, said one, *break no law. Don't touch the foid you're following, do nothing to give them a legitimate reason to call the cops. You can even apologise. Sorry love, didn't mean to scare you. Wasn't thinking.*

Wear headphones, another advised, *then when you're challenged you can say you were lost in a podcast, didn't know what was going on around you.*

Joesbury spotted one of the handles Archie used when he was trying to infiltrate these sites.

'*Where is this happening?*' Archie-in-disguise had written. '*Anywhere in particular we're doing this?*'

Central London, had been the reply from AryanBoy. *Let's keep it focused. Post your successes, brothers. Make this a night to remember.*

And then the victory posts had begun, as men had gone out onto the streets, to find lone women, follow them and terrify them.

Followed a foid along Pembridge Gardens, one had written. *Followed her for nearly a hundred yards and the stupid bitch had no idea I was there. Had to start coughing in the end. She noticed me then. She crossed the road, so of course I crossed too. She passed an alley and it would have been the easiest thing in the world to drag her in and fuck her till she bled. Remembered the rules, though. No touching, not this time.*

Stalked a classic Stacey on Clerkenwell Road, another wrote. *Bitch was tossing her blonde hair at me, until she cottoned on I might be following her. Watching her trying to run in high heels was the funniest thing I've seen in years.*

There were more of the same, each one followed by a string of congratulatory posts, as men over London revelled in frightening lone women.

A text from Archie came through on his phone. Joesbury rang him.

'I could tell you were up,' Archie said.

The team always knew when the others were online; Joesbury had found it disturbing at first.

'Are you watching this?' the lad went on.

Comments and pictures were coming in all the time, the thread showing no sign of abating.

'What do we do?' Archie asked.

'I'll get a bulletin sent out.' Joesbury reached for his phone. 'Not that it will do much good. We don't have enough cars to have a hope of keeping tabs on this.'

'Most women won't report it,' Archie said. 'They think a man is following them, but nothing happens, he even apologises for scaring them, after he's scared them witless. It's not actually a crime, is it?'

'Technically, it fucking well is, but you're right. Most women will be glad nothing worse happens. They won't take it further.'

'Have you seen some of the pictures? Jeez, there's a woman with a pram here.'

'Where?'

'Towards the bottom, posted about ten minutes ago, by some-one called LadySlicer78.'

Joesbury found the post, saw the rear view of the woman with the oilskin coat taken on a street in Battersea. He saw the make of the pram.

'Shit and corruption.'

'Sir?'

'Talk to you in the morning, Arch. Good work.

Joesbury picked up his phone to call Dana.

20

The man who, online, was known to thousands around the world (and a fair few law enforcement officers) as AryanBoy was at his own computer, watching the night unfold. His soldiers had performed beyond all expectations. If all the posts – more with every passing second – were genuine, and many had pictures or video footage to prove their authenticity, the unprecedented was happening. By morning, something would have changed forever: the men of the UK, possibly further afield, reminded of their power. An essential truth would have been reinforced in all of their minds: the women are afraid of us. The power lies with us; it's always been that way, we've just been lulled, conned, into thinking otherwise. By morning, AryanBoy knew, his army would be invigorated, eager for the next battle, ready and willing to engage. It almost made up for the failure of the Tower Bridge operation.

Partial failure, he shouldn't be too hard on himself. His endless quest for perfection didn't always work to his advantage. The first attack, to begin with at least, had gone like clockwork. The four men, selected and interviewed online, strangers to each other before they met at Tower Bridge, had played their parts perfectly. The abduction had gone without a hitch, the brat launched on the tide, the rainbow-coloured inflatable toy spinning out across the water like a symbol of hope.

It was the worst possible luck that three – for fuck's sake, three – off-duty police officers had been at the bridge that morning and that one of them had arrived in a frigging kayak and been able to give chase like in some weird British episode of *Baywatch*. Even worse that she'd caught up with the kid and fished it out of the water. Had the brat died, sunk without trace in the Thames, his stunt would have been talked about for years to come, eclipsing even the memory of Elliot Rodger's mass shooting. The world would have bowed down before a new Supreme Gentleman.

He'd had to content himself with being the lead item on the national news, but even then there'd been no mention of the community, or the cause. The dumb twats at Lewisham police station had played the whole affair down, suggesting it was the work of lone idiots, a practical joke gone wrong. There had to be a way around that. The world had to know this was only the beginning.

The problem with activity on the dark web was that it stayed dark; most of tonight's micro-attacks would go unnoticed by the world at large. Few, he imagined, would be reported, and whether the thick-as-pig-shit police force would join the dots was doubtful. There had to be a way of making the whole world take the red pill and see what was going on.

Now that was an idea.

He went back to a search he'd done three days ago, when he'd been looking for journalists who were prepared to stray from mainstream, politically correct messaging, and found the one he'd picked out. Emma Boston was a writer he'd followed for some time. Of no interest to him personally – for one thing she was ugly as shit, and for another she wrote regularly about feminism and women's issues – she never stayed clear of controversial subjects. Anything the mainstream might be nervous of touching, Boston pitched right in, not giving a toss whom she offended. And she'd built a name for herself over the past couple of years. Her byline appeared regularly in the nationals.

Boston could be the one.

There had been more posts in the few minutes he'd been away from the Rage site, but it was coming up for two o'clock in the morning and lone females on the streets would be fewer. Speculation had started about whether they would be doing the same thing tomorrow night too.

No, he wrote, knowing action lost its impact if dragged out too long. Fewer would go out the following night, even fewer the night after, and it would be harder to stir up the troops next time he needed them. Keep them hungry, impatient for the next sally, that was the way.

We keep our powder dry he wrote. *There's more to come. For now, dwell on a glorious day. Our cause has caught the eye of the world* (it hadn't, yet, but most of the losers online wouldn't see that.)

And then another post appeared.

Just wish we knew where that Stacey in the kayak lives. A couple of us could go round there, teach the bitch a lesson.

The post sent the thread off into another direction entirely, as men outdid each other to imagine the most violent and sexual revenge they could inflict on the off-duty police officer who'd saved the baby.

For a moment he was tempted to respond, to feed them information that would send them into a frenzy, but caution held him back. He was about to close his computer down for the night when an image appeared, a photograph of a woman in a white kayak. The Stacey in question. Taken by a group of surveyors who'd been on the water that morning the picture had been removed from the surface web almost immediately for confidentiality reasons, but not before his army had got hold of it.

The police officer was young, mid to late twenties, and he guessed would be very good-looking when her face wasn't screwed up with the effort of paddling hard on a big river. Her hair, long and fair, was tied behind her head in a ponytail.

Christ on a bike, it was her.

AryanBoy knew, even though she was seated in the kayak, how tall she was. He knew the sound of her voice. It had been years since the two of them had met but he'd know her anywhere.

The woman who'd rescued the baby that morning was the same one who, twelve years earlier, at the lowest point of his life, had tried to drive him over Beachy Head.

21

Since Lacey had agreed, reluctantly, that swimming in the tidal Thames wasn't entirely responsible for an aspiring sergeant in the Met's marine unit, she'd discovered London's Royal Docks, where open water swimming wasn't only permitted, but actively encouraged. The morning after her adventure at Tower Bridge, a Saturday, she swam her usual 1500 metres without incident and was out of the water before eight o'clock. Huddled in an oversized, fleece-lined robe, she arrived back at the changing room to hear her mobile ringing from inside her bag.

The caller had tried her twice already. Joesbury.

'Hi.' The changing room was suddenly too cramped and so she stepped outside into the fresh air.

'Mark?' she said, when seconds had gone by and he still hadn't spoken.

'I need a favour,' he said. 'If you're free this morning. I'm sorry to ask but—'

The sky above her was a deep, pure blue, with only a smear of cloud, its colour reflected perfectly in the river. It was rare for the Thames to look blue, but when it did, it was such a joy to see.

She waited for what came after the 'but'. Nothing did.

'What do you need?' she said, because if he needed her, she was there. It was just the way it was. Anything in the world for

Mark Joesbury, except the one thing in the world he wanted above all else.

'Can you be with Dana this morning? Helen's away in Brussels all day and I can't get there till noon. I have to take Huck somewhere.'

'I suppose,' she said. 'But—'

'She was attacked last night, well badly frightened. By the same people who were responsible for the attempted murder of the baby. Could be coincidence, but I don't want to take any chances.'

Lacey watched the swimmers and the silver trails they left in their wake as Joesbury filled her in.

'There's a uniformed car outside her house but I think she needs someone with her,' he finished. 'She didn't tell Helen what happened, because she knew Helen wouldn't go to Brussels, and she's pretending she's fine, but she's not. You know what she's like about that baby.'

'Like a parent,' Lacey said, remembering a time when Joesbury had faced losing his own precious child. The most capable man she'd ever met had lost the ability to think.

'I'll go now,' Lacey told him.

'Appreciate it. I'll be there at twelve.'

And did that, Lacey wondered, as she dressed quickly, mean that she should stay until he got there, or leave before he did?

He'd been right about Dana, she realised, within five minutes of arriving at the house in Battersea. Her one-time boss was trying too hard to be normal, forcing Lacey to eat breakfast she didn't want, producing strings of blue bunting that needed to be hung around the garden, and packets of balloons, all of which had to be blown up. The kitchen, normally so tidy, was piled high with packets of party food and the sink with dirty pans and utensils. A pool of what looked like puréed fruit lay, neglected, on the floor tiles by the sink.

For the first half hour, Lacey indulged the business of manic party preparation, polishing glasses, re-stacking champagne in the fridge, chopping vegetables for salads, but when an overfilled balloon burst, causing a sleeping Inigo to wake with a terrified wail, and Dana to burst into tears, she'd been forced to take charge.

She took the baby from a weeping Dana and carried him outside into the small, but perfect garden, knowing the dancing golden leaves and bright flowers would have a better chance of soothing him than his distressed mother. Only when his head drooped onto her shoulder did she return to the house. Dana was leaning over the worktop, staring down at the granite.

'I can't do it anymore,' she said, without looking up. 'I can't fight the bad guys, because all they have to do is threaten my child and I turn to mush.'

'All parents feel that way,' Lacey said, thinking, what did she know? 'They learn to deal with it. What do they call it, adjusting to the new normal?'

Inigo gave a heavy sigh.

'Helen doesn't,' Dana said. 'Helen went charging after those guys yesterday, like you did. I went to pieces.'

Oblivious to his mother's distress, Inigo began to snore in Lacey's ear.

'He's shattered,' Dana said. 'Too much excitement yesterday and he was awake a lot in the night.'

'Looks like you were too.'

Dana's eyes were bloodshot, rimmed with dark shadows and glassy with unshed tears.

'What if it wasn't coincidence?' she said. 'What if they tracked us down here, if they know where we live.'

'That feels very unlikely,' said Lacey, who'd wondered the same thing, as, she knew, had Joesbury. 'No one could have known you'd be on the bridge yesterday morning, so that had to be co-incidence, didn't it?'

Dana still looked troubled. 'I guess.'

'And they couldn't have identified you in such a short time. Chances are none of them even noticed you. Helen and me, maybe, but not you and Inigo.'

Nodding her agreement, but still troubled, Dana held out her arms for her son and the baby was passed from one woman to the other. Dana carried him to the pram, and was stooping to lower him in, when Lacey's phone sounded.

She grabbed it quickly, expecting it to be Joesbury again. It wasn't.

'Emma?' she said, walking out into the hallway.

Her friend wasted no time on pleasantries. 'I need to see you,' she said. 'Something's happened. Something big.'

22

The extra noise and bustle seemed to reassure Inigo; he slept undisturbed through the arrival of the journalist, Emma Boston, whom Dana had met and interviewed two years earlier during Victoria Llewellyn's killing spree, and then a few minutes later, of Mark, who rarely went anywhere quietly and one of his cyber team, the one called Archie. Mark gave Dana a quick hug, nodded politely to Lacey, and held out a hand to Emma.

'You bought me a sandwich,' Emma told Mark as they moved into Dana's sitting room. 'That time I was brought in for questioning.'

'I remember,' Mark said. 'Thanks for coming. I'm sorry to ask, but I need to be sure you're not recording the meeting. Can one of the women check you for surveillance equipment?'

Momentarily surprised, Emma nodded her agreement, and produced her mobile phone. Dana made sure it was switched off while Lacey checked her friend for concealed wires, tracking devices, and recording equipment.

'Where's Huck?' Dana asked, while the search was ongoing. 'I thought he was with you.'

'Gone to a mate's house,' Mark told her. 'He'll be here in an hour.'

'She's clean,' Lacey said after two minutes, before mouthing, 'Sorry,' at her friend.

Emma shrugged, they sat, Dana made sure she could see the baby monitor. Archie put a phone on the coffee table, angled towards Emma to record what was said.

'Fire away,' Mark told the journalist.

'He called at ten o'clock this morning,' Emma began. 'It was an unknown number, which I don't always answer, but I had a feeling about this one. He knew my name, knew all about me. My number isn't listed. When I asked where he got it he laughed and said, "Easiest thing in the world."'

'Is it?' Mark asked Archie.

'I wouldn't say easy.' Archie was making notes on a laptop computer. 'Finding an unlisted number shows some level of skill.'

'He called himself Aryan Boy,' Emma went on. 'He said he'd organised the attack at Tower Bridge, and the micro-attacks during the night. I had to ask him what he meant by that. He said that micro-attacks would be a major part of his strategy going forward, to create a healthy climate of fear. He said there'd been hundreds of his men – those were his words, his men – out on the streets last night reminding women stupid enough to be out on their own that they were never safe.'

Dana felt a stab of guilt; how could she have put Inigo at risk like that?

Emma looked around the group. 'Is that true? Were there really hundreds of men out stalking lone women last night?'

Mark sighed. 'Emma, I know you'll have a lot of questions. Can we leave them to the end?'

The journalist paused, as though to remind them that, for the moment at least, she held the upper hand.

'He said the abduction of the baby, the attacks on the women in London last night, were only the beginning,' she went on after a moment. 'He said the police were lucky yesterday morning, but that they wouldn't be again. He said he has lots more planned, things that will be much worse, that he's very well resourced and that he won't stop until his movement get what they want.'

'What can you tell us about his voice?' Mark asked. 'Young, old? British, any discernible accent? Educated?'

'White British, at a guess,' Emma said. 'He had a fairly distinctive Midlands accent, Birmingham, I thought, but I'm no expert. I'd say he was educated. A good vocabulary. Not old.'

'Doesn't mean a lot, sir,' Archie said. 'There are some pretty cool voice-changing software packages available now. He could have made himself sound like a Klingon if he'd wanted.'

'He said the next attack will be before the month is out and that things will get steadily worse between now and Christmas,' Emma went on. 'I asked him what he wanted, and what he wanted me to do.'

Emma stopped talking and bent to a black handbag on the rug beside her.

'I had to make notes.' She opened a notebook and began reading. 'He said the movement's aim is simple.' She glanced up. 'It's not, but he used the word several times, so he obviously thinks it is. They want a restoration of the rightful societal order – that's an exact quote – in which men reclaim their birth-right of leadership and control.'

'Classic incels,' Archie muttered.

'Specifically,' Emma waited until she had all of their attention again, 'they have a number of demands.'

'Go on,' Mark encouraged.

'First, that women, with immediate effect, lose their franchise. Henceforth – again his words – no woman will be allowed to vote in a general or local election or a referendum.'

Lacey gave a nervous laugh.

'Next,' Emma went on, 'that all female MPs will immediately lose their parliamentary seats, subsequent by-elections being held with candidates taken from all-male shortlists.' She looked up. 'There's more.'

Mark gestured that she should go on.

'No woman in future will be educated beyond the age of eighteen, with the exception only of nurses, teachers and social workers. Women who have previously qualified in a given profession will be allowed to continue practising, to ensure ongoing economic viability, but under the supervision of a male colleague. Newly qualified female teachers will only be allowed to teach in primary schools.'

'This is nuts,' Lacey said.

'This is nothing.' Emma glanced quickly at her friend, and Dana could tell that for all her bravado, the journalist had been upset by her conversation with AryanBoy. 'All women must marry by the age of twenty-one. Women not married by that age will be assigned a suitable spouse. Children will be the property of the father, and he will automatically be granted custody in the event of a divorce. Only men can seek a divorce. The father's permission is required before a pregnancy can be terminated.'

She waited, possibly for a reaction. No one had anything to say.

'Female homosexuality will be made illegal again,' Emma went on, 'although I'm not sure it ever was illegal. Male homosexuality will, they expect, phase itself out naturally once all men are given access to suitable female partners. Gender transitioning will be against the law. Women will be required to dress modestly in public and rape in private places will be decriminalised.'

She finished. Still, no one seemed to know what to say.

'Is that it?' Mark asked, after a moment.

'It's ridiculous.' Lacey's normally pale face had reddened. 'They'll be a laughing stock.'

'No, they won't,' Dana said. 'Most of what Emma's just related is the norm in extreme Islamic countries.'

'These guys aren't Islamists,' Lacey objected. 'They're white, aren't they?'

'They are,' Archie agreed. 'At least predominantly, but the fact that so many countries around the world already have exactly this sort of patriarchal regime will make what they're suggesting seem reasonable. In their eyes at least.'

In other eyes too, Dana thought. How many men, while not condoning for a minute the use of violence, secretly harked back to a time when life was simpler, when men were men and women knew their place? Something was shifting, she realised; the world was changing in subtle but significant ways, even while they sat here in her neat and stylish sitting room.

'They can't expect such draconian measures to be introduced here.' Lacey was starting to look frightened. 'Or anywhere in the West.'

All three women, Dana realised, herself included, were watching Mark for his reaction. It didn't matter how much women like them railed against the idea of such an oppressive patriarchal regime, they'd be powerless unless Mark and the rest of his sex backed them up. Women's safety, even their freedom, depended entirely upon the kindness of men.

'They can't, can they?' repeated Lacey. 'They can't be serious?'

'Almost certainly not,' Mark said. 'Any more than Islamic terrorists genuinely expect to overthrow the West and impose a worldwide caliphate. What they want is attention. Question is, what do they want from you, Emma?'

'He wants me to write about them,' Emma said. 'He was very pissed off that the opening strike – his words – didn't go as planned. He wants me to get a piece in one of the nationals.'

Mark said, 'Give them the publicity they're craving?'

Emma nodded.

He asked, 'Are you going to?'

Of course she was, no journalist could resist such a chance.

'As soon as I got off the phone I called Lacey,' Emma said. 'Don't think I support these losers. What they tried to do at Tower Bridge was obscene. And if they say they've got worse planned—'

She let the thought hang.

'On the other hand,' Lacey prompted.

'If I don't run with it, he'll try someone else,' said Emma. 'Most journalists I know won't hesitate. This story could make my career.'

'What did you tell him?' Lacey asked.

'I said I'd need to do some checking,' Emma replied. 'That I'd want to read up on the cause and find out if there really were any of these so-called micro-attacks last night. Were there?'

Emma the friend was receding into the background, Emma the journalist taking over.

'Are you expecting to talk to him again?' Lacey asked.

Emma nodded. 'He said he'd phone me this evening, and he'd need a decision.'

'Will he meet you?' Lacey said. 'In person, I mean.'

'I doubt it,' Emma replied. 'But I can ask.'

'Can you trace the call,' Lacey asked Mark. 'If Emma agrees to cooperate, that is.'

'Depends,' Archie answered. 'I'd expect him to use a pre-paid burner phone bought with cash and a disposable number from a smartphone app.'

'So, no?' Lacey asked.

'So, yes,' Archie replied. 'No phone is untraceable. Every time he uses it, whether to call, text or access the internet, he's leaving a trace that the telecom companies can pick up. They'll be able to tell where he is from which cell masts are picking up his signal. If he's got two phones, which is likely, his own and the burner he's using to call you, both will be passing between cellular towers at the same time. We spot a phone that's following the same trajectory as the burner phone and that will lead us to him.'

Both Lacey and Emma were frowning, struggling to keep up with Archie's explanation of how the technology worked.

'Just be glad he understands it,' Mark said, in an undertone.

'If he's with someone else,' Archie went on, 'a mate for example, we can track him through his mate's phone. This next part is a bit technical but once we get a trace on his phone, we can start to figure out some information about the device itself, which might lead us to the provider and the shop where he bought it. Most shops have CCTV and staff tend to remember customers who pay in cash. Voice-matching software might be able to help us. The chances are he knows all this though. He'll be wise to it.'

'Emma, are you prepared to cooperate with us, in return for exclusive information on the investigation?' Mark asked.

She looked him straight in the eyes. 'Why do you think I'm here?'

23

The second the journalist agreed to cooperate, Joesbury regretted asking. It was all very well expecting his team to take risks, and he'd lost count of the times his own life had been hanging by a thread, but Emma was a civilian. She wasn't trained, couldn't necessarily be relied upon, and would be another potential problem. On the other hand, she was all they had.

'Hold on, isn't this dangerous?' Dana echoed his own thoughts. 'For Emma, I mean.'

'They won't hurt me while I'm useful to them,' Emma said.

'And when you're not?' Dana retorted. 'When you've written your story and become a nice, high-profile potential victim? When you think you can trust them because you've done what they asked and they seem grateful?'

'They'll go for you in a flash if they find out you're working with the police,' Lacey agreed.

Joesbury got to his feet; it was time to move this on. Already, the two women, with the possible exception of his mum, who meant the most to him, had become far too involved. And they were both frightened. They'd tried to hide their subtle change in attitude towards him and Archie but he'd seen the same thought process running through both their heads, and Emma's. *Are these two men still allies? Can we still trust them?*

'Emma, can you come to Scotland Yard?' he asked. 'We can get you properly briefed and arrange protection.'

Glancing nervously at Lacey, Emma got to her feet.

'Uniform will be outside until Helen gets home.' Joesbury made his way to the door. 'Huck will be here at noon, is that OK? I'm not sure when I'll be back.'

'He'll be annoyed,' Dana warned, although Huck never normally minded spending time with her.

Joesbury glanced over to where Lacey stood in the doorway of the sitting room and felt, for the first time in hours, some of the tension slipping away. He liked her best without make-up, hair damp from swimming.

'Not if Lacey's here,' he said. 'He won't notice I'm gone.'

At Scotland Yard, Joesbury introduced Emma to his team, using only first names to be on the safe side. While they were talking her through the equipment they'd use that evening, he was called up to a meeting with the commissioner. He arrived to find her with Dan Owen, the head of counter terrorism.

'We'll take flack if we let her write her story,' the commissioner argued from her window overlooking the Thames. 'Either we'll look fools for not knowing what was going on, or we'll have neglected our duty by not coming clean with the public.'

Short of locking Emma up, there was no way they could stop her, but Joesbury wisely didn't point that out.

'Emma Boston's the best lead we've got right now.' He helped himself to coffee; the commissioner always had the best in the building. 'If we go public before she writes her story, we'll gain the upper hand but lose the best chance we have to track them down.'

'I'm not sure we'll take that much flack, ma'am,' Dan Owen said. 'The baby was saved by off-duty police officers, with the timely assistance of the marine unit. So far, we come out of it rather well.'

The commissioner sighed as she picked up the phone. 'I'd better let the home secretary know.'

At eight o'clock that night, Emma Boston was back at Scotland Yard, in the sound-proof booth used for telephone conversations the Met needed to trace, waiting for AryanBoy to call. Her phone was connected to equipment in the outer office, meaning Joesbury and the team could see every text message that came in, and hear any call she might make or receive.

A text pinged into Emma's phone at that moment, appearing in a highlighted box on Joesbury's screen.

Good luck, you'll be great. Lacey.

Joesbury didn't look round but was pretty certain more than one member of the team had glanced his way. Lacey hadn't, he registered, wished him luck.

The two of them really had to talk. The last few times they'd met had been earlier in the year on a job in the North West, one that had proven both difficult and dangerous. Since they'd been back in London, he'd been giving her space. If he was honest, he'd needed a bit himself. An innocent woman had died in Cumbria and however often he might tell himself he couldn't have prevented it, there would always be a small voice inside him whispering that it had been his fault.

For the first time, when his bosses had argued he needed to end the field work, Joesbury hadn't demurred. And a London-based job would keep him near Lacey. Whatever problems might stand in the way of their relationship, geography didn't have to be one of them.

Emma's phone began ringing. Through the glass screen that separated the booth from the general office, Joesbury nodded at her to go ahead.

She flicked the switch that would answer the call and said, 'Emma Boston,' into the microphone, as the sound technician began playing the low-level background noise that should fool the caller into thinking Emma was in her flat in Earl's Court.

'Where are you?' the caller asked, as Emma nodded frantically – yes, this was him – and Joesbury glanced at the trace team. None of them looked back, they were already engrossed. Two of his cyber team were present too. Georgie was online, surfing through one incel site after another, tracking any real-time response to the call; Archie had been charged with trying to identify any voice-changing software being used.

'Home,' Emma replied.

'Where's home?' AryanBoy said in a distinctive Midlands accent.

Emma said. 'I'm not telling you that.'

Joesbury nodded his approval.

'I've spoken to some contacts I have at the *Mail on Sunday*,' Emma went on. 'They're interested in principle, for next Sunday.'

'No,' AryanBoy said. 'I want one of the qualities. And I want the story to run in the morning.'

'Not possible,' Emma replied. 'For one thing, I have to write it, and that will take most of the night. There's no way we can catch tomorrow's deadline. And then they'd have to read it, check out it's for real. They'll want to talk to their police contacts. No paper will run a story that could potentially make them look fools.'

Silence.

'Monday morning then,' AryanBoy replied. 'And I want *The Times*. Front page.'

'I can't promise either of those things. If you don't want the *Mail on Sunday* – which has a massive circulation, so I think you should reconsider – then I'm starting from scratch,' Emma said. 'The editors of the dailies might not be available over the weekend, and even if I get hold of the editor of *The Times*, he might not be interested. I know it's a big story, but you never know with these people.'

More silence.

'The best I can do is try for a midweek,' Emma went on. 'Wednesday, Tuesday if we're lucky. Or we can stick with the *Mail on Sunday* next weekend.'

Joesbury could see the journalist's hands shaking, even though she sounded normal and confident.

'Unless you're planning something else this week,' Emma said. 'In which case, it probably does have to be Tuesday, so that events haven't moved on before the story appears. I see that.'

Joesbury gave her a thumbs up; she was doing everything he'd asked of her.

'I'll think about it,' AryanBoy replied, as the officer tracing the call beckoned Joesbury over. 'Give me some options, OK? Keep the *Mail on Sunday* on the table but make enquiries about a midweek on Tuesday or Wednesday. We'll go with the best offer.'

The twat enjoyed giving orders.

'OK, will do,' Emma said, in the booth. 'So, can I ask you some questions?'

'Shoot.'

'We think he might be in St James's Park,' the trace officer told Joesbury, pointing out a triangulated area on his screen that contained most, if not all, of the central London park. 'Technically he could be anywhere in that triangle, but an outdoor space feels the most likely.'

'Tell me about yourself,' Emma said.

AryanBoy laughed, 'Oh, nice try.'

'I'm not expecting name and address, but readers will want to know who's behind such a big movement. What's driving you?

Why did you feel the need to take such extreme action? Can you tell me how old you are? Have you ever been married?'

'This is not about me. It's about men enslaved by a system that is skewed against them.'

The man was letting his impatience show. Given how early in the call it was, that suggested a lack of stability.

'We're trying to access CCTV in that area,' the officer went on. 'Shouldn't take long.'

Behind him, Joesbury heard Archie speaking into a phone. 'Control, this is suite 134, can you send all available cars to St James's park? Suspect is a white male, age twenty to forty, probably alone, talking into a mobile phone. Observe, do not approach.'

It was far too vague, there would be dozens of men in the area answering that description.

In the booth, Emma was talking. 'And yet we have a male prime minister, most of the cabinet are men, two thirds of MPs are men, and most of the judiciary. How can you say the establishment is skewed in favour of females?'

'I'm not talking about the few men at the top, they're the problem.'

The caller's voice was rising, which should make him easier to spot. Witnesses might notice a man shouting angrily into his phone in a London park.

'Men with power and wealth will always have as much female attention as they want,' AryanBoy went on. 'They know women will be competing with each other to date them, marry them, have affairs with them, especially if they have good looks as well. I'm talking about men like me. The women who should be ours by right are falling over themselves to be with the top twenty per cent of men. The eighty per cent get left behind.'

'Should be yours by right?' Emma questioned, in a small voice.

'Woman was put on this earth to be a comfort to man, to be his helpmeet, read your fucking Bible, Emma!'

Silence, in the booth and the general office. There was something quietly terrifying about the man's rage.

'OK, here we go,' the trace officer muttered. Joesbury glanced back to see the half dozen screens monitoring CCTV footage showing different shots of the area around St James's Park.

'You must have been pretty pissed off when your little escapade at Tower Bridge was foiled by a woman,' Emma said. 'What would you like to say to her?'

Joesbury strode up to the glass, shaking his head.

'When the new order is established, she will no longer be a police officer,' AryanBoy replied, and his voice seemed to have calmed. 'She will be married to a suitable mate and will serve her husband the way a woman should.'

'Good luck with that one, mate,' Joesbury muttered.

'Maybe, I'll marry her,' AryanBoy said.

'What was the point of the so-called micro-attacks in the early hours of this morning?' Emma asked.

'A timely reminder of where the power lies.'

'What do you mean by that?'

'I think you know. No woman was hurt this morning; next time that might not be the case.'

'What are you planning next?'

'Something big.'

'Can you be more specific?'

'Can I? Yes. Do I choose to? Not yet.'

'Do you seriously think your demands will be met? Western governments don't have a policy of negotiating with terrorists.'

'That's because terrorist groups always represent a minority interest. We represent half the world's population.'

'No, you don't. You represent a small percentage of men who can't get laid. Real men will laugh at you.'

Joesbury made a calming gesture with both hands: *tone it down. Don't piss him off. Keep him talking.*

'You're kidding yourself, Emma,' AryanBoy said. 'How many men do you think were overlooked for a job, or a promotion, because of a politically correct need to appoint a lesser-qualified female? You think they'll be on your side? How many fathers have lost access to their children, never mind the family home and the better part of their income, in an unfair divorce? You think they're going to be rushing to defend the rights of women? How many former soldiers, who lost their health fighting for their country, and who now can't get a woman to go on a date with them because their bodies are scarred, will be saying, no, of course we have to defend the rights of women? How many men do you think secretly look back to the days when they were the bread winners, when they came home to a respectful family, a loving wife and dinner on the fucking table?'

'He's mad,' Joesbury heard Georgie mutter.

He wasn't though; the twisted git was making sense, of a sort, and that made him dangerous.

'Women don't have the intellectual rigour for the world's top jobs, they don't have the physical ability to do the tough stuff. They're emotional, intellectually stunted, and morally deficient. They're like animals; superior chimps, if you like, and they were put on this earth to be our servants.'

Joesbury watched Emma drop her head into her hands and knew he had to bring this to an end. She wasn't trained for this crap.

'Were you involved at Tower Bridge?' Emma said, changing tack.

'I planned it. The four men were working directly under my orders.'

'But you weren't there? You let someone else take the risk?'

'A general has to stay removed from his army. But I was there. I saw it unfold.'

Emma's eyes flashed up and Joesbury gave her another nod of approval. He turned round but knew Archie and Georgie would already be going back over the CCTV footage from Tower Bridge the previous day. Later, it would be compared to footage from the area around St James's Park. Should the same man appear in both places, there was a good chance he was their guy.

'What you need to understand, Emma, is that this morning was only the beginning. This country is going to see a Day of Retribution, when everything changes, when all the wrongs we've been suffering, for decades, will be put right.'

'Do you mean an actual day? A date in the calendar when something happens?'

'Of course. The Day of Retribution is real.'

'When?'

'Soon.'

'This year?'

A pause, then, 'Yes.'

It was mid-September; they had three and a half months till the year end.

'And what will happen?'

'Something big, something that will change everything.'

'Will people die?'

'Many. But what will be more significant, is who will die.'

'What do we have to do to stop it?'

'I'm glad you asked. There must be an act of parliament, brought in quickly, using emergency powers. We have lawyers in our movement, we know that can be done. This act of parliament will bring our demands into effect.'

'You expect the UK government to give in to your demands? That's crazy.'

'Then the Day of Retribution will happen. And the scale of devastation will be so great that the government will fall. A new regime will take its place, one fit for purpose. And then other countries will follow our lead. The world is changing, Emma, and it began this morning.'

'How do people find you?' Emma said. 'I mean, men you want to recruit to the cause. Where do they look?'

'They don't need to. We find them.'

'Can we meet?'

'Not a chance. You think I'm a fool? Besides, you're not my type.'

'How do I get in touch with you? To let you know how I get on with *The Times*?'

'I'll call you Monday morning. I'll give you an email address to send over your draft piece.'

'That's not the way it works, I'm afraid. You don't get approval of the piece I write.'

'It's the way it will work this time, or I won't talk to you again.'

Emma made eye contact with Joesbury, her hands held up in the air.

'After the next attack, you'll want to talk to me again, Emma, I promise you.'

Joesbury nodded.

'OK, you can see it,' Emma said. 'But you don't get to change it or rewrite it. No newspaper will print a propaganda piece and I won't let anything appear under my byline that I'm not happy with. That's a deal breaker.'

'Fair enough. That police officer, the one in the canoe. Can you give me her number?'

'What?'

'She's my type. You're not, sorry. I might consider meeting her, when this is all over and things have changed.'

Joesbury shook his head. Emma made a, *What do you think I am, stupid?* face, while saying, 'I don't know her.'

'You know who she is, though. You know where she works. Southwark would be my guess, that's the closest police station. Maybe I'll have some of my men check out the staff entrance.'

'I've no idea where she works,' Emma said.

'OK, we're done. Nice talking, Emma. Catch up Monday.'

The line disconnected. The room seemed to let out a collective breath and Joesbury sank into a chair.

'Well done,' he said to Emma, when she emerged from the booth. 'You handled that brilliantly.'

Others in the room echoed him as Emma leaned back against the door.

'You all right?' he asked her.

She made a non-committal gesture. 'I guess. He's a frigging nutter, isn't he?' She glanced over at the staff at the monitors. 'Any luck?'

'It's a matter of time now,' the officer in charge told her. 'We have to run the software, find matches. There's a fair chance.'

'I need to get home,' Emma told Joesbury. 'I have to start work.'

Georgie got to her feet. 'My car's out back. I'll run you home. Uniform will meet us there.'

Joesbury said, 'You'll have twenty-four-hour protection for the immediate future, Emma. And one of my team will be with you when schedules permit.'

'Sir, it sounds like Lacey Flint caught his attention,' Archie said. 'Can we use that?'

'Use her to lure him in, you mean?' Georgie said. 'She's done covert work, hasn't she?'

Joesbury got to his feet. 'Don't even fucking think about it,' he said, and left the room.

24

Lacey's shift finished at ten o'clock. Rain had been falling since eight, turning the river into a bouncing mass of black water, and making the decks of the Targa treacherous. As acting sergeant, she'd been in charge of the vessel, a responsibility that still filled her stomach with crawling insects, but the shift had been a calm one. They'd motored up towards Teddington, calling in at St Katharine Docks and several other moorings on the way. They'd checked the underside of bridges and warned a refuse barge, which really should have known better, that it had travelled too close to the cordon around the Palace of Westminster.

Back at Wapping, she handed over to the night shift, filed her shift report and was done. She checked her messages as she changed into civilian clothes, to find only one from Dana, thanking her for her help that day and looking forward to seeing her the next. Nothing from Emma.

Arriving back at the lock-up yard that led to the marina where she lived, Lacey went through the laborious process of unlocking and opening the access gates, driving through and parking before re-locking them. Visitors arriving at the marina on foot came in through a narrower gate that was also supposed to be locked. Often, though, it wasn't. Normally this didn't bother her. Tonight, she checked.

The tide was low and the boats had all slipped below the level of the quayside. In the next couple of hours, while she slept, almost all the water would leave the creek, leaving only the narrow, freshwater trickle that was the final stretch of the River Ravensbourne. Lacey's boat, and all the others moored here, would settle into the mud. In the early hours, the water would return; she usually felt its arrival, was lulled into a gentle half-sleep by the rocking motion as her home was lifted free.

A train, one of the last of the night, rumbled across the over-head bridge as Lacey approached the quayside ladder. The bridge, a great expanse of concrete ugliness, was possibly the only thing saving this part of the creek from redevelopment. While the bridge remained, the area of land that was the Theatre Arm marina was of no interest to developers.

Quietly, aware that most of her neighbours would be in bed, Lacey made her way across two neighbouring boats to arrive at her own, the last in line. As she stepped over the guardrail, her mobile rang.

'Twice in one day?' she said, her heart thumping. 'People will talk.' That had been flippant, surely, in the circumstances? 'Is Emma OK?'

'She's fine,' Joesbury answered. 'Hard at work, being fed coffee and sandwiches at regular intervals by a bored Georgie.'

'Did it go OK?'

'I'd have come to Wapping but I couldn't get away on time,' he said, not answering her question. 'Have you got ten minutes?'

He needed her help again. 'Sure.' Lacey sat down on the damp seat of her cockpit.

'OK, I thought I'd better call first. I didn't want to freak you out. I'm coming in.'

He hung up. Lacey looked back towards the gates. They were in darkness, almost impossible to make out, but that could be a figure, clambering over, like a thief in the night.

Joesbury. She recognised his outline as he moved through the faint glow of a streetlight. When he reached the quayside ladder, she moved quickly, jumping down into the cabin, checking the boat wasn't too much of a mess. It rarely was. Lacey had many faults, but untidiness wasn't one of them. The one mirror was in the small shower cabin but she didn't have time to check it before she heard heavy footsteps landing in the cockpit. A second later, he swung down into the cabin.

Lacey couldn't remember the last time Joesbury had been on her boat, the last time they'd been this close. Or alone. He was casually dressed, in jeans and a leather jacket; his hair was damp from the rain and he hadn't shaved that day. In the dim cabin light his turquoise eyes looked close to black.

'Coffee?' she offered.

Joesbury gave a slight shake of his head. 'God no. If I drink any more I won't be able to keep my feet on the ground.'

She had beer, had kept the bottles she'd bought when she'd thought she and Joesbury might have a future; they were in the back of her tiny fridge. Somehow, she'd never had the heart to remove them, even to a cupboard. But alcohol right now felt like a very bad idea.

'We need to talk,' he said, leaning back against the cabin steps. It was possible he meant it tactfully, not wanting to intrude further into what was, inevitably, a very small space. It was possible he didn't realise that it looked as though he were blocking her escape.

'We'll be spending several hours together tomorrow,' she said.

'In the company of at least fifty others,' he countered. 'And there's something you need to know now.'

'What?'

'The bloke in charge of these incel characters, the one who calls himself AryanBoy.'

'The one Emma was talking to tonight?'

'That's the one. Seems you've caught his eye.'

Joesbury wasn't making sense. 'How is that possible?'

'He was on Tower Bridge when you did your Wonder Woman act. He was after your number, wanted to know where you work.'

Lacey remained silent. There was no way her personal details would have been released.

'He guessed Southwark, but it's only a matter of time before he thinks about the marine unit. He can hang around outside Wapping, follow you home.'

'He won't get in here.'

'I did,' Joesbury pointed out.

'What do you want me to do?' she asked.

'Be bloody careful. I've sent a note to Dave Cook, letting him know. He'll make sure all marine unit staff keep an eye out for suspicious activity around Wapping and that no one gets drawn into giving out personal information. I'll do the same with South-wark first thing in the morning.'

'Thank you,' she said.

Joesbury moved forward, looking back up at the cabin hatch. 'This place is not secure enough, Flint. I wish you lived on the tenth floor of a block of flats.'

'I'm not wild about heights,' she replied. 'Was that it?'

She didn't mean to sound rude, and God knows she didn't want him to go, not really, but no good could come of him being here. And he'd already made clear he'd only come to warn her, to do his duty as senior officer on an active case.

Instead of answering, Joesbury moved further into the cabin, squeezing himself past the cooker and onto one of the banquette seats. Copying him, she sat opposite, and risked unzipping her coat.

'I shouldn't have asked you to marry me,' he said. 'That was stupid.'

OK, so now they were really going to talk. 'It did change the mood of the evening.'

For a moment, Joesbury didn't answer, and Lacey knew he was remembering the summer evening a little over a year ago: a reception at 10 Downing Street, attended by, arguably, the most important man in the world; a man who owed them both a huge debt. Hand in hand, after the great man had let them go, the two of them had followed the line of people out of the house and into the rose garden at its rear. The night had been filled with the scent of flowers and expensive perfume, with the chatter of ex-cited voices. A table of champagne had sent golden bubbles flying into an equally golden evening. She'd been overwhelmed by the simple, sweet joy of being with the man she loved. And then he'd ruined everything.

He said, 'I still love you.'

And that was joy again, threatening to engulf her like a strong tide. She dropped her eyes to the table top; she couldn't look at him much longer without something terrible happening.

'Nothing's changed,' she said.

Something terrible like admitting she loved him too, that she had almost since the night they'd met, and that she'd never stop. That she would give anything in the world to be with him, do anything to be in his life. Except destroy him.

'Are you married already?'

'What?' Genuinely surprised, she almost laughed. 'No, of course not.'

Joesbury leaned back. 'Damn. I thought I had it with that one.'

'You think that's the only reason a woman might not want to marry you? A pre-existing arrangement?'

'I'm struggling to think of any reason why a woman who loves me, who is free of any other commitment, is refusing to even spend time with me because I made it clear I had long-term plans.'

Lacey opened her mouth to challenge him. It was so typical of Joesbury to assume feelings she'd never expressed. 'What makes—'

And realised there was no point. She simply wasn't a good enough liar. And why add to his pain? He deserved an explanation, but if she told him the truth, he'd face an impossible choice.

I'm not Lacey Flint. I stole a dead woman's identity. If that comes to light, not only will I lose my career, even face criminal charges, but you will too. Unless you betray me.

She couldn't do that to the man she loved.

'Do you love me?' he asked, betraying an uncertainty he'd denied only seconds before.

'Yes,' she replied.

He reached out across the table; she drew both hands back and watched his eyes darken.

'Do you trust me?' she asked in turn. She'd asked him that before. On another occasion, he'd asked her the same question. When lives had been on the line, they'd each asked for total faith in the other.

Joesbury gave a heavy sigh. He knew what she was up to; he knew she'd won.

'Yes,' he told her.

'Then never talk about this again.'

His body sank, as though some invisible force had sucked all air from it. Suddenly he looked exhausted, and years older. He got up.

'See you in church,' he said.

He'd turned, had one foot on the bottom step.

'Mark.'

He stopped.

'Please don't go.'

It seemed to take several seconds for her words to sink in. He froze on the step and for a moment, she thought he hadn't heard, or that he had heard, and was going anyway and she felt the howl of dismay building in her throat. She got up from her seat at the exact second he turned to face her.

The cabin was tiny and Joesbury little more than a step away. The most important journey of Lacey's life was taken in a heartbeat.

25

The man who, from time to time, called himself AryanBoy, wasn't surfing the dark web, watching the venomous posts multiply, the hatred spreading like an oil slick across still water. He wasn't even thinking about the conversation with Emma Boston that had taken place earlier that evening. That had gone as well as he could have expected, and he had no doubt the story would be carried midweek, taking the movement to a whole new level of public consciousness. He was thinking, instead, about the night twelve years ago, when he'd almost ended his own life.

He'd thought often, since, of the psycho-bitch on the clifftop, of her utter disdain, her total disinterest in his pain. To her, he'd been an irritant, a nuisance in the way of her own plans. At the worst, most desperate moment of his life, when he'd grasped for a shred of human contact, of common decency and understanding, she'd turned away. In her eyes he'd been less than nothing, and it had been that night when his misery and loneliness had turned to rage.

And now the two of them had crossed paths – swords? – again. Her presence on the river couldn't have been coincidence. She was his nemesis, would trail his footsteps like a rabid dog. The battle between them, because that's how he'd come to see it, wouldn't end until one had crushed the other.

She was a formidable enemy, one he shouldn't underestimate. She had the Metropolitan Police on her side, along with all the trappings of the establishment. But he had an army. And a very good memory.

In the few seconds he'd been in the back of the car, before it had dawned on him that she wasn't part of the coastal rescue team, that she had no plans to save him, and that really was a corpse the mad bitch had in her passenger seat, he'd seen a scattering of documents on the back seat. He remembered a Cardiff library photo-card, a card with a national insurance number, a student rail pass. He couldn't recall in detail what all the documents had been, but he remembered the two names printed on them.

Lacey Flint, Victoria Llewelyn.

He'd assumed them to be the names of the two women in the car, one dead, one about to be, and had filed the information away to the very back of his mind. Now, as he sat at his window, staring out beyond his computer monitor to the night sky, he was especially grateful for his ability to excavate detail from the depths of his memory. He rarely forgot anything, not completely, and he certainly hadn't forgotten those two names.

Two women should have died that night: *Lacey Flint, Victoria Llewellyn.* When he'd thought of them over the years, he'd assumed both were dead, as one of them definitely had been when they'd briefly shared a car. The mad cow he'd spoken to on the clifftop, who'd locked him in the car, and would have driven over the edge with him had he not managed to break free, had been more than capable of carrying out her own suicide plans. And yet she hadn't.

He wondered, perhaps, if he'd influenced her change of heart, that their meeting had persuaded her that life could go on. How interesting it would be, if fate had bound the two of them, bringing them together on the clifftop, so that each could save the other; and then again, a decade later, for the real battle to commence.

AryanBoy hadn't got to where he was by not being thorough. Before he went any further, he had to check who, if anyone, had gone over the cliff that night. He found the website of the coroner in Eastbourne, and then the records of all inquests going back twelve years.

Most Beachy Head suicides were identified, either they had ID with them, or they left behind friends and relatives. The list was depressingly long, and he suppressed a shiver at how close he'd come to his own name being on it. No Victorias though, no Laceys. Then, a month after the night in question, he found the inquest of an unidentified female, a Jane Doe. Her body had been found inside the crumpled remains of a car, a two-year-old Lexus, trapped between the steering wheel and the driver's seat. Cause of death was listed as multiple injuries and reference was made to the quantity of heroin in the dead woman's bloodstream. It didn't say much for the skills of the pathologist, AryanBoy thought, that he'd described the death as 'probably instantaneous, on impact with the rocks, given that there were no indications that the subject had drowned'.

Such a clever corpse, to have driven herself over the edge.

Significantly, only one body had been found in the Lexus; his nemesis had walked away after all.

Excitement building, he entered Lacey Flint into his search engine and Google pulled up the listings he would have expected, including photographs of women around the world with that name. It didn't take long to see that the woman from the clifftop wasn't among them. There were Lacey Flints on Facebook and LinkedIn, and he took several minutes scrolling through possibilities. None of the photographs matched, but a few Lacey

Flints had used weird avatars, pictures of flowers or cartoon characters. Women only did that in his experience when they were ugly as trolls but he checked the details of each. None lived in London or within commuting distance; none appeared to be the right age.

He carried on, searching through Twitter and Instagram, YouTube and TikTok. When he'd exhausted the potential of the surface web, he opened his Tor browser, but after the better part of an hour, was forced to admit defeat. The Lacey Flint he was looking for had no online presence, and that was unusual, given the insatiable craving of most females for attention.

Into a fresh search page AryanBoy typed Victoria Llewellyn.

Woah!

In an instant, his heartbeat seemed to have doubled, hammering against his chest the way it had during the humiliating sports day races at school. How had he not made that connection before now? He clicked on the first link and read the Wikipedia page; his chest began to feel uncomfortably tight. This was quite some rabbit hole. He went back to the search results and opened a newspaper story; after racing through it, he considered checking he was still awake. He read another, then a third. Victoria Llewellyn was the Ripper, the killer who, not two years earlier, had slaughtered four women in some twisted revenge attack. She'd been born and brought up in Cardiff; in the back of the Lexus had been a Cardiff library card.

How had he not made that connection before now?

Hands trembling, AryanBoy switched to the page of images where the same face appeared over and over again. Young, fair-haired, beautiful; insane, although technically not, because she'd been certified fit to stand trial and was incarcerated now in Durham.

What the hell had he stumbled upon?

He clicked on one image of Llewellyn, taken shortly after her arrest and enlarged it. Not the woman who'd thrown herself into his way twice. Well, obviously not, that woman had been on the Thames two days ago, not locked up in Durham prison. And yet, there were similarities: the oval of the face, the regularity of the features, the shape of the eyes.

Spotting another image, he enlarged it too. Taken in a photo-booth, it showed two teenage girls clowning around. Victoria Llewellyn had had a sister. The younger, Cathy, at around four-teen years old was startlingly pretty, the older one, who'd grown up to be a killer, was all black Gothic hair, heavy make-up and pinched white features.

Realisation struck him hard, and for several seconds he wondered if he might be having a heart attack. He'd seen that photograph before, or one very like it. The portrait picture encased within the Cardiff library card on the back seat of the Lexus had been taken the same day, in the same photobooth. The Goth girl's hair was the same, her make-up the same, the tiny gold ring through her left eyebrow the same. Even the upturned leather jacket was the same.

The girl on the clifftop had had dark hair, but with fairer roots visible where the black dye was growing out. She'd worn no make-up or jewellery that he'd seen, but she'd worn that leather jacket. He remembered the way she'd pulled the collar up against the wind, tugged down the zip as she'd climbed back into the car. The girl in the Lexus twelve years ago, who'd nearly killed him, had been Victoria Llewellyn, had grown up to become the most notorious female serial killer Britain had ever known; and yet she'd been on the river not two days ago.

So, who the hell was serving time in Durham prison?

26

Lacey woke with her face pressed against Joesbury's shoulder, his chest hair tickling her nose. Without thinking, she rubbed her face against him. He gasped, stiffened, and from the back of his throat came a muffled moan.

The boat was rocking gently; the tide had come back. Through the tiny cabin hatch that she'd opened in the early hours, shortly before they'd fallen asleep, Lacey could smell the river: rotting moss and black mud, old timber and the faintest trace of a bonfire; strangest of all, ripe pears. The Thames carried a thousand scents in its secret folds, bringing fresh surprises with each new tide. The rain had stopped, and sunlight was casting a dusty beam across the cabin.

As Joesbury stretched, feeling his way in the unfamiliar bed, his eyes opened and a wide grin flashed across his face. 'Good morning.'

He rolled towards her. Propped on his elbows, he hovered, his face inches from her own. She could feel the heat from his skin.

'Hello.' Absurd to be shy, after everything the two of them had been through, after everything they'd done hours earlier, and yet she couldn't meet his eyes.

Joesbury bent his head to kiss her ear, her neck, at the same time shifting one of his thighs so that it slipped in between hers. He wanted her again.

No problem.

'Shit!'

He was looking at his watch, now a few inches behind her head.

'What?'

'I should have been at Dana's an hour ago.'

Lacey's body screamed in protest as he pulled away, exposing her to the chill air of the cabin.

'Nothing's happening until twelve,' she argued.

On his feet now, Joesbury stretched, reaching the yacht ceiling easily. 'They had Huck to stay over. I said I'd be back before he woke up. The last thing they need this morning is a twelve-year-old under their feet.'

Staying on the bedroom side of the doorway Lacey watched Joesbury scrambling around for his clothes. The oval cut-out of the narrow door didn't reach all the way to the yacht floor, but finished some six inches above it, creating a doorstep that she'd tripped over several times in the night before muscle memory had kicked in and taught her to avoid it. It had been one of the few things about the yacht she didn't like, but she was starting to see its possibilities. 'Huck's great with Inigo,' she said. 'Kept him entertained for hours yesterday.'

Boxers in hand, Joesbury turned back. The yacht was always cold when she woke up, and she could feel her skin goose-pimpling in the chill air.

'Helen and Dana will approve,' she told him. 'Two days ago Helen told me I should take one for the team.'

Joesbury stepped back towards her. 'She did what?'

Quick as a flash, Lacey grasped hold of him around the waist, at the same time climbing onto the narrow ridge of wood around the door frame. She was an inch taller than he was now. Using

Joesbury for balance, she rose onto the balls of her feet and manoeuvred herself into just the right position.

'What the hell are you doing?' he moaned, as she squirmed against him.

'Taking one for the team,' she whispered into his ear.

Lacey couldn't remember the last time she'd been to church. As she sat a few rows behind Joesbury in St Saviour's, Battersea, she wondered if maybe this was her first visit ever. She'd never been taken as a child, her school had been secular, and while there'd been a couple of funerals since she'd joined the Met, somehow they didn't count. A funeral had nothing in common with this joyful service, where simple, repetitive motions and chanting seemed to act as a balm to troubled spirits, where communal singing lifted the heart and where a congregation welcomed a new life into itself, to be loved and protected, to belong.

Lacey had a sense of the congregation binding together, of silvery threads reaching out from the tiny child and wrapping around each of them. How had she not known how wonderful church could be?

As they left the building Joesbury's young son, Huck, caught up with her. 'Auntie Dana has a dress like that.' He took her hand, realised what he'd done, and dropped it again.

'It was Auntie Dana's.' Lacey was conscious of the scent of a man's cologne creeping up on her. 'She lent it to me for the prime minister's reception, and then said I might as well keep it because she was pregnant and wouldn't be able to fit into it much longer.'

'She can fit into it now,' Huck pointed out.

'You think I should give it back?'

'It looks better on you.' Joesbury stepped up to her other side. 'And the last thing Dana needs is more clothes.' He too took her hand; unlike his son, he didn't let go.

*

The party, that she'd dreaded, turned out not too bad at all. Hating small talk normally, Lacey found it easy when, treated as an honorary little sister by the two hosts, she wandered from group to group, offering drinks and food. Those who knew her wanted to talk about her escapade on the river, those who didn't to compliment her on her dress, and say how lovely it had been to watch her joy during the church service.

'Are you a frequent church-goer?' an elderly neighbour asked. 'Where do you attend?'

And moving on was easy, when there were always more glasses to be filled, more trays of food to be carried around. It was round about three o'clock, when her feet were hurting in the unfamiliar heels, and she knew if she had another glass of champagne she wouldn't be able to drive home, that Lacey realised she was happy.

The thought was terrifying.

'What's up?' Joesbury had crept up on her. 'You look like you've seen the proverbial ghost.'

A hand, not his, landed on the small of her back.

'Nice work, Lacey,' Helen hissed in her ear, before moving on, casting back an evil smile. No, not a smile, a leer.

Lacey looked up at Joesbury. 'You told her?'

He had the grace to avoid her eyes. 'Course I didn't tell her. They guessed.'

'How could they guess? Did you have a T-shirt printed?'

'Well, strictly, that wouldn't be a guess . . .' he caught sight of his son at the other side of the garden, poring over a device with another boy of a similar age. 'I think Huck knows too.'

Lacey stared at the child in dismay. 'That's disgusting.'

'He's twelve, not six. He wants to know if you're coming back to our place later. We're getting a takeaway.'

To Joesbury's flat in Pimlico, a place she'd never seen. A picture came into her head of the three of them, cuddling together on the sofa, watching a movie appropriate for twelve year olds. Huck, in spite of his dad's objections, insisting on sitting between them.

'And I don't like the idea of you hanging around that boatyard at night.'

'You make it sound like I'm servicing sailors,' she said, disappointment flooding through her. 'I can't though. I have to be at Wapping by ten. I'm on nights all week.'

'Another time.' Joesbury pulled a rueful face, then leaned down to whisper in her ear. 'Another time soon.'

27

'How are you feeling?'

'Good,' replied the man whom AryanBoy knew only by his online handle, Waluigi. 'I'm feeling good. I can see the place now.'

'OK, slow down. Let's go through it one more time.'

AryanBoy told himself he had to stay calm, that panic on his part would transfer quickly down the phone line to Waluigi. Already he could hear the other man's breathing speeding up, and his voice was louder than it needed to be. The street in Peckham wouldn't be busy, not until later when the pubs started emptying and the drunken men came looking for pleasure of a different sort. The wrong comment overheard at this stage could spell disaster.

'There will be one woman on reception,' he said, although the two of them had been through this several times already. 'The security men don't arrive until later.'

'One woman, behind the desk. She won't be able to get out in time to stop me.'

Waluigi was starting to sound robotic; AryanBoy wondered if he'd taken something, although he'd been told not to.

'When you push your way through to the back,' AryanBoy went on, 'she'll pick up the phone. She'll be calling security, but it will take them a half hour to arrive. We know that for a fact.'

He didn't, but he was confident enough. He'd had another of his men visit the place a month earlier and cause a scene. The woman behind reception hadn't called the police. The place called Bubbles might be licensed as a massage parlour and spa but everyone knew what really went on behind the opaque windows and saloon-style inner doors. Trouble that led to police action could easily see the place closed down. When the same woman heard screaming, she probably would call the police, but the nearest station was several miles away and unless Waluigi got very unlucky with passing patrol cars, he'd have plenty of time.

AryanBoy tapped out a message to his lieutenants. *Ten-minute countdown. Start directing traffic to the Rage site. Men in the vicinity need to be ready to mobilise.*

To Waluigi he said, 'Go through the saloon swing doors into the back. Remember the plan I sent you? What's on your left?'

'The spa. I don't go in the spa, I might slip on the wet floor.'

'Exactly. On the other side of the corridor are the rooms where the massages take place. Ignore them too.'

'What if there's someone in one of them?'

The chances were there wouldn't be, they'd picked this time of night for a reason. The parlour hadn't been open long and there'd be few, if any, punters. It was also, coincidentally, the time of night when most of his army would be online at home. When they got word that shit was going down on the Rage site, they'd flock to it.

That would be happening right now, if his guys were doing their jobs properly. Excitement would be building.

He said, 'You don't want to get into a fight with a bloke. It's the foids you've come for. Now, you might come across one or two in the corridor, we've no way of knowing, but if you do, that's a bonus.'

'Bonus, right.' The bloke was panting. 'I'm outside now.'

The twat had been told to hang back.

'Walk past, don't go in yet, take some time. Are you moving?'

'I am, yeah. I've gone past.'

'Good. Keep walking. Is the knife where you can reach it?'

'Inside pocket. I've been practising. I can pull it straight out.'

'And you're wearing gloves?'

'Yeah. And that thing over my face.'

Waluigi had been sent equipment, including a snood that he'd pulled up over the lower part of his face as he'd left the Tube. It would be enough to fool any facial recognition software.

'And you're clear about the procedure. In below the belly button, aiming down towards her cunt, then up towards her heart. Two counts, two thrusts, are you clear?'

'Yeah, yeah.'

'Most of the foids will be in the staffroom at the back. They'll panic when you come in, especially if they've heard screams, and if there's blood on you, but panic is good. Foids are like sheep when they panic. You'll see the outside door at the opposite side of the room, and that's what you go for. Slash with the knife as you go. They won't try to stop you. We're looking for at least one death, more would be amazing, but several of them cut up would be great too.'

No response. The line was still open though, AryanBoy could hear the other man's wheezing breath.

'When you get to the door, go straight outside. There's a small iron staircase, only three or four steps, but be ready for them, you don't want to slip. The door to the yard will be locked, but you can climb onto the bins and get over that way. Once you're on the other side, head for the park. You know what to do then, don't you?'

He should know; they'd talked it through – what – four times or more?

'What if I don't make it to the park?'

'You will. The others will be out by then, you won't be on your own.'

'What if I don't?'

Fuck's sake! Twenty-four hours ago the twat had sworn he was going to hang himself live on the internet because he couldn't face another day of his lonely, pointless existence. Now, given a chance at going out in a blaze of fame, on a level with Elliot Rodger, Chris Harper-Mercer and Alek Minassian, he was worrying about being picked up by the police.

Keeping his voice steady, AryanBoy said, 'You win either way. Once you're out that door, with blood on your hands, you're one of our heroes. The first real strike will be yours. Even if you're caught, the whole world will know your name. And when the change comes, when the new order is established, all of our freedom fighters will be released and held in honour for the rest of their lives. A great home, no need to work, the best, most beautiful women. Everything you've worked for, everything that's yours by right. Are you ready to go back now?'

'I think so. Yeah, yeah I am.'

'Last time we spoke, you asked me why a massage parlour, why we were going to attack whores, do you remember?'

'Yeah.'

'Well, now I'll tell you. These places exist to degrade men. They charge us thirty quid for a hand job, fifty for a blow job, all the while treating us like dirt. Men should not have to pay for bad sex handed out grudgingly by disease-ridden whores. When the new order comes, no man will ever have to pay for sex again and women who have charged us in the past will be punished with rape by dogs.'

Bloody hell, where had that come from? Did dogs even – focus! He could not lose his grip now.

'This time last week you wanted to kill yourself. Do you now?'

'No, fuck no.'

'Good man. How far away are you?'

'Ten yards.'

'OK, switch your body cam on.'

'Right, I'm doing it. Can you see anything?'

'Hold on, wait, don't go in yet. Yes, I've got it.'

The screen on AryanBoy's monitor burst into life and he could see the grainy picture of the street in Peckham. The body-held camera had been included in the package sent to Waluigi.

'I'm outside.'

'I can see.'

The large glass window of Bubbles Spa and Massage Parlour had been painted to make it opaque. Cartoon bubbles rose from the sill, up towards the top; most had been half scratched away, and the window was filthy.

AryanBoy began typing, announcing to his followers on the Rage site that it was about to happen. 'We're going live in ten seconds,' he told Waluigi. 'The world will be watching. If you wimp out now, if you fuck it up, they'll see, but I know you won't do that. I know you'll make us all proud.'

'I'm going in.'

'Five seconds. You can do this. I believe in you. Four, three, two . . .'

AryanBoy heard the ringing sound as the door to the massage parlour was wrenched open.

'One,' he said, quietly, to himself.

28

Joesbury got back from driving his son home at fifteen minutes past ten.

Lacey would be in uniform by now, making her way down the pier at Wapping towards a waiting Targa boat. As acting sergeant she'd be its skipper for the night. She and her crew would have a stretch of the river to patrol and allotted tasks to complete; if they were lucky, it would be a quiet night out on the water, nothing much to report when the shift finished a couple of hours before dawn.

She had seven days of night shifts ahead of her, and given how busy SCD10 were right now, his own life would be hectic for the foreseeable future. It would be days before he saw her properly again, and that might be no bad thing, given how completely his life had turned around in the last twenty-four hours. He was struggling to get his head around it, frankly.

Not that he was complaining. He was grinning to himself as he locked the car and crossed the street.

He'd opened the door to his flat and switched on the lights before realising how very tired he was. Either happiness had always been exhausting and he'd forgotten, or he really was getting old. Good thing he had an early night ahead of him; one that promised very sweet dreams.

The doorbell rang. Wondering if, for some reason he couldn't begin to imagine, Lacey had arrived after all, he stepped out into the hallway again. His heart sank when he saw who was standing on the doorstep. Not Lacey.

Trouble.

'There's something new happening,' Archie began, as he, Georgie and Warwick followed Joesbury into his living room. Theo, he remembered, was taking a rare weekend off. 'We thought we should brief you before we finished for the night.'

'Cyber-flashing.' Warwick said. 'Started first thing this morning.'

Joesbury thought for a second. 'You mean sending porn anonymously to strangers?'

Cyber-flashing was nasty. First, the perpetrator uploaded images onto his device, usually his phone. Dick-pics were typical, but hard-core porn wasn't uncommon: gang rapes, violent sexual attacks. The bloke then got physically close to a woman in a public place – bus station, train carriage, busy shop – and AirDropped the picture to her phone.

Warwick said, 'Clearly meant to follow the same trajectory as what happened in the early hours of Saturday. AryanBoy tells the community what to do, men all over the country go out and create havoc, then go back home and boast on the internet.'

'Not every phone has AirDrop open,' Joesbury said. 'I've made Huck turn his off.'

'No,' Warwick agreed. 'But AirDrop-open-to-all is the default setting.'

'We've picked up a lot of noise on social media,' Georgie said. 'Especially Facebook and Twitter. Lots of very angry women out there.'

'They were told to find women on their own,' Archie added.

'And to move away quickly,' Georgie said. 'Not to risk staying around to see the reaction, because some of the foids – their words, obviously – would be wise to how it worked.'

'Why?' Joesbury asked. 'What's the point? What's in it for them?'

'Distress,' Georgie replied. 'Intimidation. They're sending out a message: we can reach you, even through your technology. You're never safe.'

Joesbury asked, 'How many incidents are we talking about?'

Georgie said, 'When we left to come here the number of comments on the thread, most claiming to have done it, had gone over fifteen hundred.'

'Problem is, we can't do much,' Warwick said. 'There's no specific law prohibiting cyber-flashing, we'd have to use existing legislation that wouldn't be ideal. Proving it would be challenging, and we'd only get a fraction of those who've been involved.'

'To answer your earlier question, sir,' said Archie, 'I think it's partly about attention. This'll get coverage in the coming days, even without Emma's piece. It's partly about keeping morale up and the troops motivated. Mainly, though, I think it's about keeping women afraid.'

'Exactly,' Georgie jumped in, and Joesbury noticed for the first time a difference in her reaction. The two lads were concerned, Georgie was visibly upset. 'If we go out at night, you'll follow us. If we're out in the day, in public places, with friends, you can still get to us. You want us to know that we're never safe, because you're everywhere. And you hate us.'

At that moment, Joesbury's phone began ringing. Then Archie's, quickly followed by both Warwick's and then Georgie's. Four phones, demanding attention, and Joesbury felt the happiness of the day slipping away.

29

Less than a half hour since the first 999 call had been received, a sizable and noisy crowd had gathered around Bubbles Spa and Massage Parlour in Peckham. Most were young men, many filming the scene on their mobile phones. As Joesbury weaved around the police cars blocking the road, an ambulance screamed away to a chorus of jeers from the onlookers. A second was parked at the kerbside. After safeguarding his bike, Joesbury pushed his way through.

'Fucking whores, serves 'em right!'

Ducking beneath the cordon Joesbury flashed his warrant card at the exact same moment that a firework exploded nearby.

'Turn round, mate! Smile for the camera.'

'How come you get to see the dead whores?'

'We've got rights too, you know!'

Jeez, he was being heckled like a Tory politician in Liverpool.

'They showed up en masse fifteen minutes ago.' The evening wasn't warm, but the sergeant in charge was red in the face and sweating. 'Didn't give us chance to secure the scene properly. Frigging social media.' He nodded towards the door of the spa. 'Ruddy mess in there.'

The crowd pressed forward again, forcing the sergeant to join his officers in the effort to keep them back. 'DI Anderson's inside,' he called to Joesbury.

Knowing he was about to see something that would ruin the best day he'd had in the last two years, Joesbury pushed open the front door. The clanging bell drew the attention of the four people in the room beyond.

A young woman of south Asian origin, scantily dressed and heavily made-up, stood huddled in the corner. An older, white woman sat behind the desk, flanked by a female police constable on one side, Neil Anderson on the other. With Dana still, officially, on maternity leave, Anderson would have been the officer called out to the scene. He approached Joesbury.

'Two dead, at least one seriously injured.' Anderson pitched his voice low. 'The whole thing was live-streamed. That lot outside arrived before we did. First thing we had to do was clear them out.' He glanced towards the saloon doors. 'No crime scene left to speak of.'

'I've got people taking the footage down,' Joesbury replied. 'Where has he gone? The perp? Is he still here?'

Anderson shook his head. 'Ran out the back door.' He glanced back at the receptionist. 'Elaine here says he seemed to know exactly where he was going. I need to have a look myself, but I can't leave until I've got all the women out of here. That lot out front are a frigging mob.'

As if on cue the men outside the parlour began chanting; they sounded like a football crowd.

'I'm not going out there,' the woman in the corner wailed. 'They want to kill us all.'

'No one's getting anywhere near you, love,' Anderson told her. 'Come on, let's find you a chair.'

Joesbury stepped closer to the window to hear what the men outside were singing.

'I wish all the ladies, were holes in the road,
And if I was a dump truck, I'd fill them with my load.'

Joesbury said, 'Are SOCOs here yet?'

Something banged against the window.

Anderson shook his head. 'Five minutes. Three of the girls are still being treated on site. The rest are having the screaming ab-dabs. No, no, love—' he broke off to stop the young woman running through to the back. 'Let the paramedics do their job. We'll get you out of here soon.'

Footsteps sounded and the low buzz of voices. Anderson and Joesbury turned to watch uniformed officers leading two young women out through the saloon-style swing doors. Wrapped in blankets, both women had blood stains on their clothes and skin.

The volume outside grew as the group left the building.

'Hard to tell who's hurt and who's not,' Anderson said. 'I'm sending them all to St Barts to be on the safe side.'

He turned back to the Asian girl. 'Love, you're next. Is there a coat we can find for—?'

Anderson didn't get to finish as, two feet behind him, the huge front window shattered. The Asian woman screamed as Joesbury pulled her out of the way. He held his breath, waiting for the broken glass to fall. It didn't, thank God, but a hard shove from the outside would send a thousand lethal shards into the room.

'What the bloody hell?' the receptionist shouted. 'Get us out of here!'

'We need more uniform,' Joesbury said to Anderson. 'That lot outside aren't harmless rubberneckers.'

'You think they could be involved?'

'This isn't normal. We should round as many of them up as we can and get them to Lewisham.'

Anderson turned away to talk into his radio and Joesbury stepped closer to the swing doors. Beyond he could see a narrow corridor; somewhere, out of sight, a woman was keening.

A paramedic appeared from a room at the back, followed by a second, carrying a stretcher between them. Joesbury pulled open the swing doors to let them pass and saw a woman in early middle age, black-haired and plump, beneath a thermal blanket. An oxygen mask covered her face; her left hand, stained with blood, fell down over one side of the stretcher. Before the doors swung shut, he caught sight of a corpse on the corridor floor: another woman, slim and small, with hair that had been dyed henna-red. Her blood formed a scarlet pool around her body. Bloody footprints tracked backwards and forwards along the corridor. As crime scenes went, this one was already a disaster.

'Neil, can I go through?' he asked.

Anderson didn't even look round. 'Mind where you step.'

Picking his way from one clean patch of floor to the next, Joesbury made his way down the corridor. Someone had propped open the doors beyond and he could see into each room he passed. The spa, on his left, was a raised jacuzzi with a couple of plastic sun-loungers on the linoleum floor. On his right, a small room with a towel-covered massage couch. A single shelf held an industrial-sized roll of absorbent paper towel and a large bottle of baby oil. He had to step round the corpse to move further into the building.

Another empty massage room, then a third. Joesbury started at the sound of a door opening and then another detective he knew, Pete Stenning, appeared from the door at the very end of the corridor. He approached gingerly, keeping a close eye on where he was treading.

Joesbury asked, 'What happened, exactly?'

Stenning said, 'Hard to tell. The women who aren't badly hurt are seriously shook up, and most of them don't have great English. From what we can gather, though, he got here about thirty minutes ago and forced his way in through the front office.'

Stenning's eyes fell to the corpse at his feet. 'He killed this one on the spot. Another woman heard the commotion and poked her head out of the end cubicle. He stabbed her too. She was still alive when the first responder got here but the paramedics pronounced her dead.'

'Any punters?'

'One, waiting for the girl of his choice to come and find him. He scarpered. We need to find him though because he almost certainly got sight of our guy.'

'Neil said he went out the back?'

Stenning nodded. 'Pushed his way into the staffroom where a few other women were waiting for the place to get busy. The two still here have some nasty cuts. We've given them what first aid we can. We're waiting for another ambulance.'

'A few other women? How many?'

'Two in there now, another you'll have passed in reception and they've been talking about a girl called Mala who ran out the back way when he broke in. Sounds like it was complete pandemonium. He was screaming at them, slashing his knife around like a maniac. He seemed to know where he was going, though. Made straight for the back door.'

'After the woman called Mala?'

Stenning gave a heavy sigh and led the way back down the corridor. Joesbury followed, past the second dead woman, a pale-faced red-head who was slumped, eyes open, against the wall of the last cubicle, and into a room with kitchen units against one wall, a TV on a formica table and several shabby chairs. A woman with silver-blonde hair, ashen pale, was clutching her upper arm against her chest. A towel that had been clumsily wrapped around it was turning scarlet.

'Not long now, love,' reassured the constable crouched at her side. 'We'll have you out of here in a jiffy.'

Two others – a knife attack victim and accompanying officer – were at the sink, treating a wound on the woman's hand. Joesbury caught a glimpse and felt his stomach heave; the woman's palm had been slashed open to the bone.

Stenning pulled open the outside door.

'Take it easy, Pete,' Joesbury called. 'We don't know for sure he's gone.'

Four iron steps led down into a flagged and very dark yard. Outside, Joesbury was reminded again of how noisy the night had become. The crowd out front seemed to have grown and a siren was approaching. Car horns were sounding every few seconds.

The yard resembled a municipal dump with rubbish filling every corner: a stained mattress, a broken massage bed, discarded electrical equipment, empty tubs that once contained pool chemicals.

'Mala?' Joesbury called. 'We're police, you're safe now.'

More fireworks shot into the sky, then a low-pitched whimpering startled both men. They followed the sound to where refuse bins stood against the wall. Joesbury's torch beam picked out the pale face of a young woman huddled between two of them.

'Are you hurt?' Stenning crouched down.

She looked past him to Joesbury and raised her right hand. 'He went over there.'

She was pointing to the wall.

'I'm going to have a look round,' Joesbury told Stenning, who was helping Mala to her feet.

'Watch yourself,' Stenning replied, as Joesbury climbed onto the same bin, probably, that the killer had used and followed him over the wall and into the alley. As he landed, he heard Stenning coaxing Mala back inside the parlour and then his own phone ringing. It was Georgie, calling from Scotland Yard.

'Couple of things, sir. We've got footage of the attacker arriving. His online name is Waluigi, you know the Mario Kart character? He got off the train at Queens Road and went on foot from there to Bubbles. His face is covered, but he was wearing a pale, lightweight jacket and what look to be hiking trousers, again lightweight, and a baseball cap and a scarf around his lower face. Oh, and he's carrying a biggish rucksack on his back.'

As Georgie spoke, Joesbury took in his surroundings. A high wall of industrial premises faced him, impossible to scale. To his right, the alley stretched a hundred metres or more, to his left, around twenty.

'I'm going left,' Joesbury said, and did so. 'He'll be covered in blood, Georgie. If he's on the streets, people will notice him.'

'That's what we thought,' she replied. 'But there's been no trace that we can find. Nothing on camera, no reports coming in.'

Reaching the alley's end, Joesbury looked up and down the street. A line of parked cars looked empty, but he could check as he went past.

To Georgie he said, 'What was the other thing?'

'We're monitoring the Rage site – you know the attack was live-streamed?'

'Please tell me that's been taken down?'

'Off YouTube and Facebook, absolutely, but it's still up on Rage and will probably stay there. It's really bad, sir.'

Georgie's voice carried the faintest hint of a tremor, a stark reminder to Joesbury that his team, brilliant and capable as they were, hadn't experienced anything like this before. They would all be changed before the night was out.

Even so, now was not the time for counselling. 'Was that it?'

'No.' Georgie sounded affronted. 'They've had another one of those call-to-arms things. They were telling anyone who lives in the Peckham area to get out on the streets and cause a distraction.

Get in the way of the police, help their hero brother get away. Are you seeing anything of that?'

Well, that explained a lot.

'Oh yes. Thanks, Georgie, I'll be in touch.'

The street Joesbury found himself in remained empty. Were he to head left, he'd hit the main road again in a few minutes; he could hear the noise of the crowds, the taunting of the police, the fireworks. It was almost as though Rent-A-Mob had been told to concentrate on the front; to keep all the police attention on the front.

Joesbury turned right, moving away from the crime scene and the commotion, into the dark street.

30

Lacey loved the river at night.

Of course, she loved it in daytime too: hot summer days, when even the Thames lost its customary muddy brown colour and absorbed the sapphire-blue of the sky; crisp autumn days when golden leaves lay scattered across its surface like confetti; she especially loved it at dawn, the early mist blushing pink as the sun came up; and evenings could be wonderful, the setting sun turning river-fronted glass into gleaming shades of bronze and copper, their reflections shimmering on the water.

Night-time, though. Night-time was special. In the dark, the river became a slow, lazy serpent, coiling its way through the heart of the capital. At night, river traffic quietened almost to nothing, and it was rare for a marine unit night patrol to spot another craft on the water. When they did, they often hailed it, especially if it was a boat they didn't know, and the exchange was nearly always friendly, like fellow travellers sharing a journey.

At night the boat slipped in and out of pools of silent, stygian blackness, so still, so deep that there were times she thought they might never emerge into the light again; but the light, when it came, glowed like treasure.

The first two hours of the shift had been quiet. Since they'd left Wapping, Lacey and her crew had encountered nothing other than a refuse barge, heading out to the estuary. As midnight approached, she steered towards the Houses of Parliament; checking on the exclusion zone was a regular and important task of the night patrol.

The call came in as the Queen Elizabeth tower came into view. The wind had been getting up for the past hour and Lacey and her two crew members were in the cabin. She was on the helm, Gemma Jackson, a new recruit, in the small galley making coffee, and Finn Turner, known as Spider-Man because of his exceptional climbing abilities, was at the work-table filling in the task sheet. Lacey felt the vibration in her jacket pocket that was her personal mobile and checked the time. One minute past midnight. Knowing that calls at this hour were rarely good news she pulled out her phone and didn't feel any better.

'Emma?' she said. 'You OK? Has something happened?'

The voice that answered was not one she recognised. 'Hello Lacey.'

'Who is this?'

Finn looked up from his work.

The voice on the phone – male, Midland's accent – said, 'Are you out on the river tonight?'

Emma should be at home now, safe behind newly installed locks, with a uniformed police presence directly outside. And yet a man with a Midland's accent – AryanBoy had a Midland's accent – had her phone.

'Again, who is this?'

'I do hope you're on the river, Lacey. I've arranged a little surprise for you.'

'Let me talk to Emma.'

Finn was on his feet, his eyes on Lacey's face. In the galley, Gemma had stopped moving around.

'Not possible, I'm afraid. Emma's tied up right now. And no, that's not a figure of speech.'

He had Emma; or wanted her to think he had; he definitely had her phone.

She said, 'What do you want?'

'Many things, Lacey, many things. First up, I want you to be the one to pull Emma's body from the river tonight.'

Ice was forming in Lacey's stomach. 'You've killed her?'

'Well, not yet, not exactly. As good as. You won't save this one, Lacey, not given the way the wind's blowing right now. And her death will be the least of it. When she goes, she's going to take a whole lot more with her. Look to the skies, Lacey.'

31

Joesbury knew London. He'd been born in the city, been to school here, and apart from the few undercover jobs that had taken him briefly elsewhere, worked here since he'd graduated police college. There was barely a street south of the river that he hadn't walked or driven or ridden along more than once and Peckham was no exception.

If the killer – Waluigi – didn't have a vehicle – an assumption, but one Joesbury knew he'd have to run with for now – the only way to get away quickly was by train or bus.

'Georgie,' he said, when she answered the phone again. 'Have a look at Nunhead station.'

'Been watching it for a while,' she told him. 'No sign of anyone matching his description.'

'Keep an eye on the bus routes, won't you?'

'Already on it.'

The blood-stained clothes would make Waluigi easy to spot, but he could have had a second set of clean clothes beneath his outerwear, or in his rucksack. Joesbury turned a slow circle as he walked, looking for rubbish bins. He passed a residential home for the elderly but didn't give it more than a passing glance. Such places were locked at night.

The next building was a school; the gate was locked, the iron railing scalable, but not easily. He walked on, past a builders' merchant, a row of terraced houses, a block of flats. At the corner a streetlamp was flickering, lending a surreal quality to the empty street.

On the opposite side of the road was a small municipal park, locked at night, but with a perimeter railing that was only waist-high. Surrounded by tall lime trees and thick bushes, the place was known as a night-time hangout for drug dealers and the homeless.

Joesbury vaulted over the railing, squeezed through a laurel bush that smelled of piss, and emerged into an open space. To one side of him was a children's playground, to the other, a basketball court. Ahead, narrow paths wove through an open stretch of lawn towards a copse of trees.

What little light there was seemed to vanish as Joesbury stepped beneath the claustrophobic dampness of the trees. Ten metres from the homeless camp, he could smell it: stale tobacco smoke and fresh weed, alcohol and rotting food, piss and body odour. Every day, the local authority sent staff to clear the park of the homeless and their detritus; every day, as darkness fell, the people and their baggage would return.

A dog growled. Tucked in a sleeping bag, its owner was a man in late middle age, his skin worn like old leather, his eyes blood-shot and yellow from disease.

Then, as though some silent, psychic message had passed among them, the other rough sleepers became aware of Joes-bury's presence. He heard rustled movement from inside two single-man tents; a young boy, slumped against a tree trunk, rolled his head up.

Four people: the dog owner, the junkie and the two in tents.

The homeless were rarely aggressive. Often drunk or stoned, they were invariably unhealthy, poorly fed, unfit. Fearful, they avoided trouble, especially with the police. Joesbury was not afraid of the homeless. The man he was hunting, though, wasn't homeless, neither unfed nor unfit, probably not on drugs, although it couldn't be ruled out. The man who might have chosen to hide out among this tiny community was young and strong, and very handy with a sharp knife.

Feeling the familiar acceleration of his heartbeat, the tingling of his skin as tiny hairs stood to attention, Joesbury reminded himself that he should have left all this behind. He should be at his desk now, directing operations from a safe distance. He thought of his son at home, oblivious to the risks his father was taking; he thought of Lacey, of the bewildering joy of having her in his life – and his bed – at last. He could not mess that up, not now.

He zipped up his jacket, although he knew that even motor-cycle grade leather wouldn't stop a keen blade. In one pocket he had handcuffs, but that was it. No gun, no taser, not even a radio for instant access to police control. He took out his warrant card and flashed it at the man who was now watching him warily.

'Police,' he said, in a quiet voice. 'I need to ask you some questions.'

As he'd known it would, his voice, and identity, created a ripple of movement. The man with the dog squirmed out of the sleeping bag. 'Need to be somewhere else,' he muttered as he walked away. The boy against the tree trunk tried to get up and failed; the drugs had too tight a grip on him. A hand appeared from one of the tents, pulling at the zip, opening up a short gap.

'We don't want trouble,' complained a female voice from inside. 'Why can't you leave us alone?'

Joesbury focused on the one remaining possibility. A cheap tent, that looked newer, cleaner than the other, that wasn't surrounded by an assortment of belongings. No remains of food, no empty bottles, no damp clothing.

Joesbury reached out his foot and nudged a dent in the nylon. 'Sir?' he said. 'I'm a police officer. Can I talk to you for a minute?'

No response.

Joesbury leaned closer. He reached for the zip and pulled it. A fold of nylon fell away.

The figure inside the tent was prone, his face hidden in the folds of his sleeping bag. After another quick glance around, Joesbury shook the man's shoulder.

'Sir, I need to speak to you. Can you get up please?'

A groan answered him.

Joesbury could smell body odour, but not the old, sour whiff he associated with the homeless. There was even a faint hint, possibly, of laundry powder. This guy smelled too good for his surroundings. Heart hammering, Joesbury stepped back and pulled out his phone. It took too long for the call to go through. He thought he heard the sound of a zip being lowered; the prone form, though, remained motionless.

'Wasgoinon?' complained the man whose face Joesbury still hadn't seen.

'Need to talk to you about an incident just off Queens Road tonight, sir,' Joesbury said, as his call was answered at last. 'Georgie, I'm in the Jubilee Park on William Street. Can you get backup sent immediately? I'm about to make an arrest.'

The homeless man burst out of the sleeping bag. Jumping to his feet, he leaped from the tent, wild panic distorting his face. Joesbury saw the knife heading for his eyes and leaped backwards. It missed him by inches. His attacker came again.

And tripped.

He was a young man with a nondescript, clean-shaven face. Regaining his balance he continued to run, this time away from the copse. Joesbury went after him.

'Georgie, I'm chasing the suspect. White male, mid-twenties, five nine, medium build. Heading north through Jubilee Park towards Bidwell Street. Suspect is armed. Repeat, suspect is armed.'

He thrust the phone back into his pocket without disconnecting.

The suspect, in a black sweatshirt and jogging pants, mousey hair streaked with sweat, was almost at the perimeter railing. Two metres away. A metre and a half. Joesbury sucked in breath and braced himself to leap.

The suspect reached the rail and spun round and that was a bloody big knife in his right hand. A kitchen blade, a meat slicer. The guy had already killed two with it, a third would make no practical difference.

Joesbury held both hands in the air and took a step back. 'Mate, it's over. The place is crawling with police. You can't get out of this park. Drop the knife.'

The suspect was panting; sweat broke out on his forehead.

'You must be Waluigi,' Joesbury said. 'Cool character. My son likes him. And Mario. Those are his two favourites. What's your real name?'

'Fuck you.'

Joesbury raised his left arm, pointed with his thumb back over his shoulder. 'Bit extreme, what you did back there. One of the girls upset you? I get it, you can't exactly complain to trading standards.'

'I wouldn't go near those fucking whores.'

'Mate, you're preaching to the choir. I'd have the lot of them closed down if I had my way. Disease-ridden dumps. Fucking rip-off, all of them. You don't smoke, do you? I'm dying for a fag.'

He patted his pockets, as though searching for a cigarette packet.

'There's this woman,' Joesbury went on. 'Been messing me around for months. Thing is, I know she's into me, but she – mixed signals, you know what I'm saying? – don't know whether I'm coming or going with her. I'm telling you, mate, it's doing my head in. Sure you don't have a fag?'

He remembered, then, that Georgie was still on the line, and that everything he was saying would be recorded. Well, he'd come this far.

'Is that why you did it?' he asked. 'Girl been giving you a hard time?'

Waluigi's eyes were shooting from left to right, looking for the new threats that hadn't yet, to Joesbury's alarm, materialised. 'They're all the fucking same.'

'Now you see, that's where you're wrong. Take my ex-wife – please! I'm kidding. I knew where I was with her, knew what she wanted. Trouble was, she wanted me home at five o'clock every night, and that just wasn't me, do you get what I'm saying? Women, they drag you down, try to make you change. You ever been married?'

The man with the knife – Waluigi – shook his head.

Joesbury lowered his voice. 'Mate, I get where you're coming from. Most of us do, the blokes I'm talking about now. Shit, police work was so much easier before they let the bloody women in. But we have to go through the motions.'

Joesbury risked looking around. Unless something had gone badly wrong, officers would be surrounding the park. There was a good chance the armed unit would be out too.

'If it were up to me, I'd let you go. Pretend you got away, but this park is crawling with CCTV, so I can't do it. We've no choice but to take you in. What I can tell you is, no one will give you a hard time.' He lowered his voice further. 'We're on your side, mate.'

He risked a step closer. Waluigi stepped back and came up hard against the railing. He raised the knife again; it was less than two feet from Joesbury's heart.

'Stick me with that, though, and it's over for you. We look after our own.'

The man, ten years younger than Joesbury, had got his breathing under control. He was sucking in air rhythmically now, deliberately, filling his body with oxygen, the way athletes did before the start of a race.

Joesbury stepped back again, hands in the air.

'Fuck it,' he said. 'Go for it. Head for Peckham Rye station, run along the track towards Denmark Hill. They'll never expect that.'

Waluigi leaped at him, knife first. Using his outstretched arms for balance Joesbury swung his right leg up. His foot struck the other man in the chest, sending him spinning sideways to the ground. Joesbury dropped flat, pinning the other man down with his full weight. He raised his head enough to look around. Where the fuck was backup?

Struggling to his knees, feeling Waluigi squirming beneath him, Joesbury reached for his handcuffs. Finally, running footsteps, urgent voices shouting.

'We've got him, guv, steady now.'

Uniformed officers wearing stab vests materialised at each of Waluigi's thrashing limbs. One forced the knife from his reach, others sat on his legs. As Joesbury staggered to his feet, Waluigi's hands were cuffed together. Only when he could no longer be a threat, did one of them begin to read him his rights.

It was done, the arrest made, and the group of five took a moment to get their breath. Joesbury looked down at the man on the ground, thought back to the two dead women at the brothel, who'd probably been trafficked, tricked into coming here by men who valued them no more than this twat did.

'You absolute fucking scumbag,' Joesbury said, as he took a step closer and swung his right foot.

'Sir!'

An officer stepped between him and the suspect; she was young, female.

'Can't let you do that, sir.' Eight inches shorter than he, some four stone lighter, she faced Joesbury down. Her bodycam was directed straight at him. As were the cameras on all three of her fellow officers.

The woman didn't take her eyes away from Joesbury's as she lifted her own right foot and kicked back, hard and fast, like a bad-tempered horse. Her boot connected with Waluigi's nose, breaking it, causing blood to explode from it like one of the fireworks from earlier.

'He's mine,' she mouthed.

Joesbury's phone was ringing again. Whatever it was, it could wait. He glanced down at the caller ID.

Lacey.

32

AryanBoy settled himself down on a bench on the south bank, one he'd previously ascertained didn't lie in any pools of light cast by street lamps or shop windows, and that wasn't within reach of any CCTV cameras. He double-checked that his phone was switched off and pulled his camera and a pair of high-resolution binoculars from his backpack. He fixed them on something on the far bank and adjusted the focus. Perfect.

Smoke and mirrors, that's what it was all about. First, send the willing stooge down to south London to wreak bloody havoc – literally – and wait for the Met's finest to pile down there in force. A much more minor distraction at Earl's Court and the stage was set.

A private motorboat passed by on the water, close to the south bank, heading upstream, which wasn't strictly correct procedure, but it was well lit and river traffic was light. AryanBoy looked down, hiding his face beneath his dark hood. A witness right now wouldn't be helpful. It would be safer, by far, to be anywhere else but here; he simply hadn't been able to resist.

The wind stung his eyes, bringing tears, causing the riverside lights to swell and dance around him. It reminded him of the drug-induced hallucinations of his younger days, before he'd accepted, reluctantly, that pharmaceuticals didn't hold the answers. He'd been clean for a long time now. He blinked, to clear his vision. It would be happening soon.

The abduction of Emma Boston had been the trickiest operation, by far, that he'd pulled off to date. Several foot soldiers
to coordinate, any one of whom could have chickened out and
called the authorities at the last minute. He'd expected Emma
herself to be warier, more reluctant to leave the safety of her
home, but in the end she'd been like so many others, refusing to
believe the worst could happen to her.

A shame her piece for the *Daily Mail* hadn't been more balanced, but her death would send a strong message to the world.
No one should take us on, least of all a woman.

The fact that she was Lacey Flint's best mate was a delicious
bonus.

AryanBoy checked his watch and glanced down river. Any
minute now.

33

Every instinct Lacey had was telling her to put the Targa into its top speed and drive back to Wapping, get over to Emma's flat and help with the search. Common sense and protocol told her to stay exactly where she was.

It was twenty minutes past midnight.

Her first call, after AryanBoy had hung up, had been to police control. Uniformed officers would be at Emma's flat now, touching base with the patrol car that should have been keeping an eye on her, making their way inside, confirming that she was really gone, checking with all her known contacts and then, if they had to, processing the crime scene. Her second had been to Joesbury. Out on another job, he'd agreed to leave it and supervise the search for Emma. He'd be on his way back to Scotland Yard now, getting his team out of bed, finding out what the hell had happened.

Her third call had been to Wapping, to request maximum assistance on the river for the rest of the night. If Mr Cook and Scotland Yard approved, every available marine unit vessel would shortly be helping with the search. She'd done all she could and now she had a job of her own to do.

AryanBoy had called her, not Scotland Yard. Somehow, he'd found out that she'd been the unnamed officer who'd saved the baby, and that she worked on the river. She'd pissed him off and he wanted payback. He'd got her number from Emma's phone and that meant he knew the two of them were friends. None of that mattered right now. All that mattered was finding Emma.

'Tell me again,' Finn said. 'You might remember something else.'

The two of them were up on the flybridge, in spite of the rising wind. Staying below in a cramped cabin had felt impossible.

'He asked me if I was out on the river, so he knows I'm with the marine unit. He said he wanted me to find Emma's body, but that she's not dead yet. He said she was tied up and that I had to look at the skies.'

'Bridge?' It wouldn't have been the first time the marine unit, specifically its line access unit, of which Finn was the star climber, had been tasked with retrieving a body from beneath one of London's bridges.

'Wouldn't be hard,' Finn went on. 'Fasten her to a long rope tied to a balustrade and chuck her over.'

Lacey opened up the radio channel to request all craft on the river pay particular attention to the undersides of bridges.

'We need to find her soon,' Finn said. 'Harness trauma.'

Harness trauma, also known as suspension trauma, was a common and potentially lethal consequence of being suspended in mid-air. The effects of gravity, immobility, and the constriction of essential veins and arteries led to severe oxygen shortages in the brain and the release of toxins into the vital organs. Symptoms typically kicked in after only fifteen minutes. If Emma were hanging from a bridge, she wouldn't last long.

'I'm not sure,' Lacey replied. 'He also said, her death would be the least of it, that she would take a whole lot more with her.'

'What the hell does that mean?'

'No idea. And he said something about the wind. He said, I wouldn't save her, given the way the wind's blowing right now.'

'So, where do we go? Upstream? Downstream?'

They were currently three hundred metres upstream of the Houses of Parliament. The wind, gusting twenty-eight miles an hour and set to increase, was coming from the north-east, cutting across the outgoing tide, causing angry waves to break over the bow every few seconds. The river temperature had dropped in the last couple of weeks to around nine degrees. No one could last long in the water tonight.

'Lacey?' Finn prompted.

If AryanBoy had brought Emma directly to the river, she'd be somewhere close. 'We stay here,' she said. 'And we wait.'

34

Joesbury arrived back at Scotland Yard as Archie and Warwick returned from Emma's flat. They met him at the door.

'We think we know how it was done, sir,' Warwick told him. 'The fire alarm went off in the house around eleven twenty hours. Some rubbish on one of the upper landings set alight. No major damage but enough to set off all the alarms and cause a mass evacuation. Some fourteen or fifteen people would have been trying to leave the building in a hurry. Including Emma, we have to assume.'

'Where the fuck was the duty patrol car?' Joesbury asked.

'Attending an incident in the next street,' Archie said. 'It sounded serious – a stabbing – and they were easily the closest. Emma wasn't considered a serious security risk before this; we were just being cautious.'

'The stabbing was a hoax,' Warwick added. 'A distraction. This was well planned.'

Joesbury asked, 'Could she have gone to a mate's?'

'Unlikely.' Archie looked grim. 'Not considering the message we found.'

Archie was carrying an answer machine, presumably the one that had been attached to Emma's landline. AryanBoy should not have had Emma's landline number; very few people, she'd told Joesbury, were ever given that number.

'How are things in Peckham?' Warwick asked, as they reached the stairs.

'Lewisham have it under control,' Joesbury replied. Already Peckham felt like a long time ago. He glanced at a clock as they passed it: 0040 hours. Not even an hour since he'd caught Waluigi. 'The bloke's in custody.'

They reached their floor and the general office. Joesbury poured himself coffee while Archie plugged in the answer machine.

'You've disappointed me, Emma.' AryanBoy's voice was unnervingly loud in the quiet room. 'This is not what I expected. You can't run this.'

Emma, not wanting to send her story on MenMatter to AryanBoy until it was finalised, had already filed it with the *Daily Mail*. The newspaper had reported themselves happy and it was due to appear on page five, trailed on the front page, the following day – Tuesday. It was going to be a big story.

She'd sent it to AryanBoy, as she'd promised, late the previous evening.

A short pause and then Emma's voice, strained from interrupted sleep. 'I'm sorry you don't like it.'

Another silence and then AryanBoy, sounding as though he was struggling to keep his temper, said, 'I've fixed it for you. It took me time I can't spare but I've got it close to acceptable. I hope you take shorthand?'

'I'm sorry,' Emma on the recording said, 'but I made it clear you don't get right of approval. No newspaper would accept a piece that wasn't impartially written.'

'You call this impartial? Take this down, and I won't repeat myself—'

'The piece I wrote has been accepted. It's too late to change, even if—'

'The war on injustice and the subversion of the natural order has begun. All over the world, men are fighting back. It began by Tower Bridge, on Friday morning, when the first blow was struck. Are you taking this down, Emma?'

The man was practically yelling down the phone.

'No,' Emma replied, her voice shaky. 'The piece I wrote will run. That was the deal. I'm grateful for your cooperation but—'

'Then the next foid to be sacrificed will be you, Emma. What, did you imagine there'd be a place for you in the new order? No man will touch you. I mean, have you looked in a mirror? No man would come near you without being sick. This is your last chance. Write what I tell you or you won't see next week.'

The recording went silent for several seconds.

'What? You think I can't do it? I can have men outside your door in seconds, Emma. They're already in your street.' He reeled off her address, even described the colour of the blinds at the window. 'We know about the police car down the road and the blond-haired boy who brings you coffee like he's some kind of lap dog. You think a good-looking Chad like that would be interested in you? We'll slit his throat first, and then we'll come for you. Make your will, bitch.'

The recording ended.

'Came in at four minutes past eleven,' Archie said.

Less than two hours ago.

'Why didn't she call us?' Joesbury asked. 'You get a call like that, hear threats like that, and it's the first thing you do. You call the people whose job it is to keep you alive.'

'They didn't give her much time,' Archie replied. 'The fire alarm went off minutes later. Which means they planned it, long before AryanBoy made that phone call. Probably before he even read her piece.'

All three of them started as the door was pulled open and Georgie strode in. 'We've traced Emma's phone,' she told them. 'It doesn't look good.'

35

'Emma's phone was last detected on the Chelsea Embankment about an hour ago.' Lacey found the same stretch of the river on the chart plotter and enlarged the area around Chelsea Harbour. 'Roughly between Edith Grove and Beaufort Street and very close to the river.' She turned the Targa towards the north bank. 'I'm heading up there now. Finn, can you get on to Wapping and let them know? Go down. You won't hear anything up here.'

The wind, building all the time, had make it tricky to hear what Joesbury had just told her. The gist of it being that, at a little after eleven, Emma had taken a call from AryanBoy, on a number he should not have been able to access. He'd been angry, made threats. And now Emma was gone.

'Come back, Gemma,' she called to the young woman at the bow. 'I'm speeding up.'

The crew had just completed their search of Vauxhall Bridge, weaving in and out of its piers, shining powerful flashlights into the arches. They'd taken their time, but had seen nothing that wasn't supposed to be there. Chelsea Bridge had been next on the list, then Albert and Battersea bridges. Somehow, though, Lacey didn't think this was about bridges. *Look to the skies.*

But there was nothing in the sky above the river. Unless the incels were planning to throw Emma off the top of a riverside skyscraper, or they'd somehow got hold of a helicopter, it simply wasn't possible to throw someone into the Thames from a great height.

And then she saw them, a cluster of lights high above the south bank, a sight so familiar she hadn't given them a second's thought. *Watch the skies.* The last few years had seen huge development in London: apartment blocks, offices, leisure facilities going up all over the city. Construction sites were everywhere, and the skies above London were full of tower cranes.

'Finn, Gemma,' she called. 'I know where she is.'

36

Joesbury parked his bike behind the line of patrol cars. Around him, the search for Emma's phone was already underway: the embankment footpath and part of the road had been sealed off and a female officer was sorting through a rough sleeper's cardboard bed. Its occupant sat a short distance away, eyes down, face sullen. Archie was on the other side of the road in a high-vis coat. He caught Joesbury's eye and shook his head.

Bloody hell, it was cold. He pulled a padded coat from the bike's luggage box and tugged it on. Then, stepping to the river wall, he looked out across the water. Few people in London, outside the marine unit and a few staff in the Environment Agency's river division, knew the Thames better than he. He could tell at a glance which way the tide was moving and when it was due to change. He could distinguish its normal muddy brown from actual pollution spills and he knew the most likely spots for the disposal of unwanted bodies. This wasn't one of them.

A moving light on the water caught his attention and he screwed up his eyes to see a marine unit Targa heading upriver between Albert and Battersea bridges. Too far away for him to make out individuals, he could see three figures on the flybridge. This had to be Lacey's boat.

Lacey had taken the call from AryanBoy. They were meant to think this was about the river and Emma, meant to look for Emma in the river. What if they were being played?

He had a sudden feeling of horror that the real plan had been to lure Lacey out into the open, that it was she, not Emma, who was the target. He pulled out his phone to tell her to get the hell off the flybridge.

He was on the point of dialling her number when it rang. Lacey was calling him.

37

'I don't think so, Lacey,' Gemma had argued, a little earlier. 'My dad works in construction. The sites are locked at night. Most have night watchmen. And cranes are always locked. You can't have just anyone accessing cranes. They're too dangerous.'

'These guys aren't just anyone,' Lacey replied.

'But where do we start?' Finn asked. 'There are dozens of cranes in London. How many have we passed between here and Westminster?'

'Her phone was on the north bank, near Chelsea Harbour,' Lacey replied. 'That's where we look.'

Hugging the bank, they made their careful way upriver. As they neared Albert Bridge they saw flashing blue lights speeding ahead of them on the A3212. Lacey slowed the vessel to give Gemma and Finn a chance to check the bridge's underside but knew in her heart they were not going to find Emma swinging from a bridge. AryanBoy had something far more ambitious in mind.

Bridge search completed, a second group of cranes came into view on the south bank. The steel construction of their towers was invisible in the darkness, but cranes, being a known hazard to low flying aircraft, were well lit at night. Bright white lights like stars ran up the towers and along the arms; tiny blue ones surrounded the drivers' cabins, huge red lights flashed at their extremities. Curiously, the long, horizontal arms on all three cranes were pointing downwind.

And then a fourth – on the north bank, only a little way ahead of them – appeared around a tall building.

'That looks the right spot,' Lacey said, pointing it out to the other two.

'There's a new hotel going up at Chelsea Harbour,' Gemma said. 'My dad's firm bid for it. I still don't think it could be done, though. They'd need a qualified crane driver, for one thing.'

The crane grew closer with every second they motored up-river; the light configuration seemed different to that of the cranes on the south bank.

'It's pointing a different way,' Lacey said.

Finn found the flybridge binoculars and raised them to get a closer look.

'Look at the arms on those three,' Lacey pointed out across the river. 'They're all facing downwind. This one isn't. The long arm's stretching out over the river. Does that mean anything?'

'Sorry,' Gemma said. 'My dad's a foreman not a crane driver.'

'Cranes are left to swing with the wind when they're not in use,' Finn said, binoculars still trained high above the north bank. 'I had to climb one once. And I think it's carrying a load.' He lowered the binoculars and looked at Lacey. 'That doesn't feel right.'

'Not at night,' Lacey agreed. 'Not in this wind.'

Finn handed her the binoculars. 'Pretty sure it's not a body, though,' he said. 'Some sort of bag.'

Conscious of her hands trembling, Lacey focused on the crane, now little more than two hundred metres away. She saw its long arm, trailing silvery lights, stretching out across the river, buffeted every few seconds by the wind. She saw the sizeable bag hanging fifty feet or so below the tip of the arm, swinging this way and that. Whatever was inside – and she had to pray to God it wasn't Emma – was in danger of being tipped out any second.

38

The construction site foreman lived close, thank God, and took only thirty minutes to arrive and unlock the padlocked gates, allowing the patrol cars through. Joesbury and Archie had already climbed the perimeter fence and dropped down into the silent and still site, but that had been as far as they'd been able to go. The crane itself was surrounded by a locked fence, too high and too sheer to climb.

'I think it's a big bag.' Archie had borrowed binoculars from one of the patrol cars. 'It looks like the ones builders' material comes in, you know, sand, gravel, top-soil sometimes. Made from a sort of woven, white nylon.'

'Anything in it?'

'Must be, or it'd be blowing around all over the place. It's moving, anything would in this wind, but it'd be flapping like a flag if it was empty.'

Joesbury took a second to check out the site. It was compact, as most sites in central London had to be, the construction still in its early stages. A base layer of concrete had been laid and a forest of steel rods, waiting to support the outer shell, sprang from it. Stacks of materials – bricks, tiles, more steel rods – most still wrapped in protective plastic lay ready for use. If Lacey was right about Emma being suspended from this crane – and he had a horrible feeling she might be – there wasn't a square foot in the vicinity that offered anything other than a deadly place to land. Not that the river was any better. If the fall didn't kill her, the tide would take her quickly with zero chance of her being recovered in the dark.

Off site, a siren broke through the night. More cars were arriving and every available officer in London would be making his or her way to Chelsea Harbour right now. Because the possibility of a young journalist falling to her death had become the least of their problems.

AryanBoy, it turned out, hadn't been making idle threats when he'd claimed Emma could take more than one life with her when she fell, and Lacey had been spot on when she'd noticed that the crane at the Chelsea Harbour site was pointing in a different direction to all the others in the area.

'You are effing kidding me!' The site foreman had yelled down the phone when Joesbury had explained. 'You need to clear the area.'

The evacuation of the nearby streets was already underway. Over the last few minutes, Joesbury had caught snatches of radio traffic from outside the site. The residents of the luxury development at Chelsea Harbour, multi-millionaires all, were not taking kindly to being roused in the small hours. He imagined they'd find it preferable, though, to having several tonnes of reinforced steel crashing onto their homes as they slept.

At increasing volume and with numerous expletives, the foreman had gone on to explain that cranes, when not in use, were always left in 'free slew', with something called the slew brake switched off. Cranes, reaching heights of several hundred feet, were extremely vulnerable in high winds. A crane with its arm or jib locked in position, as this one must be if it wasn't moving, was likely to be blown over.

'You want to hope it comes down in the effing river! Anything else would be bloody carnage,' the foreman had yelled, before slamming down the phone.

Either way, Emma's chances didn't look great.

The foreman, when he arrived, didn't bring his car onto the site. Joesbury had a feeling he'd left it some way down the road, out of range of a plummeting steel tower.

'Driver's on his way,' he told Joesbury. 'Although . . .' he looked up, didn't finish his thought. 'And you think there's someone in that bag?' he said instead.

'How long before he gets here?' Joesbury asked.

'Another five, maybe ten. You need to get your people off site. Anyone who doesn't have to be here should go. I'm not kidding, that thing could topple any time.'

'Can we unlock it from down here?'

The foreman shook his head. 'Nope. Only from the cabin.'

'Can we airlift her down?' Archie suggested.

Joesbury had already asked that very question, but his request for air support had been denied.

'Talk to me,' Joesbury told the foreman. 'Tell me what needs to be done when the driver gets here.'

'That's a saddleback crane,' the foreman replied, after a deep breath. 'The jib, what you might call the horizontal arm, doesn't rise up and down like on a luffing crane. It moves horizontally, around three hundred and sixty degrees. And there's a trolley and rope system for raising and lowering the load. Look, can you see the underside of the front jib?'

Taking the binoculars, Joesbury found the horizontal arm that the foreman called the front jib. Towards its outer end, some eighty feet from the tower, hung a box-like structure.

'That's the trolley,' the foreman explained. 'Rope runs through that, round the full length of the jib and down to the block. That's the oval-shaped metal thing you can see directly beneath the trolley.'

Joesbury found the block. 'There's a bag hanging off it. Looks like a builder's yard bag. Would it be one of yours?'

'Unlikely.' The foreman hadn't taken his eyes off the crane. 'That looks like an aggregate bag, designed for single load only. We cut the straps so they can't be used a second time.'

So the bag keeping Emma from plummeting was compromised. Like they hadn't enough problems.

'What will the driver do when he's up there?' Joesbury asked.

'Can he lower the bag here in the yard.' He looked around. 'We need to find something to pad the ground.'

The foreman was looking deeply troubled. 'Look mate, I'm not . . .'

He didn't finish. Another man had approached: small, stocky, in his late forties, wearing a hard hat and a high-vis coat.

'The driver.' The foreman introduced them and Joesbury explained what was needed.

'No chance, mate.' The driver took a step back, planting his feet in the manner of someone who was not being moved.

'You are the driver?' Joesbury questioned.

'Only one you'll get here before daylight, and I'm telling you now, no one will go up in this wind.'

'I've been trying to tell you that,' the foreman said. 'Cranes are blocked off at certain wind speeds. We can't use this one above thirty-eight miles per hour. Its gusting forty-five right now and set to get higher in the next hour. I can't authorise anyone going up there.'

'We shouldn't even be on site, Rob,' the driver told the foreman. 'That thing comes down, a gust could send it anywhere.'

Joesbury held up both hands. 'Hold on, fellas. There's a young woman in that bag, and she could be alive.'

'Are you sure?' The foreman asked. 'Have you actually seen her? Because all I can see is an aggregate bag that could have anything inside.'

'She won't be alive,' the driver added. 'Not if she's been up there any length of time. Exposure will have killed her.'

'She'll die for sure if we leave her up there,' Joesbury said.

'Even without the slew lock on, I wouldn't go up there in these winds,' the driver said. 'I wouldn't be able to control it. Best I could do would be to take the lock off and drop her in the water.'

Joesbury closed his eyes and took a deep breath, feeling his entire body becoming cold and clammy. Then he opened them. 'Give me the keys,' he told the foreman.

The man stared at him. 'You what?'

'Archie, give the driver your radio and stay with him. Make sure he knows how to use it and don't let him leave the site. He can talk me through it.'

Eyes wide, Archie nodded.

'What the hell?' asked the foreman.

In reply, Joesbury took his arm and frogmarched him over to the base of the crane. 'Open it,' he said. 'I'm going up.'

39

'He's doing what?' Lacey said, feeling every last trace of warmth leave her body.

While they'd been waiting to hear from the team at the construction site, Gemma had phoned her site foreman father, who'd explained to them precisely what the implications of a locked crane in high winds could be.

'You can't let him,' she went on, when Archie, on the other end of the phone, didn't reply.

'He's the most senior officer on site.' Archie was having to shout above the wind. 'He's calling the shots.'

'Let me talk to him.'

'He's twenty feet in the air. He said to make sure all craft on the water are at least 300 feet away until he gets the thing unlocked. Look, I've got to go.'

'What can we do?' Lacey asked, wondering if she were about to be sick.

'Pray.' Archie was gone.

'Finn, take the helm,' Lacey said. 'Head out towards the middle of the channel. And give me those binoculars.'

As the Targa motored away from the bank, Lacey focused on the crane's tower. At first, she saw nothing, as its lower part remained hidden behind the river-fronted buildings. Then a hard hat came into view, followed by a high visibility coat. She wouldn't have known him from this distance if she hadn't been told it was Joesbury. Even as she watched, the tower seemed to lean, way off vertical. She held her breath, convinced it was toppling. The wind dropped and it straightened again. Next time it might not. Next time it could come down.

This was her punishment then, for daring to risk a few hours of complete happiness. The man she loved, the bravest, most reckless, stupidest man she'd ever known, was about to die. And she had to watch.

40

It had never occurred to Joesbury how long it would take to climb to the driver's cab on a crane. This one, he'd been told, was 150 feet in the air and that made him lucky. Many London cranes were a lot higher.

He'd never had a problem with heights, had several times been hoisted to the top of a mast at sea, but nothing could have prepared him for the way the tower he was climbing was moving in the wind. He'd scaled only the first three of the zig-zagged stretches of ladder before his torso felt slick with sweat. And he was shaking like a leaf.

He'd been told not to look down, so of course he did exactly that each time he stopped to get his breath back. Already the few people left on the ground were hard to make out. The site had been cleared apart from the foreman, the crane driver, Archie and a couple of uniforms on the gates. All of them knew to run like hell if the crane looked like it was falling.

His hands were freezing; no one had thought to give him gloves.

Beyond the site, houses, shops and parked cars flickered blue in the lights of patrol cars, while torch beams danced around the surrounding streets. The evacuation of nearby homes was still underway. All local roads had been closed, as had the river. Lacey's Targa, plus a couple of marine unit RIBs, were the only craft in the vicinity and he'd already spotted them making their way out to the middle channel.

The normal sounds of a London night faded as he climbed, replaced only with that of the wind, and, increasingly, the beating of his own heart.

'You're doing well, Mark,' the driver told him over the radio. 'Climbing like a champ.' He could have said 'chimp', but the wind made catching every word spoken over the airwaves close to impossible. Either way, the comparison didn't feel remotely apt. His coat was weighing him down, but he'd been warned not to leave it behind. It would be, 'bloody freezing up there', according to the driver, who would know.

Thirty minutes, he'd been told it would take him, to reach the driver's cabin; another ten to sort himself out, plus an extra ten to work out where everything was. Already he felt as though he'd been climbing for hours.

A gust caught the tower.

'Hold on, mate,' came the driver's voice. 'Stay where you are for a second.'

Joesbury didn't need telling twice. He clung to the ladder and held his breath as the tower rocked. After several seconds, when he was certain he was about to fall, it righted itself again.

'You're over halfway,' the driver told him. 'Making good time. Don't worry about falling. The squirrel cage will catch you and you'll only go as far as the next platform. Concentrate on getting up.'

Easy for him to say. Already his legs felt weak, his breathing more and more laborious.

The higher Joesbury climbed, the more of the city unveiled itself beneath him. The lights on the Thames' bridges turned vast stretches of the river a deep cobalt, while lapis and turquoise lights shone out from thousands of windows. Running between the jewel-coloured buildings were the countless gold ribbons that were London's streets. Car headlights gleamed silver and sky-scrapers carried warning lights like gleaming bubbles of blood.

'You're at the cab,' the driver said, startling him, and Joesbury realised he'd actually zoned out as he'd climbed, mesmerised by the dark kaleidoscope beneath him. 'Careful with those keys.'

Joesbury forced his frozen fingers to unlock the driver's cab before pulling himself inside. His relief at being out of the wind was short lived. At this height the movement of the tower was continual and he was still in imminent danger of collapse.

There was a single seat in the cab. He staggered into it and pulled the cabin door shut. 'I'm in,' he told the man on the ground.

'Good man. You need to switch on the ignition. Left-hand console, it looks like any you'd find in a car. Use the smaller key.'

Joesbury found the key, inserted and turned it; a low rumbling noise sounded and his seat began a gentle vibration. At the same time, he sensed a change in the cab's lighting. On the console were a range of instruments, including one indicating wind strength and direction.

'Done,' he said.

'I can see. Now, find the slew lock. Right-hand console, there's a row of three switches. Middle one, with the padlock symbol. It should be pressed away from you, is that right?'

'Yep.'

'Press it the other way. Do it now.'

Joesbury flicked the switch and the jib of the crane swung violently clockwise, spinning over ninety degrees, taking the cab with it. Suddenly he was facing a very different direction, away from the river.

'Shit!' He'd grasped the seat handles, had felt a moment of sheer terror.

'No, that's good. It's correcting itself for wind direction. You're facing south-west now, the wind's coming from the north-east.'

Fighting a wave of nausea, Joesbury glanced down. The river was on his left side.

'We're all a hell of a lot safer now.' Relief was clear in the driver's voice. 'We still need to get this done, though. It's too windy to be up there. OK, you've got two handles, like the gear sticks in a car, one on each side.'

'Got 'em.' Joesbury stretched out his arms and let his fingers tap gently on both levers.

'The left-hand one is your swing control. That turns the jib, and I'm going to be asking you, in a minute, to push it to the left, so that you move the jib anti-clockwise, back over the river and towards us here on site. The other stick controls the trolley. Pulling it back towards you will bring the load closer to the tower, which is what we're looking for, but don't worry about that for now. Right, left-hand stick, move it gently to the left.'

Joesbury did what he was told. Nothing happened. 'It's not moving.'

'You're going against the wind. Increase the pressure, nice and easy.'

Joesbury could feel the wind resistance fighting him as the jib began to move. It might be his imagination, but the wind speed seemed to have increased, even in the short time he'd been in the cab. With his free hand, he wiped sweat off his brow.

He wasn't sure he'd ever been this scared before. Telling himself he wasn't going to die, that cranes, properly left, didn't tumble, even in gale force winds, he kept the pressure on. The jib swung further anti-clockwise and the river reappeared in his direct vision. He spotted a light on the water that could be Lacey's boat and told himself he was going to see her again, and that if he could, he was going to save her friend.

A few more degrees. The jib was facing south-east now and the wind resistance was increasing.

'Keep going,' the man on the ground told him.

'It's not moving.'

'Increase the pressure. Steady now.'

He tried, and a fresh burst of sweat chilled his entire body. 'I can't. That's it. All it's got.'

'Shit.'

Silence. Fifty feet below the end of the jib, the bag that might – or might not – contain Emma Boston swung violently.

'What? Talk to me.'

For several seconds, he got no response.

'Archie, what the fuck's going on?'

'Hold on a minute, sir. They're talking it through.'

'OK, Mark, we can't get the jib back over the site.' It was the driver again. 'The wind's too strong. We need you to put it down on the river.'

'I'll take it the other way,' Joesbury argued. 'Clockwise.'

'Exactly the same thing will happen. You've boats out on the river, right? You need to lower it, and one of your boats can pick it up.'

Put Emma in the river? She wouldn't survive.

'I don't think I can do that.'

'Only way you're getting her down, mate. Right, I need you to move the lever back the other way, just five to ten degrees, can you do that? Careful now, it'll swing back quickly.'

Moving the other way was easy.

'That's it, mate. You're a bit more stable now, and still above the river.'

'Sir, there's a Targa getting into position now,' Archie told him. 'The skipper's been briefed. It's PC Flint, sir.'

Of course, it was.

'OK, mate, hold it together, you're doing well. Now, the block is lowered by twisting the lever on the left-hand side. Anti-clockwise to go down, clockwise to come back up. When you're ready, twist slowly anti-clockwise.'

Joesbury did what he was told. At the end of the jib, the block, with the aggregate bag hanging from it, began to sink lower, heading straight for the Thames.

41

'It's coming down now, Lacey.'

'Understood.'

Lacey tightened her grip on the flybridge helm and glanced to starboard. On the embankment wall was a carved stone face, lit from above, that she'd been keeping lined up with the stern rail. The wind was blowing the boat towards the south bank, waves were pitching it from side to side every few seconds, and the tide was pushing it back downriver. On top of everything else, rain had started to fall, blurring visibility and making the decks treacherous. These were the worst possible conditions for holding a boat on the water. She felt the vessel slipping back and increased the revs.

Finn and Gemma were at the bow. The plan, agreed a few minutes ago with Archie, was to lower the aggregate bag onto the flat area of deck between the tip of the Targa's bow and the front wall of its cabin. In theory, there would be space for it. In practice, they were working at night, in very rough conditions, and Gemma, while a good officer, had neither the height nor the strength they needed. Finn, at nearly six foot five, and with the agility of an athlete, was ideal, but he could be stupidly reckless.

She said, 'Are you two fastened on?'

'You asked us that already,' Finn replied. 'Answer's still yes. I think you need to steer to starboard, maybe three metres. And head up a bit.'

Lacey and her crew were speaking over the radio; the wind was too loud to make shouting from one end of the boat to the other feasible.

She glanced behind. The two RIBs had positioned themselves to either side of the Targa, a few metres downriver, as she'd requested. There, they'd be best placed to retrieve anything – or anyone – that went in the water.

Finn was right, she was too far downriver, but the outgoing tide was at its strongest, ripping out towards the estuary and the wind was coming hard at them from the north bank. She would have to wait until the bag was almost on the water before moving into position. And she would need to approach from the leeward side, so that the bag was blown onto the vessel.

'We're staying here for now,' she said. 'Do you have an idea of distance?'

Finn was looking skyward. 'Hard to say. Maybe it's come down twenty metres, maybe a bit more. Still a long way to go.'

The radio crackled into life. 'Marine unit Targa, marine unit Targa, this is DCI Mark Joesbury. If you can hear me, go to channel 18.'

'DCI Joesbury, this is Constable Lacey Flint on the river. Going to channel 18 now.' She switched channels. 'Mark, you there?'

'I'm here. How you doing?'

'Holding up. You?'

She heard what could have been a soft laugh. 'Had better evenings. Listen, we have a visibility problem. I can't see you anymore with that building in the way and I won't be able to see the bag make contact with the boat. The crane driver and site foreman have eyes on you, but from where they are they can't judge distances too well. You're going to have to talk me down, are you OK with that?

God no, if it all went wrong now it would be on her.

'Understood,' she said. 'I think you've about twenty-five metres to go. Keep it coming.'

The ghostly white bag, flapping and swinging in the wind, continued to descend.

'Twenty metres,' she said. 'Do we know if what we're looking for is actually in there?'

Knowing that even secure police radio channels could be intercepted, no one involved in the operation had named Emma, or even given away that the bag might contain a human cargo.

'Negative. I've got Archie on my phone. The men from the site say you're too far downstream. You need to head up a bit and move to starboard.'

No, she was the one on the helm, the one who could feel how the river was moving beneath her.

'I know what I'm doing. Keep bringing it down and keep the speed constant. You're at ten metres.'

The plan – if they managed to get the bag onto the boat, if Emma was in it, and if she was still alive – was to proceed a short distance upriver to Chelsea Harbour Pier where paramedics were waiting.

Lots of ifs in that scenario.

Were it to be a corpse they retrieved from the bag, they would head back to Wapping police station. Bodies pulled from the river were processed there.

A rogue wave rocked the boat and Gemma stumbled. She grabbed a side rail and steadied herself. Finn's eyes were darting from the suspended bag to Lacey at the helm. He still thought she was too far downstream but was too good an officer to argue again.

Lacey looked over at the river wall. The carving was still immediately behind the rail. She was holding her position.

'Five metres,' she said into the radio. 'Keep it coming. Keep your speed and position constant. Three metres. I'm heading up. Finn, Gemma, stay on the boat!'

She pushed the throttle forward and the boat slid through the water. For a second, she thought she'd misjudged it, that the bag would swing into the cabin wall and then bounce over their heads, but Finn – the idiot – leaped into the air and caught hold of its fabric. He dragged it back, away from the cabin. Gemma caught the other side and the two of them pulled it onto the deck.

'Mark, hold steady,' Lacey called, as she eased back the throttle. 'Don't move.'

'Have you got her?'

'Stand by.'

They had seconds to get this right. Finn reached up, fumbled with the crane's hook, and swore. He yelled at Gemma, who handed over something she'd pulled from her jacket pocket. Finn reached up towards the hook again and Lacey saw the flash of a knife as Finn cut through the bag's straps and the hook swung free.

'Heads down, both of you,' she yelled, as the heavy steel hook trailed over the cabin roof. 'Mark, we've secured the bag. Get that hook out of here.'

The hook swung up and away. At the front of the boat, Finn and Gemma were on their knees, reaching into the bag of white nylon.

'Have you got her?' Joesbury repeated over the radio.

Finn and Gemma had peeled the white nylon back like petals, to reveal the trussed body of an unconscious young woman. Lacey's heart sank. What little of the face she could see beyond the brutal gag tied around Emma's jaw looked a waxy white.

Then Gemma gently pulled the gag away and Lacey saw Emma gasp for breath. Finn turned to the flybridge. He gave a thumbs up.

'Full speed ahead, skipper,' he said. 'We have a passenger to drop off at Chelsea Harbour.'

They were seconds away from the pier. No time for Finn and Gemma to do anything but use their own bodies to keep Emma secure and warm for the short trip. Resisting the temptation to drive at top speed – the water was still rough – Lacey drove to the pier, pulled up alongside and threw the stern line to a waiting constable.

'Mission accomplished, DCI Joesbury,' she said, as Finn tied up the bow and a paramedic prepared to come aboard. 'Now, for the love of God, get down from there.'

42

Fifty-two seconds after the scheduled time, Helen walked through the front door.

'Did I miss it?' she called. Dana heard the sound of a coat dropping onto the hall floor and then footsteps running upstairs. The study door was pushed open.

'Still waiting,' Dana replied quietly, because Inigo was sleeping yards away. 'A minute late.'

Helen came up close behind her and let a hand drop onto her shoulder. 'Any news?' she asked.

'Jason Hancock's been charged with two counts of murder,' Dana said, without taking her eyes off the computer screen. Jason Hancock, aka Waluigi, was the man who'd wreaked havoc in the massage parlour. 'Counter terrorism have finished with him, though. He knows nothing, had no direct contact with AryanBoy or any of the other MenMatter leaders, and there's nothing useful on any of his devices that we can find.'

'Cannon fodder, then?'

'As we thought. On the plus side, it's an open and shut case. We found his blood-soaked clothes in the park so we can tie him to both victims. The woman on the reception desk at Bubbles picked him out of over a dozen possibles. We have the footage from his body cam, plus the various cameras that picked him up on the way there. It really doesn't need a crack team of London's finest.'

'Know any more about him?'

'He's twenty-five, a computer science graduate from De Montford University, whose career never really left the starting blocks. Currently working from the Amazon depot at Bromley. Few friends in real life, a keen gamer, and I probably don't need to add, no girlfriends that we can track down. Classic incel.'

Helen pulled up a chair and sat down beside Dana.

'We did find several dark web conversations between him and AryanBoy,' Dana went on. 'He was being groomed, no doubt about it, wound up like a spring, all his grievances multiplied until he was ready to explode.'

The digital clock in the corner of the YouTube screen showed that 'the event' was currently running two and a half minutes late.

Dana asked, 'Did you see the girls?'

Since Emma's abduction and attempted murder, three days earlier, she and Lacey had been living in Mark Joesbury's Pimlico flat. It had state-of-the-art security, and Mark had persuaded Lacey that it made sense for the two women to stay together for the immediate future. Mark himself had moved onto Lacey's boat.

Lacey, temporarily, had been moved out of the marine unit, also for her own safety, and seconded to the Major Investigation Team at Lewisham, under Dana's command.

'Emma insists she's fine,' Helen said. 'She's not, but she's determined we think so. She's still refusing to leave London. She says, and it's hard to argue, that if these guys can get to her here, with the Met watching her, they can get to her anywhere.'

Emma had been able to tell them frustratingly little about the men – three or four she thought – who'd kidnapped her. Only that, barely minutes after she'd put the phone down following AryanBoy's tantrum, the fire alarms had rung out in her building.

Unsure whether to leave or not, she'd been on the point of calling Scotland Yard when she'd heard a knock at her door. The unknown male in the hall had used, or so she thought at the time, the agreed code words to indicate a trusted visitor.

Emma's recollections of the abduction, though, were so vague and disorientated, that the conclusion Mark and his team had come to was that she was in the grip of a form of PTSD and probably couldn't be relied upon.

'Still no news on how they infiltrated the construction site?' Helen asked.

Dana shook her head. 'We're trying to trace everyone who's worked on the site over the past year, anyone who could have stolen keys to the crane, but that's a lot of people.'

The bland backdrop on the TV screen changed. 'Here we go,' Dana said, and felt Helen's hand close over her own.

On the screen appeared a scene from a room in a normal-looking house. Centre stage was a sizeable leather armchair, a small circular table to its right-hand side. Behind the chair a tall, angle-poised lamp loomed over the seated man, turning him into a black silhouette. He spoke:

'Some of you may know me. You know me as AryanBoy. We've spoken online, we've formed a community, and I value all of you. But I'm speaking now to every man in the United Kingdom, to say this . . .'

He paused. His voice carried the same Midlands accent that experts had pin-pointed to the western reaches of the Black Country.

'Our time is nigh.'

Those same experts had failed to identify the voice-changing software that produced AryanBoy's distinctive accent. In any case, Dana had learned, most serious, dark web level voice-hiding software would be resistant to infiltration attempts.

'Too long now, we've waited in the shadows of those who are lesser. We've been courteous, respectful. We've acted like gentlemen and been repaid by betrayal. We've been shown no courtesy in return, no respect, no kindness. The women we wanted to protect, to love and cherish, the women we worked hard for, risked our safety and even our lives for, have turned from us, greedily seeking out the bigger mate, the richer, the more powerful.'

Dana could see two pale, square hands now. Was the light building? Were they actually going to see AryanBoy? She felt a warmth from Helen's body as her partner leaned in closer.

The figure on screen said, 'I'm here to say to you that it will end, very soon. There will be a day of reckoning, or should I say, a Day of Retribution.'

The light was definitely building. Dana could see the outline of the man's hair, the width of his shoulders. It would be possible to estimate his height, maybe even his weight.

'On that day, the men of the United Kingdom will take back our birth-right. Others, all over the world will follow until the natural order has been restored. Many countries, more enlightened than ours are already ahead of us. We look to our brothers in the Middle East to show the way, to support us in our endeavours, to be a gleaming light that we follow.

'So, brothers, be ready. Arm yourselves, organise your finances. If there are women in your life – wives, mothers, daughters – tell them you love them but they must accept the new world order. Keep them at home to keep them safe. This is a war, and the battles will take place on many fronts, even our own homes. Many will die, even some of our brave soldiers. If, like many of us, you've struggled to find meaningful relationships because of women's greed, fickleness and inconstancy, take heart. Your loneliness will soon be a forgotten dream.

'Be ready and join the struggle. Share this video as widely as you can before the corrupt, female-dominated authorities take it down. Save it on your private servers. Join us on the dark web if you can. Above all, be ready for the signal. The Day of Retribution will be soon.'

The screen went dark.

'Well,' said Helen. 'Shit just got real.'

Part Two

43

October gales brought havoc to the capital city. Lacey's former colleagues in the marine unit spent much of their time retrieving dangerous debris from the water and rescuing small crafts that, literally and figuratively, were out of their depth. Roads were blocked as ancient trees couldn't hold out against the onslaught, and Londoners trudged through piles of rotting leaves that no amount of street sweeping seemed able to stay on top of.

Rainfall reached its normal level for October and kept on coming. Sewers backed up. Several London Underground stations found themselves under water and the mayor demanded more money from central government to deal with the crisis. He was always doing that though, so no one took much notice.

The UK mourned when an elderly man and his spaniel were blown into the river at Teddington. The dog clung to a fallen branch and was pulled from the water, sodden, by some workers from the Environment Agency; the body of his owner wasn't found for days.

In the weeks following Emma Boston's kidnap and attempted murder, her explosive story in the *Daily Mail* and the release of AryanBoy's call-to-arms video, incidents of domestic violence rose by over fifteen per cent, as angry men saw their grievances legitimised. It was the sort of increase normally associated with Christmas and England losing an important football match.

Women's charities argued the figure could be even higher, as many cases went unreported. Reports of rape were up too, and even the relatively rare crime of women attacked by strangers had seen an upturn. Vacancies in women's shelters had become rarer than the Gutenberg Bible.

The video, sadly, had given few further clues as to the identity of AryanBoy, but Joesbury and his team knew it had been viewed, on both dark and surface webs, nearly forty million times by men all over the world, and that downloading of Tor browsers had increased by nearly thirty per cent. Traffic on the dark web incel sites, particularly the Rage site, had similarly multiplied.

Experts were divided as to whether the rise in violence was directly related to the MenMatter movement, but it was hard to argue with the stats. Women were being punished, for the crime of being women.

The social media giants were employing extra staff to deal with managing and removing a constant flood of hate content, either directed at women, or representing an anti-male backlash. Every day, in some form or other, the topic was discussed on current affairs shows, questions were asked in parliament, and a commission had been set up to look into violence against women.

Everything Joesbury had feared, and more, had come about.

On the other hand: finally, at last, after two years of misery, disappointment and frustration, Lacey Flint and Mark Joesbury were a couple. Both were still a little bewildered that the entirely unexpected emotion of joy had stolen into their lives; both knew that, in spite of their intimacy, they were each keeping a great deal from the other; and both were terrified of what they now stood to lose.

There were times when, were he to be entirely honest with himself, Joesbury missed the old days, when he'd been – if not happy – content with less.

On the second Tuesday of the month, he put on a suit and tie and caught a cab to a small, upmarket hotel on the Strand, showing his convincing press credentials to the young, dark-haired bloke guarding the door of the function room. He spotted Georgie and Warwick, sitting separately, three and five rows from the front, and Emma Boston two seats from Warwick.

In many ways, recent events had done Emma no harm: she'd become the go-to writer on the subject of incel violence, employed regularly by the national papers for articles and opinion pieces. Surviving the kidnap attempt had turned her into something of a national heroine. She'd appeared on *Question Time*, on the *Daily Politics* show more than once, and on *Woman's Hour*. She was busy and successful, and that helped keep her mind away from the torrent of abuse and threats that flowed her way.

Because Emma, to Joesbury's great regret, had become a constant feature on the dark web. Articles, most badly written and with no basis in fact, appeared on a regular basis, always with unflattering photographs of the scarred side of her face. Spurred on by AryanBoy and the other three incel leaders, the men of the cyber underworld competed to be as obnoxious and threatening as they could. The abusive posts appeared on social media too, quickly taken down, but adding up to a relentless campaign of bullying and intimidation.

She was still refusing to leave London, or to quit her job.

The room was continuing to fill and Joesbury estimated fifty chairs. From the crowd already gathered in the thickly carpeted, heavily curtained room, and the sound of others arriving, he guessed most would be filled.

The man they'd come to listen to was backed by a self-made billionaire and rumoured to be as well-funded as a US presidential candidate.

At the front of the room, a temporary stage had been constructed in shades of blue and mauve. The word UNITY was being projected onto its back wall, and the same logo had been fixed to the solitary podium. Upbeat music was playing, a tune Joesbury found naggingly familiar but just out of reach. He recognised several well-known journalists and political editors.

An amplified voice cut into Joesbury's thoughts, inviting those present to take their seats. The auditorium lights went down, those on the platform brightened and the star of the show – former TV and film actor Fergus Lord, walked to the podium.

Joesbury was surprised, never having seen Lord in the flesh before, to find that he wasn't a big man; tallish, maybe a little over five eleven but slender, perfectly proportioned, and his neat-fitting blue suit and stark white shirt spoke of Savile Row and Jermyn Street. Not conventionally handsome, he had curly, dark auburn hair and deep-set, brown eyes. He was a striking-looking man, one who seemed younger in real life than he appeared on screen.

The *Question Time* appearance, over a month ago now, had – temporarily, at least – brought his stellar acting career to an end. The world of film and TV drama, dominated by those whose politics inclined towards the left, couldn't forgive or forget Lord's less than politically correct views. As the acting work had dried up, Lord's political activism had taken off, and he'd been invited, with increasing regularity, to appear on news and talk shows to discuss feminism, male issues and the gender wars.

He was about to step it up a few notches.

'I'm here today,' Lord said, after he'd thanked everyone for coming, 'to speak for a forgotten minority. Men.'

A low-pitched buzz flew around the room; a female voice was heard to laugh, but quietly, nervously. Lord didn't miss a beat.

'The male suicide rate is at an all-time high,' he told a room that had fallen silent. 'Men are twice as likely to die violently than women. In the armed forces, many times more death in service happens to male soldiers, even allowing for their greater representation. White and Black British boys underperform their female counterparts in the majority of schools; if you can't afford a fancy private education, don't expect your son to thrive. Divorce laws are disgracefully skewed against men. I know, from experience, that losing our homes and our children is entirely the norm in our legal system. Family life is suffering, one in three marriages ends in divorce and children from single-parent families are always outperformed by those from more stable backgrounds. Our society is broken, because we've allowed its natural balance to be upset.'

Joesbury followed the example of those around him and typed on his laptop keyboard.

'I want to say upfront, and without equivocation, that I do not endorse the MenMatter movement,' Lord said. 'I condemn their use of violence and intimidation to further their ends. I will never be affiliated with such a dangerous and destructive ideology.'

'Bullshit,' a woman behind Joesbury muttered.

Up at the podium, Lord gave the impression of having heard the comment too, although that was surely impossible. He stopped speaking for a moment, and it seemed as though he was making eye contact with Joesbury.

There was something quietly menacing about the man.

Glancing down at his notes, Lord went on, 'But I want to make clear that I understand where the people behind MenMatter are coming from. I get their frustration and their anger. I share their hunger for change, but I happen to think there's a better way of achieving it. Which is why, today, I'm launching a new political party called UNITY.'

On the backdrop the word UNITY began to glow; the lettering morphed from blue to bright silver.

'In the coming weeks,' Lord said, 'we'll be publishing our manifesto. For now I can tell you that UNITY will be about fairness. Fairness for men, for young, working-class boys, for traditional manufacturing communities, for retired servicemen who struggle to rebuild their lives after sacrificing so much for their country, for men going through traumatic and difficult divorces, often divorces they don't want. We'll also offer fairness for those women who recognise that society has lost its way, who embrace the chance to return to a more traditional and fulfilling way of life. I'm convinced there are many of them.'

As Lord spoke on, talking about the new party's generous funding from a donor who preferred to remain anonymous and about their plans to field candidates in local elections the following spring, Joesbury sneaked a look around the room. Every important political reporter in the capital was present. Lord's personal profile, and the fact that social media had been talking of little other than the rise of the incel threat for weeks now, had guaranteed interest. Lord might not be taken seriously in political circles – the prime minister had been characteristically dismissive – but he was news.

Up at the front, he was drawing his address to a close.

'To those behind the MenMatter movement, I say this: I will be your voice. I know your cause is just and I will speak for you. The time for suffering in silence is over but we talk now through the ballot box. Put down your weapons and join me, because together we can retake the earth.'

'Fuck's sake,' a woman behind Joesbury muttered.

'We've time for some questions,' Lord said. 'Laura?'

The cameras moved towards the slight, blonde woman in the front row.

'You say you're not affiliated with the MenMatter movement,' the BBC reporter said. 'But surely in the minds of the public there will be a natural connection? Your aims are practically identical, and the timing suggests that the political party has sprung from the terrorist movement. Aren't you Sinn Féin to their IRA?'

Lord gave a slow, firm headshake, one of his signature moves that Joesbury recognised from TV. He said, 'Absolutely not. I condemn the attacks carried out by MenMatter. But what we've seen emerge in our society in recent months is nothing short of fury because the men of the UK don't have a voice. UNITY will give them that voice. UNITY will listen to them and speak up for them. There is no need for MenMatter now that we're here. Robert?'

The ITV political correspondent was handed the mic. 'We've seen growing calls on social media, even from some mainstream commentators, for the government to consider some erosion of women's rights,' he said. 'For example, introducing a require-ment to dress modestly, restrictions on abortion, a 10 p.m. curfew for women out at night not accompanied by a man, a ban on women renting property together. The thinking behind it being that conceding some of the MenMatter's demands will result in them stepping down their campaigns. Would you support the introduction of such measures?'

Lord said, 'No credible government will negotiate with terror-ists, nor should they. UNITY isn't about restricting women's free-doms or making life more difficult for women. It's about levelling up, giving men equal opportunities and rights. Take abortion: how can it be right that a potentially loving and supportive father is denied the right to see his child born, purely because the parent gestating the child – the so-called mother – wants to bring its life to an end? UNITY will call for fathers to have equal say in the termination of pregnancies. Beth?'

The dark-haired woman took hold of the microphone, 'What do you think MenMatter have planned for the Day of Retribution?'

'I've no idea. The people behind MenMatter don't share their plans with us. What is important though, is that in order to prevent the attacks getting worse men of the UK must be given a voice. That's where we come in.'

44

'So, what do we think?' Joesbury said, when he and Georgie arrived back at the office; Warwick had gone with Emma to the Pimlico flat. 'Is Fergus Lord part of the MenMatter movement or jumping on the bandwagon?'

'Bandwagon,' Georgie said without hesitation. 'His career's in tatters after his disastrous appearance on *Question Time*, but he's still young. He needs a new purpose.'

'I'm not sure,' Archie countered. 'You can't set up a political party in weeks. I think he's been planning this for a while.'

'It's not a political party though, is it?' Georgie argued. 'It's him, a private-school Man Friday and a swanky room in a hotel.'

Theo looked up from his desk. 'His GoFundMe page was set up two weeks ago. It's currently standing at a quarter of a million quid with nearly ten thousand donors.'

While the others had been at the press conference, Theo and Archie had been monitoring social media reaction to it, including the launch of the political party's online presence. 'His website's pretty cool,' Theo went on. 'And it's open for membership. Nearly seven hundred people have joined in the first two hours. Mind you, membership's cheap, only a tenner.'

'Emma's apartment in Earl's Court has been vandalised again,' Archie said. 'A can of red paint flung at the front door. Her landlord wants to send us the bill.'

'I thought we were putting it out she doesn't live there any more,' Joesbury said, in exasperation. The novelty of living on Lacey's boat, with constant reminders of her absence, was starting to wear off. He wanted to be back in his own flat, with Lacey as a regular visitor, if not a permanent resident.

Since she'd been seconded back to CID meeting up had become harder. She rarely agreed to leave Emma alone in the evenings and staying over – either at his place or hers – was proving challenging.

Lunch though; lunch was something. They could still do lunch.

He crossed to the window. Unlike the uninspiring view in his own room, the larger general office looked out over the river. A young woman with fair hair and wearing a coat the colour of maple syrup was approaching from the south, probably from Westminster Tube station. She had chosen to cross the road so that she could walk closer to the water. She carried a bag, from one of the sandwich shops, so they didn't have to waste time finding a café. They could grab a bench and eat and talk while they watched the water.

'I don't think they care, boss,' Archie was saying. 'It's a place the incels connect with Emma so they target it. She's still their public enemy number one, although the home secretary comes in for her fair share.'

The woman on the embankment pulled out her phone and tapped out a message. Joesbury waited to hear the resultant ping coming from his own phone and realised he was smiling.

'You don't think it's still Lacey they hate the most?' Georgie asked.

Archie shrugged. 'Toss-up. God help us if they ever find out the two of them are living together.'

Outside, Lacey was looking up at the building, might even be able to see him, but he was some way off the ground, and she wouldn't know which windows belonged to SCD10.

He turned away. 'Catch you later, guys,' he said. 'Got a date.'

45

She had a boyfriend. The bitch actually had a boyfriend, and a recent acquisition at that, judging by the way they were all over each other, with their lingering glances and their surreptitious touching when they thought no one was watching. AryanBoy had seen them together, several times now: watching kids play football in a south London park on a Saturday morning, sharing a late supper in some dump of a Chinese restaurant in Kennington; they'd even gone swimming early one Sunday morning at London's Royal Docks.

He was nothing special at all. Not that good looking, certainly not that bright, bit of a thug by all accounts, and yet the sort that women, inexplicably, were drawn to.

She was even living in his flat now. He wasn't there himself, he was tucked up on her boat in Deptford Creek, and she was cosied up with that ugly bitch Emma Boston. But it was only a matter of time before they moved Boston out and then the two of them would be left in peace to shag themselves witless.

Well, it wasn't going to happen.

Don't get cosy, Lacey Flint. I'm coming for you.

46

On her way back to Lewisham, Lacey took a call from the office, and then a detour. She showed her warrant card to the young man on the door at The Mudlark, a pub and restaurant on the south bank by London Bridge.

'She's this way,' she was told, and followed the staff member through the long bar, beneath sturdy oak beams and brass ceiling lights, to a table at the furthest corner from the door. A female police constable sat at it, her male colleague standing a few feet away. Also seated was a young woman with her head down, eyes on her phone, tapping away furiously.

'Belinda Scott?' Lacey approached. 'I'm from Lewisham's Major Investigation Team.'

The young woman pushed long dark hair aside. Her nose had been bleeding, and the flesh around both of her eyes looked reddened. Her mascara had run, creating tear streaks through her make-up. Several blood-stained napkins lay on the table.

Lacey took a seat. 'We can talk on the way to hospital, if you prefer,' she began. 'But I have to speak to the staff here, and to any customers who were witnesses, so I'll need you to wait a few minutes more, I'm afraid.'

The girl fixed her eyes on her phone again. 'I don't want to go to hospital. I want to go home.'

'I understand. Can you tell me what happened?'

A sharp, tearful glance up. 'I arranged to meet someone here. For a drink. And then this guy showed up and started yelling at me. When I told him he couldn't talk to me like that, he thumped me.'

The incident, phoned through to Lewisham CID, had been described as a vicious assault on a young woman by a man she didn't know.

Lacey asked, 'Who was the man you came here to meet?'

'This guy I've been talking to. He said we should meet here because it's always busy, and I wouldn't feel nervous about meeting a strange man.'

Already the story was depressingly familiar. On the day Lacey had returned to Lewisham's MIT, MenMatter had launched their latest offensive – Operation Catfish, inspired by the online activities of an incel in Connecticut in the United States. Needing to monitor it, and find something for her new recruit to do, Dana had given the job to Lacey.

In this, its latest context, catfish was a verb: it meant to deceive with an intent to humiliate.

Lacey said, 'You'd never met this man before today?'

Reluctantly, the girl pushed her phone across the table. On the open Tinder app Lacey saw the profile picture of a man in his late twenties with great teeth. His black hair was combed back off his forehead, his beard close-cropped. He wore large-framed, tinted glasses. His name, supposedly, was Charlie Coates.

'He told me he was a consultant with Deloitte,' Belinda sniffed. 'We've been chatting for nearly a month. I'm not a fool.'

'I know you're not,' Lacey said. 'These people are very clever. You're not the first woman this has happened to, not by a long way.'

Catfishing worked by the perpetrator setting up a fake online presence. Usually it was based on Tinder, the dating website, but the more sophisticated ones were reflected on Twitter, Facebook and Instagram. The key was to give the impression of an attractive, successful, single man – a typical Chad, to use incel speak – looking to make female connections. When a woman 'took the bait', she began messaging him. They talked, he came across as funny, intelligent, with lots of active, interesting hobbies. He was 'reeling her in'. After a while, they arranged to get together in person.

'So, you were supposed to meet here,' Lacey said. 'What happened?'

'He was late. Not much, maybe around ten minutes, but I was starting to get worried, wondering if I'd been set up. You never know with Tinder do you?'

Lacey agreed that, no, you never did.

'And then this other guy arrived. I saw him come in, because I was watching the door, but it obviously wasn't Charlie, so I carried on texting a friend. Next thing I knew this new guy was standing next to me, filming me on his phone.'

The female constable interrupted. 'Belinda was sitting by the window.' She indicated a table, currently roped off. A glass of what looked like red wine had been upturned.

Belinda went on, 'So, I said, can I help you, mate, and he started talking loudly, so that everyone could hear.'

'Can you remember what he said.'

'Something like, so you're Belinda Scott, twenty-two years old from Wandsworth, work at Hamden Dental Clinic in Battersea. I'm not sure what came next, something about do my work colleagues know I pick up men on the internet. Everyone was looking by this time.'

Of course, they were. The catfish dates were always arranged in busy public places, to maximise humiliation for the woman.

'And then he said Charlie wasn't coming, that Charlie didn't exist, that he'd invented him to show everyone what a shallow, self-centred bitch I was.'

'We've spoken to the manager who confirms this,' the male constable added. 'At this point staff got involved, but he was pretty abusive to them too.'

'I'll talk to them all later,' Lacey said. 'Go on, Belinda.'

'He said he was filming everything and he was going to put it on the internet so everyone would see what a stupid loser I was. I lost it at that point.'

She looked down.

Lacey said, 'I'd have lost it before that. I'm not judging you, but I need to know what happened.'

Belinda sniffed, and then winced; her nose was hurting her. 'I got up and swiped my hand at his phone. I'm not sure what I was planning to do, maybe try to delete the footage. His phone fell onto the table, onto my glass, knocking it over, and he yelled something at me. The next thing I knew I was on the floor. People say he hit me.'

'He did,' the male constable said. 'It's on CCTV, we've seen it already.'

'He'd gone by the time people helped me up,' Belinda finished. 'Will he do what he threatened, put the footage up on social media?'

Lacey shared a look with the female constable. 'Possibly not. The fact he hit you in such a public place means he knows we'll be involved. He may shy away from putting evidence out there. If he does, we can ask the social media sites to take it down and as it's linked to a crime, they probably will. But you know what, even if it's out there, no one will blame you.'

'Yes, they will,' Belinda said.

Lacey didn't bother arguing because she knew that, yes, they would; when the victim was a woman, when the attack was sexually motivated, she invariably got the blame. It was just the way it was.

47

Dana closed, locked and bolted the front door to the house, slipping the chain in place, even though she knew she'd be admitting visitors later. The shutting out of the world had become an essential part of her evening ritual. Only when the door was shut – properly shut – when she, Helen and Inigo were safely on the inside, could she even begin to think about relaxing. Twenty-six days since AryanBoy had sent his call to arms across the internet, almost a month since he'd threatened the country with a Day of Retribution, and with each day that passed, Dana felt disaster moving closer.

Endless speculation in the media about what form the big day might take was hardly helping. A total failure of the technical support behind the NHS? A meltdown of the UK's financial markets? A 9/11-style catastrophe? Every morning when she woke, the first thought in Dana's head was: It could be this day. This could be the day I lose everything.

She'd said nothing of this to Helen, to anyone, because she couldn't help the feeling that voicing her dread would make it real.

Raindrops were gleaming on Inigo's eyelashes as she carried his car seat into the kitchen. Seeing his other mum, the fun mum, setting up his high chair, which of course meant food, Inigo began squeaking to be lifted from the seat. He'd had tea at nursery but the child never seemed to stop eating. Since he'd started crawling, a week ago, towards Helen not her, which frankly was hard to forgive, his appetite, substantial to begin with, was close to matching that of a child of two.

Helen had stopped by the deli on her way home from work, stocking up on wine, bread, cheeses, hummus and olives, all of which, admittedly, were delicious. She'd also defrosted a jumbo tub of homemade soup from the freezer; homemade by Dana, who found the predictability a bit annoying – would it kill the woman to make a spaghetti? On the other hand, the house was spotless, fires had been lit in both dining and sitting rooms and lamps were casting golden light into all the dark corners. It looked like home.

'Hello brat.' Helen beamed down at the baby before dropping a kiss on Dana's forehead. 'Lacey called to say they'll be late. Emma has to finish a piece landed on her after this morning's press conference. I'll feed the ankle-biter.'

'You know you've roughly a year before he's repeating all these insults.' Dana hung up her damp coat.

'Fuck me, as little as that.' Helen lifted the baby out of his car seat, tossing him into the air. She was always doing it, and every time she threw him, Dana's heart stopped. It took all her resolve not to scream at her partner to be careful.

'Hancock have his half hour in court?' Helen asked.

'Remanded in custody until the new year.' Dana found herself oddly reluctant to leave the warm kitchen. 'Progress on the Tower Bridge baby, though. We've charged the third suspect.'

'Three out of four ain't bad.' Helen took a tub of baby food out of the microwave. 'How'd you find this one?'

'Lacey and Gayle again, same way they did with the bloke posing as a dad, through his shopping history. They searched for an identical inflatable unicorn and eventually narrowed it down to a site on eBay that claimed to have twenty in stock, so they drove down to Kent to talk to them.'

Helen was testing the temperature of the purée. 'And they'd sold the one in question? God, what is this muck?'

'They'd sold only one in the previous six weeks, to a cash buyer, who'd walked in off the street. Didn't leave any identifying documentation but there was CCTV footage of him in the shop and, get this, in the car park. We got his registration number. After that, it was easy. And it's puréed swede.'

Helen mimed vomiting, the baby squealed with delight and Dana helped herself to wine. The man who'd pretended to be a dad on the morning of the Tower Bridge abduction had been tracked via the pram. He'd bought it second-hand, for cash, but had used a work email to make first contact with the seller. That had been enough. The team had traced his company, his company had traced the IP address to the man's desk, and as a bonus, Dana's team had matched his prints with a partial found behind one pram wheel.

Fingerprints had similarly led to the capture of the third suspect. Following David Cook's suggestion, the team had checked CCTV footage around St Katharine Docks for several weeks prior to the incident and had found pictures, taken ten days previously, of all three men gathered around the gates. That time, they hadn't bothered with face coverings. Best of all, Lacey had spotted that one of them wasn't wearing gloves and had touched the metal railing running down the side of the pier. His print was still recoverable and matched a set on file; the man had been arrested two years earlier in connection with football hooliganism. It was a good result, and more than once Dana had been grateful for Lacey's dogged attention to detail. She was seriously thinking of having words with David Cook; Lacey was a born detective, wasted on the river.

On the downside, none of the three men knew each other and genuinely had no idea of the identity of the fourth, or of the masterminds behind the planning. AryanBoy, MadHatter, Joker and BlackPill88 were still eluding them.

And every day, the Day of Retribution was drawing closer.

48

Not for the first time, the man who'd taken to styling himself AryanBoy was pondering his lack of success with women. He knew it wasn't about looks any more. He'd grown three inches since school, lost his puppy fat and gained muscle in its place. More than one girl had told him it really wasn't the way he looked that was the problem, his looks were fine, better than average, it was just . . .

They could never finish the sentence; never tell him what he needed to know. And after the incident at uni when – well, he didn't need to dwell on that.

He bent to retrieve a bottle left abandoned on the pavement, glanced around, and then hurled it out across the void in front of him. He had a good throwing arm; the bottle soared through the air before gracefully arching down and vanishing with an audible splash.

It wasn't that he didn't try. Jeez, if medals were handed out for effort. It had cost him several expensive mistakes, but he'd learned to dress well. He had a flat in a good part of town, drove a decent car. He ought to be tripping over available women. Yet still they flocked to the Chads who treated them like shit.

It was so fucking frustrating, to know he was doing something wrong, something he couldn't quite put a finger on, something beyond his view, because if he knew what it was, he could put it right.

There were times when the unfairness of it all enraged him.

AryanBoy picked up his pace, heading downstream towards the lights of Tower Bridge. As the days had grown colder, the evenings shortening, he'd taken to hanging around the river, drawn by its darkness and its ever-changing moods. He didn't expect to see her, especially now the Met had moved her to another division for her personal safety, but the marine unit Targas passed by every now and again; he knew it was stupid, but they helped him feel closer to her somehow.

Besides, he thought, as he stalked the silent banks of the Thames in the dark, staring down at the black water, he had a feeling that, finally, he had it. Everything that was still wrong in his life was the fault of the girl on the clifftop twelve years ago, the girl who against all odds had come back into his life.

It was all the fault of the woman now calling herself Lacey Flint.

49

'So,' Helen said, two hours later, when Inigo was tucked up in bed, dinner had been eaten and they'd broken apart a bar of Cadbury's Fruit & Nut, which was Helen's idea of dessert. 'You wanted to ask about financing terrorist operations?'

Emma shook her head at the offered bar of chocolate. 'Lacey said it was your specialism at Interpol.'

Helen threw Lacey a glance. 'She's flattering me. I can probably give you enough background though, so shoot.'

'Terrorism is expensive,' Emma began, after glancing down at her notes. 'Where are MenMatter getting their money from?'

'It can be,' Helen agreed, 'but what we've seen so far from the incel crowd is low budget stuff. The cost of the inflatable, the pram, the fake baby. Even with the web presence, you're talking low thousands at most.'

Emma said, 'If they scale things up, which they keep threatening to do, they'll need more money. Bombs won't come cheap.'

Helen said, 'A lot of terrorism is state sponsored, but that's unlikely to be the case here. Some groups use commercial activities to fund their attacks, either legal or otherwise. The IRA notoriously owned a couple of hundred taxi cars, a few pubs, some gaming machines. The trouble with money-making businesses is that they require a lot of work in themselves, initial investment money, time and attention to make them successful.

I'd be amazed if a group as new as MenMatter were funding their activities commercially. Which leaves two routes. One, setting up one or more registered charities and seeking donations. Several Islamic terror groups are funded that way. The other, which is the only one I think could work in this instance is crowdfunding. The thousands of men around the world that allegedly support the movement can be asked to fund it too. A lot of small donations can add up.'

'You mean like a GoFundMe page?' Emma asked.

'That would be dismantled very quickly,' Dana said. 'Most crowdfunding platforms keep a watching brief over who's using them. I can't see a terror group lasting long.'

'There are some far-right platforms that would be more tolerant,' Helen explained. 'Hatreon, WeSearchr, Counter Fund. The problem with those is that once the banks and the credit card companies get wise to what's going on, they stop processing the payments.'

'Some switch successfully to cryptocurrencies like bitcoin,' Dana said. 'But not everyone's comfortable using them.'

'They're getting more popular, though,' Helen said. 'And there's no shortage of tutorials available on how to use them. So, that would be my guess: MenMatter are crowdfunding, using a far-right platform and a cyber currency.'

'They are,' Lacey said. 'Sorry, Dana, I haven't had time to brief you. I had a phone call from Theo Cox today, you know one of the guys in Mark's team. Theo's their finance guy. He did a master's at UCL after Cambridge.'

Dana nodded.

'Well, finance-guy-Theo said an appeal had been launched on the MenMatter website, the one called Rage,' Lacey went on. 'They want donations to fund the defence of those three men we've charged in connection with the Tower Bridge abduction.

And a separate one was set up a while ago to fund Jason Hancock's defence. There are links appearing on the surface web too.'

'So, we should know how much they've raised,' Dana said. 'All cryptocurrency transactions are public.'

'Theo said new campaigns are springing up every hour and that it's close to impossible to keep tabs on them all. He said he'd keep me posted.'

Helen said, 'There's also a possibility, and I stress possibility, that this new political group, UNITY, are linked to MenMatter. UNITY have over ten thousand members, all paying ten quid each. That's a hundred thousand quid in a few days. If you print that, Emma, you'll be sued for libel, so don't. But bear it in mind.'

'It could work, though,' Lacey said. 'Men who are sympathetic to the aims of MenMatter but shrink from the violence could feel they're doing their bit by contributing to UNITY. When UNITY doesn't get anywhere politically, they might be more inclined to support a bit of direct action. Whatever happens, the money flow continues.'

Lacey's phone began to ring. Her face seemed to pale as she glanced at the screen and got to her feet. 'I need to take this,' she said. 'Excuse me.'

50

For a long time, the girl on the clifftop, with the long, two-tone hair and the leather jacket, the one he must now learn to think of as Lacey Flint, had been a bad but distant memory for Aryan-Boy; an annoyance he could safely keep at the back of his mind, because that night on Beachy Head had no relevance to the man he was now.

These days, though, he found himself thinking about her increasingly, and getting more and more angry. Because she'd done it all wrong!

She should have seen in him, as he had in her, a kindred spirit. They should have comforted each other; sat together on the clifftop, held hands and talked until each knew the other inside out. He would have realised, as the darkness turned into the soft gold of dawn, that he wasn't alone after all, that fate had stepped in, and that at the very worst moment of his life, he'd found his soulmate.

They should have left Beachy Head together. (The Lexus with the dead girl was a logistical problem he'd yet to resolve satisfactorily.) They could have found breakfast in an overnight café in Eastbourne and then slipped into his room before the household was properly awake. They should have slept in each other's arms and known, as they woke, that neither had to be alone again. She belonged to him. Why the fuck hadn't the bitch seen that?

Well, this time it was going to be different. This time, she wasn't going to get away.

51

Lacey left Helen and Dana's house, grabbing her coat. Outside, she crossed the road and walked down the street. Only when she was sure there was no one around did she answer the call.

'Toc?' It was an old nickname, because she and the woman known to the world as Victoria Llewellyn had agreed never to use their real names, even when they couldn't be overheard. 'You OK?'

Toc was a caller she never ignored if she could help it, no matter what she was doing.

'Fine and dandy.' The familiar voice sounded reassuringly normal. 'Something's come up, though.'

In the background Lacey could hear orders being barked, female voices arguing, a heavy door slammed shut, the entirely normal soundtrack of a high-security women's prison.

'What?' Lacey could feel the muscles in her shoulders tensing. 'What's happened?'

'I've been contacted by a man who claims he's an author. Bloke called Adam Ryan. We've had a few email exchanges.'

High-security prisoners could receive emails, but only indirectly. They came into a central account and, once approved, were printed off and handed to the prisoner, a process that often took days. Prisoners were allowed to respond, but only under close supervision at allocated times. As a result, email correspondence with a prison inmate wasn't much faster than snail mail.

Toc said, 'He's writing a book about female murderers, called Lady Killers, which I told him was a long way from original but I'm not sure he took it on board.'

Lacey said, 'Don't you get that a lot?'

'Oh, all the time. But there's something different about this one. Something off.'

The rain was becoming heavier. 'How so?' She looked around for shelter, saw none.

'He won't name his agent, or his publisher, but claims to have a huge advance, fifty grand, that he'll share with me, fifty-fifty, if I cooperate. He's offering me twenty-five grand, Lacey, authors never do that. I don't even think I'd be allowed to take it, some bollocks about not profiting from my crimes.'

Lacey pulled up her coat collar and bent forward to keep the rain off her face and phone.

'And I can't find anything about him on the internet. All authors have a massive online presence, even the ones you've never heard of. I think this Adam Ryan bloke's a fake.'

'I'm guessing there's a reason you're not simply telling him to get lost?'

'We've talked on the phone twice. Both times I had to call a different number, which made me suspicious. Who changes their number in a week?'

'He's using burner phones.'

'That's what I thought. He doesn't want me – or, more likely, the prison authorities or the police – to be able to trace him. And his questions were odd. He was asking a lot about my early life, where I grew up, did I have any surviving family, did I get any visitors, who did I feel closest to.'

'A biographer would want background,' Lacey said.

'Yeah, but it wouldn't be the first thing he'd ask, would it? He'd start with the juicy stuff. How does it feel to stick a knife into someone's belly? What's it like having another human being at my mercy? How quickly does blood cool when it's spilling out all over you.'

'Toc—'

'I know, you don't like all that, but the people who want to talk to me always do. They're like, proper weirdos. And then he wanted to know what I thought about the whole incel business.'

Lacey was upright again, the rain no longer mattered. 'He talked about incels?'

'Now you're getting it. He wanted to know what I thought about the attack on the massage parlour, and the kidnap of that journalist, and whether I'd have done either differently, and did I have any advice for men who want to take out their frustration on women who've let them down.'

'What did you tell him?'

'I told him Emma Boston is one of my personal heroes and Jason Hancock's a sad wanker who'll get what's coming to him if he comes anywhere near me.'

'That's the spirit,' Lacey said, but with a wave of sadness. There were times when she found it almost impossible to reconcile the cold-blooded killer with the girl she'd once known.

'Then he said I was becoming something of an incel icon, that thousands of men all round the world looked up to me, because I'd killed four women who'd destroyed their sons' lives.'

'That's not what you did.'

'Hey, you don't need to tell me what I did, I was there. And then he wanted to know if I'd used my looks to manipulate men. Well, Christ, who hasn't? I was getting suspicious by this time. He wasn't interested in me so much as how he could link me to the incel movement. So, I was about to tell him to go fuck himself, because I'm not having anything to do with those dangerous bastards, when he said something that made my blood run cold.'

Lacey had never heard Toc use that expression before.

'He said he wanted to visit me, but he didn't want to interfere with other visitors I get. He asked whether I have family who keep in touch, parents maybe, brothers or sisters. I said I don't have any family, because that's what we agreed. And he said, was I sure? Was I sure I didn't have a sister?'

So, this was how it felt then, when your blood ran cold.

'He's called Adam Ryan, Lacey. Mr A Ryan. Do you need to write it down?'

Lacey stretched out a hand and wrote on the passenger window of the closest car. The letter A, for Adam. Then his surname. The lettering immediately began to leak, as droplets of water sped down the glass.

A Ryan. AryanBoy.

Toc's next words were hardly necessary, but she said them all the same.

'It's not me he's interested in, Lacey. It's you.'

52

AryanBoy had worked it out; it hadn't taken long. The two young women in the car that night had been Lacey Flint and Victoria Llewellyn. The one still living had to be Victoria (leather jacket, traces of black dye in otherwise fair hair, faint Welsh accent) so the Jane Doe who'd gone over the cliff in the stolen Lexus had been Lacey Flint. For some reason, after she'd chickened out on her suicide plans, Victoria had assumed her friend's identity.

He was less sure about the real identity of the woman serving several life sentences in Durham prison. Victoria's sister Cathy remained his best guess. The two women, especially as girls, had looked alike enough to get away with it.

He'd been nonplussed, at first, by the discovery that Cathy Llewellyn had supposedly drowned in a houseboat accident on the Thames, some months before the night at Beachy Head, but had concluded that faking their own deaths and assuming a stolen identity must be a Llewellyn family trait. Quite why Cathy had taken her older sister's name was another matter. What he hoped – really, really hoped – was that they'd both been involved in the murders, because that totally would be something he could leverage. A woman guarding that sort of secret would have to do whatever he asked, wouldn't she?

Hey, maybe she'd even had a hand in killing her friend, the real Lacey, the one she'd sent plummeting over the clifftop. Wouldn't that be something?

AryanBoy spent a lot of time, these days, fantasising about having the woman from the clifftop answerable to his every whim.

In the meantime, he had to test his theory. He'd made contact with the woman in Durham, the woman known to the world as Victoria Llewellyn, and set a few hares running. How long did he give it, before the hound came bounding after?

53

Dana said, 'Emma, has Lacey kept you up to speed on what happened today, the latest sally in the so-called Operation Catfish?'

Emma nodded. 'She says there's very little you can do about it. Do you think that's right?'

Silence greeted her question.

'You can't quote me,' Dana said.

Emma gave a rapid nod of her head. 'I know. You'll be an unnamed source in the Metropolitan Police.'

There was an impatience apparent in Emma that evening; Dana had noticed it within a half hour of her and Lacey's arrival. She spoke quickly, interrupted more frequently and started at loud noises. Over a month of knowing that people – a lot of people – wanted her dead, had had its inevitable impact. Also, Dana realised, she'd insisted on sitting facing the door.

Lacey had just left the house. She might have left the front door ajar.

'None of us think it's right,' Dana said, after several uncomfortable seconds of resisting the temptation to get up and check. 'It isn't right that women on their own at night can be followed and intimidated, it isn't right that girls as young as ten get hardcore porn AirDropped into their phones, and it isn't right that women can be publicly humiliated when all they're trying to do is make a meaningful connection with a guy. But legally these are very grey areas and as a rule, as long as the woman isn't harmed or threatened, it's not technically a crime.'

'And where it is, it's very hard to prove,' Helen added. 'You're talking about dozens, maybe hundreds of offences, many of which seem minor in isolation, but together they add up to a big problem.'

'Lacey said you've been seeing a backlash? Women actually fighting back?'

'Good,' Helen snapped, through a mouthful of chocolate.

'No, it's not, because they're putting themselves in danger,' Dana said. 'They've been trying to do the catfishing thing back to the men, setting up fake accounts, seeing who bites, then confronting men who clearly aren't who their profile claimed to be. The trouble is when men are humiliated and pissed off by a woman, especially in public, they can fight back in a way we can't. Women are getting hurt.'

And she hardly needed to tell Emma that; Emma, who daily received video clips of her hours spent suspended above the river Thames.

'What impact do you think this new political party, UNITY, will have?' Emma asked. 'I mean, it's been over a month since the spa murders and my little adventure. The following-women-at-night and the cyber-flashing fizzled out after a few days. Even the catfishing isn't as prevalent as it was. Maybe a new political party was the change they needed.'

'AryanBoy hasn't gone away,' Dana said. 'He's telling his followers to bide their time, to keep their powder dry for now, to watch and wait.'

'He's planning something else, isn't he?' Emma said. 'This is the calm before the storm.'

'Yes.' Dana agreed reluctantly, because even admitting this much felt like giving power to her fears. 'We think that's exactly what this is. Again, not to quote me, Emma, but another really worrying thing for me is that the big stuff – what happened to you, and the baby, and the women in Peckham, even the lower-level intimidatory stuff is having an impact. Terrorism always does. The IRA atrocities strained relations between the British and the Irish to breaking point. Islamic terrorism stirs up anti-Muslim feeling and that leads to racial attacks on all people of colour, regardless of their faith. The incel movement is creating division between the sexes and that's more worrying than anything that came previously because we're entirely dependent on each other.'

'And because men will win,' Helen added.

54

Lacey drove the short distance home from Battersea to Pimlico. Emma, as always when she was processing new information, was silent in the passenger seat. That suited Lacey fine, because she had a lot to think about herself.

It felt like a long time since she'd been this afraid.

It was too much of a coincidence. Far too much. A man known as AryanBoy, believed to be the brains behind MenMatter, had been trying to track her down for some time, and with some success; and now a man called Adam Ryan, with an unhealthy interest in the incel movement, and an unconvincing cover story, was talking to the incarcerated murderer with whom she had an intimate connection. Not only talking, but dropping hints about family, about sisters.

'Could someone have dropped you in it?' Toc had said over the phone, as Lacey was considering the practicalities of running, now, tonight; not to mention the morality of doing so, given she'd be leaving Emma alone and unguarded. Her grab bag, the one she'd packed years ago with money, a change of clothes and fake documents wasn't anywhere handy – she'd had to move it when she'd learned Joesbury would be staying on her boat – and accessing it quickly would be next to impossible.

'Well, could they?' Toc had had to prompt her for a response.

It felt unlikely. Hardly anyone knew about her Durham visits. Dana and Helen, Joesbury of course, and her boss, Superintendent

Cook: people with whom she'd had to come clean, who knew and believed the story that Lacey and Victoria had known each other as young women. None of them would have spoken out of turn. Except . . .

'It's not impossible, I suppose. Dana told me not so long ago the powers-that-be have been asking questions about my visits to you, suggesting it's not a good look for an aspiring sergeant. Careless talk has a way of getting around. He definitely mentioned sisters though? Those were his exact words?'

'Yep.'

'How can he know that? How can anyone know that?'

'He might not. Look, it's too soon to panic. He's got more to lose than you have. He's a murderer and a terrorist. All you did was lie on your job application form. People do that all the time.'

'Not to the Met, they don't.'

'Even so, if he's seriously planning to visit me, that's something you can use, isn't it?'

Something they could use. It would be dangerous, would involve going it alone, without the protection of the Met.

Did she really, though, have a choice?

55

On the Thursday of that week, storms were threatening, matching Dana's mood perfectly. It was twenty-eight days since Aryan-Boy's threat to unleash havoc. Twenty-eight days on which, barring weekends, Dana had dropped her child off at nursery without any confidence that she'd return to pick him up again. Twenty-eight days of starting at a car back-firing, of being reluctant to take the Tube lest she get trapped underground, of hurrying from one barrier to the next on pavements, in case a passing van chose to mount the pavement and head straight at her. Twenty-eight days of living in fear.

And now it seemed she might not be the only one, because there was an obvious nervousness about Theo Cox; one that had nothing to do with expertise, because he clearly had that in droves. As he spoke, he played with his hair, pulled at shirt cuffs, didn't hold eye contact: all classic signs of someone ill at ease. She glanced down at the briefing note Mark had sent her about him. Originally from Oxford, but a Cambridge graduate, Theo had read computer science and finance. He'd worked in the city for a while, as a quantitative analyst at Goldman Sachs, before leaving to seek what he'd described as a 'more worthwhile' career.

Unlike Archie and Warwick, Theo and Georgie were civilian members of the Met, not having been through the usual police training at Hendon. A child of the armed forces, Theo had spent much of his childhood in boarding school. His listed hobbies included amateur dramatics, and he was an excellent mimic, according to Mark. He was considered a good future candidate for actual, as opposed to online, undercover work. He was single, as were all four of the cyber squad.

With his own time limited, Mark had sent Theo along to Lewisham to update Dana and her team on the latest developments in the MenMatter case.

'Shortly after the attack on the massage parlour,' Theo was saying, 'we spotted a new development. Teachers and parents were noticing teenage boys getting involved in a new online game called *Rage and Rampage*. It's downloadable from the surface web despite our attempts to take it down. As you're about to see, it simulates a violent attack on a private secondary school. This is a recording we made of an actual gameplay a few days ago.'

He leaned over his laptop for a second or two, and then the screen behind him came to life and the recording of an online game began. Dana and her colleagues watched as the protagonist, a teenage boy with the handle Nate666, entered a school building. From the entrance doors he hurled a knife that hit the middle-aged female receptionist square in the chest. As she collapsed behind the front desk, he set off. Making his way around the school, he slaughtered all the unsuspecting girls and female teachers he came across, hunting out terrified ones hiding in cupboards, battering down doors of changing rooms, taking out a few boys for good measure. A running commentary accompanied his rampage; as he claimed each victim he listed his grievances against them, the girls who'd rejected him, the boys who'd looked down on him.

Gayle Mizon said, 'I can't believe this shit stays online.'

Theo paused the game. 'My colleague, Warwick Bowman, is working with the legal department to get it off permanently. The problem they have, though, is that on the surface it's not so different to other games that simulate violence for fun.'

'Any idea how popular this game is?' Dana asked, when Theo had closed it down. She was feeling slightly sick.

Theo said, 'I had a headteacher contact me this morning and that makes six in the last three days. If we can't shut it down, the thing's going to be bigger than *Minecraft* before we know it. Worryingly, though, we're starting to think the game could be more significant than we realised at first.'

'How so?' Dana asked.

'These games generate millions,' Theo replied. 'Billions sometimes. We've no way of knowing how many subscribers this one has, but we're seeing it pop up in the US, Canada, Australia, South Africa. And it's only been out a few weeks. A few more, especially with the publicity the incels are getting, and we could be looking at tens of thousands of players.'

'But it's free to download and play,' Neil Anderson said. 'It's a brainwashing device, that's what we were led to believe. Terrorist groups use them all the time to radicalise young potential recruits.'

'It's free to play,' Theo acknowledged. 'That's the business model most of these games follow, but they make their money from what they call microtransactions.'

Dana could feel a headache building. 'Explain.'

'The basic game gives each player a couple of machetes and some knives he tucks down his boots, plus that sword thing they wear on their backs, but they're encouraged to pay money to upgrade with guns and grenades – little extra things that make their fantasies more powerful, more fun. And there's a whole new level being launched next week that involves a school production and a swimming gala. The new level will cost £10 per player.'

'Not a massive amount,' Pete Stenning said.

'No, so most parents might not even notice it going out of their son's account,' Theo replied. 'But ten thousand players upgrading and you've got a hundred grand, plus all the income from the other weaponry and special skills. It's showing signs of building into a very sophisticated game with massive income-generating possibilities.'

'Mark told me they're on top of the possibility it might be taken down,' Dana added. 'He said they've started issuing warnings about what to do when it happens so that playing enjoyment won't be disturbed.'

'Teenage boys all over the world are downloading Tor browsers ready to continue playing on the dark web,' Theo said. 'That's the really scary thing. It's taking thousands of young lads and dragging them into a very dark place. Some of them might not make it out again.'

'What's frightening me . . .' Neil got to his feet, '. . . is what the buggers are planning to do with all the money they're raising. How do we know if these guys are building bombs?'

56

When Lacey boarded the train at London's King's Cross the following Saturday few people, even those who knew her well, would have recognised her.

Her clothes were baggy and loose, the sort worn by teenage boys who hung around the embankment late into the evening. Her long hair, fastened back into a loose, wide plait, was invisible beneath the beanie cap. She wore no make-up but a pair of reflective sunglasses that she didn't take off the whole journey. She had a backpack and a skateboard to complete the look.

In the days that followed the dinner at Dana and Helen's house, she and Toc had come up with a plan. Toc would contact Adam Ryan, agree to meet, and send a visiting order. Lacey, incognito, would travel to Durham the same day and wait outside the prison.

Toc would meet Ryan. Once he'd left, she'd race to the phone – having bribed other inmates to keep it free – and call Lacey with a description. Lacey could then follow the man back to London, and to where he lived.

'You don't think you should do this by the book?' Toc had asked. 'From what you've told me about surveillance, it'll be bloody hard work with just you. If you get your police mates involved, they'll do a better job. We could have the bastard locked up by the end of Saturday.'

'And if he knows everything? About us, I mean? He's not going to keep quiet once he's under arrest, is he?'

Toc had fallen silent.

'I don't think we can risk it,' Lacey had said, as though trying to convince the other woman.

'What if he does know everything?' Toc had asked after breaking off to tell someone that no, she wasn't done yet, and she'd be finished when she was bloody well finished. 'What will you do? I mean, if positions were reversed, I'd soon sort it. I can't see you taking the law into your own hands, though.'

'I'll have to leave,' Lacey had said. 'Cut and run. We always knew it could come to that. If you don't hear from me again, for a long time, you'll know what's happened.'

Too much of a coincidence, the two women had agreed, and yet here she was, days later, desperately hoping it was coincidence, that Adam Ryan was nothing more than a wannabe author, that he'd simply been fishing when he'd asked about sisters, and that Lacey's life wasn't about to fall down around her ears.

He wasn't though. Toc had been right. Adam Ryan had no online presence, couldn't be found anywhere. Adam Ryan the author wasn't real.

By the time the queue began forming outside the prison, a half hour before two o'clock, Lacey was physically tired. She leaned against a railing fifty metres up the street and watched the visitors arriving: older women with grandchildren, men in their forties, fifties and sixties, several of whom she knew by sight, one or two by name. Lacey was looking for a younger, white man, because most incels fit that demographic. He'd be well dressed, maybe arty, a bit bohemian; he'd be trying to maintain the fiction that he was a writer.

A little after two o'clock the doors opened, and the slow process of admittance began. Only when the last visitor had gone inside the building could she relax. She jogged down the hill, found a pub and ordered a sandwich and a drink. With the tension and the constant walking around, she was exhausted. Keeping an eye on the time, knowing she'd have an hour, more or less, she sat back, letting her eyes close.

Her phone was ringing. It was Toc. 'Lacey, he didn't show.'

'Are you sure?'

A faint sigh, then, 'We've been doing this visitor thing for a while now. We don't lose them. He isn't here.'

She'd come all the way to Durham for nothing. 'He got cold feet?'

'Maybe. Or maybe this was the plan all along. Doesn't it strike you – in hindsight, I admit – that he was indiscreet? He gave me his name, Adam Ryan, he must have known I'd make the connection – unless they really do think women are thick as pig-shit – and making his interest in the incel movement clear. Dropping hints about sisters.'

'You think we've been played?'

'I'm bloody livid with myself but, yeah, I think we have. Where are you now?'

'In the pub.'

'Have a look around. Don't make it obvious.'

With a creeping feeling of dread, Lacey took stock of her surroundings. She'd found a corner table, so could see the whole of the room and half of the bar. A group of students sat by the window, a middle-aged couple in walking clothes were at the next table, a lone man was reading a newspaper. She couldn't see his face.

'I've got to go,' Toc went on. 'These people hurt women, Lacey. Watch your back.'

She was gone. Lacey was on her own.

And so now she was the prey. They'd lured her into the open, alone, unprotected, and hundreds of miles from her patch. Every man she went close to was a potential threat; the man she'd sit next to on the train home could be carrying a knife, or worse.

Appetite gone, Lacey made her way towards the ladies, taking in as much of the pub as she could. Two lone men were sitting at the bar.

The corridor was cold after the over-heated interior of the pub lounge. At the far end a fire escape led to the yard at the back. Knowing she was panicking and not caring, Lacey made for the open door. Reaching the street, she picked up her pace.

She barely looked back on the way across the small Cathedral city, reaching the station out of breath. She was one of the last to take her seat; on the platform the guard was slamming doors shut. Two groups of women sat nearby. One lot – across the aisle a little way up the carriage – were obviously students; the others, immediately in front of Lacey, equally obviously not. The non-students were dressed to the nines and already opening prosecco. Further down the carriage were a young family, an elderly couple, a father and son in matching football gear.

'Excuse me.' A man in the aisle was looking down at her. 'Sorry,' he went on. 'Didn't mean to make you jump.'

He was young, late twenties, clean shaven and white; about five foot nine, and of a slim build, casually dressed in clothes that were entirely unremarkable. His dark hair was a little too long, his eyes a light grey. His face was wide at the temples, narrowing towards the jaw; ordinary looking, not particularly handsome, some way from ugly.

He said, 'Is this yours?' He had her skateboard.

Still, she couldn't speak. She was watching his hands, waiting for them to dart towards the hidden knife, the gun, the axe.

He said, 'I was in the pub just now, and I thought I saw you in there. I skate myself so I noticed your board. When you didn't come back, I thought I'd bring it on the off-chance.'

She said, 'Off-chance of what?'

The hand that wasn't holding the board came up in a pacifying gesture. 'Sorry, I don't mean to be weird. I saw you on the train coming up so I thought there was a chance you'd be on your way back down. If it's not yours, I can find a home for it. I've a lot of friends who skate.'

'It's mine. Thank you.'

Smiling, he reached across. She flinched again, but he merely lifted the board up to the rack above her head, before pulling off his jacket and stowing it above his own seat.

A dark green jacket, lined in brown fabric; very similar to one she'd seen before.

'I'm Jack,' he said, smiling down at her.

'Are you sure?'

He gave her an odd look, and, OK, she was being weird, but if he wasn't AryanBoy, she had nothing to lose; and if he was, well she had nothing to lose. The two of them might as well level with each other.

He said, 'Do you want to see ID?'

'No, I'm good. Thanks for the board. I appreciate it.'

'No problem.'

The whistle blew, the train began to move. It would take three and a half hours to get back to King's Cross and for all that time she'd have no means of knowing whether the man sitting inches away meant her harm. She could move. If he followed, that would prove something. Or she could stay and play the game.

Lacey made up her mind. Pulling off her beanie cap, she shook out her plait, before unzipping her jacket and putting it on the next seat. She could sense eyes watching her from across the aisle.

Turning, she smiled at the boy. He had a paperback book on his lap but hadn't opened it. 'Visiting friends in Durham?' she said. 'Family?'

He inclined his head. 'Got a mate at uni there.'

'Must be a good mate. It's a long trip.'

'So, what's your excuse? Boyfriend?'

'Loved one.' She smiled again. 'In the prison.'

A look swept over his face – surprise, followed by unease. It looked genuine but it was hard to be sure. 'That's tough.' His eyes fell to the book and he shifted in his seat.

'Going all the way?' she said, brightly.

'Excuse me?'

'To London. Do you live in London?'

He nodded, nervously. She'd freaked him out. That probably meant he was genuine.

As the train picked up speed, a Tannoy announcement informed them that the buffet was open for tea, coffee, light refreshments and alcoholic drinks.

'I'm Laura,' she said, giving the name she'd used in the past when she'd been roped into undercover work.

The man who'd called himself Jack got to his feet. 'Can I get you a drink?' he offered. 'You ran out on your last one.'

'Thanks,' she said. 'I'll have a beer.'

While he was gone, Lacey had a chance to look at the paperback he was reading – the twentieth anniversary edition of Eve Ensler's *The Vagina Monologues*. It seemed an odd choice, on the face of it, for an incel. On the other hand, maybe a good cover prop. He'd taken his rucksack with him but his jacket was in the luggage rack. She stood and, keeping a close eye on the corridor, ran her hands over the fabric, green on the outside, lined in brown with a beige trim. Something in the right-hand pocket that felt like keys. Taking the risk, she pulled the jacket off the rack, sinking into her seat again, unzipping the pocket. Keys, a packet of chewing gum, some loose change. Nothing in the other pockets. She stood and returned the coat, sitting down as the automatic door between carriages whooshed open.

He was back, with two bottles of Cobra and a packet of cheese and onion crisps. 'You left yours in the pub,' he said, as he handed her the packet. 'I'd have got you a sandwich but I didn't see what kind it was. Also, you might be veggie, but they only had ham.'

She was hungry, but too on edge to eat. And she had no idea whether he was being kind or creepy. He'd actually noticed the flavour of crisps she'd bought?

She said, 'This is great, thanks. My round next. Unusual reading choice.'

He glanced down. 'You think so? I'd say men get more out of this than women. Have you read it?'

Lacey shook her head.

'A lot of women say its empowering.'

'And for men?'

He shrugged. 'Enlightening. So, where do you skate?'

'Stockwell, Clapham,' she said. 'Sometimes the embankment. Depends who's there, of course. It can get a bit blokesy.'

'So, what can you do?'

'I learned the ollie this year.'

He made an impressed face, although it was a fairly basic move according to the internet sites she'd looked at. Fortunately, there wasn't much chance of being asked to perform it. Then the door opened again and the guard made his way through the carriage, inspecting tickets, forcing them to break off conversation. By the time he'd gone, the man claiming to be called Jack had picked up his book again. Pretending to study her phone, Lacey discreetly took his photograph, then one of his jacket.

As she was filing the pictures away, a news flash appeared on her phone.

Major incident in London. Multiple casualties. Police say terror related.

57

Joesbury had taken to working on weekends when he didn't see Huck, and during the times, increasingly frequent these days, when Lacey either felt she had to keep an eye on Emma or had other plans. Today, those plans involved a train journey to Durham to visit that maniac Victoria Llewellyn.

She'd made it clear long ago that her relationship with Llewellyn was not up for debate and he'd gone along with it. But that was before. Now, he wondered how big a deal it would become, now that they were together, knowing that one day in every month she'd choose to spend with the woman who'd shot him.

Hell, he'd probably have come into work anyway. With no evidence other than a feeling in his gut, he could sense something coming. The incel noise had been growing, and there was a gleefulness about it. The team agreed with him, an excitement was building. Almost a whole month now, since AryanBoy had threatened the new apocalypse. Something had to happen soon.

'Mark, we're picking up chatter,' his contact at GCHQ was saying to him over the phone. 'It's been going on all week but a sizeable shift upwards today. I've let the commissioner know. She's going to talk to the home secretary about putting pressure on JTAC to get the threat level raised. We think something could be imminent.'

'Sir.' Warwick had appeared in the doorway. 'I think something's going down.'

The lad was unusually pale. He held a mobile phone in both hands, turning it about like a deck of cards he was about to shuffle.

Joesbury said. 'Now?'

'Someone's live-streaming on the Rage site. The fuckers are going mental.'

Joesbury spoke into the phone. 'Did you hear that?'

The answer came back. 'Yeah, we'll get on to it.'

The call ended and Joesbury followed Warwick through to the main office. It had been almost empty – just him and Warwick – but as they made their way towards a row of monitors on the central desks, other staff members from nearby offices slipped through the door. Word was getting around.

'I'll stick it on the big screen.' Warwick's fingers were moving faster than Joesbury could follow. A second later, the large overhead screen on the back wall sprang into life and Joesbury was watching a live stream on the Rage website. He saw a city street with slow-moving traffic. It looked like London – yep, a red, double-decker bus was edging into shot. The picture bounced around, swinging from side to side, as though whoever was carrying the camera was moving quickly, and walking rather than cycling. Pedestrians heading the other way came into view and vanished.

'Chest camera,' Warwick said. 'Like the feed we got from Jason Hancock at the massage parlour. I'm switching on audio.'

A second later, they could hear the sound of a busy London road: traffic, the base thump of music in a passing car, the high-pitched yell of a small child.

'I'm calling it.' Joesbury leaned across the desk and opened the line to Scotland Yard's central control. As he did so, in the bottom corner of the screen comments started to appear.

Fuck, I am so here for this.

Tear 'em apart, mate.

Joesbury saw a building he thought he knew and could hear heavy breathing. He glanced at Warwick, then realised it was the suspect behind the camera that he could hear. The man was almost panting.

The comments were still coming:

Foids going down.

Die bitches.

'Imminent suspected terrorist attack in Central London,' Joesbury said into the open microphone. 'Being live-streamed on the internet. Get all units on alert. Could be near the Elephant and Castle. Yes, confirm that. Suspect probably male but we have no further information at this time. He's on the A3 heading south, about to go under the underpass. Get cars down there. Proceed with caution. Expect suspect to be armed.'

He closed the line. 'Bring me up to speed,' he told Warwick as, up on the screen, the man carrying the chest camera turned down a side street. Raising his voice he called, 'Someone find out what's down that road.'

'MadHatter posted a couple of minutes ago.' Warwick's voice was unsteady. 'Said something big was about to happen and to get everyone on the site to bear witness. Over three thousand people are online right now.'

'There's an arts centre,' a voice called. 'Sports centre, too. He's not far from South Bank University.'

Three thousand was already an underestimate. The number active on the site was building faster than Joesbury could keep track of. Whatever was about to happen would be watched by a lot of people.

'Get the others in,' Joesbury told Warwick, who moved to another desk and picked up a phone.

The comments continued, increasingly excited, frequently obscene, and the man with the camera picked up his pace. Without turning round, Joesbury was conscious of people gathering behind him.

'He's going to the university,' a voice said.

Joesbury re-opened the line to control. 'Suspect making for the university. Can we alert their security? How far's the nearest response?'

'Fifteen minutes,' came the reply. 'Do you have a description?'

'Negative.'

'That's the sports centre,' someone behind Joesbury said. 'He's going into the sports centre.'

'Shush, he's talking.'

Silence fell; then a voice: male, but high-pitched, breathless and with a south London accent, seemed to fill the room.

'I'm good. I'm stoked. Let's do this.'

The entrance doors of the South Bank University sports centre filled the screen.

'We need a number for that sports centre. Has anyone got a number?'

Behind Joesbury, someone was instructing control to warn the sports centre.

Too late. The automatic doors slid open. A reception desk, large and circular, lay ahead of them. The camera turned right, making for a turnstile meant to control access to the centre's facilities.

A male voice called, 'Can I help you, sir?' and was ignored. A black leather glove came into view as the man with the camera pushed at the turnstile. It didn't move.

'Sir? Can I help you?'

The picture swung and lurched as the suspect leaped the barrier and turned down an internal corridor. A woman coming the other way with a young child pressed herself, and her daughter, against the wall.

'He's armed,' someone muttered.

'Sir, I've got the front desk of the sports centre on the line?' a voice called from the far side of the room. 'What do I tell them?'

'Where's first response?' Joesbury asked.

'Five minutes. Bad traffic. They physically can't get through.'

'Nobody approaches the suspect,' Joesbury said. 'If people can be evacuated quickly, without going anywhere near him, do it. If rooms can be locked, do that. Basically, stay clear until backup gets there.'

A black holdall swung into view and a gloved hand reached inside it. The weapon pulled out was huge and brightly coloured. A pump-action water pistol.

'You are fucking kidding me,' Joesbury muttered.

Someone said, 'What is this, a wind up?'

'Do I stand down response?'

'No!' Joesbury snapped.

The suspect stopped. They could hear him breathing. He turned so that the lettering on the door immediately facing him appeared in the centre of the screen.

Women's Changing.

'Jeez, no,' someone sighed in Joesbury's ear, as a foot, heavily booted, kicked out and the door sprang open. The suspect strode through, kicked at a second, inner door, and was in the women's changing rooms.

It was a large space, designed to take two or more sports teams. To the left, a row of shower cubicles and a matching one of lavatories. At the far side of the room, hazy in the steam from the hot showers, were the lockers. Most of the room was taken up by four rows of benches, with coat hooks at head height.

'Hockey team,' someone mumbled, as the camera caught sight of a tall cylindrical drum from which the curved ends of hockey sticks sprang.

The comments, appearing almost too fast to read, took on a lewd turn.

Oh mate, give me a minute. Let me enjoy this.

Foid city. Look at those bitches.

Even through the steam they could see the changing room was full of young women in varying states of undress. One girl, her hair in a blonde ponytail, stepped out of a shower stall, a towel barely covering her body from upper thighs to armpits. Another stood in bra and pants, reaching one arm towards the ceiling as she applied deodorant.

Joesbury saw two very distinct hockey uniforms: one blue and black, the other red with yellow insignia. Assuming up to twenty players on each team, including reserves, that could mean forty young women at imminent risk.

The intruder had been noticed. Noise levels built and towels were grasped; slender forms slipped into cubicles. So far, though, the mood was annoyed, indignant, not scared.

'Mate, I think you're in the wrong place.'

One of the teams' goalkeepers – Joesbury could see her helmet and faceguard on the bench close by – had challenged the man. She looked to be in her late teens, tall, with glossy dark hair loose around her shoulders.

The camera swung and the water pistol appeared in shot. The suspect snapped, 'Shut the fuck up, bitch!' and a jet of liquid shot towards the young woman. Matching the man's speed, she side-stepped. It missed her.

'Get out of here, you fucking perve.' She stepped closer, challenging him. 'Are you actually filming us, you creep?'

'No, get back,' Joesbury found himself whispering, as an ear-splitting scream rang out from somewhere out of sight.

The pistol swung back towards the goalkeeper, but she was too close; it hit her on the arm. Elsewhere in the room more than one woman was screaming. The shooter stepped back to give himself room to aim; the goalkeeper darted out of the way. He spun back the other way and opened fire.

Liquid shot out and hit one of the closest girls in the chest, a few inches above the towel she was clutching to her body. Her skin glowed red, seemed to give off steam. She screamed, clamped her hand to her wound and fell over backwards.

Joesbury and his colleagues watched in horror as the suspect began working the pump-action water pistol. His hand jerked back several times to fill the chamber and then he fired – twice, three times, again – aiming at those closest. The weapon might be a kids' toy, but the pump action made it powerful, especially in the confined space. The shot of liquid could leap the length of the room. Girls fled, falling over boots, clothes, each other; screams became deafening.

'It's acid,' someone muttered behind Joesbury. 'The sick fucker's firing acid at them.'

The girls had nowhere to run. Those closest to the cubicles slammed the doors shut and locked them, but the flimsy hiding places were soon full. The rest pressed against the far wall. The screams didn't let up.

'He's blocking the door,' Warwick said, when the shooter didn't pursue the girls further into the changing room. 'He's stopping them getting out.'

'We need armed response,' Joesbury said. 'Someone tell me nineteen are on their way.'

SCD19 was the Met's specialist firearms command. They couldn't possibly get there fast enough.

The shooter stopped firing. Screams became terrified whimpering, moaning, cries for someone to help them.

'Why's he stopped?' a man behind Joesbury asked.

'He's run out,' another replied. 'My son has one of those guns. It's called a super-soaker. The tank doesn't hold that much. He has to keep filling it up.'

Joesbury called, 'Do we have officers in the building?'

They heard a clattering sound as something heavy fell to the tiled floor and then the picture on screen lurched as the shooter bent down. They saw his holdall, his gloved hands pulling it open. To one side lay the discarded super-soaker. From the holdall he lifted another.

'Shit!'

A loud banging; someone hammering on the outer door. 'Can you tell us your name?' a voice called. 'We want to talk to you. Just talk.'

'OK, OK.' It was the voice of the shooter, straightening up, aiming the weapon. 'OK, let's finish this.'

He pumped the pistol again. Stepping away from the door, he jumped onto the bench and looked towards the first of the shower cubicles. The upper edge of the cubicle door ended two feet below the changing room ceiling, leaving a sizeable gap. He fired. The stream of acid flew into the air, curved and began its steady fall towards the women crammed into the cubicle.

Agonised cries.

The shooter sidestepped along the bench and fired again.

Then he fell. One second the camera was fixed on the cubicle door, the next it was flying through the air and then they could see nothing but damp floor tiles.

'He's down,' Warwick said.

'Get them in there!' Joesbury yelled.

The picture cleared. Now, through the still-functioning camera they were looking up, could see the florescent lights on the changing room ceiling. They heard a man's voice moaning in pain. Then the water pistol came into view again.

Another figure stepped into the frame. The young goalkeeper. She was standing above the shooter, a hockey stick held aloft. She swung it, connected with the water pistol and it left the shooter's grip.

The camera left her face, found her legs. The shooter was trying to sit up. They saw the stick swinging, heard a resounding crack and then the camera, once more slumped sideways.

'She's got him,' someone said.

The appearance of several pairs of dark trousers, and heavy-duty black boots, told them the police, finally, had dared to enter the changing room.

58

Three and a half hours stretched on, becoming four when the train was held up at Grantham, and information out of London was frustratingly sparse. The news channels repeated the same few details: a sizable area around the South Bank had been cordoned off by police; an attack seemed to have been centred on a sports centre; several casualties, all young women, had been taken to hospital; believed to be no fatalities as yet.

Lacey's text to Joesbury had earned a three-word reply: *Where are you?* Having learned she was on a train from Durham, he hadn't replied further. A similar text to Dana had gone unanswered; neither Emma nor Helen knew more than what they were hearing on the news.

Big leisure centre in Newington, Helen had texted. *Dana got called out an hour ago. Mark there too. Sounds nasty.*

Twitter wasn't much help either: shaky video footage of police cars hurtling along London streets, an ambulance with blue lights flashing, people running.

'Shit,' muttered the man across the aisle. 'That is seriously fucked up.'

As she looked over, he made eye contact. 'Have you heard?' he asked.

'I know there's been a suspected terror attack. What's happening?'

Jack handed over his phone. 'Press play,' he told her. 'Should warn you, though, it's not pleasant.'

Lacey took the phone and tapped a finger on the play arrow. The footage was poor quality, but clear enough to see the suspect walking into a sports centre and spraying acid. When the women started screaming, she stopped it.

'This is on YouTube?' she asked as she handed it back.

'I saw it on Facebook. Some guy I barely know shared it. Pretty messed up, hey?'

'Acid?' she said. 'Is that what they're saying?'

'Hydrochloric acid,' he replied. 'Not the most toxic but one of the easiest to get hold of.'

'Wouldn't it melt that thing he was using, that water pistol? Aren't they plastic?'

'Hydrochloric acid won't burn plastic,' Jack replied. 'He'd have to be careful not to get burned himself, but he looked to be wearing thick gloves.'

'You're well informed.'

'I studied natural sciences at uni. At Durham. We did a lot of chemistry.'

'So where would he have got the acid?'

Jack gave a slow, easy shrug. 'He'd have entered hydrochloric acid into the search engine and pressed the tab for shopping.'

'That easy?'

'Weapons are everywhere, Laura. Just about everything can be a weapon in the wrong hands.'

And was that an observation, or a threat? The countryside, meanwhile, had given way to the bland brick, plastic signage and commercial premises that signalled the outskirts of London. They weren't far from King's Cross.

Jack said, 'So, do you live in London?'

'I'm staying in Pimlico at the moment. Friend's flat.'

'Boyfriend?' He allowed a hopeful expression to creep across his face.

People around them started tidying their tables, packing stuff away in bags. Lacey relaxed her lips to form a half smile. 'That's twice you've mentioned boyfriends.'

'Can't blame a man for trying.'

'Actually, the flat does belong to my boyfriend.'

Did it, though? Was Joesbury her boyfriend?

Jack's mouth pursed into a mock pout. 'Story of my life.'

And what was that – normal disappointment or resentment?

'He's not there at the moment,' Lacey added. 'We're kind of having a break.'

Jack had been leaning forward to pull his jacket around his shoulders. He looked back at her.

She said, 'You could give me your number? You know, in case the break doesn't work out.'

He mimed thinking about it, then grinned and slipped a hand into an inside pocket. He pulled out a card and handed it over. Jack Brine, website design and management, it said, along with contact details and a web address.

'You know, you look familiar, Laura,' he said as he fastened the zip of his jacket. His demeanour had changed; he was brighter, somehow, cockier, because a good-looking woman had asked for his number. 'I was thinking that in the pub,' he went on. 'One of the reasons I noticed you. Where did you say you worked?'

She hadn't. 'I'm an office manager,' she said. 'Recruitment company in Whitechapel.'

He shook his head, 'No, can't be that. Where are you from? Originally, I mean.'

She pulled a town out of the air. 'I grew up in Milton Keynes.'

Jack's face remained clouded over. 'Never been there in my life. Ever hang out around Shepherd's Bush, White City?'

'Opposite side of town from me.'

The recorded announcement told them they were arriving at King's Cross and to be sure they had all their personal belongings before leaving the train. Lacey stood, found her jacket and skateboard. It would look strange to leave it behind again.

'Thing is,' Jack wasn't letting it go. 'I feel as though I knew you a while ago. When we were much younger, I mean.'

She pulled her jacket on. 'How could that be?'

'You didn't spend any time in Eastbourne, did you? That's where I grew up. I look at you and I think, Eastbourne.'

The train stopped, the door locks disengaged, and people began moving. Jack, already in the corridor got swept along towards the exit. He nodded at her, mimed phoning, and then turned to leave the carriage. Lacey didn't move. Through the train window she saw him disappear along the platform towards the ticket barrier. Only when the carriage was empty did she leave it.

In the main concourse she found a bench, sat, and pulled up the picture she'd taken of him. It told her nothing she didn't know already. A man of around her age, and of medium height. His thick, dark hair grew back over his forehead to curl softly around his ears. He had a pronounced nose, with a slight hook, an oval face and full lips. His eyes – rather nice eyes – were deep set and dark blue. Not especially handsome, but a long way from plain, Jack Brine wasn't someone she ever remembered meeting before. And yet he'd placed her at Eastbourne.

Only one time in her life had she been to Eastbourne.

No one knew about her drive to Beachy Head; she'd never even told Toc the full details. No one alive knew what had happened that night, except the weird kid who'd almost got in the way. Had he grown up to be AryanBoy? And had he found her again after all this time?

Twelve years ago. A needy, unhappy teenager, she'd taken so little notice of him.

She looked up then, around the station concourse, in case he was hanging around watching her. No sign of him.

It wasn't possible. At the same time, it was the only possibility. And it would explain his unnatural interest, if she meant more to him than being merely the policewoman who'd saved the baby.

There had been documents in the car, on the back seat where he'd sat, if only briefly. Shortly after she'd got back to London, she'd burned her own, the ones in the name of Victoria Llewellyn, keeping only those of her dead friend Lacey. He'd seen them, it was the only possible explanation. He'd remembered and he'd worked it out. He knew exactly who she was.

59

'No fatalities, thank God,' Joesbury told the commissioner an hour later, when they met at Marsham Street. 'Two of the women have some bad burns. They're in surgery as we speak. Seven more have minor burns.'

The commissioner, who hadn't been on duty, swore under her breath, something Joesbury had never known her do in uniform. 'He's in custody?'

'Yep. Thank God for that goalkeeper.'

The goalkeeper, an eighteen-year-old student from Leeds University called Kate, had knocked the attacker off the bench. He'd broken a wrist in the fall and let go of the acid gun; she'd sent it spinning across the tiled floor out of reach. Seeing the attacker down, momentarily helpless, girls had fled the changing rooms and armed officers had gone in.

'Amen to that,' the commissioner said, as they were shown into the home secretary's office. 'Is she OK, the goalkeeper, I mean?'

'She's unhurt.' Joesbury spotted the home secretary in the corridor outside. 'Let's hope that's enough. Georgie's with her as we speak, talking to her about the importance of keeping a very low social media profile in the coming weeks. The last thing we need is her becoming an incel target the way Emma and Lacey have.'

'I went out on a limb for you, Mark,' Alison Brabin said, as she strode through the door. 'You've brought me nothing. Now I've

60

'Gayle, what are you doing here?'

Startled, Gayle Mizon spun round on her seat. She looked tired, but then they all did. They'd all been putting the hours in.

Strictly, Dana hadn't needed to leave home – and Helen and Inigo alone – for the attack at the sports centre. No one had been critically injured, the offender was in custody and Neil, who was on duty, was more than capable of handling everything.

But this could be the start; the acid attack could be the opening strike. Thirty days after AryanBoy's video release and the Day of Retribution had to be coming soon.

'I needed some quiet time, boss,' Gayle said as Dana approached. 'I wanted to have another look at the Tower Bridge footage.'

A couple of weeks after the baby's abduction, a late witness had given the police a description of a man seen filming the incident. Gayle had subsequently found CCTV pictures of a lone white male leaving Tower Bridge shortly after the attack.

Dana pulled a chair across. 'Find anything?'

Gayle said, 'Look at this clip, south bank, about a hundred metres upstream from the bridge. See that bloke with the camera over his shoulder?'

This wasn't a new find.

'The one you've been hunting for a while? I thought you lost him in Potters Field Park.'

On a laptop, Gayle brought up the Google map of the area around Tower Bridge. Switching to satellite view, she indicated an L-shape of green space between the bridge and City Hall. 'We did,' she agreed. 'No sign of a bloke in a grey baseball cap and green jacket, with a professional-looking camera, coming out of the park. We figured he'd done a reccy previously and found a route where he wouldn't be picked up. But what if he had a change of clothes?'

'No backpack,' Dana argued. 'He wasn't carrying anything but the camera. Where would he get his costume change from?'

'Say he had a bobble hat in his pocket, it wouldn't be too big a deal to swap it with his cap, would it? And suppose the jacket was reversible, suppose it was, say, brown on the other side.'

Opening up another screenshot Gayle said, 'Lacey found this piece yesterday. This guy was picked up on one of the cameras outside City Hall. Does he look a similar build to you?'

Dana focused on the male figure, some fifty feet from the camera, wearing a brown jacket and matching bobble hat. 'He does, but isn't he heading back towards the Tower?'

'Looks that way, which is why we didn't spot him before. And look, we've got him again here, heading towards Borough High Street and from the front he's got one hell of a beer belly.'

Dana looked closer. The man, possibly conscious of cameras and their surveillance capability kept his head down, his face invisible, but he did seem to be strangely misshapen around the chest.

'He'd put the camera down the front of his jacket,' she said.

'That's what we figured. So Lacey has been searching for green and brown reversible jackets and she found this, look.'

Another screen shot, this time a shopping website. A reversible jacket, retailing at £59.99, green on one side, brown with a beige trim on the other.

'She couldn't come in today, so I said I'd follow it up,' Gayle explained.

Dana said, 'OK, that helps. But do we know where he went from Borough High Street?'

'Not until this afternoon.'

Gayle brought up one final screenshot. 'Does that look like him, going into that building?'

Dana took her time. The figure was a long way from the camera, but the jacket he was wearing looked brown, as did the bobble cap. 'That's a public library,' she said.

'Yes. The John Harvard Library on Borough High Street, open until seven this evening. What do you say we pop down?'

'You're fishing, aren't you, officers?'

The elderly librarian was a short, solid woman. Her ice-grey hair was cut into a smooth bob and her eyes were a cold blue. 'You'd be here with a forensic team and a warrant if you had the power to search our hard-drives, wouldn't you?'

The room that Dana and Gayle had been shown into was more storeroom than office. Crates of books scattered the floor, and cheap shelving units buckled beneath the weight of box files, paper reams and random pieces of library equipment.

'Will you get a warrant?' the librarian went on. 'If you apply for one?'

'Probably,' Dana replied, although she was far from certain. 'We can demonstrate a trail from Tower Bridge to this building on the morning of 11 September, following a serious attack at St Katharine Docks. A man we very much want to speak to came into the library that morning.'

The woman raised two perfect silver eyebrows. 'But that will take time?'

'Warrants can take a few days,' Dana admitted.

'And in the meantime, dreadful attacks like the one ongoing at the South Bank University will be taking place. What time window are we talking about?'

'Between nine and eleven,' Gayle jumped in. 'That's when the images were first posted online.'

Cold blue eyes blinked at them. 'You mean the pictures of the baby being washed downriver? They were posted here?'

'Possibly,' Dana replied.

Taking a seat, the woman clicked on an icon from the sidebar. 'This is the back door into our operating system,' she said. 'We can see all internet activity on any particular day. Mind you, I'm not an expert on how it works. You might have to come back on Monday when Sally's at work. She designed most of the system.'

'I'm not bad,' Dana replied, telling herself not to get her hopes up. 'Do you mind if I have a look?'

The librarian got to her feet. Taking her place, Dana began combing through the record of internet activity on the morning in question: websites accessed by library visitors, emails sent and received, bills paid. Fortunately, at that hour of the morning, the library had been quiet.

'Here,' she said, after a couple of minutes. 'MadMax101 sent an email at zero nine twenty hours.'

She was conscious of Gayle leaning over her shoulder, screen-shotting the recipient's email address. MadMax101 meant nothing, but these people had all sorts of online identities.

'With images,' Dana went on, clicking on the attachment.

A shot of the river appeared, the same that men all over the world had cheered, the record of the first blow being struck.

'Is that it?' the librarian said. 'Have you got the bastard?'

61

'Bloody good work, Dana,' Joesbury said. 'And Gayle too of course.'

He heard a car horn, the revving of an engine; Dana was driving.

'Did it help?' she asked.

'Definitely. I've just heard back from the tech team. The footage was sent to a dead drop account, as we expected, but they'd slipped up. They hadn't deleted it.'

The line cut out and he had to ask Dana to repeat herself.

She said, 'Can you see who accessed it?'

'An IP address we're tracking right now. It could be the slip-up that lets us through. Fingers crossed. Where are you heading?'

'Back to the leisure centre. I need to check on my lot. Catch up soon.'

Dana was gone and, as though she'd taken his energy with her, Joesbury was suddenly shattered, with no real idea why. It wasn't as though he did much these days except wait around while others did their jobs.

Joesbury was used to being in the thick of things, not hanging around on the side-lines. Increasingly, his nights were plagued with dreams when he saw Lacey, his son, even Dana get washed away on a swollen, angry tide while he stood by, watching. Most of his days were spent feeling helpless in the face of the growing threat to everyone he cared about.

And since when did standing around doing nothing become so bloody exhausting?

He sighed, knowing he probably wouldn't get away from work until the small hours.

'Sir, we think we might have something.'

Joesbury looked up to see Georgie and Archie in his office doorway. He gestured them towards the round table and got up to join them. They sat. He waited. Georgie glanced at Archie, who nodded back at her. She took a breath, held it for a second.

'I think,' she began. 'It's possible – I'm not really sure.'

'Georgie may have found BlackPill,' Archie said.

Joesbury told himself he could not get excited, then doubted he had the energy anyway.

'You remember we did that analysis on how the four main players post,' she began.

Joesbury nodded. Georgie had used the word 'we', but the work had been her own; with a degree in psychology, she was the one best qualified for the task. Studying the activities of the four men, she'd created profiles based entirely on their internet behaviour. AryanBoy was the leader, the dominant member, educated, a bit of a show-off, frequently throwing classical references into his posts. Georgie had concluded he was self-employed, possibly unemployed, as his posts appeared at all hours of the day and night. Joker, like AryanBoy not in a regular-hours job, was angry, his posts belligerent, with frequent references to violence and rage. MadHatter was the fool of the group, taking little seriously, constantly cracking jokes. In fairness, MadHatter was genuinely witty, albeit invariably mean. Unlike the other two, his posts were restricted to after seven in the evening and weekends. BlackPill88 was the odd one out, poorly educated, making frequent spelling mistakes.

'I've suspected for a while that BlackPill might be dyslexic,' Georgie went on. 'There are certain spelling mistakes that are very typical of that condition. He'll be aware of it and will be taking steps to hide it, but every now and then, signs slip through. He also mixes up upper- and lower-case letters, another common dyslexia trait. So, I've been looking on the surface web for dyslexics with an interest in incel issues. The program threw up a couple of dozen possibilities, and I've been keeping track of those.'

'She spotted something a few hours ago.' Archie said. 'We've given it a serious looking at.'

'We didn't want to jump the gun,' Georgie said.

'Understood,' Joesbury replied, wishing they'd get a frigging move on.

Still nothing.

'Go on,' Joesbury encouraged Georgie.

'It's something really small,' she said. 'Which is why I didn't say anything before, but given who it involves.' She gave a nervous glance at Archie.

Joesbury had had enough. 'George, I love you, you're brilliant, but I can't take any more of this. Arch, tell me, and do it fast.'

Archie took him at his word. 'A chap called Jack Brine shared the YouTube footage of the acid attack about half an hour after it was posted,' he said. 'He seemed to be condemning it, but he used three words that Georgie's been searching for.'

'Two words and a mixture of upper- and lower-case letters,' Georgie said. 'Sorry Arch, go on.'

'So we dug a bit deeper,' Archie said. 'And there's no doubt about his interest in the incel movement. He plays it down, hardly commenting at all, but liking a lot of posts and sharing quite often. Some of the things he shares are a bit dodgy.'

'His writing patterns are very similar to BlackPill's,' Georgie said. 'Not identical, I found a few anomalies, but similar enough to take him seriously. Even before—'

'He posted earlier today using his phone,' Archie said. 'He used a public Wi-Fi on North Eastern Railway, from somewhere near Peterborough.'

'He was on a train?' Joesbury said.

'Not just any train,' Archie told him. 'The two fifteen from Edinburgh to London King's Cross. Calling at Durham.'

Georgie said, 'Didn't Lacey go—'

Joesbury was on his feet.

'Sir, she's fine.' Archie stopped him as he was halfway to his desk. 'We checked before we came in. She's at your place now with Emma.'

Joesbury stopped moving and let out a long breath.

'It's good news, sir,' Archie said. 'There'll be CCTV footage and Lacey herself might have spotted him.'

It was good news. Possibly their first real break. It also meant that Lacey had been followed all the way to Durham and back.

And that was helplessness flooding through him again, in a crippling series of flashbacks: Emma, waxen-faced and shaking in a hospital bed; Helen and Dana fighting back tears on the Thames foreshore; the blood-stained walls of the massage parlour; and today, the brave young goalkeeper brandishing her hockey stick in the face of an armed attacker. Lacey would show exactly the same courage faced with danger. And it would get her killed.

62

'I'd no idea,' Toc said, after a silence so long Lacey thought the two of them had been disconnected. 'I'd no idea you'd done that. I thought Lacey – the real Lacey, I mean – I thought she died in London.'

'She did.' Lacey closed her eyes, reliving again one of the worst nights of her life. 'It happened during that time I was looking for you. One night – I was on the point of giving up, it was obvious you didn't want to be found – I got back to the squat to find her in a bad way. I don't know whether she'd deliberately overdosed or just taken some bad shit by mistake. She looked dead, her eyes wide open, no obvious signs of breathing. I managed to get her to the street but there was no one around. No phone boxes either. So, I nicked a car. But by the time I got back to her, she was dead.'

'So you drove to Beachy Head?

'I'd lost everything,' she said to Toc. 'Lacey dying was the last straw. I didn't want to live any more. Beachy Head was the only place I could think of.'

'You were going to drive over the cliff?'

Knowing Emma was somewhere in the flat, Lacey kept her voice low. 'I thought I was, but maybe I'd never have done it. Maybe I'd have found some other reason not to, if he hadn't been there. We'll never know, and I don't think that's what's important right now.'

'I suppose not. I just can't bear to think of it. And that was him on the train?'

Movement in the corridor; Lacey got up and opened the door a fraction. Emma, her back turned, was engrossed in her mobile phone. Once a day, for up to an hour at a time, she 'sanitised' her Twitter account, working her way through endless replies and direct messages, deleting the abuse, liking the supportive stuff, blocking the serial abusers. She'd shown Lacey once. It had been sickening. After a post suggesting Emma be put out of her misery and her internal organs offered up for donations, Lacey had stopped reading.

'Who else could it be?' she said to Toc, after easing the door shut again. 'The way he said Eastbourne, it was so pointed.'

'So Adam Ryan, AryanBoy, the UK's most wanted, is really a website designer called Jack Brine who followed you to Durham and bought you a beer this afternoon?'

'Looks like it.'

A long, slow whistle came down the telephone line. Then Toc said, 'It would explain why he's fixated on you, especially after you foiled his first big stunt on the river that day. Are you going to tell Lover Boy?'

'If I tell him any of it, I'll have to tell him all of it.'

And with every minute that passed, not telling him was leaving a dangerous terrorist on the loose. How many more lives would be lost while she guarded her sordid little secret? What she was doing was unforgivable.

Somewhere in the background a female guard was encouraging the women to *hurry it along now, ladies.*

Toc said, 'But you didn't recognise him? You'd have known him, surely? It wasn't that long ago.'

It had been the one ray of hope Lacey had been clinging to. 'People change a lot in twelve years. And I didn't get a good look at him back then. It was dark, and I had other stuff on my mind.'

'And there were definitely documents in the car?'

She'd already explained all this; Toc wasn't usually slow. 'I think we have to accept he knows who I am, and he knows who you are.'

'You need to talk to him,' Toc said. 'I have to go. He gave you his number, right? You need to meet him and ask him what he wants.'

'That simple?'

'Sometimes it really is that simple.'

'And then what?'

'Yeah, well – that bit won't be simple.' Toc gave a soft laugh. 'Maybe you'll have to be Victoria again.'

63

'Lacey!' An urgent whisper. 'Lacey, are you awake?'

She was now. Away from the boat she rarely slept well, and the odd, random noises of Pimlico woke her frequently. This was new though. Tap, tap, tap: someone rapping on her bedroom door.

'Emma? What's going on?' Lacey could make out her flatmate's silhouette in the open doorway.

'Don't put the light on.' Lacey's outstretched arm froze in place. 'I think there's someone outside.'

Joesbury's bedside clock – in the shape of Buzz Lightyear – told her it was three fifteen in the morning; a time when, usually, even busy Pimlico streets could be relied upon to have fallen quiet, if not silent.

'I heard the side gate opening,' Emma's outline said. 'It's right below my window. I went into the bathroom and I could see someone in the yard.'

There were eight flats in the Georgian house and each stored their rubbish in the same back yard, accessed via a narrow foot-path to the side of the house.

'He was looking up at our windows. I think he could see me.'

Unsurprisingly, Emma had been exhibiting high levels of anxiety in the weeks following her kidnap. She jumped when the doorbell sounded, striding to the big bay window to see who might be at the door; she was fastidious about locking up at night and even started when her phone rang. Having spent the last several years at risk of physical danger, Lacey had forgotten that, for most people, it was an unusual state of being. Emma was probably unnecessarily alarmed. Even so, there was no good reason she could think of for someone to be in the back yard at this hour.

She found a sweater and trainers.

'What are you doing?' Emma sounded horrified. 'You're not going out there?'

'Probably not.' Lacey left her bedroom – Joesbury's bedroom – and turned left into the bathroom, the only room in the flat that directly overlooked the yard. She climbed onto the lavatory seat and pressed her face towards the top window that was always kept open. From down in the yard came the sound of something metal banging against stone.

Foxes, she told herself, they were a bloody menace, then a muttered curse; she'd never heard a fox swear before.

'Can you see anything?' Emma was in the doorway.

Lacey held up one hand for quiet and saw the flickering light below. It was gone in an instant. Two tiny a light to be a torch, maybe the flash of a mobile phone screen.

'Shall I call Scotland Yard?' Emma hissed.

Lacey squeezed past Emma and stepped into Huck's room, temporarily Emma's. In a basket in one corner the young boy kept his sport's equipment, including, she was pretty sure – yes, there it was – a full-sized cricket bat. Back into her own room to collect her phone and she was ready.

'What are you doing? You're not going out there?'

One advantage of moving the two young women into Joesbury's flat, the one that had convinced Lacey, was that it was easier to secure than just about any other property in London. The locks and alarms were state-of-the-art; there was even a panic button by Joesbury's bed. It had meant the twenty-four-hour protection that Emma had needed since she'd first been contacted by AryanBoy was no longer necessary. During non-working hours, Lacey had become Emma's close protection officer. She'd even been given a pay rise and the extra money was useful. So, now she had to do something to earn it.

'I need you to watch from the bathroom window,' she instructed. 'If you see or hear anything that alarms you, or if I yell at you, hit the panic button – you know where that is, right?'

Wide-eyed, Emma nodded.

'Then you call the Scotland Yard number on your phone. You don't answer the door to anyone but me, or one of Mark's team. Basically, someone you know, right? And make sure this time.'

'I don't think this is a good idea.'

'Emma, I'm a police officer. This is what we do. I won't be long.'

Unlocking the flat door, Lacey stepped out into the darkened hallway. 'Make sure this closes properly behind me.'

As she stepped towards the front door, feeling the draft from outside on her bare legs – Lacey always slept in sports shorts – she realised her mistake: she had no pockets. Her phone was necessary, and she wasn't going out without the cricket bat. That meant her keys would have to be left behind. Tucking them beneath a pile of uncollected mail on the hall table, she found the door-stop, used to keep the heavy front door open during big deliveries and wedged it in place. Then she slipped out into the night.

The fierce winds of the past few days had died down, leaving the night unusually and unnervingly still. There was even a hint of frost in the air that tingled as it slipped into her nose and throat. The moon, high above the long line of rooftops was about a week off full, its cold glow echoed in a receding line of streetlamps. Somewhere close by a dog barked.

Both sides of the street were lined with cars. She looked for interior lights, for shadows that could indicate occupants, for movement. Nothing that she could see. A few windows in the houses opposite showed light behind blinds or curtains but there was no sign anywhere on the street of a living person.

She tapped out a quick text to Emma. *You OK?*

A response came back immediately. *Yeah, you?*

Sending Emma the thumbs-up emoji, Lacey stepped down the half-dozen steps that led to street level and turned left towards the side passage.

It was very dark. With little more than two feet between the side of the four-storey house and the twelve-foot wall that divided this property from the next, the streetlights hadn't a hope of getting anywhere close to the ground. The gate, painted a deep blue, was barely visible, although Lacey knew from several weeks of rubbish duty that it was little more than twelve feet away. She used the torch on her phone to light the way. The gate was open, and that was unusual, but not alarmingly so.

Fully aware that she was walking into a dead end, also known as a trap, Lacey went through. High above her left shoulder, something hissed; she looked up to see the emerald eyes of a dark-furred cat. Conscious of the animal watching, she reached the back corner of the house.

The yard, about ten metres square, stretched across half the rear of the house; on the other half was a private courtyard garden owned by one of the basement flats. By pressing her face to the window of Joesbury's bedroom, Lacey could just about catch a glimpse of the corner of it. What she hadn't noticed before was that a gate led from the bin yard into the garden. A way out, possibly, for the intruder?

Glancing up, she thought she could see Emma's outline in the bathroom. Lacey raised one hand in a gesture intended to reassure and then got to work. She had sixteen bins to check, eight of them overly large for recycled rubbish and she'd have to look inside them all. By the time she was done and had shone her torch into all the corners and shadows, she was shivering. She tapped out another message.

Still OK?

Fine. Anything?

Getting colder by the minute, with neither the time nor the inclination for a text chat, Lacey tried the garden door. To her surprise, it opened.

The garden beyond, at first sight, had been left to run wild; gradually, after several seconds, an order of sorts appeared. A path, overgrown with creeping plants and moss wound its way from a tiny, flagged patio towards a miniature gazebo, almost invisible beneath ivy and honeysuckle in the opposite bottom corner. Bushes and shrubs fought for space, pushing back against the boundary walls and forwards towards the path. Late-blooming dahlias and roses gleamed from among the leaves in pale metallic shades and somewhere, out of sight, water was trickling over stones. Solar lights shone from their hiding places among the huge and exotic leaves, creating pools of cold green light.

Lacey stood and listened. The wild garden was in constant movement; leaves scratched and unseen creatures scurried along pathways too dark and low for her to see. She glanced back at the basement flat – no one relished the thought of waking up to find a stranger in their garden – but it remained in darkness.

Only the gazebo to check.

Her footsteps crunched along the gravel path, warning anyone hiding out in the summer house that she was coming. The small narrow door had a Perspex window. Stepping to one side, in case anyone burst out, Lacey shone her phone light in, and then looked. A wicker armchair and matching coffee table. Nothing else.

On my way back, she texted Emma. *All good. Get the kettle on.*

Tea would be good, she thought, as she made her way back along the path, a hot water bottle even better. Did Joesbury even have one? It didn't seem his thing, somehow. A warm body would be very nice right now. Creeping back into bed, snuggling up beside Joesbury felt like the best thing in the world.

She pulled open the gate, checked the bin yard one last time, and stepped into it. Joesbury, though, would never have let her investigate a night-time intruder. She would have been the warm body, waiting to welcome him back into bed. Allowing a smile to slip across her face, she closed the adjoining gate. She was directly beneath the bathroom window when she heard Emma screaming.

64

Lacey ran. She'd fallen for a classic distraction. Emma had been the target all along, the man in the yard the lure. They'd known she'd investigate, leaving Emma alone.

And she'd left the front door wedged open, her keys on the hall table. How could she have been so stupid? She reached the steps and raced up. The front door was as she'd left it.

Inside the house, Emma's screams sounded louder. Lacey found the keys where she'd left them, which didn't make sense, but there was no time to think about it. The flat door was still locked, and that made no sense either.

Emma's screams were gaining in volume and inside there was banging, glass shattering, all hell breaking loose. People were awake in the other flats too.

'Emma, I'm coming! Police, stay where you are!'

She was shouting into the void, nothing but screams came back. One lock turned; she dropped the keys. The screaming went on, and screaming meant alive, didn't it? Lacey turned the second lock and thank God Emma hadn't fastened the chain because then she'd never have got inside. She threw open the flat door.

The smell hit her first. Organic, disgusting. Fighting back the urge to retch, she found the light switch.

The screaming was coming from the front room. Lacey ran towards it, cricket bat aloft, as tiny missiles hurtled towards her.

Things – living things – struck her face, too small to hurt, but nightmarishly freaky. She fought the urge to turn and flee.

Emma, close to hysterical, was in the middle of the living room, slapping hands against her body, waving them in the air, trying to drive away the creatures that seemed to be attacking. They whirled around her, like bees or wasps, but worse somehow. Emma was in the midst of a swarm of large and exotic insects.

One of them, inches long, the colour of sand with a black muzzle and huge black legs, landed on Lacey's shoulder. She batted it away. It came back, hovering above her head.

Flying insects, dozens of them, maybe more, were spinning around the room, hurling themselves against the wall lights, the windows and mostly, against Emma.

Someone was banging on the flat door. 'You OK in there? Mark?'

'Don't come in,' Lacey yelled back. 'Call the police. Quick as you can.' Something else – small, black, disgusting, – was crawling up the bare skin of her thigh.

Forcing herself to move, because while she'd seen some things in her time, this took some beating, Lacey grabbed her friend's arm, dragging her down the corridor and into the bathroom. Slamming the door shut on the insects that weren't yet attached to the two of them, Lacey turned on the shower and pushed Emma beneath it.

The stream of water stopped the other woman screaming. She clamped both hands to her face and began sobbing instead, but at least it was quieter. Knowing that she too had small creatures all over her body, Lacey joined Emma in the shower stall, unhooking the shower head and directing the full force of water onto Emma's body.

'Turn round.'

Emma did what she was told, allowing Lacey to wash the insects from her hair, her shoulders, the length of her body. The creatures, too large to disappear down the drain, gathered in a crumbly insect soup in the shower tray. Stepping on them, feeling them crunch underfoot, was unavoidable.

'You're clear.' She turned Emma, who still hadn't shown her face, and pushed her out of the shower.

Focusing on herself, avoiding the drowning insects around her feet, Lacey rinsed off and stepped out of the cubicle, closing the door tight.

Joesbury's robe hung on the back of the door. Lacey pulled Emma's pyjamas off, towelled her dry, and then pulled the robe around her. She found a small towel and wrapped it around her friend's head.

'Now they can't get in your hair,' she told her. 'There's no bugs on you now. I know it was horrible, but I don't think they can hurt us. Try and hold it together, OK?'

Emma nodded. Sitting on the lavatory seat, she curled her feet beneath her, making herself as small as possible.

More banging on the flat's front door. Lacey, dripping wet, opened the bathroom door a fraction.

'What's going on in there? What's happening?'

'We're OK,' Lacey called back. 'Don't come in. Are the police coming?'

'I called them. I don't know when they'll get here.'

A 999 call to Joesbury's flat would take priority; they would be here in minutes.

From the lavatory seat Emma sobbed something that sounded like, 'They were in the tea bags', but it didn't make much sense and Lacey had more urgent things to focus on. She found a towel from the airing cupboard and tried to rub herself down.

The smaller, black insects had fled; she could see a couple in the corner between the shower tray and the wall, but the others had vanished. The bigger insects, though, they were seriously creepy, and unnaturally focused on her. One on the edge of the sink seemed to be watching her. Another was fluttering around her head, its wings making an eery, jittering sound.

Peeping out again, she saw that the door to Joesbury's room was closed. Also, her phone was in the corridor by the front door where she'd dropped it, and someone was calling her.

'We have to move,' she told Emma. 'My room. Head down, keep your eyes shut if you want, we go fast.'

Without giving Emma time to object, she dragged her to her feet and out into the corridor. Stooping on the way to pick up her phone, she made it to the bedroom, pulled Emma in and closed the door.

The caller was Joesbury on his work number; he was still at Scotland Yard.

'What the hell's going on?' he demanded when she answered. 'Are you OK?'

Glancing round to see if any of the insects had followed them in, Lacey spotted one squatting by the wardrobe. She pulled off her sweater, soaking wet now, and dropped it on the creature. Emma dropped onto the bed, sobbing again.

'Lacey, talk to me.'

Exhausted, Lacey sank down behind the door. 'You are not going to believe this,' she said.

65

'They were in the tea bags.'

Emma had climbed quickly into one of the twin beds in the room that Joesbury had found in Barons Court. The hotel was a depressing place: the soft furnishings frayed at the edges, the hard surfaces scuffed, and the room was tiny, especially for the five people crammed into it; but the night manager hadn't objected to a uniformed officer being stationed in the foyer for the rest of the night, nor a patrol car at the rear. The two women would be safe enough.

That said, they should have been safe in his flat, the ruddy place was like Fort Knox. He glanced over at Lacey; she'd barely been able to meet his eyes since he'd pitched up to find the two of them huddled on the outside steps.

'Tea bags?' he said. 'I'm going to need a bit more than that.'

'Lacey texted from the yard to say I should put the kettle on.' Emma supressed a shudder. 'We keep the tea bags in a PG tips tin on the top shelf of the cupboard above – well, you know, it's your kitchen. And your tin.'

'Not your tea bags, though,' Lacey added, with an attempt at a smile. 'I bought my own.'

Joesbury said, 'Glad to hear it. And the insects were in the tin?'

'Locusts and crickets.' Warwick had been engrossed in his laptop since they'd entered the room. 'Readily available by mail order at a number of outlets that supply food for exotic pets.'

Emma sniffed. 'I reached up, opened the tin without thinking and put my hand in.' She broke off, shuddering again.

'They seemed to be attacking,' Lacey said. 'Are they aggressive?'

'Not to people.' Warwick was reading from the screen. 'They're well known for devastating crops, but for the most part they're solitary animals. Under certain conditions they'll eat more, get bigger, reproduce faster and start to act in a herd-like way. A typical swarm. What you probably saw was collective panic, triggered by finding themselves in a new environment, and faced with a lot of threatening sound and movement.'

He looked up. His back was to the room, so he made eye contact in the mirror. 'Perfectly harmless, if it helps.'

'It doesn't,' Emma grumbled.

'When did you last open that tin?' Joesbury asked.

Emma looked across at Lacey. 'I drink green tea, chamomile sometimes. Only Lacey drinks builders' tea, and she's been out all day.' She looked at the clock on the table between the two beds. The digital face showed 04.16. 'All yesterday,' she corrected herself.

Lacey said, 'Maybe on Friday. I don't think so, though, because I've been going in early all week and getting breakfast on the way. I don't usually drink tea in the evening.'

'I'm not sure it's relevant,' the uniformed sergeant in charge of the incident said. 'The insects were obviously placed in the flat when constable Flint was out checking the back yard.'

Lacey shook her head.

'Probably a simple tin switch,' the sergeant added. 'The perpetrator hanging around outside waiting for Miss Flint to leave. CCTV will pick it up.'

'Not so far it doesn't.' Warwick's eyes were still on his laptop. 'I've got Lacey leaving the house and vanishing around the back. I pick her up again in the back yard, lose her when she goes next door, then track her again running round the front. No one else.'

'They didn't swap the tins while I was out,' Lacey said. 'Emma locked the door. It was still locked when I got back.'

'You left your keys by the front door,' the sergeant pointed out. 'And the front door wedged open. Easiest thing in the world to get in.'

'I shouldn't have done that,' Lacey agreed. 'But no one touched the keys, they were exactly how I left them. And Emma would have heard someone entering the flat.'

'Why insects?' Joesbury said. 'Seems an odd thing to do.'

'Women hate insects,' Emma replied. 'It wasn't about hurting us, it was about freaking us out.'

'It worked,' Lacey admitted.

Joesbury got to his feet. 'Can I have a word?' he said to Lacey, indicating that they should go out into the corridor.

He led her a few paces from the door and then turned to face her. She dropped her head and stepped towards him in that way she had when she was coming in for a hug and he was happy to oblige. She was cold beneath the sweatshirt, her hair damp.

'I'll have people go in tomorrow and get some stuff for you both,' he said. 'If you're not working you could come and spend the day on the boat with me.'

'Sounds good,' she mumbled into his chest. 'Not sure I can leave Emma, though.'

An excuse he was hearing all too often these days.

'We'll find somewhere a bit more cheerful than this place,' he said, glancing round at the scuffed walls, flickering lights and threadbare carpet.

'I know I messed up,' she said. 'But I don't think someone came in the flat this morning. Emma would have heard, Warwick would have found them on camera.'

'You shouldn't have gone out,' he said. 'That's not what you're there for.'

She raised her head to argue. 'There's something else,' he said, before she could speak. 'Did you spot anything on the train back to London yesterday?'

Her eyes fell. 'What do you mean?'

'Lacey, look at me.'

When she did, something in her eyes had changed. And then she stepped back, away from him.

'A bloke called Jack Brine was on the train with you,' he said. 'We think he might be one of the incel leaders. Georgie did something brilliant with patterns and searches, don't ask me to explain it.'

'It was a busy train,' she said after a pause that went on far too long. 'There was one chap I spoke to briefly. He gave me his business card. He seemed, I don't know, a bit creepy. You think he could be AryanBoy?'

'Georgie thinks BlackPill, one of the others. Can you describe him?'

'I got his picture.' Pulling her phone from her pocket she scrolled through the photo library. When she held it up Joesbury saw a man in his late twenties, with dark hair and a thin face, looking down at a book. 'It was his jacket that made me suspicious. It looked reversible green and brown, like the one worn by the man on Tower Bridge we've been trying to trace.'

As Lacey AirDropped the picture to his phone, Joesbury said, 'And you were going to tell me about this, when, exactly?'

Her face took on a closed look, one that could almost be described as sullen. 'I was going to think about it and tell Dana on Monday,' she said. 'She's my line of command now. Look, I was a bit uncomfortable about it, but to be honest, it seemed too much of a coincidence. I mean, how could AryanBoy, BlackPill, who-ever, know I'd be on a train to Durham?'

He couldn't. Even so, there was something she wasn't telling him.

'Did he say what part of London he's from?'

'Shepherd's Bush, according to his card, why?'

That was a pity. 'The team found an IP address of interest a few hours ago,' he said. 'An internet café in Fulham. It was used to put footage of the baby abduction on the internet. If we can tie this Brine chap to it we've got a solid piece of evidence against him.'

She nodded, but absentmindedly, and he felt her distance again. It felt, sometimes, as though the more intimate they became physically, the more she was pulling away from him.

'You need to get some sleep,' he said. 'We all do. I'll clear that lot out.' He reached for the hotel room door.

'Mark.' She stopped him, catching hold of his wrist. 'I do love you. You know that, don't you?'

It was the first time she'd ever said as much, in so many words. Christ, now he really was worried.

66

The flat was in darkness when AryanBoy got back. He left it that way. He needed to shower, because he was filthy and dripping with sweat; he needed to eat, because his blood sugar had dived, to drink, because his hands were still shaking, and to sleep, because he had one hell of a day to get through in a few hours' time. He did none of those things. Instead, he crouched, for long minutes, in his living room, head resting against his sofa. He could never tell anyone, especially his nearest associates, how close he'd come to ruining everything.

She'd almost caught him.

The overgrown garden had saved him. She hadn't seen that the gazebo didn't sit flush against the back wall of the property. There was a gap, some ten inches wide, hidden by the shrubbery and he'd squeezed into it. She'd come close enough for him to hear her breathing.

Stupidly reckless, to go himself, to search her waste bin for something, anything, additional he could use against her. He should have sent someone; he had dozens of cannon fodder only too desperate to help the cause. But Lacey Flint was a secret he wasn't prepared to share and besides, if he were really honest with himself, he got a buzz from being close to her.

He'd got too close. If she'd seen him it would have been the end of everything.

Slowly, gradually, his breathing was calming. The entirely un-expected bonus, of course, had been the screams he'd heard as he'd scrambled over the back wall. He'd been starting to think the insects would die before the two women found them. Unleashing them in the middle of the night, with both women already on edge, was better than anything he could have planned.

Maybe it hadn't been too bad after all. Maybe fortune really did favour the brave.

He was feeling better, as though he might sleep after all. First though, a check online, find out where the two women were being taken.

And maybe, if he felt up to it, a little more poking of the wasps' nest.

67

Joesbury and the others had gone, and Lacey had turned out the lights and told Emma to try to sleep. The constant movement and irregular breathing coming from the other bed told her that her new roommate was having as little success as she was.

Run or stay? Which? Two years ago, when 'Victoria Llewellyn' had conducted her murderous rage around London, Lacey had run, only to be stopped, inadvertently, by Joesbury. Ironic, then, that it was simply the thought of him that was stopping her this time. If she ran now, she'd never see him again. Worse, he'd despise her; in his eyes she'd be a liar and a coward.

The phone rang.

'It'll be Mark.' Lacey pushed back the covers, trying to remember the route to the desk where she'd left her phone on charge.

Emma's voice corrected her. 'Lacey, it's mine.'

The glow from her phone created a small pool of light around Emma's hand. The ringing continued. For some reason, she wasn't answering.

Lacey reached for the bedside light. 'What's up?'

'This number. I think it's him.'

The phone rang twice more, and the look on Emma's face – alarm, revulsion – told Lacey that the 'him' in question wasn't a welcome caller. Not Mark then.

'My phone has a new number,' Emma reminded Lacey. 'He can't have this number.'

The answer message kicked in, giving them a few seconds of breathing space.

'How sure are you?' Lacey asked, above the recorded voice instructing the caller to leave a message.

'I'm good with numbers. This is the one he used before.'

The recorded message ended. The two women waited. Nothing.

Lacey said, 'To be clear, do you mean AryanBoy?'

As Emma nodded, her phone began ringing again.

'Answer it,' Lacey said.

Emma pressed two buttons and put the phone on the bedside cabinet between them.

'Hey, Emma!' The familiar Midlands accent rang out. 'How'd you like my little surprise tonight?'

'Fuck you,' Emma replied.

'Told you already, you're not my type. Let me speak to Lacey.'

Emma looked over for instructions. Into the phone she said, 'What makes you think she's here?'

'You were both seen being bundled into that fleapit in Barons Court,' he replied. 'I only waited for your bodyguards to go. Put her on.'

Lacey reached out and switched off the speaker. 'It's me,' she said into the phone. 'What do you want?'

'Now, is that any way to greet an old friend?'

Turning her back on a troubled Emma, Lacey left the hotel room, leaving the door on the latch. As she walked down the corridor, she said, 'Was that you on the train yesterday?'

'Might have been.'

She doubted it. Jack Brine hadn't had a Midlands accent. And Joesbury thought Jack Brine was BlackPill88, quite how and why, he hadn't explained. It made more sense, now she thought about it, for one of the others to follow and approach her; and it explained why she hadn't recognised Brine. She genuinely hadn't seen him before.

It also might mean more than one person knew her secret.

The voice down the phone – AryanBoy – said, 'So, you didn't go over the edge after all. Tell me, did I have anything to do with that?'

It was him then, definitely him.

She said, 'I have no idea what you're talking about.'

'You disappoint me, Lacey. Or should I say, Victoria?'

'What do you want?'

'I'll let you know. And I hope it goes without saying, if any of your Met friends find out about our history, or if you try to leave town, things will go very badly wrong.'

68

Thirty-two days since AryanBoy had declared war on the female sex and still they clutched at straws.

Fergus Lord was a person of interest simply because his move into politics had coincided with the emergence of the MenMatter movement; and because the aims of his party were, if not identical to those of the terrorist group, then at least complementary. They had no other reason to suspect him and this was probably a complete waste of time. Dana might even have cancelled the appointment or sent a junior along in her place, but Lacey, for some reason, had been very keen on the idea and Dana had learned to trust Lacey's instincts.

Lord lived in Fulham, not far from Parsons Green station, so Dana and Lacey took the Tube. They arrived early and had to wait for Lord to arrive back from Television Centre where he'd been a guest on a morning news show. A dark-haired man in his late twenties led them into a comfortable sitting room and turned on a TV that was showing the last three minutes of the interview.

'You want men to be men again, I get that,' the presenter was saying, as his co-presenter's eyebrows disappeared into her hair. 'But for some of us, that isn't a problem. Don't the men you say are downtrodden just need to man up?'

'I think that's exactly what some of them will claim they are doing,' the co-presenter snapped. 'And women are getting hurt.'

The sitting-room door opened and the smell of fresh coffee preceded Fergus Lord's assistant into the room.

'The biscuits are homemade this morning,' he said, as Fergus Lord on screen talked about misguided men resorting to violence because they saw no other way forward. 'You're watching on catch-up by the way. Gus will be here in less than five. I'm tracking him on Find My Friends.'

He turned to leave. Dana called him back. 'You didn't explain your role here, Mr . . .?'

'I'm Charlie.' The man gave them a wide smile. 'Just Charlie. And I do . . .' he held both hands up as though trying to clutch an answer from mid-air. 'Whatever,' he decided upon.

'I'm going to need a bit more than that,' Dana said. 'I'd like your name please, and your relationship to Mr Lord. Are you a personal assistant, agent, friend, boyfriend?'

The man gave a heavy, exaggerated sigh. 'Gus isn't gay,' he said. 'And I suppose you could call me his manager. Before he went into politics I handled his diary, and his finances, his personal admin, that sort of thing. I still do all that, but we've got a lot busier since we launched UNITY, of course.'

At that moment, they heard the front door opening and a familiar voice calling out, 'It's me.'

With a muttered, 'Excuse me,' Charlie vanished.

'He's called Charlie Frost,' Lacey said in a low voice. 'His name was on the press invitation sent out before the launch. I looked him up on LinkedIn. He and Lord go way back.'

The door swung open. 'He's just changing,' Charlie informed them. 'Gus hates suits.'

The door closed tight again.

'Well, we'd better hope what he said was true and that Gus isn't gay,' Dana said. 'Or a lot of prep work will have been wasted.'

Lacey looked down at herself and pulled a face. 'I think it kind of works.'

It had been Helen who'd spotted the similarity between Lacey and Lord's ex-wife, a social media influencer who'd divorced Lord – publicly, expensively and humiliatingly – a couple of years earlier. Using photographs from the internet and the combined contents of five wardrobes – hers and Helen's, Emma's, Gayle's and Lacey's own, which had been close to hopeless, the woman seemed to wear nothing but jeans – they'd recreated the ex-wife's signature look. When Lacey had appeared from the women's toilets at Lewisham that morning, with her hair loose and curled, wearing far more make-up than she ever normally did, her body covered in layers of tight, fondant colours, Dana had felt an uncomfortable stirring in her gut. She'd never known a woman downplay her looks the way Lacey did, so that when she dressed to impress, well, frankly, it was disturbing. She just had to hope it would have the desired effect on Lord.

'Nice biscuits,' said Lacey, offering the plate. Dana shook her head. She could never eat when she was anxious.

Footsteps sounded and then murmured voices. The door opened once more and Fergus Lord himself walked in, pausing on the threshold, forcing Charlie to hover half in, half out of the room. Lord was deliberately standing in the light from the window, Dana realised. Once he sat, he'd be in shadow. He was letting them see him at his best.

He wore black jeans and a simple white shirt, collarless and cut on the bias around a wide yoke. Tall, with hair the colour of a fox's coat, and chin stubble that had a ginger tone, he looked like Hamlet, a role he'd played more than once.

To her surprise, Dana found herself on her feet. A couple of seconds later, Lacey followed.

'Thank you for seeing us, Mr Lord,' she began. 'My partner and I saw you in *Hamlet* at the Globe a couple of years ago. We enjoyed it very much.'

He held out a hand. 'Thank you, that's kind.' His smile seemed genuine, but his eyes flicked quickly to Lacey and hardened.

'I'm Lacey.' She looked confident, unfazed, the opposite of Dana. 'Great biscuits.'

'Please, sit down.' Lord waited until they'd obeyed him before sitting himself. He crossed one ankle over his opposite knee. His feet were bare.

'I hope you don't mind Charlie sitting in,' he said, as the other man took a chair by the door and opened a laptop. 'He knows more about me than I do.'

They couldn't object. Lord was seeing them willingly in his own home and had every right to set the conditions.

'We'd like to know where you were on the morning of Friday 11 September,' Lacey said, after a moment, and Dana realised she'd allowed an uncomfortable silence to fall. 'Specifically, between the hours of eight and ten.'

Friday 11 September had been the day the baby was abducted from Tower Bridge.

Lord turned to the other man and raised his eyebrows in a silent question. Frost opened the laptop.

'Bear with . . . here we go. You were at the LBC studio in Leicester Square, waiting to go on the Nick Ferrari show.' He glanced up at Dana. 'I can confirm that, I was there too. As indeed was Mr Ferrari and a modest production team. The interview's still on the LBC website so you should be able to ascertain the exact time we went on air, but we had an Uber booked for seven forty-five to take us there.'

'The morning of Saturday 12 September,' Dana asked, after a glance at her notes. 'Between ten and eleven o'clock.'

The following morning, when AryanBoy had first made contact, phoning Emma Boston at her home in Earl's Court.

'You had the girls that weekend,' Charlie said, after a few more seconds staring at the laptop screen. 'So, that would mean, Saturday morning, let me think—'

'Ballet lessons,' Lord replied. 'At Pineapple Studios. I stay in the building because their mother is very safety conscious. I usually order a coffee in the cafeteria and read.'

'Can anyone confirm that?' Dana asked.

Charlie let out what sounded like a squawk. 'Are you kidding me? The place is packed with yummy mummies, all pretending they're totally cool about Gus being there, and trying to work up the courage to invite his daughters on play dates.'

'They're all very nice,' Lord objected. 'Any more dates you want to check?'

'Later that day, between six and seven o'clock?'

The time AryanBoy had phoned Emma at Scotland Yard, when their surveillance had tracked him down to a large triangle around St James's Park.

'Awards ceremony at BAFTA,' Charlie answered.

'Did you win?' Lacey asked Lord.

'I was presenting the award for best actress,' Lord told her. 'Suranne Jones won; again.'

'Those events rarely end before midnight,' Frost added. 'Next?'

These two were too smug. The genuinely innocent would be perplexed, even alarmed by the questioning.

'Sunday 13 September, nine o'clock in the evening onwards into the small hours,' Lacey said, after waiting a couple of seconds for Dana. The night AryanBoy had guided Jason Hancock, aka Waluigi, to the massage parlour in Peckham; the night Emma had been abducted from her Earl's Court flat and suspended above the Thames.

'Nothing in the diary,' Frost said. 'Can you remember, Gus?'

Lord shook his head, mimed not having a clue.

'Day after the awards,' Frost said. 'Hangover, by any chance?'

'Wouldn't have lasted all day. Oh, I remember, I spent the awards night at a friend's house, we went out for breakfast, I got home about midday.'

'Did you see your children?' Lacey asked.

Lord shook his head. 'No, they went back to their mother's because I knew I'd be out. I was knackered to be honest. I went to bed for a couple of hours, had dinner, watched TV, got an early night. So, what do you think? I passed three out of four.'

'It feels coincidental,' Dana said. 'The incel movement start their campaign of terror and, within weeks, you launch a political party aimed at satisfying their demands.'

'Not so. We have aims, not demands, and ours are quite different.'

'What are your aims?' Lacey asked Lord. 'What is it you think UNITY can achieve? Because we all know the incels are bonkers and don't have a snowball's chance in hell.'

No, Dana was shocked to find herself thinking, *don't wind these men up. They're dangerous, they could hurt us; they could hurt my child.*

'Quite,' Lord said, not looking at all put out. 'Did you catch my GMTV interview this morning?'

'We were en route,' Lacey replied. 'I'll get it on catch-up. Just for now, though, humour me. I mean, taking the vote from women, banning women from becoming MPs, these things are never going to happen.'

Lord looked carefully at Lacey and must have decided that he did want to humour her.

'UNITY will press for legislation that equals up government money for both men's and women's causes,' he said. 'At the moment, women's causes and charities get far more attention than men's, with a negative impact on men's health. We also want more resources put into boys' education, particularly the struggling working-class areas and an investment in traditional male-dominated jobs. We want to end talk about the gender pay gap, because it's bollocks, excuse me being so blunt, and a return to the days when people earned according to their merits.'

'So, it's basically about money,' Lacey said.

'It's always about money,' Frost snapped. 'And I'm afraid Gus has another appointment.' He got to his feet.

'One last thing.' Dana ignored Frost. 'Can you do a Midlands accent?'

Lord smiled, a long, slow, easy smile, as though she'd said something initially quite diverting, that became funnier the more he thought about it. He let several seconds go by. Finally, he said, 'I'm an actor, I can do any accent you name.'

'Midlands will do.' Dana threw a look at Lacey, who switched her smart phone to record.

Lord turned his gaze to Lacey. 'Everyone's a whore, Lacey,' he said, in a very convincing Birmingham accent. 'We just sell different parts of ourselves.'

Lacey held Lord's stare for a fraction longer and then turned to Dana. '*Peaky Blinders* quote, ma'am,' she explained, seeing Dana's mystified expression. 'The character addressed is called Grace, not Lacey. Mr Lord was improvising.'

'I auditioned for the part of Tommy,' Lord said, still in his gangster voice. 'They told me I was too posh.'

'Their mistake.' Dana got to her feet. 'Do you like women, Mr Lord?'

He rose too, but slowly, unwrapping his long legs. 'What makes you doubt it?'

'Bad divorce, a career in trouble because of a public conversation you had with a woman, launching a political party that, however much you protest otherwise, can only damage women's rights if successful.'

'So wrong are you, Detective Inspector, that if Constable Flint will agree to have dinner with me, I'd be happy to demonstrate how much I enjoy women's company.'

Taken aback, Dana could only glance at Lacey for her reaction; it was a waste of time. As usual, the woman gave nothing away.

'The outfit is a bit obvious,' Lord went on. 'But you're right about one thing, she's absolutely my type.'

'Thank you for your time, Mr Lord,' Dana said, stepping forward and forcing Frost to open the door for them.

'Charlie has my diary,' Lord said, behind her back and Dana could only guess that he'd been speaking to Lacey.

Dana walked several yards down the street before she spoke. 'There's something not right about him. Did you get that voice recorded?'

'I did,' Lacey confirmed. 'But he's got alibis that sound solid for three out of the four occasions when we know for a fact that AryanBoy was on the phone. He cannot be AryanBoy.'

'He knows something,' Dana insisted as they reached the end of the street.

'Which is why I should have dinner with him,' Lacey replied.

'Mark will go apeshit.'

'Not his decision. I'm not even sure it's yours, with respect. It was a social invitation.'

They crossed the road and made for the Tube station.

'We know AryanBoy has a thing about me,' Lacey said. 'Jack Brine came on to me on the train on Saturday. Now, Fergus Lord asks me out. That's stretching coincidence, don't you think?'

Have you seen you, Dana wanted to say. It was no surprise at all to her that two men, maybe more, found Lacey attractive. The woman was right though, they should follow it up.

She was right too, Mark would go apeshit.

'We do it officially,' she said. 'If at all. Full Scotland Yard clearance. I'll sort that out. We know where and when you're going and we get you tailed.'

'No problem.'

They walked a little further in silence, then Lacey's footsteps slowed down.

'What is it?'

Lacey nodded across the street towards an internet café. She said, 'Is that the one Mark's team linked to the dead drop account? The one used to post footage of the Tower Bridge abduction?'

'I think so.' Dana looked back up the street. 'Not ten minutes from Fergus Lord's house.'

They set off again.

Dana said, 'He has a presence, doesn't he?'

Lacey didn't reply.

'Odd relationship, don't you think? Him and that Charlie bloke.'

'Gus isn't gay,' Lacey said. 'Trust me on that one.'

'Fergus Lord won't earn mega bucks. Few British actors do, unless they break into the big films. How can he afford a full-time Man Friday?'

'Charlie Frost isn't full-time for Lord,' Lacey replied. 'He's a certified financial advisor with a number of clients in show business. He and Lord seem close because they were at school together.'

'In the Midlands?' Dana asked. That had been a very convincing *Peaky Blinders* accent.

For a moment, Lacey didn't speak. Then, 'No,' she said. 'In Eastbourne.'

69

From the outside the independent school in Eastbourne looked more like a Tudor palace than a modern educational establishment. The main building was brick, gleaming red in the late October sunshine, with stone-lined windows and deep, inset arches leading to a covered walkway. Its square tower overlooked vast playing fields, tennis courts, athletics track and accommodation for the boarders. A bell rang as Lacey left her car and the place burst into life. The dark-blazered children with their shining hair and clear skins all ignored her as she made her way to the main door and she was glad of it. Increasingly, these days, she felt tainted, unfit to associate with these fresh young people. She was a fraud, a liar; a coward whose silence could lead to many more people getting hurt.

So you didn't go over the edge after all?

She couldn't even be completely honest about her visit to Eastbourne, admitting only that Jack Brine, too, had mentioned the place. Dana had agreed, eventually, to Lacey's visit today, probably because the team had so little else to go on, but hadn't been able to hide her true feelings: that it was a massive waste of time.

Dana was wrong. Eastbourne was the key. Whatever was going on had started here, possibly in this school; and how ironic it would be, were she to be the one to track down AryanBoy, only for him to destroy her. That might even be his plan, to make her the instrument of her own downfall. She was in free fall, she realised, almost as though she'd gone over the edge after all, plunging ever downwards.

'I was hoping to talk to the headmaster,' she said to the grey-haired woman in her fifties who led her down several long corridors that reminded Lacey, surprisingly, of her own school days. The interior of schools smelled the same, it seemed, regardless of the social class of the students.

'His diary's rarely anything but chock-a-block,' the woman countered. 'I'm the archivist. As your enquiry is about people who were students here some time ago, I'm probably the best placed to help you. Although there will be limits to what I can share. Data protection and all that.'

So few people understood data protection legislation and what it really meant, as opposed to what they assumed it meant.

'Can you confirm that Fergus Lord was a pupil here?' Lacey asked, when they'd reached a small, square office with an untidy desk and several overflowing bookshelves.

The archivist squeezed her way behind the desk and nodded to Lacey to take the seat in front of it.

'Yes, that's a matter of public record,' she said. 'It's on his Wikipedia page. He was here from age thirteen to eighteen. Colourful character.'

A colourful character who'd asked her on a date, the day before.

There was a stack of papers on the chair. Lacking instructions, Lacey placed them on the desk. 'I'm guessing he was a boarder,' she said. 'His family lived in Northamptonshire at the time?'

'Seems reasonable,' the archivist replied, a second before catching sight of something happening outside. She got to her feet and waved frantically.

'Is it possible to check?' Lacey asked, when she had the woman's attention again.

The archivist retook her seat. 'That probably falls under the heading of confidential information,' she said.

Lacey let it go. Somehow, she didn't think either Fergus Lord or Charlie Frost were AryanBoy. She'd seen no spark of recognition in their eyes the day before. Frost had focused attention on Dana, the senior officer, while Lord's interest had seemed, on the surface at least, to be of a different kind. Likewise, Lacey was pretty sure she and Jack Brine had never met before. There was another name to be found.

'What I came for is a list of all male pupils who were contemporaries of Fergus Lord,' Lacey said. 'Ideally, I'd like the year above him and the year below, as well as those in his academic year.'

She already knew there were around a hundred children in each year group. Without photographs a list of names wouldn't help that much, but it would be a start. If only the boy on the clifftop had given her his name.

'May I ask why?'

The woman had small, grey eyes, and a round face that had probably never been attractive, even in her youth.

'Surely this is information in the public domain,' Lacey argued. 'The school produces an annual yearbook, listing every graduating student. I saw reference to it on your website. Can't you let me have a copy of the one produced for Fergus Lord's year?'

The yearbooks did include small portrait photographs of each student.

The archivist smiled. 'I'm afraid that's not a publicly available document. Only members of the school community receive a copy.'

Maybe he had given her his name, and she simply hadn't taken it in.

'Nevertheless, the fact the document is published means it's not confidential information. So, there should be no reason why you can't let me have it.'

'Again, may I ask why?'

'We have reason to believe Mr Lord may be connected to a series of crimes we're investigating. It would be helpful to be able to rule him out.'

The archivist leaned back from her desk with an air of immense satisfaction. 'Then I doubt there's anything else I can tell you without his permission or before seeking legal advice.'

'Was Charles Frost a student here?' Lacey asked, although she knew the answer. That information, too, had been on LinkedIn.

'I'm afraid I can't say.' The woman got to her feet. 'You'll have to excuse me now.' She came out from behind her desk and walked to the door. Knowing she had no choice, Lacey got to her feet.

'What about Jack Brine?' she asked. Jack Brine had no LinkedIn profile, and the details on his Facebook page had been vague. 'And Adam Ryan? I'm particularly interested in an Adam Ryan.'

Adam Ryan had to be an alias though. If only she could remember whether or not the boy on the cliff had mentioned a name.

'Come back with a warrant,' the woman told her, with an air of someone who'd always wanted to say such words. She made an extravagant gesture with her right hand. 'After you.'

Knowing she was beaten – probably – Lacey stepped into the corridor. In reception she had to queue to hand back her visitor's pass. The walls of the large open space held huge photographs of students in various aspects of school life: sailing, bent over Bunsen burners in the chemistry lab, an orchestra, several theatrical productions.

The archivist was hovering, determined to see her off the premises.

Leaving her pass on the desk Lacey crossed the space towards a photograph on the far wall that had caught her attention. A scene in a school play: a forest grotto, lit only by lanterns, populated by fairies. A beautiful blonde girl, scantily clad and wearing a crown fashioned from leaves and berries took centre stage. Facing her, similarly crowned, bare-chested, stood a young Fergus Lord. At the fairy queen's feet knelt a plump boy with a donkey's head over his own. *A Midsummer Night's Dream.*

Lacey scanned the other actors for familiar faces. One of the boys, his eyes down, could have been Charlie Frost but it was hard to be sure.

And now something was nagging at the back of her mind. *I didn't ask,* she'd snapped at him. What hadn't she asked? Had he offered his name? Shit, why couldn't she remember?

'Can you sign out please?' The archivist had followed her. 'I have another appointment.'

'Don't let me keep you.' Lacey took out her phone and took a photograph of the larger image. 'That's Fergus Lord in the role of Oberon, isn't it? And if I'm not mistaken, the boy playing Puck is Jack Brine.'

70

'I'm not sure how much it helps, Lacey,' Dana said, when they met in her office later that day.

Mark had called earlier, furious that she'd let Lacey drive to Eastbourne by herself, and she was still smarting from the feeling of being ticked off. Maybe she had been wrong though. Lacey was a natural target for the incels. Well, at least the woman was back in one piece.

'It helps a bit,' Neil Anderson disagreed. 'Lord, Frost and Brine were at school together. They've known each other for years. They could easily be AryanBoy, MadHatter and BlackPill88.'

'Or Joker,' Pete Stenning reminded them. 'We're looking for four men, not three.'

They were right, it could be important, but they were at day thirty-four after AryanBoy's video release and something had to happen soon. Dana had taken to writing the number on her office calendar, in tiny digits in the bottom right-hand corner of each day. As though she might forget! She knew, the moment she woke, how many days into the new normal they'd gone.

The door opened and Gayle Mizon stuck her head around it. 'DCI Joesbury just called for you, Dana,' she said. 'We have to put the TV on.'

*

In the main office Gayle had the TV tuned to the BBC. The news headlines had finished, and the camera focused on the anchor – an attractive, dark-haired woman – for the day's biggest story.

'A private members' bill, scheduled to be brought before parliament in the coming days, will call for unprecedented measures to ameliorate the so-called incel problem,' she told viewers. 'The intervention, headed by the Anglican Bishop Desmond Sittingbourne, has called for tighter restrictions on the freedom of women and girls to be introduced under parliament's emergency powers. Our Westminster reporter has more.'

As they gathered around the TV, the scene switched to the green outside the Houses of Parliament where a middle-aged man in a business suit was holding an umbrella against the rain.

'This is an unprecedented move,' he began. 'A cross-party, multi-faith group of MPs, religious leaders and social media commentators has called for the introduction of immediate restrictions on women's freedoms in order to quell the rising incidents of violence. At a press conference this afternoon Bishop Sittingbourne was joined by other religious leaders, and by Conservative MP James Hunter-Dean and right-wing social media commentator Tobias Coburn.'

Another scene switch, this time a room inside the Palace of Westminster. A raised platform held a long table, behind which sat three men: a bishop, a rabbi and an imam.

It was happening then. The establishment were starting to consent to the incel demands, to ask themselves: *What harm can making a few minor changes do? And don't we all want the same thing? To keep our women safe?* That's how they'd justify it. *This is for your own good.*

'All we are asking for is a moment of calm.' The bishop spoke in soft, melodious tones. 'Our proposals are simple, non-onerous and temporary. We are simply suggesting that for the time being the women of this country adopt a more restrained way of behaving.'

'Fuck you,' Gayle mouthed at the TV screen.

'The women of Islam have long understood the value of modesty,' the Imam said. 'Consequently, the women in our society are valued and protected.'

'Exactly,' the bishop jumped in, as the rabbi nodded his agreement. 'All we are suggesting is that for the foreseeable future, women adopt a habit of dressing modestly in public, that they don't leave their homes after ten o'clock in the evening without a male guardian, and that fines are levied for being intoxicated in public. There is no hardship in any of this.'

Maybe this was it, what MenMatter had planned all along, that the mainstream would come round to the incel way of thinking and make it easy for them. Maybe this was the Day of Retribution, when the world Dana knew fell: not with a bang, but a whimper.

The scene switched back to College Green. 'The group are claiming to have the quiet support of a number of MPs on all sides of the house,' the reporter said. 'And, they say, not all of them male. Earlier this afternoon, I spoke to the home secretary about it.'

The scene switched once more to show Alison Brabin sitting against a wood-panelled background. Facing her, all but his left shoulder out of shot, sat the reporter.

'Home Secretary, this private member's bill will put women on a less equal footing to that of men for the first time since the sex discrimination act in 1975. Is there any chance of it passing?'

What future could there be for her and Helen, in a world where women only existed to comfort and support men?

Brabin gave an icy smile. 'None at all. A bill like this flies in the face of everything we stand for in the United Kingdom.'

'But male MPs outnumber female members by two to one,' the reporter said. 'Is it possible you simply don't have the numbers to fight this off?'

'I think most members of the house, regardless of their sex, will see this bill for the absurdity it is,' the home secretary replied. 'And those who might be wavering would do well to remember that when it comes to the ballot, women are equally represented. No serving MP can afford to alienate women, no sensible one would even seek to.'

Brabin was wearing a dark blue suit, very unlike her usual bright colours.

'The MenMatter movement are calling for women to lose the vote,' the reporter said.

'I'm not going to dignify their nonsense with a response.' The home secretary got to her feet, effectively ending the interview.

She looked older too or might be wearing less make-up. The home secretary, possibly the most powerful woman in the land, was just like the rest of them, Dana realised. She was scared.

71

Lacey Flint had been to Eastbourne, had visited his old school. Shit, he should have expected this. She was a police officer, had been a detective, and a good one at that. Her solve rate was impressive. He should have known she'd try to track him down, just as he'd done her.

He reached out for the empty coffee mug on his desk, on the point of hurling it across the room, but managed to stop himself in time. How would he explain that to the others?

AryanBoy was, he realised, as close to panicking as he'd been since they'd started all this. And they weren't nearly close to home yet. Taking several deep breaths, he forced himself to be calm.

The school couldn't have given out his name; if they had, he'd have been brought in already. Her colleagues over at Lewisham could be applying for a warrant, but the chances of her telling them why she really suspected the school were slim. Without more to go on, without being able to demonstrate a real and imminent risk, a warrant wouldn't be issued urgently. Maybe not at all.

After all, she couldn't exactly tell them about the night she'd pushed a stolen car with a dead woman at the wheel over Beachy Head. She couldn't tell them she'd stolen a dead woman's identity, that her real name was Victoria Llewellyn, and that the convicted murderer in Durham prison was her kid sister, Cathy.

Lacey Flint was hamstrung and there was too much at stake for him to give in to panic now. Sooner or later, though, he was going to have to deal with her; and that, sadly, meant the two of them probably didn't have a future together after all. No, Lacey Flint had to be taken out of the picture.

72

'I need to tell you something,' Lacey said, late the following day.

Joesbury sighed, and stretched, his body moving beneath hers. He was rarely still after sex, the opposite in fact, fidgety, restless, almost energised.

'Is it about the phone call you took in the early hours of Sunday morning?' he asked.

Grateful that her head was still on his chest, that he couldn't see her face, Lacey said, 'There was no point calling you about that, I knew Emma would report it as soon as her daytime bodyguard arrived. I want to talk about when those insects were left here.'

Joesbury said, 'Still insisting it didn't happen while you were in the back yard?'

'I am. Because no one touched the keys while I was outside. I put them in the inside pages of a catalogue. From David Austin Roses to be specific.'

'Sounds like Miss Pinney in flat six,' Joesbury replied. 'She has a roof garden.'

'I remember the exact page.' Lacey twisted herself round so that she could see him. 'You know I notice things like that. I think mostly the pictures were just rose bushes or blown-up shots of flowers, but this one showed a bride with a bouquet of pale pink roses. I saw it and, well it made me think of – you know . . .'

Joesbury raised one eyebrow.

'When I got back to the front door, I know I was rushing, but I saw the same picture again. The keys were exactly where I'd left them. What are the chances of someone sneaking into the house, finding the keys, letting themselves in here, replacing the tin with one of their own, leaving again, locking the door, without Emma hearing or seeing anything, and putting the keys back on the exact same page?'

Joesbury pulled a face. 'Slim. But there's a more important question you should be asking.'

'What's that?'

'How did the man with the bugs know what type of tea I drink, and that I keep my tea bags in a big, branded tin?'

Lacey sat up. That was exactly what she should have been asking; if she hadn't been so fixated on – well, on other things, she'd have thought of it.

'No one would know that.'

The realisation stunned her. The knowledge that she'd been right would, in time, be some consolation; for now, there was something much more serious to worry about.

Joesbury spoke her thoughts out loud. 'Only people who've been in here.'

'Blimey.'

'So, you could well be right. There was probably no tin switch after all. The critters were brought in well before they made their escape. By someone who can access my flat.'

For a second, Lacey thought she might be about to throw up. All the time she and Emma had thought they were safe, they were the very opposite.

'I knew it. I knew their surveillance was too good.' She raised a finger on her right hand. 'They knew where Emma lived, and her landline number.' Another finger. 'They knew the codeword to get her to leave when the fire alarm went off.' A third. 'They found out who I am, they followed me to Durham, they saw us being moved to the hotel in Barons Court.' She'd run out of fingers. 'They'd need an army to keep on top of us like that.'

Joesbury had already worked this out for himself. He said, 'Or one man in the right place. Our friend AryanBoy might have an inside track to the very heart of Scotland Yard. Hell, he might even work there himself.'

'Jesus.'

'Yep.'

Joesbury looked unhappy, even deeply worried, but it was worse, far worse, than he knew. He thought someone he trusted at work was betraying him; how would he cope when he learned she was too? Catching sight of the bedside clock – she had to go – she looked around for her clothes. 'Any idea who?' she said.

Joesbury shook his head. 'It could be any of a couple of dozen people, frankly.'

'Have you told anyone?'

'Not yet. I keep hoping he'll give himself away. If I start a manhunt, I put him on red alert.'

'So, wherever Emma and I go, they'll find us.'

She couldn't help the sudden surge of panic. She'd assumed AryanBoy's worst threat was to expose her. What if it was more? What if he really meant her harm? He'd already nearly killed Emma.

This could be it, the time to run. Since the insect attack, Joesbury had moved back into the Pimlico place. Her boat was empty. She could be back at Deptford Creek in an hour, find her bag and leave.

But she'd agreed to meet Emma, in less than an hour. And running away? It didn't feel like the sort of thing she did any more.

'Maybe not.' Joesbury picked up a business card from the bedside table and handed it over. 'This is your new place. You move in tonight.'

She glanced down at the card. It showed a large hotel not far from Tower Bridge.

'Looks expensive,' she said.

'Let's hope you're not there long. In the meantime, their security will be better than most. You need a key card to access the stairs and the lifts. I sent your stuff round by courier earlier. No one knows where you are but me.'

Lacey said nothing.

'You're safe,' he said. Then, in a possible attempt to lighten the mood. 'From everyone but me.'

Joesbury's eyes fell dark when she didn't respond. She couldn't tell him.

She would never be safe.

73

While Lacey had been spending time with Joesbury, Emma, in a small rebellion against constant surveillance, had insisted on having dinner with some of her journalist friends and Lacey had arranged to meet her a little after ten o'clock. Because her car was still at Lewisham station, she and Emma caught the Tube back to their hotel.

'We're the Farrow sisters at this new place,' Lacey explained, as the train pulled away from Leicester Square. 'I'm Laura, you're Ella, so be sure not to use any credit cards in your own name.'

'Like anyone will believe we're sisters.'

Emma had been drinking, but given how stressed she'd been of late, that had to be a good thing; maybe she'd actually sleep for a change.

'Pleasant evening?' Lacey asked, as movement at the far end of the carriage caught her eye.

'Don't judge.' Emma's eyes closed.

A new group – around eight to ten identically dressed women – had illegally entered the carriage from the one following and were squeezing their way through the crowd.

Emma mumbled, 'How was lovely Mark?'

'Busy.' Lacey's attention remained on the disruption at the other end of the carriage.

Not too busy to grab hold of her the second she'd stepped through the front door of his flat, to tear the clothes off her body, all the while kissing her until her lips felt bruised. 'Not seeing you is killing me,' he'd muttered into her ear, his breath warm on her cold skin.

He still thought this was a temporary hiccup, a problem they could solve and move on from. He still believed the two of them had a future.

'You still going in to Scotland Yard tomorrow?'

Lacey had been summoned to a meeting, to discuss whether she should take up Fergus Lord's invitation to dinner.

'I'm not supposed to talk about that,' Lacey replied.

The uniformed women were accosting strangers in the way of a religious group, or over-aggressive charity collectors. Most were clad in pink sweatshirts and berets, but any intended femininity ended with the colour scheme. They wore jeans or combat style trousers, heavy-duty boots, and carried backpacks. Most had very short hair. As they moved through the carriage, Lacey could see them handing out printed leaflets to the women travelling alone or in small groups.

As they neared the open space around the central doors, where a group of young men were gathered, Emma gave a soft snore. Avoiding eye contact, the eight women tried to make their way round the group of men. The men didn't make it easy; they blocked the way, moving reluctantly, facing the other group down. As the women squeezed past, the men turned and watched them move away.

'Good evening, ladies.' One of the women stood directly in front of Lacey. 'Everything OK?'

'Yes thanks.'

Ages of the group ranged from late teens to late twenties. All were clear-eyed, focused, confident. The spokeswoman was around twenty-seven, short and stocky. What little hair was visible beneath her beret had been dyed a patchy lilac.

She said, 'Where you heading this evening?'

In the carriage window opposite, Lacey saw Emma's eyes drift open, then widen. Meanwhile, the group of men – five of them, all young, all white – were watching.

'We're on our way home,' Lacey replied. 'May I ask who you are?'

A slip of paper was thrust at her.

'We're the Mama Bears,' the lilac-haired woman replied. 'Can we escort you somewhere when you get off the train?'

'Why do we need an escort?'

'London's not safe for women any more.' The new speaker was a young woman, bespectacled and overweight. 'Have either of you been drinking? We don't recommend that, not if you're travelling on public transport.'

'Do Transport for London know you're doing this?' Emma's journalist instincts had kicked in. 'Do you mind if I get a picture?' Turning to Lacey, she said, 'I've been following them on Facebook. I left a couple of messages but no one's got back to me yet.'

Emma pulled her phone from her bag. 'What about British Transport Police? How do they feel about you patrolling the Underground?'

Lilac-hair raised a hand, palm out. 'No faces in the picture please. We have a lot of enemies and we don't want retaliation. We're only thinking of your safety.'

From the area around the doors a male voice sounded. 'Leave the girls alone.'

Another called, 'You lot are causing the problems, not us.'

'Can I ask you some questions?' Emma had switched her phone to record. 'How long have you been doing this? Would you describe yourselves as a vigilante group?'

Lacey got to her feet. The group of men by the door were huddled together, muttering, shooting sly glances their way. She put a hand on the arm of the lilac-haired woman. 'Maybe move along now,' she suggested. 'My friend can contact you tomorrow to do any follow-up.'

The woman gave her a dismissive glance. 'I don't mean any disrespect, but your friend's been drinking. That's asking for trouble.'

'I'm not sure you lot are women.' One of the men, a bloke in jeans and unzipped anorak had moved closer. 'Any of you care to prove it?'

The train was slowing down. Lacey caught the lilac-haired woman's arm again and discreetly pulled her warrant card out of her bag. 'I'm a police officer,' she said, in a low voice. 'I think the situation here could escalate. I'd like you and your group to leave the train at this station and board the next one to come along, please.'

More catcalls came down the train as it entered the station.

'Fair enough,' the lilac-haired woman said. 'Thank you for your assistance, officer.'

The train stopped and Lacey stepped aside to let people get off, more, she suspected, than had originally planned to, leaving the carriage almost empty. The group in pink were the last to leave.

'Lacey,' Emma called. One of the men had jumped onto a seat near her, had pressed his groin against the window and was exposing himself at the group in pink. Emma got to her feet, steadying herself against the metal pole.

The doors closed. At the last moment, the women in pink leaped back aboard the train into the next carriage.

'Shit,' Lacey muttered, as the train began to move.

The women's about-turn hadn't been lost on the men. They were all facing the carriage in front, deliberating: did they go after the women or not?

'There's no signal down here,' said Emma, telling Lacey what she'd already guessed for herself.

As the train picked up speed the few remaining passengers moved away.

None of the men looked like incels, not on the surface anyway, in fact more like football supporters, hooligans in the right circumstances. Big, red-faced, with tattooed knuckles, they looked more likely to join an English Defence League march than support the incel cause but they wouldn't like being told what to do by women. They were working-class white men and probably had a whole host of grievances, real and imagined, that were looking for an outlet. And they'd been drinking.

They were all making obscene gestures at the women in pink; the women, sensibly, turned their backs and began to engage with the occupants of the next carriage. The bloke who'd flashed had his hands on his waistband, as though about to repeat the offence.

The situation was seconds from spiralling out of control.

'Stay here.' Leaving Emma, Lacey took the few steps that would bring her face to face with the men. 'What's up, lads?' She stretched out both arms to grasp the side rails, so they couldn't move forward without pushing her out of the way. The man in front – heavily built, a crucifix tattooed on his left cheekbone – looked her up and down. 'Were that lot bothering you?' he asked, before glancing over her shoulder at the pink crew.

'They don't mean any harm.'

'Cause more trouble than they solve,' the bespectacled bloke next to him argued.

'Fucking lesbians,' another yelled.

Lacey gave an awkward smile. 'Please guys, just turn round and sit down. When we get to the next station, I'll have them removed from the train.'

The man with the facial tattoo made an incredulous expression. 'How you going to do that then?'

'I'm a police officer.' She took her warrant card out again. 'And you sir,' she gave a quick glance at the flasher. 'Fasten your pants and leave them that way. We're all civilised people here.'

Tattoo-face reached for the warrant card. 'Give's a look at that.'

Police officers do not surrender their warrant cards. As their hands met, Lacey stepped back, shoving her card away. She held a hand up. 'Stand back, please sir.'

He wiggled his shoulders and stepped forward, not back, enjoying the confrontation. He was too close to her now, using his size to intimidate; the others were drawing in too. One of them said, 'It's an offence to impersonate a police officer. Show us that card.'

'Hey!'

The shout from behind was followed by a loud banging on glass. Lacey turned to see the women in pink were pulling open the doors between the two carriages. It took several seconds, the doors weren't frequently opened, and then the first of them – lilac-hair – stepped into their carriage. 'Stay away from her,' she called.

The idiots thought they were coming to her rescue.

Rough hands pushed Lacey aside as Tattoo-face called, 'What the fuck you gonna do about it?'

The women in pink pushed their way back into the carriage, a couple of the men pressed forward, past Lacey, and stopped. Both groups, annoyed, resentful, were nevertheless holding back as a trace of common sense prevented the descent to violence. A social construct was holding steady, Lacey realised – men and women do not fight each other – but only just.

And this was partly her fault.

'Emma,' she called. 'Pull the emergency alarm.'

The train would travel on to the next station, and they were probably a minute or two away, but the driver would know something was happening. He could radio ahead for help.

On her feet now, Emma had spotted the closest alarm above the side doors, but Tattoo-face reached her first and pushed her back down. 'Not now, Quasimodo.'

Emma flushed scarlet. 'Someone activate the alarm, please,' she called.

Over by the far door a woman in her forties reached up to the alarm lever and pulled it.

The women had taken weapons out of their rucksacks, short stubby coshes secured to their wrists with leather straps. They held them upright, like wooden phallic symbols, several slapping them against their open palms. They were being stupidly provocative.

Holding up one hand, Lacey called, 'Ladies back off'; turning back to the men she said, 'You too, gentlemen, or this won't end well for anyone.'

The train was slowing again.

To the men she said, 'I'm a police officer and emergency response is on its way.'

A beer can hurtled past, heading towards the women. Lacey felt spray hit the side of her face before it clattered to the floor, the beer fizzing out.

Lilac-hair stepped forward; Emma blocked her path. 'Not a good idea,' she said, shaking her head.

Hands fell on Lacey's shoulders. She was seconds from being thrown aside. She spun round to face Tattoo-face, grasping his arms and looking up into his eyes. Out of the corner of her eye she could see their reflection in the carriage window. They appeared to be embracing.

'Men don't beat up women. Not in this country.' She spoke softly, like a defenceless female, pleading with a man not to hurt her. Even as she despised herself, she could see it working. His eyes softened, the tension in his body relaxed. He dropped her arms and turned.

'Leave it lads,' he said. 'Not worth it, not for a bunch of girls.'

The train stopped, the women in pink got off, followed by Lacey and Emma. A member of Transport for London security and an officer from British Transport Police were waiting on the platform. It was over.

Lacey had never been more furious in her life; never so bitterly ashamed of herself.

74

Heads around the room were nodding, eyes flicking between Lacey and Joesbury. Most thought she should do it, she could tell, set up a date with Fergus Lord, get to know him better, become – if she could – their woman on the inside.

The meeting – the day after her encounter with the Mama Bears – was taking place in Joesbury's office at Scotland Yard. Archie had met her at reception and escorted her upstairs. She'd known it was Joesbury's room from the second she'd walked in, even though he'd been elsewhere, from the collage of Huck photographs on his desk and the sailing pictures on the walls, and from the smell of it.

In another life, she'd come to this room often, would know the people in the outer office like old friends, and there'd be a photograph of her on the desk, maybe of the two of them together; but that was another life, and for the moment, she could see no way out of this one.

And now they wanted to turn her into a spy, without knowing how much of a liability she could be to the investigation. Did that make her a double agent, albeit a reluctant one? Weren't most double agents reluctant though, at least in the beginning? Forced this way and that by forces with leverage.

She glanced around the small conference table: Mr Cook, to her left, Dana on his left, Dan Owen from counter terrorism opposite and Archie, taking notes, next to him. Joesbury had been pacing the room for the last five minutes.

David Cook, still officially Lacey's boss, opened his mouth to speak, but Joesbury got there first.

'Our priority should be keeping Lacey out of trouble, not throwing her into the thick of it. It's not happening.'

'Isn't that for Lacey herself to say?'

The new voice took them all by surprise; none of them had noticed the door quietly opening. Lacey turned to see the commissioner as, around the room, people got to their feet.

'Constable Flint?' The slim, slight woman with short, grey hair held out her hand. 'Well done last month. On the river, I mean. Both times.'

Lacey took the hand that felt small and cold in her own. She and her ultimate boss, she noticed, were exactly the same height. 'Thank you, ma'am.'

'Please sit down, all of you. I only came to say hello to Lacey.'

The commissioner glanced around the room, her eyes landing back on Lacey.

'Put the investigation aside for one moment,' the commissioner said. 'A good-looking, well-known actor has asked you out. The two of you are single, of a compatible age. All other things being equal, would you have said yes?'

It was interesting, Lacey thought, that it should be a woman who thought of that.

'No ma'am,' she said. 'I wouldn't. I have a boyfriend.'

Over at the window, Joesbury didn't move. She waited for him to step in, to say that he was that boyfriend.

'They know she's police,' he said instead. 'They know she's involved in the investigation. There's no way Lord will give anything away. We'll gain nothing and could be putting her at risk.'

'I think I should do it,' Lacey said to the commissioner. 'It's too much of a coincidence that Fergus Lord and Jack Brine went to the same school. Lord must be involved and maybe I can tease it out of him.'

No sooner had the words left her mouth than Lacey realised their truth. This was what she'd been lacking, a sense of agency; a feeling that she could make a difference, that she was something more than flotsam on a strong current.

The commissioner made up her mind. 'I agree,' she said. 'It's worth a try. Strictly by the book, full backup.'

Joesbury didn't argue, and Lacey wasn't surprised. Fewer than two minutes in the woman's presence and Lacey could tell this was not someone whose orders were up for discussion.

The commissioner glanced at the clock. 'Right, keep me posted.'

'I guess we're done,' Joesbury said, as the commissioner left the room. 'And Lacey has a call to make.'

75

'Mind if I join you, mate?'

The café in Shepherd's Bush was almost empty, so there was no reason, really, why Joesbury should want to sit at the same table as the young white male who, until a second ago, had been engrossed in his laptop.

'It's Jack, isn't it?' Joesbury said, after the younger man's mystified stare around the room had been exactly the reaction he expected. 'Jack Brine?'

Brine was wearing, Joesbury noticed, the reversible brown and green jacket that Lacey had photographed on the train twelve days earlier. The same jacket worn by the suspect in the CCTV footage captured around Tower Bridge the morning the baby had been abducted. Given that thousands of the same coat were made and sold in the UK every year, it wasn't proof, but it would help. Slowly, the case against Brine was building.

Too slowly for comfort though, which was why Joesbury had decided to do the meeting himself this morning. He had to push things forward somehow.

'Do I know you?' Brine pressed a few keys, closing whatever page had been open on the laptop.

It was a good question. Brine might know exactly who Joesbury was; in which case, sometime in the next few minutes, he'd give himself away. A slip of the tongue, an obvious lie, even defensive body language. It would happen and when it did, he'd spot it. Joesbury had been playing the game of secrets far longer than this kid.

He gestured towards the counter. 'I was talking to the girl who works here sometimes. Told her I was looking for a website designer. She said to speak to Jack, that you're in most days and that you might be able to help me out.' Uninvited, he pulled out a chair and sat. 'Mick Jackson,' he said.

Suspicion remained in the other man's eyes. 'What you looking for?'

'Like I say, new website. I've had two companies the last two years doing, what do you call it, hosting. Both made a cock-up and truth is I don't know enough about the business to know where they're going wrong. I need to start from scratch, with someone who knows his stuff and can explain it to me in noddy language.'

Few fake personas he'd adopted over time had come more naturally than that of the clueless technophobe.

Brine said, 'What line of business you in?'

'Antiques,' Joesbury replied. 'And house clearance. Bric-a-brac. I buy up cheap, sell on at online auction.'

'Stolen?' Brine questioned.

Joesbury fixed the other man with a stare, 'Would it matter?'

Brine shrugged. 'Show me what you've got now.'

Joesbury pulled a laptop from his bag, one of the older, decommissioned ones from the storage facility at Scotland Yard and opened up the website that Archie had spent the last couple of days setting up.

Brine began making his way around it. 'Home page is clunky,' he said. 'Top menu's not clear, links are slow. How are you getting payment? PayPal?'

'Seemed easiest.'

After a few more seconds Brine looked up. 'Yeah, it's a bit crap. I can do something better. Not for a couple of weeks though, I'm in the middle of a big job, with a deadline.'

'No sweat. Couple of weeks will be fine. If you give me your details I can get in touch. So, can you tell me a bit about yourself? Show me some of your work?'

Brine tapped a few keys on his own device before turning it round. 'This is my website client list,' he said. 'I do a lot of scientific and technical sites, because my background is science. A couple of GP practices, some clinics.'

'What are you working on now? If you're allowed to say.'

'Not a secret. You've heard of International Men's Day?'

Joesbury felt a tightening in his stomach. 'Can't say I have, but it feels long overdue.'

Brine scratched the side of his face. 'It's a fund-raising thing. People encouraged to donate to a variety of men's charities. Look, I'll show you.'

Grabbing the laptop back, he tapped away for a few seconds then spun it round. Joesbury saw a photograph of men, of varying ages and ethnicities, standing against an ocean backdrop. The page heading read: International Men's Day UK.

'This isn't live yet,' Brine explained. 'It's sitting behind the corresponding site for last year. I have to get it up by the end of next week. Look, this is the key bit.'

He pressed a button on the top menu marked DONATE and a sub-page headed Charities to Support appeared. Beneath the heading Joesbury saw a list of website links, subdivided into sections. *Boys and young men's personal development* was one, another was *Domestic abuse and violence, Fatherhood* was a third, then *Health, including mental health.*

'Thirty different charities listed,' Brine explained. 'All related to men and men's issues. The publicity around International Men's

Day encourages people onto the website, where they can choose the charity they prefer. The tricky bit is directing the donations to the right charities. You can imagine the furore if they get mixed up. That's what I'm finalising now. It has to be live three weeks before the day. Which is basically today. I have a midnight deadline.'

'Impressive. So how do I get in touch?'

Brine handed over a business card; Joesbury shook his hand and got to his feet. Outside on the street he phoned the office.

'International Men's Day,' he told Georgie over the phone as he walked to his bike. 'Find everything you can.'

'Do we pull him in?' the commissioner asked, thirty minutes later when Joesbury had arrived back to find her grilling three quarters of his young team. Just the boys; Georgie was absent.

'We haven't been able to link him to the internet place in Fulham,' Theo said. 'We know Fergus Lord goes there a lot because all the local yummy mummies flood in when he's due, and that Man Friday of his, the bloke called Charlie Frost, but nothing to place Brine there.'

'The jacket, the similarity of his posts to BlackPill's, even his meeting with Lacey Flint on the train, it's all circumstantial,' Archie said, before adding, 'capable of being explained in a different way,' as though the commissioner of the Metropolitan Police needed to have 'circumstantial evidence' explained.

'Have we anything concrete?' she asked.

For several seconds no one spoke.

'The case is building,' Joesbury said. 'We've checked the known movements of Fergus Lord, Charlie Frost and Jack Brine against the posts of AryanBoy, MadHatter, BlackPill88 and Joker. We've looked at timings, locations when we have them, style and tone.'

The commissioner didn't look impressed. 'And?'

'Nothing to indicate Jack Brine isn't Blackpill,' Joesbury said.

'Anything to indicate he is?'

'Charlie Frost could be any of them, although Georgie thinks she's spotted a similarity in phrasing between his regular emails and some of Joker's posts. We have nothing to link Fergus Lord to any of the four.'

'Even if all three of them are involved, we're looking for four people,' the commissioner pointed out. 'We could be a hundred per cent right about Lord, Frost and this Jack Brine character, but there's still one of them eluding us.'

And that one could be among them, Joesbury thought. In which case he'd been fed information they wanted him to have.

When no one replied, the commissioner shook her head and made for the door, almost colliding with Georgie on the way out.

Knowing his team were feeling as bruised as he was, Joesbury gathered them around his table. When they were settled, he said, 'So, International Men's Day? What have you got, Georgie?'

Georgie had made handwritten notes. 'It started back in the 1990s as a sort of celebration of boys and men and their achievements,' she said. 'Sometime over the years it became an annual event and now it happens every year on the 19 November, with events all over the world. Each year has a theme, sometimes sort of loose like *Working Together for Men and Boys* and sometimes worryingly focused, like *Stop Male Suicide*. Do you think this is it, sir? That 19 November is the Day of Retribution?'

'That would give us three weeks,' Archie said.

Joesbury said, 'Tell me what's planned in the UK.'

Georgie said, 'Back in the spring the PM announced that he was going to throw his full weight behind it this year. Apparently, some of his back benchers have been nagging him about poor mental health in young boys. So, there's a conference at the Queen Elizabeth II Centre on that day, with hundreds of fifth and sixth formers being bused in to listen to speeches from the PM and his cabinet, leading businessmen and entrepreneurs, health professionals and so on.'

Theo said, 'Why would a day intended to be all about making things better for men be the target of the MenMatter campaign?'

'Good question,' Georgie said, 'but it's attracted a fair bit of backlash from women's groups. Their beef is that with all the violence being threatened and committed against women just lately, the last thing the government should be doing is pandering to men. The Mama Bears – the group that Lacey had a tussle with on the underground last night – they've said they'll be there in force.'

Archie said, 'So what? They won't be allowed in.'

'No, but they can picket, shouting abuse at delegates, drawing attention to themselves and causing a lot of trouble. A group of women's associations applied to the mayor for permission to hold a demonstration in Westminster Square. It was denied but they may turn up anyway. Oh, and the home secretary has got involved.'

Joesbury said, 'Brabin? What's it got to do with her?'

Georgie said, 'She's claiming it's time to stop talking about men's issues and women's issues and accept that both sexes are mutually dependent and have to support each other. She's throwing her full support behind the day and has persuaded, with the PM's backing, a lot of influential women to attend and speak in support of men's issues. I asked Warwick if he could get a list of high-profile female attendees, I don't know how far he got.'

'Came through ten minutes ago.' Warwick opened up a tab on his laptop. 'Brabin herself, obviously, and most of the other female cabinet ministers are planning to pop in. The commissioner will be there for some of the day. Prince Charles will open it, but Camilla is expected to be with him and to say a few words herself. Then we've got Emma Watson, the *Harry Potter* actress – she was behind the HeForShe movement a few years ago, Laura Bates from the Everyday Sexism project, JK Rowling's hoping to come. There's even talk of Malala being there.'

'Jesus,' Joesbury said. 'How many red flags can we wave in front of these guys?'

'No one can argue with the intention,' Georgie went on. 'But we do have to ask how wise it is in the circumstances.'

'Could be seen as women trying to take over yet another male space,' Theo said. 'Or hector them on the one day that's supposed to be all about men.'

'I need to talk to the boss,' Joesbury said, knowing they probably had zero chance of persuading the home secretary to change her plans. 'Anything else?'

'There's a dinner the night before at the Guildhall,' Warwick said. 'Strictly for the big guns, something like three hundred quid a ticket, but mainly male so probably not something we have to worry about as much.'

'So, the following day?' Joesbury said. 'That's our best guess at when something happens? Anyone disagree?'

Faces around him looked troubled.

'I don't know, boss,' Archie said. 'MenMatter aren't Al Qaeda. They don't have the funds, the training or the discipline. Everything they've been doing has been low-level, amateur stuff.'

'Tell that to the women who were scarred for life in the acid attack,' Theo said. 'Or the ones stabbed to death at the massage parlour. Oh wait, you can't, they're dead.'

'They might have the funds though,' Warwick said. 'That video game could have raised a shedload. We know UNITY, if they're involved, are well resourced. Plus, all the crowdfunding initiatives to pay for the defence of the men who've been arrested.'

Archie dug his heels in. 'My point is, I don't think they're up for a full-on terrorist attack on the Queen Elizabeth II Centre. Security is always massive wherever the PM goes, and the Prince of Wales is guarded within an inch of his life.'

Georgie said, 'They're not after the PM or the Prince of Wales though, are they? They're after the home secretary, or the Duchess of Cornwall, or Malala. Imagine the embarrassment if the girl who survived the Taliban gets shot on British soil as a guest of Her Majesty's government.'

Joesbury got to his feet. 'Not going to happen,' he said. 'But that's our focus from now on. We look for anything that suggests something might be happening on 19 November. George, get on to Dan Owen at counter terrorism, Theo, talk to MI5, Arch – GCHQ.'

'What about me, guv?' Warwick said.

'Carry on being brilliant. Come on, guys. We've got three weeks before the shit really hits the fan.'

Part Three

76

November crept in like a ghost. Early mist lay damp and heavy, more than a match for the frail, pale sun. Every day the chill grew. The city turned leaden and its edges sharpened. Frost gleamed on buildings like the sweat-glow on the sick. Londoners coughed, wheezed and sneezed, and hospital admissions surged. The Thames put on its winter cloak of iron grey and became invincible: once its temperature dropped to single figures, few who entered its murky waters survived. The corpse-processing facility at Wapping police station became a little busier.

On the plus side, nothing major had happened in the twelve days since Joesbury and his team had identified International Men's Day as the most likely focus for the next attack. The microaggressions, though, had not only continued but increased. Incidents of women stalked at night were being reported all over the UK, as was cyber-flashing, with the images becoming more and more obscene. Catfishing – humiliating women on blind dates – was still rampant, despite Tinder's attempts to warn women of the risks.

Lacey was struggling in the alien surroundings that others called four-star luxury. The airy hotel room felt claustrophobic, because she was never in it alone; the windows didn't open and the river, fifty feet below, felt as far away as the moon. It was a toss-up, between her and Emma, as to who was most on edge.

Neither slept well, neither felt comfortable being outside alone and both pored over the national news and social media constantly.

Each time the phone rang Lacey expected it to be AryanBoy. His silence over the last couple of weeks was the opposite of reassuring and she knew in her bones that the threat hadn't gone away. Every morning when she woke she asked herself if this was the day when her life came tumbling around her ears.

She was seeing very little of Joesbury.

He wasn't stupid, he knew she'd been avoiding him, using Emma as the excuse to spend most of her time in the hotel. He couldn't possibly know she was trying to protect him from the inevitable fallout, and also herself a little, because losing him now might just be the hardest thing she'd ever done. He couldn't know the truth, so she had to watch him coming to his own conclusions. She was losing him, she knew, even before AryanBoy did his worst.

On the tenth of the month, nine days before the anticipated Day of Retribution, she did something she knew would really piss Joesbury off. She had a date with another man in a fancy London restaurant.

'So, am I still public enemy number one?' Fergus Lord asked, as the waiter poured champagne.

'I think that's what we're here to decide.' Lacey raised her glass. 'Cheers.'

'And what are you hoping? That I am, or that I'm not?'

That he was, of course. That during the course of the evening he'd slip up, give something away, anything that took them a step further to tracking down the incel leaders, because if she could be instrumental in that then it might help, a bit, when AryanBoy revealed everything and her world came crashing down.

'Nice place,' she said, ignoring his question. 'Judging by what little I can see of it.'

They were at a window table. In the huge pane of glass the reflections from the brightly lit room fought with the city lights outside, creating a bewildering mass of shape and colour and movement. The Millennium Wheel was a massive circle of violet while the Georgian buildings on the north bank gleamed a pale gold. By contrast, the river beneath them was huge and empty, a void at the heart of the city.

They'd been seated, at Lord's direction, so that Lacey's back was to the busy room and his face the more visible.

His eyes narrowed. 'We can swap seats. I just didn't think you'd appreciate being caught up in the inevitable social media posts that follow every time I eat out.'

He drank down most of his glass, and Lacey noticed his hand trembling. Lord wasn't quite as self-assured as he pretended, but whether it was nervousness about being on a date, or something else entirely, she had no way of knowing.

She said, 'I didn't think of that. Sorry.'

'No worries. You look great. Are you wired?'

She wasn't. She'd argued with both Joesbury and Dana that it was unnecessary. She had a fully charged-up phone and a police radio in her bag, there were plain-clothes police officers in an unmarked car directly outside the restaurant, and one other couple in the restaurant, she'd been assured, were SCD10 officers.

She was very aware, though, that she looked good, in another borrowed dress of Dana's – midnight blue with miniscule silver sparkles – and with her hair and make-up done by Emma, who turned out to be surprisingly good at both.

'No,' she said, in answer to Lord's wire question. 'But you should assume I'm on duty.'

'Again, no problem. So, ask away.'

Lacey took him at his word. 'You were at school in Eastbourne?'

'I was.' He named the school. 'Nice place. I go back some years to present prizes.'

'Your associate, Charlie Frost, was there too?'

'Yep. A couple of years younger than me. We got to know each other in the drama club.'

'I saw a photograph. You were playing Oberon.'

A tight smile. 'I remember. Titania looked a bit like you. I fancied her rotten.'

And this was why she hadn't wanted Joesbury and his cohorts listening in. She'd known she'd have to flirt, and that wasn't something Joesbury needed to hear.

'Was Charlie in the play too?'

Lord pulled a thinking-about-it face. 'Probably. Maybe one of the artisans – Peter Quince, Nick Bottom. The main parts went to the older kids.'

'I thought I recognised Jack Brine as Puck.'

'Who?'

She repeated the name.

'Rings a bell.' Lord pulled another face. 'Yeah, there could have been a Jack. Small guy, thin, good gymnast, one of the reasons they cast him as Puck. Why the interest?'

She reminded herself that Lord was an actor, and a good one at that.

'Are you in touch?'

'Haven't thought about him in years. Why? What's he up to?'

'He's a website designer, lives in Shepherd's Bush. I met him on a train a few weeks ago.'

'Small world.'

'Possibly. Do you remember an Adam Ryan?'

Leaning back, he made a *give-me-a-break* face. 'Couldn't the school help you out? It was some time ago.'

'Our warrant request is being processed. Anything you remember will speed things up.'

Their warrant request had been denied. And Georgie had
made no further progress in trying to identify the four incel leaders from their online personas.

Lord said, 'No Adam Ryan in my year that I can remember. He
could have been one of the younger guys.'

Lacey inclined her head. Fergus Lord, she'd already decided,
was not – could not be – the boy on the cliff from twelve years
ago, the man now going by the name of AryanBoy. Even allowing
for a teenager to grow several inches, in itself possible, the boy
she'd met had dark hair whereas Lord's was obviously a natural
red. The plump lips were similar but the face shape wasn't right.
Lord's seemed longer, thinner, and his nose didn't have the slight
hook she was certain she'd seen that night.

Besides, Joesbury's team had already concluded that Lord could
not be their prime suspect, based on his known movements when
AryanBoy had been online. Spending time alone with him, she
had to agree. Fergus Lord was good-looking, successful, albeit
that his acting career had stalled; he had no difficulty attracting
women. In the short time they'd been in the restaurant she'd
spotted several sidelong glances from women at nearby tables.

'I've been doing some research of my own,' Lord said. 'You
rescued the baby from the river.'

'Right place at the right time.' Lacey gave her standard answer.
'And I know the Thames. I've been with the marine unit for over
a year.'

'And you have your own canoe. Does that mean you live on the
water?'

'You'll forgive me if I don't answer that. Until I know you're
not a terrorist.' She smiled, to take the sting away.

He said, 'Every message I've put out has deplored violence.'

'The membership of your party stands at a hundred thousand. People think that's remarkable, given the short time you've been up and running.'

'We struck a chord. And we have female members as well as male.'

'You've raised over a million pounds in membership fees alone. Is that paying for the champagne?'

Now she'd annoyed him. Leaning back in his chair he said, 'Do you have any idea how much it costs to run an election campaign?'

For a second, she thought about appeasing him, and decided she was done being nice to win men's approval. She said, 'Oh, drop the attitude, Lord. Do you think I'm here because I fancy you? I want information. You know that.'

His eyes remained narrow, his shoulders stiff. 'I don't like being accused of embezzling.'

'Then I apologise. But what happens if you change your mind and pull out? You are the party, it collapses without you. That's a lot of money looking for a home.'

'If we don't fight the local elections next May, which we've pledged to do, the money will all be redirected to men's charities. Charlie's set up the trust, it's watertight.'

Lacey said, 'Are you involved in International Men's Day on the 19 November?'

Lord said, 'I've been invited to the dinner at the Guildhall the night before. You could come with me.'

His eyes left hers at the same moment Lacey became conscious of someone standing behind her. She looked round to see a man in his forties, with long hair and a close-cropped beard.

'Sorry.' He held up both hands in a pacifying gesture. 'Don't mean to interrupt. Just wanted to say I'm a big fan. Of the politics, I mean, not the acting. Although that's good too.'

Lord gave a polite smile. 'Thank you, I appreciate it.'

The bloke held out his hand over Lacey's shoulder, as though he'd barely noticed she was there, or had noticed and didn't care. 'Well done, mate,' he said. 'Keep up the good work.'

'Happens a lot.' Lord looked smug as the bloke walked back to his own table. 'So, what about the Guildhall dinner? 18 November. Wednesday, I think. A week tomorrow. Are you free?'

Their starters arrived, giving Lacey some thinking time. More fazed than she'd have wanted to admit by the extravagance of the menu, and its prices, she'd opted for the cheapest item, a vegan dish of oyster mushrooms with pea gel and asparagus foam.

When the waiter left them, she said, 'You're asking me on a second date?'

The vegetables on her plate looked like the scum she saw on the creek most days when the tide was on its way out.

Lord picked up a fork. 'Well – you haven't said you *don't* fancy me.'

Tentatively, Lacey tried the asparagus foam. It was delicious.

77

Joesbury was at his desk, long after most of his colleagues had left for the day, conscious that a little way upriver Lacey was being wined and dined by Fergus Lord who might, if he was really unlucky, turn out to be a regular guy; and one who was above averagely good-looking and famous.

His foot caught the waste bin as he pushed his chair back from his desk; he kicked at it, sending it tumbling across the room.

He barely saw her any more, other than professionally. Apart from one weekend when Emma had gone to visit her parents in Derbyshire, she'd been taking her close protection duties seriously, reluctant to leave Emma alone at any time, especially at night.

There had been times when Joesbury had asked himself whether the Emma situation was a little too convenient for Lacey, the perfect excuse to avoid him. Increasingly, he'd sensed her withdrawing, holding back, and when it came to keeping stuff from him, God knows she had form.

He glanced at the clock, just to make sure his watch was correct.

Lacey and Lord had met at eight. Joesbury had called in a favour with David Cook and arranged for her to be transported via marine unit Targa to the Oxo Tower wharf. The same boat would pick her up at ten and take her back to her hotel at Tower Bridge. He'd argued it was for her personal safety but had a feeling everyone knew it was really about making sure Lord didn't take her home.

An hour earlier, on CCTV, he'd watched her tread carefully along the pier after the boat dropped her off, unsteady on unfamiliar heels, her hair coiled at the back of her head, and Dana's dress blowing around her slim frame. He'd felt as though he didn't know her at all.

Another hour to go.

And Lacey, yet again, was proving a distraction. What should be at the forefront of his mind right now, absorbing most of his attention, was the possibility that MenMatter had a man on the inside: a presence at Scotland Yard; someone dangerously close to the investigation, who knew and could plan for every action they took to track the terrorists down. It would explain so much, how they always managed to stay one step ahead.

Joesbury had taken, the last few days, to wandering through his department, scanning the men and women of the covert operations unit. All of them specially chosen because of their powers of dissembling; all of them more than capable of living a lie, sometimes for years on end.

It could be anyone.

And nine days to go before the Day of Retribution; always assuming they were right about it being 19 November.

'Sir?'

Joesbury looked up. 'Archie, what are you doing here?'

'Same as you, boss. Trying to get ahead. I've had a call from the Hilton at Tower Bridge. Problems.'

The Hilton was Emma and Lacey's new hotel.

'What sort of problems?'

'Minor at this stage, but the enemy have found out that's where the girls are.'

'How the fuck?'

'AryanBoy announced it on the Rage site a couple of hours ago,' he said. 'The Hilton reception have had five blokes asking for either Emma Boston or Lacey Flint in person this evening, and a few other phone calls. They know not to put them through, and they got straight on to Southwark who sent another car round. We have to move them again.'

This was all he needed. 'Have you spoken to Emma?'

Archie nodded. 'She says she's OK but I'm not sure she is.'

Joesbury sighed. 'Lacey says she's being attacked by her own side now. Other journalists saying she's acting irresponsibly, inflaming the situation. She's facing regular calls for her to be cancelled.'

'Yeah, I think that's what's really got to her, that people she knows have turned on her. And there's talk of another of those websites being set up, you know, like the one for the female MPs, only this time for high-profile journalists. Emma's name is going to be at the top, along with the likes of Laura Kuenssberg, Susanna Reid and Emily Maitlis.'

An alert sounded on both Joesbury's and Archie's phones at the same instant. Both looked down.

'Holy fuck,' Archie said, while Joesbury was still trying to absorb the short text message. The words were simple enough, and not many of them, but there'd been a mistake, there had to have been. This couldn't be right.

'Sir,' Archie said. 'What the hell do we do now?'

78

Helen was in the kitchen, intent on her laptop. 'It's up again.' She held her face up to Dana for a kiss; she tasted of red wine and dark chocolate.

'What is?' Dana took her wife's empty glass over to the sink. 'Ini OK?'

'Decided he hates his bath, screamed all the way through it and took nearly an hour to settle. I haven't finished with that.' She got up, took the glass from Dana and refilled it.

'Did you take his temperature?'

'Bang on normal. No sign of teeth coming through, his nappies are no more disgusting than usual and he hasn't made a sound other than a gentle snore for two hours. Dinner's by the microwave.'

'Thanks. And what's up again?'

'That bloody website.'

Leaning over Helen, Dana scrolled up to see the website's title: *No Girls in Government*. Beneath a paragraph explaining why women were unsuited to leadership and representative roles, the site became a register of female MPs, each entry accompanied by an unflattering photograph. The first was of the member for one of the North-Eastern constituencies, an overweight woman, slumped on the green bench; a second showed an elected member stumbling out of a black cab; the face of a third yelled something across the House of Commons.

Next to the photographs were the listings: movements of every female member of parliament from the home secretary down: constituency meetings, surgeries, dinners, even local fetes, along with information on how to get to the place in question, vulnerable points in security and ideas for how the MPs' working lives could be disrupted. Some of the entries gave the names and ages of the women's children, with side notes on how threatening a woman's kids would totally freak her out.

The intention had been plain from the outset: to facilitate intimidatory attacks on women in the public eye. As most back-bench MPs couldn't dream of cabinet-minister-style security, they'd become sitting ducks. Constituency offices had been spray-painted, car windscreens broken and tyres slashed. One liberal democrat MP in her late fifties had had ink thrown over her, another had been pushed to the ground during a school visit.

'I texted Mark,' Helen said. 'He was already on it. It won't stay up long but before it comes down it will have been copied a thousand times.'

'And hard-working women all over the country will be re-arranging their schedules again,' Dana said. 'The honourable member for Solihull resigned today.'

Helen said. 'Another one?'

A Welsh MP had stepped down the previous week, citing unacceptable stress. Two more were taking sick leave for the same reason.

'Three constituencies are considering replacing their female MPs with men until the situation calms down,' Dana told Helen.

Her partner pulled a surprised face. 'Can they do that?'

'A constituency can replace a sitting MP by majority vote,' Dana told her. 'And it's quite possible local party members will vote to do so if they believe their MP is in danger. The trouble is, once these women lose their seats they may never get them back. Men-only parliaments will become the new normal.'

Climbing the stairs, Dana realised she'd been fighting a low-level depression all day, probably for several days. The new normal was already upon them. She couldn't remember the last time she'd seen a woman out on her own after dark. For a while, women had banded together on the streets, assuming safety in numbers, but the opposite had been proven. The girl gangs had become targets in themselves, set upon by male counterparts. Young women had been beaten up and sexually abused for the crime of being out of their homes at night.

Inigo was sleeping peacefully, snuffling, arms flung above his head. Reaching down, she teased a curl away from his forehead. It sprang back immediately.

'I'm so glad you're not a girl,' she whispered.

Downstairs, Helen had warmed up the food, a veggie lasagne that Dana had cooked and frozen herself and poured her a glass of wine.

'We had a briefing at Scotland Yard,' Dana said, when she'd swallowed several mouthfuls and her hunger had vanished. From now on, she'd be eating only to keep Helen off her back, and because she knew it was the right thing to do. 'Mark's team have finished their report on Fergus Lord, Jack Brine and Charlie Frost.'

'Anything?' Helen asked, not hopefully.

'Nothing good,' Dana replied. 'None of them are AryanBoy.'

'Are they sure?'

'As they can be. They have several dates and times when they know for a fact that AryanBoy was online or on the phone to someone like Emma. All three suspects have alibis for at least some of those times.'

'Any got alibis for all of them?'

Dana thought back for a moment. 'No,' she said. 'But they don't need to. If Lord, for example, can prove he absolutely could not have made a phone call that Mark's team have on record, then he cannot be AryanBoy. Even if he was theoretically available on another occasion.'

'Guess not. What about the other characters? What are they called again?'

'MadHatter, Joker and BlackPill88. Nothing to link Fergus Lord with any of them. And all four have been active online tonight, while we know Lord is wining and dining Lacey in the Oxo Tower.'

'To be a fly on that wall,' Helen said.

'Plus, of the four of them, only AryanBoy has actually committed a serious criminal offence,' Dana went on. 'Only AryanBoy has claimed responsibility for the movement, only AryanBoy has threatened Emma. Only he helped Jason Hancock plan the attack on the massage parlour. Even if we do link the other identities with actual people, there's not much we can charge them with.'

At that moment, an alert sounded on Dana's phone. Glancing at the screen, she said. 'It's Mark.'

'Christ, what now?'

Dana opened the text. 'Oh no,' she said. 'Oh, God no.'

79

Do I fancy Fergus Lord? Lacey asked herself, as their main course was cleared away and she'd said thank you, while it all looked lovely, she really couldn't manage a pudding. Lord, who'd avoided carbs the entire meal, nodded his agreement and ordered coffee for them both.

There was something compelling about Lord, she had to admit; and a boyfriend who wasn't a senior police officer would be a whole lot less complicated. If it turned out he really did have nothing to do with the MenMatter movement, would she?

He'd been fun company, once he'd answered all the questions she'd come primed with and they'd moved on from politics. He didn't hold back when it came to sharing showbiz gossip and he had a self-effacing manner that wasn't without its appeal.

From across the city came the sound of Big Ben striking the hour and below them, at the wharf, her carriage home would be waiting. She was, she realised, a tiny bit disappointed.

And fair play, he was hot.

'Anything to do with you?' he said, pulling her out of the momentary daydream. His eyes were fixed on something over her shoulder, towards the restaurant's entrance.

Lacey looked up at the reflection in the window to see a uniformed police officer had taken up position to one side of the door. She sighed. Weren't SCD10 supposed to be masters of subtlety? Taking her home along the river was one thing; sending uniform to escort her out another entirely.

And wasn't that Archie Leech, one of Joesbury's young factotums, standing by the reception desk, tucking his wallet away in his jacket pocket? Then another figure appeared in the dark glass. Joesbury was walking towards her, watched – a bit nervously – by the maitre d'.

OK, this was going too far.

Joesbury came right up to their table.

'Mr Lord,' he said. 'I hope you've had a pleasant evening. Your bill has been paid. And now I need you to accompany my associate to Scotland Yard. We have a few questions.'

Lord dropped his eyes from Joesbury to Lacey. 'Seriously? Was this the plan all along?'

It was a good question.

'I'm perfectly serious,' Joesbury replied. 'But for what it's worth, Lacey is as surprised as you. Now, you can come with us, quietly and peacefully, or I can arrest you.'

As Archie joined them, hovering a foot behind Joesbury, Lord sneered. 'On what grounds?'

'Terrorism offences. I'll do it loudly and forcefully. I might even throw in some broken glass and overturned furniture. And that won't be a good look for an aspiring politician.'

'He means it, Gus,' Lacey said, no longer able to meet Lord's eyes. 'He'll do it.'

Joesbury was ostentatiously looking at his watch. 'I'm giving you five seconds to be on your feet, Gus,' he said. 'And then I start shouting.'

'What the hell was that about?' Lacey demanded, minutes later, when she and Joesbury stepped outside the building. Archie and Fergus Lord were already climbing into a waiting police car.

Sensibly, Lord had opted not to be arrested, but the look on his face as he'd walked away from the table would stay with her for a long time.

Joesbury was looking everywhere – down the road, across the river, to the top of the building they'd just left – everywhere but at her. 'On the boat,' he said, taking hold of her arm and pulling her forward. 'Now.'

The marine unit Targa was moored at the end of the pier.

Lacey went along with him for three steps and that felt like enough. 'No, this is ridiculous. You're not my boss – in any sense of the word – and you don't get to push me around like this.'

Still, he wouldn't look at her. He seemed to be scanning the length of Blackfriars Bridge now. 'This is an active operation, so I am your boss. Now will you get moving. I'll explain on the boat.'

For the first time, Lacey noticed the other police car, a few yards down the street. And then a third. A constable had taken up position at the wharf end now, facing outwards, as though to prevent anyone following them. This really was overkill.

Or something else. Picking up, at last, on Joesbury's tension, she turned and walked quickly along the pier towards the boat.

'Lacey!' The Targa skipper was Fred Wilson, Joesbury's uncle. 'Quick as you can.'

A crew member – Gemma – handed her a lifejacket, then released the mooring line as she and Joesbury climbed aboard. The boat drifted away from the pier.

'Below,' Joesbury snapped. 'Everyone below.'

In the cabin Fred took the helm, steering them at speed towards the centre of the river. Lacey sank onto one of the bench seats.

'What?' she said. 'What's happened?'

Emma? Dana or Helen? Even Toc – oh God, not Toc.

'Alison Brabin,' Joesbury said, before adding, 'the home secretary', as though she might have forgotten who Brabin was. 'She was shot at a constituency meeting in Dagenham this evening. We've just had an update. She died in theatre.'

Emma had the TV on, was watching an alternative news programme on her laptop, and peering every few seconds at her phone. She gave Lacey the briefest of glances. 'Did you hear about the home secretary?'

The news of Brabin's death hadn't been made public, and Lacey couldn't bring herself to be the one to share the news.

'Only what I could find on my phone. What's the latest?'

'She's in surgery. Critical injuries. She's in her early forties, Lace. Two young kids. Nice woman, too. I met her a couple of times. Not that it would be OK if she were sixty-five and a miserable old cow.'

Two young kids, who sometime in the next few hours, would learn they no longer had a mother.

She said, 'Do you know what happened?'

Joesbury would have known, but she hadn't asked. She hadn't wanted to talk once she'd heard. It was enough, surely, to know one innocent woman had died that night, and that Joesbury had been genuinely afraid for Lacey's own safety. If Lord had had anything to do with this, if – God forbid – the two of them having dinner was some sort of distraction, they could lock him up and throw away the key for all she cared.

'She was addressing a local meeting in the town hall,' Emma told her. 'As she started to speak there was a kerfuffle outside. The security staff, and one uniformed police officer went to investigate, leaving the field clear for the perp who shot her from the public gallery with his dad's shotgun. He's in custody, of course, but the damage is done.'

Sitting on the bed, Lacey pulled off her shoes. 'We're checking out of here in the morning.'

Emma looked surprised. 'We are? Where are we going?'

On the journey back across the river, Joesbury had advised against telling Emma that their whereabouts had been discovered. 'No point freaking her out until we need to,' he'd said.

'I may stay with Dana and Helen for a few days. They're both going to be busy and they need some help minding the baby. Maybe I'll get some time with Mark, although he has a lot on too. You're going home to your parents.'

Emma did a double take. 'I'm what?'

Lacey said, 'We know something is going to happen in the next couple of weeks and you're too high profile. You're an obvious target.'

'So are you.'

'Handling this shit is my job. It's not yours.'

Emma closed her laptop. 'No, writing about it is mine. I can't do that if I'm not here.'

'You know you can.'

'I'm going to the conference at the QEII Centre.'

'You're absolutely not. Don't glare at me, Emma, this came from the commissioner not from me. She wants you out of the city. And she's right. It's not safe for any of us any more.'

80

'We need to make this quick,' the commissioner said the next day. 'I'm due at the cenotaph in fifteen.'

It was Remembrance Day; anyone who might be seen in public was sombrely dressed in black. The commissioner was in full uniform.

The others were looking at Joesbury; for some reason he'd been deputised to speak for all of them.

'Ma'am, after last night, we think you should reconsider,' he said. 'You're one of the most high-profile women in London. We can't risk anything happening to you too.'

The commissioner's face blanched.

He should have told her, should have confided his fears that it was worse than any of them knew, that the enemy was among them. Hell, could even be in the room with them. He'd been a fool to think he could handle it himself.

Too late now. In fifteen minutes the head of the Met had to go out into the street, and the men who wanted her removed from her post, maybe even dead like Alison Brabin, might know exactly where she would be standing, and what form her protection would take.

If anything happened to the commissioner, it would be on him.

'Tough,' she said, as he'd known she would. 'Now, talk to me someone. The bloke we arrested last night. Lloyd Massey, is that his name? Can we link him to any of our four suspects?'

No one replied. She looked from one face to the other. 'Come on, someone tell me we've got AryanBoy. MadHatter at the very least.'

'Nothing to connect Massey with the leaders of MenMatter,' Dan Owen from counter terrorism said. 'We'll keep looking but there's no sign, at this stage, of anything comparable to the trail we found between Jason Hancock and AryanBoy prior to the attack on the massage parlour. If you want my guess, I don't think this was centrally planned. I think our shooter last night was a lone wolf.'

'A lad with serious mental health problems and access to his dad's shotgun,' Joesbury said. Having spent the night combing through Lloyd Massey's online history, he had to agree with Owen.

'The prime minister called me first thing,' the commissioner said. 'There'll be a vigil for Alison Brabin in the Abbey tonight at six. We need to be there. Everyone who's free.' She looked around. 'OK, I've got ten minutes. What else?'

'Fergus Lord will be released without charge this morning,' Joesbury told her. He and others had been speaking to the actor/politician throughout the night and had come up with nothing. Lord was still insisting he had nothing to do with MenMatter and they had no proof at all that he was lying.

'The PM wants to go ahead with the International Men's Day events,' the commissioner said. 'So where are we with that? Come on, people. Dan, talk to me.'

Dan Owen was on Joesbury's right hand. 'We're not expecting much trouble at the Guildhall,' he said. 'The guest list is high profile, but predominantly male.'

Joesbury allowed his eyes to meet those of Dana sitting opposite; she and Helen were both due to attend the Guildhall dinner, Dana in a work capacity, Helen as a senior officer of Interpol.

'The tables are sponsored by companies who invite guests they want to impress,' Owen said. 'The event's categorised priority one, David Cook's line access team will be doing a sweep a few hours before it all kicks off, and we'll set up a cordon a half mile from the entrance, with only authorised vehicles allowed through. The risk assessment report's on your desk, ma'am.'

The commissioner nodded her thanks. 'So, the following day's the one we need to worry about?' she said. 'The conference at the QEII Centre?'

'Less easily contained,' Owen agreed. 'We've spoken with all the high-profile guests, and none of them are prepared to pull out. We can make sure all boxes are ticked, but with that number of people, it's always going to be risky.'

The commissioner looked at Joesbury. 'Mark?'

'No let-up in the chatter,' Joesbury said. 'A lot of outrage about the women attendees. How dare women muscle in on our one day, etcetera. There are calls for blokes to be on the street, picketing, keeping the foids out. Usual bollocks, but it's got some traction. We can expect a substantial presence, and the potential for things to kick off.'

The door opened and the commissioner's PA poked her head into the room. 'Commissioner, your car's at the door.'

Joesbury couldn't help himself. 'Ma'am, are you sure?'

For a second, maybe two, the commissioner's mask slipped. Her face clenched and reddened. Tears sprang into her eyes and then she seemed to lose focus. As she swayed on her feet, Joesbury took a step towards her. She held up a hand to stop him, but the look she gave him would have done that anyway. He'd never seen such anger in a woman's face before.

'I liked Alison Brabin,' she said, before turning her back on them all and walking out.

81

The Black Friar, a stone's throw from the river on the north bank, had long been one of Joesbury's favourite pubs. Built on the site of an old monastery, the weird flat-iron shape with its art deco signage was appealingly incongruous with its surroundings.

Opting for the obvious ecclesiastical theme, the interior decorators had toyed with the idea of over-the-top and thought sod it, let's go for completely absurd. There was something almost Disneyesque about the arched ceilings, sweeping mosaics and endless stained glass. Monks were everywhere: glaring out from alcoves, cavorting across the ceiling, carved into smoke-stained oak.

At nearly nine o'clock in the evening on a Thursday, most of the city folk had gone home.

'Just in time, boss,' Warwick announced, as Joesbury joined his team in the dining room. 'Food's about to come.'

They'd got the drinks in too. Joesbury sank two inches of his pint before speaking. 'Nice work folks.'

'Wait till you see what George's got for you,' Warwick said, without smiling.

The guys were in an odd mood, he thought. Excited, but anxious too. The news wasn't all good. 'I'm listening,' he said.

Georgie was balancing her laptop on the few inches of table that remained clear. 'Sir, you'll remember the psychological profiles I created for each of the four main suspects?'

'AryanBoy's the classicist, Joker hates the world, MadHatter takes nothing seriously and BlackPill88 is on the verge of killing himself.'

'Nicely summarised. Well, I've been working on them since, trying to spot anything distinctive like BlackPill's dyslexia that we can use to track them down in real life.'

The food arrived, forcing the group to make small talk. Knowing the boss well, the team had ordered him steak pie and chips.

'So, a couple of things,' Georgie went on, when they were alone again. 'First, just about everything I found only seemed to confirm what we knew already. But then it occurred to me in the middle of the night.'

'Stay with it, boss, she'll get there in the end,' Archie said.

Joesbury told himself to be patient.

Georgie said, 'What if these personalities aren't real?'

He thought about it. 'You mean, what if you've seen stuff that isn't there?'

'No, it's absolutely there. But what if we're thinking what they want us to think – looking for a suicidal depressive and a classically trained scholar and a raving lunatic, only because that's what we've been led to look for. What if we've been played?'

He was too tired for this. 'I'm not sure I'm following.'

'Right, so, I made a list of the Latin words and phrases that AryanBoy has used since he first came to our attention. *Carpe diem* appears four times, *bona fide* three times, *ergo* at least six that I could find. We've also got *de facto* a couple of times, *verbatim* at least twice. Then, I googled *Common Latin Words and Phrases* and guess what, there's a website that lists all the words that Aryan-Boy uses.'

Joesbury put down his fork.

'So, then I looked at his classical references. Most of them are from Homer, a couple from the *Aeneid* and one from Aeschylus's

Oresteia. All of them appear on the first page of a Goodread's search for quotes from those respective texts. AryanBoy may not be a classicist at all. It could be a smokescreen.'

'Everything all right for you?' The waitress had arrived back at their table. Warwick smiled and thanked her, and she left them alone again.

'So, then I looked at the others,' Georgie went on. 'And once I knew what I was looking for, it was obvious. On Joker's posts I found five lines that are direct quotes from the *Joker* film.' She glanced down at the laptop. 'For instance, *Is it just me or is it getting crazier out there?* And, *You don't listen, do you?* This guy has created a persona based on the film character.'

'Same with the other two,' Archie jumped in. 'MadHatter is modelling himself on the character from *Alice in Wonderland*, talking bollocks, cracking jokes. BlackPill talks non-stop about depression and loneliness and suicide. Only, all four of them do it a bit too much. Once you know what you're looking for you can't not see it.'

Joesbury said, 'Why? Why create elaborate virtual personalities that no one other than a genius like George would spot?'

'Because they knew a genius like George would spot it,' Warwick said.

Archie said, 'They knew George herself would spot it. Face it, boss, they've been on to us this whole time.'

'They've got a man on the inside,' Warwick dropped his voice. 'Someone close.'

Silence fell. Joesbury kept his eyes fixed on his barely touched plate.

'You already knew that, didn't you?' Archie said, eventually.

Joesbury let his head rise and fall.

'Does anyone else know?' Theo asked.

Joesbury shook his head.

'You've been hoping he'll give himself away,' Archie offered. 'Once word gets round, we've lost our chance to spot him.'

'Exactly. For the record, I still have no idea who he is. This guy is good.'

Several more seconds went by.

Theo said, 'So, BlackPill's dyslexia, that led us to conclude he's Jack Brine, is entirely fake? Brine is no more likely to be BlackPill than I am.'

'No, the dyslexia is real,' Georgie said. 'He's tried to cover it up with some bad spelling thrown in, but some of the things he does aren't really common knowledge. For example, mixing up the letter t with the letters ed, so that *looked* is spelled *l o o k t*. Both BlackPill and Jack Brine do that. I think he's genuinely dyslexic.'

Joesbury gave up with his food. He wasn't hungry any more.

'Cheer up, there's more,' Archie told him. 'Go on George.'

'It was actually the word *looked* or *lookt* that did it,' Georgie went on. 'Because I spotted exactly that on a post that appeared last night. At two o'clock in the morning to be exact.'

She gave a nervous glance at Warwick then Archie.

'A post by AryanBoy,' she went on, turning the laptop so that Theo and Joesbury could see a screenshot of the Rage site. There it was. AryanBoy, posting about the imminent Day of Retribution, had misspelled the word *looked,* using a t instead of e and d.

'So, is AryanBoy dyslexic too?' Theo asked.

'He can't be. I went back through all his posts that we have on record. I found a few mistakes and spelling errors but not nearly enough. And, when they do appear, they're clustered in the same posts. So, I found a post with three errors, including the phrase *should of* instead of *should have* and another with two mistakes, then one with three. Other posts, including some of the long diatribes he does, are perfect.'

Suddenly, he saw what she was driving at.

'BlackPill occasionally posts as AryanBoy?' Joesbury said.

'Well done, boss, quicker than Warwick and me,' Archie said.

'So, then I thought, if BlackPill can do it, maybe the other two can as well,' Georgie went on. 'Maybe they're all four sharing their internet handles. So, I looked at words and phrases that are commonly used by the other two and I made a list. Then I checked them against AryanBoy's posts.'

'And?'

Georgie nodded her head. 'Definitely. Once you know what you're looking for it's obvious. It could be another reason why they created quite elaborate and distinctive personalities, to make it easier to slip from one role to another.'

'Why?' Theo asked. 'Why would they bother?'

'They're covering for each other,' Archie said.

'We've ruled Fergus Lord out of this because he has cast iron alibis for times when we knew AryanBoy was posting,' Joesbury said. 'But if one of the other three was posting in his name, Lord could be AryanBoy after all.'

'And you let him take your girlfriend out to dinner,' Archie quipped. 'But you haven't heard the best bit yet. Come on, George, big finish.'

'I found traits belonging to Joker, MadHatter and BlackPill in AryanBoy's posts, but nothing the other way,' Georgie said. 'No Latin phrases or classical references in any of their posts. They might be posting for him, but he isn't returning the favour. Also, they're not posting for each other. MadHatter doesn't occasionally assume Joker's persona, Joker doesn't sometimes become BlackPill. It's just the three of them, sometimes posting as AryanBoy.'

Joesbury shook his head. 'I'm going to disappoint you. I'm not seeing it.'

'We've been looking for four men,' Theo explained. 'But there's only three of them. AryanBoy doesn't exist offline. He's a fictional construct of the other three.'

'We've been chasing a ghost,' Archie added. 'No wonder he keeps eluding us.'

It was possible, Joesbury realised, to feel both exhausted and exhilarated at the same time.

'What are you going to do?' Theo asked.

'Tomorrow morning I'm going to use emergency powers to have Fergus Lord, Charlie Frost and Jack Brine arrested and their devices seized,' Joesbury said. 'And Georgie, bloody good work.'

82

They were getting too close. Damn Georgie with her endless poring over minutiae. It would sting if it were a foid, an ugly one at that, who tripped them up at the last hurdle. They were a week away. Seven frigging days.

And damn Jack for his bloody carelessness. He'd been warned so many times. Check everything, read through posts several times before sending; he'd even been told to read backwards, a classic proofreader's trick.

The one good thing, the only good thing, was that the idiots had put two and two together and made three. Because several people shared AryanBoy's online identity, because he occasionally lent his personality to others, they'd assumed he wasn't real.

He was real, all right, they'd find that out soon enough.

Seven more days, though. Time wasn't on his side. And Joesbury might not be the sharpest knife in the box, but he wasn't stupid.

Well, it was lucky he'd planned for exactly this scenario.

Time to kill two birds with one stone. Time to get Lacey Flint's boyfriend out of the picture.

83

This should be happiness: her boat tipping on the incoming tide, the man she loved a warm presence beside her, his son in the stern cabin. The three of them, safe from the world, complete.

The tide was at its strongest rush, a couple of hours off full; that would make it between midnight and two o'clock in the morning. Lacey's eyes opened to see blackness through the half-open bow hatch.

This was the very opposite of happiness; this was dread. Joesbury and the others thought AryanBoy wasn't real. How had he described him – a fictional construct of the other three? He couldn't be more wrong. AryanBoy was entirely real, he was full of rage, and – sooner or later – he was coming for her. When Joesbury knew what she'd held back from him, he'd never forgive her.

Fergus Lord, meanwhile, was back in the frame as prime suspect. And now she was questioning her own conviction that he couldn't be the boy from the clifftop. Men changed more than women in the years from late teens to late twenties. Fergus Lord – AryanBoy? Was it possible?

Joesbury stirred, and cool air met Lacey's skin as he left the bunk. She watched him fumble around for his clothes and ease open the cabin door. He trod lightly across the main saloon and opened the hatch. She heard another voice. A woman.

Lacey pushed back the duvet and found jogging pants and a sweatshirt. The main cabin was full of fresh, cold air and the sounds of the night. Joesbury was on deck.

From halfway up the cabin steps Lacey could make out a slim shadow on the next boat, dark hair, the gleam of eyes. A torch.

Lacey said, 'Mark?'

He glanced back, and then stretched out a hand to help the woman climb across. The torch beam came first, then two sneakered feet. His body blocking that of their visitor from view, Joesbury kept hold of the woman's hand as he led her down from the side deck into the cockpit. Lacey, finally, could see who their late-night visitor was: Georgie, who worked with Joesbury at Scotland Yard.

When all three were in the cabin Joesbury closed the hatch.

'I'm so sorry,' Georgie began, her eyes flitting between the two of them. 'I wouldn't be here if it wasn't important.'

'We know,' Joesbury said. 'Have a seat.'

Georgie squeezed onto one of the bench seats. Lacey sat opposite. Joesbury leaned back against the cabin steps and said, 'You haven't been home?'

Georgie shook her head. 'After we said goodbye at the pub . . .' she glanced anxiously at Lacey. 'Not just Mr Joesbury and me, the whole team were there, all five of—'

Joesbury cut her off. 'She knows that, George. God knows I haven't gone through the last two years to start playing around now.'

He took a moment then, to glance at Lacey, to let the corner of his mouth twitch, his right eye to flicker in a wink.

Georgie said, 'Sorry, I know. Well, after we all said goodbye, I got myself in a bit of a state about what I'd told you. I was thinking, what if I'm wrong, the shit's really going to hit the fan, sorry about the language, and it could be hugely embarrassing for all of us, the Metropolitan Police I mean, not just our people, so I thought I'd better double check.'

'You went back to the Yard?'

Looking miserable, Georgie nodded.

'And were you wrong?'

Georgie shook her head. 'Sir, I really wish I was. But everything I told you about the way the three men behave online is right.'

Joesbury didn't move; he invariably froze when he was thinking hard.

Lacey took over. 'So, where's the problem?'

When Georgie didn't reply Lacey got to her feet. 'You want to talk confidentially? I'll be in the cabin.' She forced a smile, knowing that something had crept into the boat interior with their night-time visitor. Something dark. Things had changed.

'Stay,' Joesbury ordered her, like she was a dog. He'd sensed it too, possibly faster than she had. What Georgie was about to tell them would change everything. 'George, spit it out. I'm not keeping anything from Lacey.'

'I had to go onto the Rage website,' Georgie began. 'There was a lot of activity a few days ago and I wanted to check it again. The thing is . . .'

Joesbury's face was like stone. 'What?'

'What you need to understand, sir, is that when I look at the posts these people are making, I'm doing it differently. I'm examining every letter, every punctuation mark, because everything could be relevant. It's like, I'm deliberately not seeing the woods because I need to focus on the trees. I think, eventually, someone else might have seen what I saw tonight, but maybe not. Maybe it would never have been picked up.'

'What did you see?'

'A new edit on one of the posts, the tiniest one imaginable, left a few days ago. Literally just a smiley face at the end of the comment, in among dozens of other comments and replies, and replies to the replies. You know how these threads can go.'

'I do,' Joesbury said.

'Do you mean an edit done by AryanBoy?' Lacey asked, her heart hammering.

Georgie almost seemed glad to look at someone other than Joesbury. 'Yes, and I didn't spot it before tonight, although it's been there for a couple of days. Even when I'd seen it, I almost passed over it, because it's nothing, but—'

'It's not in your nature to let something go,' Joesbury said.

Georgie nodded, unhappily. 'No, so I did what I always do. I checked the IP address, just to see if he'd slipped up, if he'd posted from another place and guess what – he had.'

Joesbury sighed. 'From the look on your face, George, I'm guessing this isn't the breakthrough we've all been hoping for?'

She shook her head. 'I thought it was at first. I almost rang you and the others. But something made me check. You see, the IP address looked a bit familiar. I look at so many of the things I wasn't certain, and they're all just strings of numbers, but something was niggling. And then I realised. It's a Scotland Yard address.'

On the instant, Lacey felt her whole body tensing. This was massive. If AryanBoy had posted from a Yard computer that meant only one thing. They'd found him and their mole at the same time; AryanBoy himself was their mole! Lacey had learned enough about IP addresses the past weeks to know that every computer had its own unique string of numbers. Scotland Yard would have a block of common numbers, with maybe the last three digits differing for each device. Georgie would have been able to identify the actual machine that AryanBoy had used. So why had Joesbury become so very still?

'Go on,' he told Georgie. 'Who posted it? I know you've track-ed it down.'

Georgie looked on the verge of tears. 'Sir,' she said. 'You did.'

Lacey felt the cabin slipping away from her. Joesbury hadn't moved a muscle.

'Obviously I was shocked,' Georgie went on. 'I thought I must have made a mistake, but I checked and checked and I hadn't. So, I looked back further.'

'And what?' Lacey asked.

Georgie said, 'I found three more interactions in AryanBoy's name, going back over two months, made from Mr Joesbury's computer. Three interactions in among hundreds, all of them edits to previous comments, or tiny little emojis, all of them posted days after the original post went up. All during the day, at times you were in or around the office, sir. I checked in your online diary. According to the evidence . . .'

'I'm AryanBoy,' Joesbury finished for her. Turning from them both, he leaned forward over the steps, dropping his head onto his arms.

'It was brave of you to come here,' Lacey said, feeling as though she were speaking through a mouthful of cotton wool. 'Probably not wise though. I hope you won't get in trouble.'

Georgie shrugged as she shot nervous glances at her boss. 'Obviously, it's bullshit. He's been set up.'

Of course, he had. But proving that would take time, and they were only six days from the Day of Retribution.

Joesbury pulled himself together and turned to face them both. 'You need to arrest me,' he said to Georgie. 'Lace, can you stay with Huck? Take him back to his mum's in the morning. Then go and see Dana, she'll know what to do.'

Dana wouldn't have a clue. Dana, like Joesbury, was working half blind.

Georgie had got to her feet. 'I came here to give you time, a chance to get away, to – I don't know – to sort it out.'

Silence.

'Wouldn't be the first time,' Lacey said, and as Joesbury looked back at her she knew they were both remembering him going on the run, a little over a year ago, accused of killing a police officer. He'd hidden on an abandoned dredger not far from her boat, and she'd kept his secret. They could do that again.

For a moment, she thought he was considering it, then he shook his head.

'I can't fight a cyber war in hiding,' he said. 'Shit, I'm not sure if I can fight a cyber war if I'm not. These guys can run rings round me. Come on, George, arrest me. There can't be any question you came here to do the right thing.'

A tear ran down Georgie's cheek. 'Mark Joesbury,' she began, 'I am arresting you on suspicion of . . .' she stopped. 'I can't, sir. I'm a civilian, remember? I don't have powers of arrest.'

'Mark Joesbury, you are under arrest on suspicion of terrorist activities.' Lacey's voice sounded as though she'd borrowed it from a second-rate impersonator. 'You do not have to say anything, but it may harm your defence if you do not mention when questioned something which you later rely on in court. Anything you do say may be given in evidence.'

Silence in the boat.

Lacey let her eyes fall. She said, 'Take him in, Georgie.'

'That's my girl,' Joesbury said. 'Now, and I mean this, don't do anything stupid.'

Without saying goodbye, he turned and climbed the boat steps. Georgie followed, leaving Lacey alone.

Only when she was sure they'd left the boatyard did Lacey climb on deck and let the chill air cool her down. The boat bumped and rolled on the swelling tide as she waited for misery to flood through her. AryanBoy had done this somehow, he'd done it to get at her, and there was no possible way she could see of fighting back.

This wasn't misery though, this feeling growing in the pit of her stomach, burning like an ulcer, setting her limbs ablaze. This wasn't misery, making her heartbeat race and her nerve endings tingle. Misery pulled you down, threatened to engulf you, paralyse you. It didn't fire you up, make you want to run straight at the enemy, to fight, to wreck everything in your path.

This wasn't misery; this was fury.

84

Dana said, 'When did you last have a girlfriend, Mr Brine?'

He stared at her for long seconds. 'I'm not sure I understand the question.'

Dana knew, the three other people in the interview room knew, that she didn't have nearly enough to charge Jack Brine. She could hold him for longer than usual, but with nothing further to go on than she had, what was the point? There were only so many times you could ask the same questions.

In the meantime, they were days away from the possibility of a major terrorist incident, the head of the investigation – her best friend – was under arrest; and it was Friday the thirteenth.

'And I'm not sure I can make the question any clearer. When did you last have a romantic relationship with a female? And I'll be asking for her name and contact details.'

Brine gave a perplexed look around the room. 'Is it a crime to have a girlfriend now? Are you going to charge me with enjoying female company?'

The bloke was far too cocky. 'If I charge you,' she said, 'it will be with terrorism offences. We spoke to your flatmates. They say you haven't brought a woman home in over a year. That's quite some dry spell.'

Brine spent several seconds examining his fingernails. She was on the point of pushing him for an answer when he said, 'I'm not looking for anything serious. Plenty of girls are happy to hook up on Tinder, or in clubs. That suits me. I met a nice girl on the train the other week, she asked for my number. I'm keeping my fingers crossed for that one.'

He meant Lacey. Brine was taunting them, knowing his trip to Durham checked out. He had friends in the city, former students, he visited several times a year and his being on the same train as Lacey proved nothing.

Lacey was another concern. She'd been unnaturally calm when she'd knocked on their door early that morning, before Dana had even finished feeding Inigo.

He said you'd know what to do, she'd told them.

To Jack Brine, Dana said, 'And yet your flatmates have noticed none of this rampant sexual activity.'

'Girls feel more comfortable if you go to their place. I prefer that too. I can get up and leave when I want.'

'You've posted on incel sites several times. Why would you do that if you don't consider yourself to be one of them?'

'I spend a lot of time on the internet. Sometimes I'm drawn into some odd places, get involved with chats that start out OK and somewhere down the line, take a turn. You know how it is. I'm pretty certain I've done nothing illegal though.'

He hadn't. When Jack Brine was posting as himself, he was careful.

'You have a Tor browser, I see.'

'Nothing illegal in that.'

'How often are you on the dark web?'

'Almost never. It's a shitshow. I can't be bothered trying to navigate it half the time.'

'So, why the Tor browser?'

'Security. You never know when Big Brother is going to come looking.'

'What are you trying to hide?'

He shrugged. 'OK, you got me. I'm into octopus porn.' He gave her a slow, nasty smile.

Dana felt despair creeping. If she'd conducted interviews less successful than this one, she couldn't remember them.

'Where are your other devices?'

'Don't know what you mean.'

'Your other phone, tablet, whatever you use when you're being BlackPill88.'

He looked genuinely perplexed. 'Who?'

'Do you sometimes post using the handle AryanBoy?'

'Nope.'

'Who are Joker and MadHatter?'

He shook his head. 'I'm sorry, detective, my quality filter is clogging up.'

'When did you last see Fergus Lord?'

'In real life? At school, I guess. He was a couple of years older than me.'

'Are you a member of his political party?'

'UNITY? No, I've no interest in politics.'

'And yet you've heard of it.'

'I notice what Gus does. And he's come out in support of International Men's Day, which is good for me.'

At Brine's side the duty solicitor looked a little less bored.

Dana said, 'How exactly?'

'I designed the fundraising page. If it works well, and raises a lot of cash, they're more likely to use me next year.'

'Ah yes, I had a look at that. Nice work. You've good IT skills.'

His face stiffened. 'I have computer science skills. The IT guys fix the printer.'

'I stand corrected. How much money will International Men's Day raise?'

Brine shrugged. 'Hard to know. Last year it channelled just under twelve million to around thirty charities. They're hoping for more this year.'

'So, it's not in your interests to be held in custody for the next fourteen days? If anything goes wrong with the website at this stage, it won't look good for you.'

Brine gave a heavy sigh. 'It's all up and running and tested within an inch of its life. My being here will make no difference. You can keep me as long as you like.'

'Is she doing any better than I did?' Dana asked, when she'd terminated the interview with Brine and found her team watching a live transmission of Gayle Mizon interviewing Charlie Frost.

Pete didn't bother with platitudes. 'Not sure she is, boss.'

'We've had word that Mark's been moved to Charing Cross,' Neil said. 'He'll be there for the foreseeable.'

The foreseeable meant for up to fourteen days under the terrorism act. During which time, whatever was going to happen on International Men's Day would be over.

'My plans for this Thursday?' Charlie Frost was saying on-screen. 'Off the top of my head, a few client phone calls, checking the various markets, a meeting or two. I'll probably spend the evening at Gus's place. The new party's bringing in a lot of work at the moment. Why, is anything happening?'

'This is going nowhere, boss,' Neil said. 'Their devices are all clean, all the ones we've found anyway, and they've all got alibis for some of the time when AryanBoy was active.'

'Which proves nothing if Georgie is right about them sharing that identity,' Dana said.

'We can't prove they are. If you want my pennyworth, boss, I've watched all three interviews and the only one close to cracking is Fergus Lord. He's the one we should put pressure on.'

In the interview room, Charlie Frost raised his voice, even glanced at the camera, as though he wanted those watching to take note of what he was saying.

'Seems to me,' he said, 'the solution's simple. If you think something big is going down on Thursday, keep me and Gus here until then. If we're in custody, we can't blow up the Houses of Parliament, or lead a raid on Buckingham Palace, or whatever it is you think we have planned.'

Dana said, 'Whatever they have planned has been set in motion. The three of them being out of action won't change a thing.'

'So, what do we do?'

'I think we have to let them go.'

85

The keys to Joesbury's flat still worked when Lacey tried them on Sunday evening. Lights were on inside, bright lights in the hallway, a low-level lamp in the sitting room. Furniture had been moved around; pictures removed from walls. The place didn't feel empty.

'Dana?' she called, unsure who else might have keys.

Movement in the main bedroom, then the door opened and a man Lacey didn't know appeared. White, around her age, maybe five ten, five eleven, wearing a suit, shirt and tie. A good-looking bloke, his startlingly blond hair strangely at odds with his deep blue eyes. He had a prominent nose and thick, full lips.

His head tilted, like that of a reptile sizing up its prey. 'Lacey, is that right? Lacey Flint?'

His manner did nothing to calm her unease. 'Who are you?'

'Theo Cox. I work with Mark Joesbury at Scotland Yard. Hang on a sec.'

He slid his hand into his jacket pocket. She fought the instinct to step back, but what he retrieved was nothing more than a warrant card. She approached cautiously; it was legit. He was Theo, the fourth member of the undercover cyber team.

'You're the only one I haven't met,' she said, as some of the tension drained away. 'I think we spoke on the phone, though.'

He gave a shy, lopsided smile. 'I guess we could have hoped for better circumstances. Are you moving back in?'

With Joesbury's arrest, Lacey's personal safety had slid down the list of Scotland Yard's priorities; a fact she wasn't entirely ungrateful for.

'I said I'd collect a few things for his son. And I left a hairdryer behind.'

'Have you seen the boss?' Theo asked.

'I tried. He wasn't allowed to see anyone over the weekend apart from his solicitor. You?'

Theo shook his head. 'Strictly, we're on the investigating team, we can't go anywhere near him. None of us like it, but . . .' Theo didn't go on, but he didn't have to. None of them could risk their jobs, however loyal they might feel to Joesbury.

'Why are you here?' she asked. 'Are you looking for something?'

'No, the cyber forensic team have already been in. They've taken his computer and laptop and given the place a complete going over. I'm here because we thought – the others and me – that we should tidy the place up a bit. Actually, it wasn't too bad. The search teams were pretty respectful.'

An awkward silence fell. 'I won't be long,' Lacey said, stepping towards Huck's room. She added, 'I'll let you see what I take,' to save him telling her he'd need to.

'None of us believe the boss is guilty,' he called. 'You must know that. Look, do you mind if we sit down? I feel a bit uncomfortable doing this in the corridor.'

Without a word, Lacey led the way into the living room, where the low-level lighting felt strangely intimate. She switched on the overhead lights and took a seat on the arm of one of the sofas. Theo sat opposite.

'The boss has a habit of leaving his office without logging off,' he said. 'The computer shuts down automatically after fifteen minutes but that still leaves a gap when someone could have slipped in. Over a dozen people work alongside the four of us in the outer office. And there are other offices close by. We think these supposedly AryanBoy posts have been happening when the five of us went to meetings together.'

If this was ever over she'd tear Joesbury a new one for being so bloody careless.

Theo glanced down at the carpet, frowning, as though thinking about something. Then, 'One thing I should warn you, Lacey,' he said.

'What's that?'

'We know you met Fergus Lord yesterday, not long after he was released.'

She shouldn't be remotely surprised. 'Is there a tail on me? Am I a suspect now?'

'No, it was just one of those things. You were spotted on CCTV. You're probably going to be asked about it though. Why he wanted to see you, what you talked about.'

'Actually, I contacted him. I wanted to ask him if he was OK.'

Theo's face registered surprise, even distrust; maybe seeing lack of loyalty to the boss. But Fergus Lord was one of the few leads they still had.

As it turned out, Lord had been far from OK. He'd been totally freaked out at being arrested.

Didn't make him innocent.

'I'm not convinced he's not involved,' she said.

'Neither are we, but we've got nothing on him.'

She looked him directly in the eyes. 'Maybe I can ask questions you can't.'

Theo looked nervous. 'Is that a good idea?'

She shrugged. 'I guess we'll find out.'

It was dark when Lacey got back to Deptford Creek, and raining lightly, but the early evening activity of her neighbours was strangely reassuring as she climbed down the quayside steps and made her way along the raft of boats. On the first boat she crossed, children were watching TV; nearby someone was practising the clarinet. The smell of frying onions danced out of the hatches to meet her as she made her way round the bow of her closest neighbour and onto her own yacht. She was digging in her bag for keys when her phone rang.

'Hello, Lacey,' said the distinctive Midlands accent of Aryan-Boy.

Heart thudding, she waited.

'Sorry about your boyfriend, but frankly you can do better.'

'I'm curious to know how you did it,' she asked, knowing few men could resist the opportunity to show off.

'Nothing to do with me,' came the reply. 'Guess he's a wrong 'un. Not the first time he's been in trouble from what I hear.'

'What do you want?'

'Many things. Let's start with loosening your hair. I don't like it scraped back.'

Lacey's hand flew to her head, felt the dampness of rain on her hair. She thought for a second, then climbed back up onto the side deck. The man on the phone wanted her to think he could see her.

The tide was out, leaving just the trickle of the river Ravensbourne in the bottom of the channel. It was possible to walk up Deptford Creek at low tide, the nearby educational centre even ran guided walks from time to time, but it was dangerous without the right equipment and not knowing the terrain. It was unlikely that he was in the creek.

'You won't find me,' he told her over the phone. 'I'm using binoculars with a night vision attachment.'

Even if that were true, there were relatively few places he could be. Most of the land on the opposite bank was private, difficult to access. Pulling open the main hatch Lacey swung herself down into the cabin.

No reaction from the man on the phone.

The interior of the boat was as she'd left it, nothing out of place, everything looked, felt and smelled the same. He hadn't been here.

She said, 'You have ten more seconds and I'm hanging up.'

'I hear your friends at Scotland Yard are wise to our plans on Thursday,' he said.

He meant International Men's Day, the conference at the QEII Centre. She said, 'If they are, they don't tell me.'

'I need a distraction.'

'A what?'

'Something to occupy their minds. Divide their resources. Give us a fighting chance.'

She said nothing.

He spoke again, 'Here's what you have to do, Lacey. On Thursday morning, you'll paddle that canoe of yours along the south bank to Tower Bridge and tie it up there. At eleven thirty exactly you'll show up at the Southwark nursery on Gainsford Street and collect Inigo Tulloch-Rowley. The nursery will have received an email from his mother an hour earlier authorising you to collect him. They won't give you any trouble.'

Lacey felt a dull cold creeping over her.

'You'll climb back into your canoe, with the baby – I recommend you get hold of one of those papoose things – and paddle out into the central channel. You'll stay there and wait further instructions. Make sure your phone is charged and secure.'

'You're out of your mind.'

'There's a pleasing symmetry, don't you think? This began with a baby on the river. What should have been a brilliant opening strike in our campaign was foiled by you, in your little dugout, and those two lesbians you're chummy with. They'll learn to stay in their lane when their own child is at risk. And we're sending out a very clear message to all the other uppity women who think they can take us on. Don't.'

'It's not happening. Even if I agreed, which I won't, a canoe in the central channel would be swamped in seconds, especially with the added weight of a baby. We're in late November, in case you hadn't noticed, and there's been a lot of rain. The river is very full and very fast. And if I stay close to the bank, I'll be picked up in minutes. The marine unit will send one of their RIBs out. They're less than a mile away at that point.'

She could hear her voice getting faster, more shrill. AryanBoy, by contrast, when he spoke again, was chillingly calm.

'We've checked the tide, and it will be an hour off low at that point. Someone like you should have no trouble holding a boat in the central channel. And you won't have to worry about the marine unit. They'll be hearing from us too, and they'll be told that if anyone approaches you, a sniper will blow a hole in your skull. You and the baby will both be lost.'

'What?'

'Well, that's what we'll tell them. And it could be true. There are a lot of tall buildings around there. They'll never be able to check all of them in time. You should assume it's true, to be on the safe side.'

'What on earth makes you think I'm going to agree to this?' Lacey asked, knowing exactly why he thought she would.

'Because if you don't, we'll issue a press release detailing your real identity and your close relationship to the most notorious serial killer in the last decade. You'll be finished.'

'I'll be finished if I kidnap a baby and put his life at risk.'

'No, you won't. You'll claim and we'll back you up, that you were acting under duress. At gunpoint. And you'll obviously do everything in your power to protect the baby once the two of you are on the river. We're not monsters, Lacey, we don't intend that the baby actually dies. Or that you do.'

They were monsters though; the other baby would have died if she hadn't got to her in time. Women had been killed and maimed, beaten up, raped and terrified, mainly because of this man. He was lying.

'So, what is the point?'

'Do keep up, I told you already. You're a distraction. Once the Met know they have a hostage situation, involving one of their own officers, they'll send all available resources to the river.'

'Leaving the field clear for whatever you have planned at the QEII Centre,' Lacey said.

'You'll be on the river for thirty minutes, forty at most. Then we'll give you the all-clear. You'll be fine, Lacey. Just make sure you're both well wrapped up.'

The line went dead. He was gone. And suddenly, the cabin was suffocatingly hot. She went back up top, no longer remotely afraid of who might be watching. The trembling in her fingers that had been a constant since Joesbury's arrest had gone and in its place was an icy calm.

Not once, in two years, had she understood how someone so closely related to her, so like her in so many ways, could take the life of another human being. Well, she'd got it now.

She was going nowhere. AryanBoy could do his worst and he'd learn exactly what he was dealing with. She'd go down gladly, just as long as she could take that dangerous bastard with her.

'You in there, Victoria?' she whispered to herself. 'I think I'm going to need you.'

86

'You're probably wondering why we haven't spoken to you already.'

They'd sent a commander to interview him. She was in her mid-forties, with dull brown hair and bad skin. A younger man accompanied her. Joesbury had been told his name and rank but couldn't be arsed remembering either. Without making eye contact with Joesbury, he opened a laptop and began tapping away at keys.

Joesbury said, 'I assumed you were letting me stew. Consider me stewed. Have you arrested Fergus Lord, Charlie Frost and Jack Brine yet?'

The commander nodded at her subordinate and said, 'This Fergus Lord?'

When the laptop was turned Joesbury saw a grainy, black-and-white photograph of two people in a Costa coffee bar. Fergus Lord, casually dressed, faced the camera. His companion was a woman. Joesbury recognised the pattern on the sweater, the long fair hair. Lacey.

'Taken on Saturday afternoon,' the commander said. 'Shortly after he, Mr Frost and Mr Brine were released without charge by your friends at Lewisham. A second date, from what I understand.'

Joesbury looked her straight in the eye. 'Those three men are the brains behind the MenMatter movement. They're planning an attack on the city, probably at the QEII Centre in three days' time and they have an inside man at Scotland Yard. If you find all their devices there's a chance my team can link them to the online posts of the four characters we know are driving the incel movement.' He paused, took a breath. 'You're welcome.'

The commander gave a tight smile. 'Inside man at Scotland Yard, you say? Someone who can post as, say, AryanBoy from Met computers?'

He'd walked right into that one. 'We were getting close,' he said. 'We know we're looking for three men, plus the guy on the inside. We have three names. That's why they had to stitch me up.'

She said nothing.

'I didn't make those four posts. If you dig deep enough you'll find I have alibis for the times and dates they were posted.'

'Oh, we checked that. Richard?'

The man with her – Richard – read from the screen. 'One of the posts was five minutes before you were due to host a meeting in your office, DCI Joesbury, a meeting we know took place. Another was several seconds after you sent an email to your ex-wife about picking up your son after school. So, on at least two of the four occasions, you were in your office when the posts went out. On one of them you were at your desk.'

Shit, the bastards were good.

The woman said, 'What we do find interesting is that Aryan-Boy has been uncharacteristically silent since your arrest in the early hours of Friday morning. Don't you find that interesting, Detective Chief Inspector?'

'No, I find it entirely predictable.'

She stared at him for several seconds then, possibly without realising what she was doing, began picking at a blemish on her chin. She said, 'Constable Flint's led you a bit of a dance the past couple of years, hasn't she?'

'My relationship with Lacey is nothing to do with you.'

'Well, I beg to differ. Your colleagues say your interest in her is verging on an obsession, a rather unhealthy one.'

'I'd like to know their names.'

'So, I'm guessing it wouldn't be too surprising if you developed an antagonism aimed at the female sex.'

'There are some women who could make me feel antagonistic towards their sex. Lacey isn't one of them.'

'And yet she's dumped you for an actor, not days after you were arrested.'

'If she's dumped me, she's yet to tell me. Why don't you let her visit and we'll see?'

'Dana Tulloch too? Another woman you were supposedly keen on. Must have been disappointing when she turned out to be a lesbian?'

'She didn't turn out to be a lesbian, she is a lesbian. She's also my best friend. We're godparents to each other's children. It's really not my place to teach you your job, Commander, but this line of questioning is going nowhere. I'm not an incel.'

Thin lips stretched into a tight, humourless smile. 'You're right. It's not your place. Richard, do you have that recording handy?'

'Yes, ma'am.'

'Could you play it, please?'

More tapping of the keys on Richard's laptop and then Joesbury heard his own voice.

'There's this woman. Been messing me around for months. Thing is, I know she's into me, but she – mixed signals, you know what I'm saying? – don't know whether I'm coming or going with her. I'm telling you, mate, it's doing my head in.'

The commander's eyes remained fixed on Joesbury, as the tape, edited to remove the other man's replies, continued.

'Now you see, that's where you're wrong. Take my ex-wife – please! I'm kidding. I knew where I was with her, knew what she wanted. Trouble was, she wanted me home at five o'clock every night, and that just wasn't me, do you get what I'm saying? Women, they drag you down, try to make you change. You ever been married?'

The man with the knife – Waluigi – had shaken his head at that point. But he'd been listening.

'Mate, I get where you're coming from. Most of us do, the blokes I'm talking about now. Shit, police work was so much easier before they let the bloody women in. But we have to go through the motions.'

'Richard, does that sound to you like a man who likes and respects women?'

'No ma'am, it doesn't.'

'Does it to you, DCI Joesbury?'

'I was trying to make a connection with a man who'd just murdered two women and attempted to kill several more. It worked. We carried out a successful arrest.'

No response from the commander.

'I've spent fifteen years in covert operations,' Joesbury went on, hating that he felt the need to convince her. 'I know how to assume a role.'

'Hmmn.' She looked down, then back up at him again. 'Where are your other devices?'

'My what?'

'Devices, Detective Chief Inspector: phones, laptops, iPads. We have your home and work computers, a Met-issued laptop and a smartphone, what make is it, Richard?'

'An iPhone, ma'am.'

'Yes, an iPhone. Where are the others? We know they're not at your flat, or on Constable Flint's boat, because we've searched both thoroughly.'

'And you haven't been able to link any to incel activity? What a shame. Well, sorry to deepen the disappointment but I don't have any other devices.'

'Might they be with your son, perhaps, what's his name, Richard?'

'Huckleberry, ma'am.'

'Yes, that's right, known as Huck, sweet name. Will we find them in his bedroom at home, do you think? Did you give them to him for safe-keeping?'

The bastards were going to search his ex-wife's home. 'If you scare my son, fuck it, if you so much as unnerve his mother, I will personally see to it that you go down.'

'Make a note that DCI Joesbury is threatening me, Richard.'

'Be sure to include yourself in that threat, Richard.'

Richard kept his head down.

'Richard,' the commander said. 'Could we have a look at that piece of footage you saved? I'm sure DCI Joesbury will find it interesting.'

The laptop was turned round again. This time, Joesbury saw a clip of CCTV footage of London traffic at night. He recognised the road, one not far from Parliament Square.

'The vehicle of interest should be coming into shot now,' the commander said, as Joesbury saw a white transit van drive past the camera and take a left turn along Broad Sanctuary.

'The van approached along Birdcage Walk,' the commander informed him. 'Turned right into Little Sanctuary and then left along Broad Sanctuary before heading north along Parliament Street.'

The significance wasn't lost on Joesbury. Little Sanctuary would have taken the van around the back of the QEII Centre.

'No deliveries took place at that time,' the commander went on. 'So we had to ask ourselves why the van would take such a particular route around this part of London. Especially when we found out it was the second time that night it had done exactly that loop, and that the number plates are fake.'

'They're trying to throw you off track,' Joesbury said. 'These guys are smart enough to stitch me up, they wouldn't do anything that obvious.'

'Or maybe that's what you want us to think.'

'We might be wrong about the QEII Centre and the conference,' he said. 'Is there anything happening at the Abbey that day? They could be targeting the Houses of Parliament.'

'Your team, what is it you call them, the undercover cyber squad? – I'm very impressed with them by the way – they've been picking up a lot of chatter about explosives and home-made bombs over the weekend. Can you tell us anything about that?'

Joesbury's sense of unease was growing.

'It sounds to me like MenMatter are giving a lot away about what they're planning, which is unusual for these guys. They could be trying to send you off on a wild goose chase.'

'And yet you had advance warning about the attack on Tower Bridge,' Richard chipped in. 'Which is why, you claim, that you and one of your associates – Theo Cox I think it was – were able to be on scene so quickly. And both the attacks on the massage parlour and the sports centre were trailed beforehand on social media.'

'Hours beforehand, in the case of the sports centre and the massage parlour, not days,' Joesbury countered. 'After the Tower Bridge attack they got more careful. There was talk that Lacey, Helen and Dana had been on the scene officially, as a consequence of online warnings. They weren't, it was coincidence, but it made the incels more cautious. And good to know you can think for yourself, Richard.'

Joesbury turned to the commander. 'Talk to my team. Tell them to find out how someone managed to send those messages from my computer. They'll work it out.'

The commander got to her feet. 'They're my team now, DCI Joesbury. Have a pleasant evening.'

Joesbury had been arrested before, been held in cells before; it was practically in the job description when you worked in covert operations. Never for so long though, and never without knowing that someone on the outside would pull him out at the right time. Left alone, the bravado that had sustained him during the interview drained away, leaving him feeling helpless.

The white van circling the QEII Centre felt all wrong. It was too obvious a pointer that something was going to happen there. What if it was a distraction? A sleight of hand?

And what the fuck was going on with Lacey and Fergus Lord? She'd been dismissive after the OXO Tower dinner, claiming it had been work, that Lord hadn't been particularly good company. And yet she'd seen him again, not days later. Either she'd liked him more than she'd let on or she was working the case alone. Joesbury really couldn't have said which he'd prefer.

Footsteps echoed down the corridor and stopped outside his door. Keys rattled, and the lock was turned. The custody sergeant, a bloke he'd known for years, who'd treated him well over the past couple of days, appeared.

'Visitor for you,' he said. 'You've got ten minutes.'

The sergeant backed out, leaving space for his visitor to enter the cell. It was Lacey. His brief moment of elation soon evaporated. She looked deadly serious.

'We need to talk,' she said.

87

'Let me see,' Helen instructed.

Dana turned the phone round so that the camera was directed at the full-length mirror. Downstairs she heard the music that preceded the evening TV news.

'Hmmn,' Helen sounded.

'What?'

'You could just borrow my tux and have done with it.'

'Your tux is too big for me.'

Helen had a point though. In a full-length, long-sleeved, black silk dress, Dana would be barely distinguishable from the several hundred dinner-jacketed men she was expecting to meet at the Guildhall. The dress even had a white Peter Pan collar. Her hair, drawn into a tight bun at the back of her neck, completed the androgenous look.

'I don't want to stand out,' she said. 'Standing out doesn't feel wise.'

Helen was silent for a moment, then said, 'Probably not. How's the changeling?'

Dana directed the camera lens towards the cot that was still by her side of the bed. The tiny form lay motionless in the over-sized sleeping bag dotted with blue penguins. His arms stretched above his head in the classic infant sleeping pose and his mittened hands were scrunched into fists. A blue cap covered his dark hair, leaving only closed eyes, the curve of his cheeks and his perfect rosebud mouth visible. A sound, somewhere between a snore and a whimper, broke the silence.

'Sleeping like a baby,' Dana said.

'Shouldn't give Lacey too much trouble. How is she?'

Dana turned her back on the cot. 'You know Lacey, gives nothing away. Quieter than normal, I'd say, but holding up well. Look, I've got to go. Call you later.'

Dana lowered the light so that the room was in semi-darkness. A cry sounded as she eased the door closed, as though the infant in the cot sensed her leaving and was distressed by it. She felt a tug in her gut and told herself she was being stupid. Her child was perfectly safe.

Downstairs, she peered into the sitting room. Lacey, pale and tired-looking, was curled up in Helen's armchair. A uniformed female constable sat on the sofa. Neither of the two women looked comfortable, either with each other or the situation.

Lacey forced a smile. 'You look . . .' her voice tailed off. 'Great,' she added, without enthusiasm.

'Don't bother. I've heard it all from Helen.' Dana stuck out a foot. 'Trainers,' she announced, showing the black running shoe. 'In case I have to move fast.'

The woman in uniform looked troubled. Lacey said, 'Nothing's going to happen tonight.'

'Your car's outside,' the constable said.

'There's dinner in the fridge.' Dana pulled on her coat. 'It will microwave in a couple of minutes. The baby will be fine till around ten when he might start screaming. The bottle's in the fridge too. Thirty seconds in the microwave, shake it thoroughly and then test it on your wrist.'

Lacey held eye contact without blinking. 'We'll be fine. Have a good time.'

There was nothing else to say. With a nod, Dana left the room, pulling on her coat as she opened the front door. The night outside was cloudy, with rain threatening. She'd never in her adult life felt so reluctant to leave the house.

She climbed into the waiting car to be driven to the city.

88

BlackPill88 was typing. AryanBoy waited while the ellipsis refreshed itself: twice, three times, then . . .

Last check done. All good. I'm heading out first thing.

Nice work, buddy, Joker replied. *You packed?*

Copy that. All OK for tomorrow, boss?

Everything in place, AryanBoy wrote. When he was talking to the other two, he used the moniker MadHatter, only without the tiresome jokes. AryanBoy was, as Georgie had annoyingly worked out, an internet identity the three of them shared; or rather, he loaned it to the other two, allowed them to use it from time to time. It was his though, more than theirs. Increasingly, as time had gone on, AryanBoy had started to feel like who he really was.

You think she'll do it? Joker asked. *For real?*

I think she will, AryanBoy replied. *She's moved in with Tulloch and Rowley, is practically the kid's nanny right now. She's made it easy for herself.*

OK, this is it, he wrote, because he needed to get rid of the other two. He had stuff to be getting on with. *See you on the other side, gentlemen.*

The other two signed off, wishing each other well for the following day, and AryanBoy breathed a sigh of relief.

For the rest of the night, he was on his own.

He couldn't care less whether or not Lacey Flint planned to go along with his river stunt the next day. He wasn't going to give her the chance.

He was just waiting for one last signal. A lone foot soldier, posted on a street corner in Battersea.

Here it was. A one-line text. Dana Tulloch had left the building, en route to a fancy dinner at the Guildhall.

Time to move in.

89

'How old is he?' the constable, whose name was Elly, asked, as she and Lacey sat at the kitchen table finishing dinner. The intercom had just emitted a soft cry.

'About eight months,' Lacey replied.

'He's been quiet enough. Not that I know anything about babies.'

'Me neither,' Lacey admitted.

'Just saving them?'

Lacey got up to take her plate to the sink.

The constable said, 'That must have been terrifying?'

She wanted to talk about the rescue of the baby on the river, everyone who met Lacey these days did.

'I don't mind admitting, the river freaks me out,' Elly went on. 'Especially in winter. You'll be used to it though, working for the marine unit.'

Elly had been talking continually since Dana had left. It had helped, in a way, to have something to focus on, other than—

'It could so easily have gone wrong, when you went after the baby. I've seen the footage. The waves were massive. How did you keep the boat upright?'

Not waves, not really, just a bouncing of water where the wind lifted it, and the wind hadn't been too bad that September morning. It had been the wash from bigger boats that had been the real danger, and the risk of hitting a floating obstacle.

The wind was forecast to rise during the night and be close to force six by noon the next day. She would be taking her canoe out in a force six wind, something she'd never normally consider, even alone. And yet, in a little over twelve hours she would tie up on the south bank, collect that tiny infant upstairs from his nursery and take him out with her onto the river. The chances of either of them surviving unscathed were slim.

And that was assuming AryanBoy had been telling the truth, that he didn't have something else planned, something intended to take her entirely by surprise.

'How long have you been living here?' Elly asked.

'I moved in Monday night,' Lacey replied. 'Inigo came down with a cold, so couldn't go to nursery. Dana and Helen were a bit stuck, so I said I'd help out.'

'Good of you.'

'Not really. Things have been a bit mental at work. I was glad of a break.'

The last two days had been anything but. Stuck in the house with the baby and their police protection, pushing his pram for what felt like miles around the streets of Battersea, expecting, any moment, for AryanBoy to make his move, Lacey had never been so on edge.

Hourly calls from Dana hadn't exactly helped.

And nothing had happened. It was starting to look like Aryan-Boy had been serious, that he really did intend her to take Inigo out on the river the next day.

'That's yours,' Elly said, startling her.

Elly meant her phone. She reached across, lifted it and in the act of handing it to Lacey, sneaked a look at the screen. 'Oh my God,' she said. 'I know that face. That's, what's-he-called?'

It was Fergus Lord.

'Hi.' Leaving the kitchen, closing the door on a curious Elly, Lacey walked the length of the hall.

After asking her how she was, he said, 'What are you up to tonight?'

'Babysitting.'

A second's pause. 'For real? God, do you have a kid?'

'Dana's baby. That's my boss, you met her that day we came to your house.'

Another few seconds of silence. 'Want some company?'

Lacey felt her ribcage tightening. She'd known AryanBoy could make his move any time. Was this it?

'You mean now? I thought you were going to the Guildhall dinner.'

He gave a heavy sigh. 'Couldn't face it. Not after everything that's happened. Truth is, Lacey, things have been getting me down. Being arrested on Friday, it was a bit of a wake-up call.'

This wasn't news. Lord had been very obviously shaken when the two of them had met for coffee the following day. The police became blasé about arrests, not realising the impact the process could have on people who weren't used to the judicial system.

He said, 'I'm beginning to wish I hadn't started this whole UNITY business. You're a good listener, Lacey. I can't be the first person to tell you that.'

She said, 'Where's Charlie?'

'We don't live together. He has his own life. Seriously, an hour? The baby must be in bed. I can bring a bottle?'

She'd set out on a course; no choice now but to see it through. 'We'll be chaperoned,' she warned. 'I have a police constable with me. She's my bodyguard. And the baby's too, I guess.'

A note of amusement crept into his voice. 'Again, I ask, for real?'

'I'm a person of interest to the MenMatter movement and the city is on high alert. I'm not being left alone at the moment.'

If Lord backed down now, that would tell her something, wouldn't it?

'Well, I guess I get two for the price of one. So, can I come round?'

Sometimes, the only way to fight the lion was to walk right into its den. She gave Dana's address; he told her he'd be thirty minutes.

As she returned to the kitchen, the baby monitor sprang into life.

Elly looked alarmed. 'It's nowhere near ten o'clock. Are we supposed to feed him?'

Lacey turned on her heels. 'Dana said this might happen. I'll go up.'

The cries gained in volume.

'Good luck.'

In Dana and Helen's room, Lacey lifted the child. He was warm and heavy in her arms as she paced, his cries gradually weakening and fading, as Dana had told her would happen. When he'd been quiet for several seconds, she lowered him slowly, surprised at how empty her arms felt after she'd returned him to the cot.

From downstairs she heard the sound of knocking. Lord had arrived early. Leaving Elly to enjoy his company for a few minutes Lacey crossed to the bathroom. She heard Elly greeting the new arrival, the door closing and then two sets of footsteps on the hall tiles. After checking she didn't have spinach in her teeth, Lacey gave a last glance towards the cot.

An odd silence greeted her downstairs. Elly had cleared the kitchen, putting crockery and cutlery in the dishwasher and wiping down the surfaces. No sign of either her or Lord. There was a hint of fresh air in the room, as though the back door had been opened within the last few minutes.

'Elly?' she called.

No answer.

Nervous now, Lacey left the kitchen. The front door was closed, the chain still attached. She pushed open the door to the sitting room, saw a corner of the room, Helen's empty armchair.

'You two in here?'

No response. Heart thumping, Lacey stepped inside. The slumped body of the policewoman lay half across the sofa. Lacey darted forward, crouched at the woman's side and reached for the pulse point on her neck.

She heard the creaking floorboard, was on the point of turning round, when the agonising pain shot through her body.

The world went dark.

90

The mediaeval great hall at London's Guildhall could seat up to six hundred people. Even at less than capacity, it felt hot, over-crowded and claustrophobic. The stone arches didn't seem high enough to take away the buzz and crackle of hundreds of male voices, and the huge statues of Nelson, Wellington, both Pitts and the founding giants, Gog and Magog only emphasised the maleness of the place. Even the evening's colour scheme felt oppressive, the great stone façades washed alternately in purple, deep blue and bottle green. A screen beneath the stained-glass windows showed clips of high-achieving men and boys on a loop: they won races, scaled impossible peaks, vaccinated black child-ren in faraway lands.

Dana's instinct to wear anonymous black had been the right one; this was not an environment where women were welcome. More than anything she regretted the last-minute developments that had taken Helen away. Helen wouldn't have been fazed by all this. Nothing got in Helen's way.

A hand touched down lightly on her shoulder and Dana turned to see Georgie, the young woman from Mark's team. Putting a sealed envelope on the table Georgie turned and made her way through the cluster of tables towards the exit. Dana ripped open the seal. The handwritten note inside read:

We need to talk to you. Urgent.

*

Georgie was waiting in the entrance hall. In a low voice, she said, 'When I drove DCI Joesbury back to Scotland Yard last Thursday night he said that if any of us thought of anything, we should speak to you.'

Dana said, 'And have you?'

'Possibly. And if I'm right, we need to move quickly. Can you come with us to Scotland Yard? Archie's there too. He's been following a lead of his own. He thinks he knows how Mr Joesbury was set up.'

Dana's coat was in the cloakroom, but precious minutes would be lost while she retrieved it. 'Do you have a car?' she asked.

Georgie nodded.

'Let's go.'

91

Blackness all around. Lacey couldn't get her breath, couldn't move. A terrible pain in her head. And the baby crying. What the hell was happening?

A distant roar. Movement. A smell of engines and fuel. Lacey was thrown forward, came up against something solid, then thrust backwards again. Spasms of pain shot through her body, this time from her arm, trapped beneath her. Something was pressing against her face; what little air she had was hot and sour.

Was she awake or trapped in a horrible dream? Cramp grabbed hold of her lower leg. More pain, and rising panic. She was encased in something – a sack, a bag – she could feel the soft sheen of artificial fabric against her face.

The policewoman – Elly – slumped face down on the sofa. She couldn't remember reaching her, had no idea whether she was alive or dead.

The crying continued. The baby was close by.

Lacey grasped the fabric with both hands and pulled it apart in a desperate attempt to tear it. The fabric held but one of her hands brushed against something cold, rough, familiar. A zip.

Telling herself to be calm, to breath slowly, her fingers traced the course of the zip up and above her head. She reached the end but couldn't feel the metal tag that would open it. Finding the other end was harder, especially in the cramped space, but after several panic-stricken minutes, the fingers of her right hand closed around the tiny piece of metal. She eased it up, past her knees, her waist, her face. The air became marginally fresher, but she was still in a confined space, still in the dark.

She reached out, touched something hard and cold. Her kicking feet met resistance. Her back ached, her head felt like her skull had been prised apart. She was curled up in a foetal position, could feel rough matting under her cheek.

And she was moving. The metal box she was trapped inside was in motion.

She was locked in the boot of a car. And the baby she'd been charged with protecting was somewhere in the car too.

92

Grateful for the trainers, Dana followed Georgie at a half run along the corridor and into the office at Scotland Yard where Mark's cyber squad were based. The big room was empty apart from Archie Leech at his own desk.

'Hundred per cent,' he told Georgie, after nodding a greeting at Dana. 'The boss is in the clear.'

'What? How?' Dana looked from one to the other. 'What have you found?'

'We should go into his room,' Archie said. 'We can talk in there.'

He led the way, Georgie followed and Dana brought up the rear. Chairs were pulled out. Archie and Georgie sat down. Reluctantly, Dana did the same.

'Who's going first?' Georgie said.

'You,' Archie told her. 'Yours is more significant.' He glanced at Dana. 'No offence, I know we need to get the boss out, but this needs urgent action.'

'We think, perhaps, we might have been on the wrong track all along,' Georgie said. 'We've been preparing for a terrorist attack, because these people have been behaving like terrorists since they came to our notice, but what if it's something different?'

Dana said, 'I'm not following.'

Georgie said, 'Right from the start, there's been something of the charade about the MenMatter movement. They've been trying too hard to create an illusion of something they're not.'

'Smoke and mirrors,' Archie added. 'It's all been about attention. Like a good magician, directing us to look a certain way, so we don't see what he's really up to.'

'I should have spotted it sooner.' Georgie looked miserable. 'But they're good. That stunt with the baby, we'd never seen anything like it. And then the massage parlour, Emma's kidnap, the acid attack. All the really aggressive messaging. Of course, we took them at their word.'

'They've been drip-feeding us,' Archie said. 'Hitting us with new threats, keeping up the pressure, continually talking about a Day of Retribution, so we all started second-guessing and panicking about a massive attack. They knew we'd home in on International Men's Day, it was too obvious, and that took us to the conference at the QEII Centre. Then they started the chatter about home-made bombs. They had that van driving round Westminster, knowing it'd be picked up on camera. They wanted all our focus on stopping a major incident tomorrow, so we wouldn't see the real game.'

'Which is?'

'I only started to suspect when I realised they'd created these elaborate online personas,' Georgie said. 'And that they were taking it in turns to be AryanBoy. I figured if they could do that, they might be deceiving us about something else too, something bigger.'

Archie jumped in again. 'And they had this massive resource of frustrated and unhappy men who were like a powder keg, waiting to explode. They've exploited miserable young men all over the UK, goaded them into lots of small-scale intimidatory attacks and some serious criminal offences. They've all been fooled too, they thought they were part of something big, something that would change the world.'

Georgie said, 'I've been what we call deep-mining into the online posts of Jack Brine, Fergus Lord and Charlie Frost. Some of it, like Snapchat, I can't access, but they've all been active on Facebook, Twitter and Instagram for years. I was looking for stuff that I could link to the posts made by the four leaders of MenMatter. You know, repeated phrases, the same opinion expressed by, say Brine and BlackPill. If Jack Brine had repeatedly expressed an interest in suicide, for example, it would be another piece of circumstantial evidence against him. If Charlie Frost's posts exhibited the same sort of rage we see in Joker's, again, a steer in the right direction.'

'Close to meaningless individually,' Archie added, 'but with enough examples, we would have been on the way to building a case.'

Dana nodded to show that she was following.

'And I found nothing,' Georgie said.

'Nothing?' Dana wondered where the hell this was going.

'Nothing to suggest that Brine, Frost or Lord had ever been even remotely sympathetic to the incel cause. Quite the opposite, if anything. Lord has a history of long-standing girlfriends, he married young, he's not been short of female companionship since his divorce. Brine and Frost aren't in the same league but they've had girlfriends, even steady ones from time to time.' Georgie shook her head to emphasise her point. 'They're not incels.'

Dana took a moment. 'So, we're wrong. They're not the ones behind MenMatter? We're looking for someone else entirely?'

She felt despair sweeping over her. Except, these two weren't despairing, far from it. She'd rarely seen people more keyed up. Georgie was practically squirming in her seat.

'No, they are,' she said to Dana. 'It's just their motivation is entirely different.'

'So, what are they really up to?'

Georgie looked at Archie, he gave her an encouraging nod.

'We think it's about money,' Georgie said.

'Money?'

'That's what they've obsessed about over the years. Even Lord, who doesn't do too badly for himself, has been complaining about how little British actors earn compared to their US counterparts. They post houses, fast cars, yachts in the Med: aspirational, envious posts. They're all very financially motivated.'

Archie said, 'They've been particularly interested in high-level heists and fraud. They watch movies in which glamorous players pull off clever ruses and walk away with a fortune. They've played it down a lot this last year, but I'd say in the past, they've been close to obsessed. Oh, and up until a year ago, they were all friends on Facebook, and followed each other on Instagram and Twitter. When Brine claims he's not in touch with the other two, he's lying.'

Well, that was something at least, they could use that.

'Hold on,' Dana said. 'How does that square with AryanBoy's telephone calls? With the videos he's released. I've been over them so many times I can quote them word for word. His rage is palpable. He really hates women. You can't fake that strength of feeling.'

'With respect, ma'am, they're actors, all three of them, not just Lord,' Georgie told her. 'They were all in that photograph Lacey saw, of the production of *A Midsummer Night's Dream*. AryanBoy's been reading from a script.'

It didn't feel right, somehow, but these two seemed so sure of themselves.

'But MenMatter isn't a well-resourced organisation,' Dana complained, remembering Helen's explanation of how terror groups were funded. 'Everything they've done so far has been pretty low key. Nasty, but low key.'

Georgie shook her head. 'Not so,' she said. 'Potentially, they're sitting on a fortune,' she went on. 'Archie's pulled it all together. Look . . .'

She shoved a notepad in front of Dana.

'The crowdfunders for the people arrested so far on terrorism offences have raised nearly half a million quid, mainly small donations from individual people,' Archie explained. 'The online games could have generated several million, and over a million is sitting in UNITY's coffers.'

Dana shook her head. 'That's not a lot of money. Not to risk something like this.'

'International Men's Day raises upwards of ten million annually,' Archie said. 'Twelve million last year and that could skyrocket this year. Think about it, ma'am. For months now the country's been talking about men's issues and whether men have a hard time of it compared to women. Awareness is massive. And, this is the crucial part, most of the money generated by International Men's Day comes in on the day itself, and in the few days immediately afterwards. It's one of the biggest charity fundraising events in the UK.'

'MenMatter and UNITY have been working in tandem,' Georgie said. 'MenMatter raise awareness, using shock tactics, and then UNITY channel it into official outlets. How many times have we heard Fergus Lord say, *If you're concerned about men's issues, do something positive? Donate to men's charities. Volunteer for men's causes.* That twelve million could double this year. Add that to what's come in through the other channels and you're looking at sums upwards of twenty-five million.'

That was a lot of money; more than enough.

'And Jack Brine has designed the website that supports it,' Dana said. 'But how can MenMatter access that cash? The donations all go directly to the charities.'

Archie turned his laptop so that Dana could see it. 'This is their home page. You can see the thirty different charities here.'

Dana glanced down at the list of charities that people all over the UK would be encouraged to support that week: *Lads Need Dads, Future Men, The ManKind Initiative, Baggy Trousers, Prostate Cancer UK.*

'Here's what I think they've done,' Archie said. 'Because, frankly, it's what I'd do, and it wouldn't be hard. I think they've built another payment system, virtually identical to the official one currently sitting behind the International Men's Day website. Sometime soon they'll deactivate the official system and replace it with the compromised one. When all the donations start flooding in tomorrow, they'll be channelled off to a bank account that these guys own.'

Georgie said, 'The recipient charities will receive a notification that they're about to receive money, so they think all is well, and it might be several days later before they realise it isn't actually in their bank accounts. By the time the owners of the main website – the trust behind International Men's Day – cotton on, the money is long gone.'

'When?' Dana said. 'When would they do this?'

'My guess is tonight,' Archie replied. 'Donations have been coming in steadily over the last few weeks as awareness has built. I know this because I've checked directly with several of the charities today. I'm thinking sometime in the early hours, when no one from any of the charities will be awake and checking, and when they'd naturally expect donations to stop anyway. When the money starts to flood in tomorrow, it won't be going to the charities.'

'So, no big terror attack?' Dana said.

'No, but a bloody big money heist in the next few hours,' Archie said.

Dana got to her feet. 'We need the commissioner. She can authorise the suspension of that website account. And we can pull all three of them in again so they can't do any damage.'

'Ma'am, we found something else,' Georgie said. 'At least I think we have.'

Archie took over. 'I think I know how they've framed the boss. I found something—'

'Save it,' Dana said. 'Mark isn't going anywhere. We need to get that website closed down.'

Her phone started ringing. It was Neil Anderson.

'We're at your house, Dana,' he said, as something cold and hard gripped hold of Dana's stomach. 'I'm not going to sugarcoat this, it's a massive cock-up.'

Neil Anderson and Pete Stenning had been in an unmarked car in Dana's street, an unofficial addition to the uniformed presence there. They were supposed to be watching Lacey and the baby.

Dana put her phone on the table and switched it to speaker. 'Go on,' she told him.

'Fergus Lord parked his car a short way from your house about twenty minutes ago,' Neil went on. 'Trouble is, uniform spotted him first and challenged him. We didn't know what to do for the best, to be honest. He was arguing, uniform looked on the verge of taking him in, so I sent Pete out to intervene. I took my eyes off your house. Not for long, but it was enough. When I looked again, Lacey's car was gone.'

'Lacey left?'

'We had to check at that point. I didn't get an answer, either from knocking or ringing her mobile, so I looked through the front window. The female constable keeping an eye on Lacey was slumped over the sofa.'

Dana was conscious of scared glances shooting between Archie and Georgie.

'She was unconscious,' Neil went on. 'The ambulance is taking her away now.'

'What about Lacey?' Dana said. 'And—'

'No sign of Lacey or the baby,' Neil said. 'I'm sorry, Dana, they're both gone.'

93

Lacey lost track of time, drifting between layers of consciousness, summoning up the energy to hammer on the metal roof of the boot when she sensed the vehicle had stopped. Once, she heard screaming, and knew the baby was close, inches away on the back seat, but the cries died away.

There should have been two police cars in the street outside Dana's house, one marked, one unmarked. No one should have been able to get her and the baby out of the house. She trusted Neil Anderson and Pete Stenning with her life. Where the hell were they?

Eventually, the smooth motion and subdued hum of wheels over tarmac gave way to a bumpier movement, with no sound but that of the engine. They'd left the road. The car lurched and swung, the engine revved hard; the vehicle dipped, the wheels spun. It struggled on and, finally, came to a stop. The engine was switched off. A car door opened.

Lacey tensed and flexed the muscles in her feet, hands, shoulders. Other than the dry-cleaning bag, which she'd shrugged off, she wasn't bound. She had to be ready.

A click. Fresh air on her face. The boot was open.

She raised one hand; it met the metal of the lid. More cold air; a slice of night sky visible. She pushed, opening the boot. Wind grabbed her hair, a smell – strange but bringing with it a distant memory – rushed up to meet her, and high above her head, avian creatures screamed their welcome back.

She knew where she was, even before she looked around. She was at Eastbourne, high above the sea at Beachy Head, where her life as it was now had begun. Where Lacey Flint – the real Lacey Flint – had tumbled to a watery grave.

Knowing she was a jolt of pain from throwing up, she climbed out of the boot and let her unsteady legs make their best effort to support her. By clinging to the rim of the boot for several seconds, she realised she'd been abducted in her own car.

That wasn't good.

At a distance, she could see the man who'd brought her here: a shadowy, distorted figure on the clifftop. He seemed to be swaying in the wind, as though moving to a music only he could hear, and in his arms he clutched a bundle.

He had the baby.

Lacey moved slowly, making her way over the uneven heathland, keeping one hand on the car at first, because she didn't quite trust her balance. The keys were in the ignition. He obviously thought the baby in peril would be enough of a lure to get her to the cliff edge.

He was wrong about that. She almost jumped into the driver's seat and reversed back to the road, leaving him to do his worst. But AryanBoy, Adam Ryan, the man at the centre of all this, was standing with his back to her, a dark coat masking his shape, and if she were to confront him, once and for all, if she were to bring his power over her to an end, she would have to approach.

Ten large strides would take her to his side.

She took the first step, feeling the wind pulling her back. The night was dark, darker even than the last time she'd been here, with cloud cover hiding moon and stars. She could barely see the ground at her feet. Only a subtle colour change marked the cliff edge.

Her ears were filled with sound: the bluster of the wind, waves crashing, gulls screaming at her to get back, get in the car and drive away, what the hell did she think she was doing. So very different to the silence that had greeted her last time.

Five strides to go and the man on the clifftop hadn't moved. He was very close to the edge, although he must know the cliffs around the south coast were notoriously unstable, that they crumbled continually, that the wise kept their distance. The wind picked up, her foot caught in a tangle of coarse grass. Three strides to go.

Two strides. She could see the paler gleam of his skin between coat collar and hat. One stride. She took it and joined him on the cliff edge. His face was still in shadow.

'Hello Lacey,' he said, with no trace of the Midlands accent that had fooled them all on the phone.

He held the child, swaddled in the blue check blanket that Dana had hung over the foot of Inigo's cot. As though to greet her, a sound drifted over on the wind, something between a hiccup and a cry. And then he bent and laid the bundle on the ground at his feet. The baby was less than two feet from the cliff edge.

He said, 'Except that's not your name, is it?'

'In the end, we decide our own names,' she replied. 'Whether we stay with the one we were assigned or take a different path, we make the choice. I choose to be Lacey Flint.'

And it was true, she realised, even as she spoke the words. She had become Lacey Flint on this very spot, and it wasn't a façade any more. Lacey Flint was who she was.

'Question is,' she said. 'Who do you choose to be?'

He turned and she knew him at last. She knew the shape of his face, the sweep of his hair, his hooked nose and full lips. The boy from the clifftop twelve years ago and the young civilian member of the Met who worked alongside the man she loved.

'Theo.' She'd been right then, days ago, when she'd guessed AryanBoy's identity. 'You weren't blond. Twelve years ago, you weren't blond.'

'Neither were you,' he said. 'It was another bond between us, or so I thought.'

He'd been shorter too, and fatter, but boys grew even in their late teens, and with a bit of hard work, they could change their shape.

He broke eye contact, staring instead out to sea. 'We were doing *A Midsummer Night's Dream* at school,' he told her. 'I was Nick Bottom. The director didn't think Aryan blond worked for the role so he talked the house master into letting me dye it.'

Of course. He had told her a name after all. *I'm Nick,* he'd said, too nervous to tell her his real name. *I didn't ask,* she'd replied, and wiped it from her mind.

He'd been in the school photograph too, along with Fergus Lord, Jack Brine and Charlie Frost; unrecognisable, because he'd worn a donkey's head over his own.

'You broke me, that night,' he said. 'All I needed was a kind word, and I'd have been OK. I thought you were there to save me.'

'Maybe I did. You seem to have done OK. Maybe we saved each other.'

He shook his head. 'It took me years to get over that night. Actually, I'm not sure I ever did. Everything that's gone wrong for me since, I can trace back to that night.'

'Nothing to do with me.'

He turned to face her fully then, fury in his eyes. 'Everything to do with you. I asked you, would you date someone like me and you could have said yes. You could have lied.'

His self-obsession was close to laughable, or would be, if it weren't so dangerous.

Inches from his feet, the baby uttered a plaintive cry.

She said, 'Believe it or not, I had more things on my mind than soothing your ego. And, for what it's worth, I worked out who you were days ago. I've been expecting this.'

True, she'd expected a challenge, but not one that would succeed so well. She hadn't expected he'd be able to bypass her protection and get her out of the house.

'How?' The question burst from him, as though he'd spoken without thinking. 'I look nothing like how I did back then.'

Lacey told herself that backup might not be far behind; the number-plate recognition systems on many of the UK's main roads could have picked up her car.

'You gave yourself away on the phone with that comment about my hair,' she told him. 'It was up when we met in Mark's flat, because I'd just come from work. But it was giving me a headache, so I took it down in the car. When you phoned me at the creek it was loose. I knew you couldn't see me then, but I knew you'd only have risked claiming you could if you'd seen me within the hour. Plus, we've known for a while one of the incel leaders works at Scotland Yard. It all pointed to you.'

He gulped in air, seemed on the verge of spitting at her, but spoke instead. 'It makes no difference. You won't have told anyone. You've too much to hide.'

'I haven't told anyone who you are, that's true.'

'Jump,' he said.

'What?'

'Jump. Go on, do it. It'll be over in seconds. Or not. I haven't forgotten what you told me that night. Maybe you'll lie on the beach in agony for hours before you die. Either way, you're going over the edge.'

The wind picked up, catching hold of the baby's blanket, making both of them glance down. The child was too close to the edge; a strong gust could send it over.

'If you jump, I'll let the baby live,' he said. 'I'll put it in the back seat of your car and make an anonymous phone call to the local plod. It'll be fine.'

'And if I don't?'

'The brat goes first, then I come for you. You took a blow to the head earlier. I can run the 400 metres in 55 seconds. I really don't think you can outpace me.'

He'd throw the baby anyway; he'd already tried to kill one infant. Unable to stop herself, she glanced round at the road.

'There's no one coming,' he said. 'Those uniformed idiots back in Battersea were too busy arresting Fergus Lord to see me leaving.'

Neil and Pete would have seen though. Where were they?

'So, which are you?' she said. 'When you're not being Aryan-Boy. Are you Joker or MadHatter?'

'MadHatter,' he said with an odd note of pride. 'Charlie's Joker and, as you guessed, Jack's BlackPill88. He's the weak link, to be honest. If it weren't for his website skills we'd have dumped him months ago.'

'Fergus Lord?'

Theo gave a disparaging toss of his head. 'The useful idiot. Genuinely thinks he's doing the right thing by men and boys in the UK.'

Well, that was something. She'd liked Gus.

'Seems to me you're the weak link,' she said. 'Letting personal vengeance get in the way of whatever you've got planned tomorrow.'

He laughed. 'You're not here for vengeance, Lacey.' And then he smiled, a long, slow, nasty smile. 'Well, not just vengeance, that's the icing on the cake. You're here because I work with your boyfriend. I've avoided bumping into you the past few weeks but I knew sooner or later, you'd remember me. You have to go. Sorry and all that.'

He took a step towards her. Then another. She backed away.

'I agree with you on one thing,' she said. 'One of us isn't walking away this time. I think it should be you.'

He shook his head. 'Not going to happen.'

'Funny you should mention my boyfriend,' she said, keeping on the move, conscious she could trip easily on the rough ground. 'He said something months ago, when we were on another job. I've never forgotten it.'

She risked another quick look round, at the car. Her keys were in the ignition, but it was too far away and he was gaining on her.

Lacey held up a hand, a stop-where-you-are gesture. 'You need to hear this.'

He paused.

'He said, whenever you can, use the enemy's playbook against them.'

Theo shook his head, opened his mouth to speak, and took another step towards her.

'You didn't look at him, did you?' Lacey went on. 'Not properly. You just grabbed him from his cot and threw him in the back of the car. It's to your credit, I suppose, that you didn't want to look at him.'

Theo's eyes narrowed. He stopped moving, then turned and retraced his footsteps back to where the child lay on the cliff edge. As though sensing what was coming, it started crying again.

Unable to help herself, Lacey followed.

She watched Theo stare down at the baby for a second, then bend and move the blanket aside. He gave a howl of rage, and picked the child up again.

She watched as he threw the bundle into the air and kicked at it. The tiny form, still wrapped in a blue checked blanket, soared through the dark sky before sinking from sight.

The kick threw Theo off balance. His arms began to flail. For a second, she thought he'd fall backwards, landing heavily but safely on the rough heathland. He didn't. He regained his balance.

A split second before the cliff edge began to crumble.

He scrambled back then, but each step he took dislodged more of the unstable chalk ground. He twisted to face her, as though to throw himself forward, and his hands reached out. They were inches from her own. Their fingers met, and she knew if he grasped hold of her, they'd both tumble.

She did what she had to.

Theo's eyes, horrified, disbelieving, met hers for a fraction of a second. Then feet first, he vanished.

He was much heavier than the baby, Lacey thought, as she heard the sound of waves crashing against rocks. He might even land first.

94

Helen picked up the phone after seven rings, when Dana was on the point of screaming.

'Show him to me,' she demanded. 'Show him to me now.'

Her partner sounded half asleep. 'Dana, what the hell?'

'Just do it.'

'He's upstairs. OK, hang on.'

Helen stopped talking as she moved quickly through the house in Lanarkshire where her parents lived. Dana caught glimpses of stairs, a landing, a bedroom door, then finally, at last, her sleeping son in the travel cot in Helen's parents' spare room; entirely oblivious to the adventures his doppelganger had been having hundreds of miles away.

Helen held the camera in place for several seconds, then raised it to her own face.

'If it helps, I can confirm he's breathing,' she said.

Dana burst into tears.

After a few moments, Helen said, 'I'm guessing something's happened?'

'He came to our house two hours ago. He took Lacey and the – the other one.'

'The changeling?' Helen said, referring to the nickname the two of them had given to the fake baby, otherwise known as an infant simulator, the same one that had plummeted over the Thames embankment wall, and that Dana had retrieved from evidence after learning of AryanBoy's latest threat.

'What's going on,' Helen said. 'Is Lacey OK?'

Fighting for breath, Dana told Helen about Lacey's encounter on Beachy Head with Theo Cox, one of the key members of Mark's cyber squad, who was now believed to be the man known as AryanBoy.

'There's a team trying to recover his body,' she said. 'He threw the baby over the cliff, Helen. He just threw it. It would have been Ini.'

Helen moved back to the travel cot and leaned in to feel the warmth of her safe, living son. For several seconds, she seemed unable to speak.

Then, 'He's OK, Dana. He's really OK.'

Dana was still crying. 'We're not, though, are we?'

'No,' Helen agreed, as tears started to roll down her cheeks too. 'But we will be.'

95

A few days later . . .

They said goodbye to Emma at the park entrance and watched her hurry away in the direction of Chelsea Bridge, scrolling through text messages as she went.

'She'll be too important to know us soon,' Helen said, tucking her arm through Dana's.

Emma was on her way to Marsham Street to conduct the first televised interview with the new home secretary, a black woman whose grandparents had been of the Windrush generation. The camera was to be positioned on the scarred side of Emma's face, supposedly sending out a very clear message that women should be valued for their talents, not their looks.

'It's a step in the right direction, I suppose,' Emma had conceded. 'But I'm going to get some flack for it on Twitter.'

Less than a week after International Men's Day, there were signs that the online bile directed at women was starting to die down. The publicised arrests, and one death, of the Men-Matter leaders had helped, but it would take time. A similar story could be told about real-life violence against women. There'd been fewer incidents over the past few days than in the weeks leading up to International Men's Day, but they were still occurring.

Mark's team was still monitoring incel movement on the dark web and were reasonably confident it was losing steam. Dana had to hope they were right.

The two women – Dana pushing Inigo in his pram – returned to the park. It felt like the first fine day in ages – blue sky, no wind, the air sharp on exposed skin – and yet she still had an unreasonable urge to get home, away from the random men who might look normal, but who secretly harboured a grudge against her, her partner and their child.

It wasn't over yet.

The conference at the QEII Centre had attracted the anticipated protests, with several arrests and injuries, but Archie and Georgie had been right when they'd worked out that MenMatter had been all about money. No bomb had exploded, no gunman had run amok, no royal princess or female rights campaigner had been murdered. The day hadn't been nearly as bad as feared and that, in itself, had felt like a victory, albeit a small one. Maybe it was a sign of the new normal, that they expected less, were grateful for small mercies. *You haven't hurt us today; you've allowed us some measure of freedom back. Thank you.*

The website heist had been successfully foiled in the early hours of the morning and a record thirty-two million pounds had been raised for men's charities. One MP – male – had said publicly that he thought it a decent enough silver lining.

'It's good news that female MPs are coming back to parliament,' Helen said, as they left the north carriage drive to head towards the lake. Inigo always adored the waterfowl and Dana was half dreading the day he would walk, because she knew he'd be heading straight into the water at the first opportunity. 'And most have started holding surgeries again.'

'They're all being very brave,' Dana said. 'So is Emma.'

It wasn't over yet.

Sometimes, she feared it never would be, that something dark had been unleashed over the last few months, and that all over the world unstable, grievance-filled men had felt legitimised. Pandora's box was standing wide open.

96

A few minutes before sunset, a man and a woman were sailing a dingy on the lower reaches of the Thames, round about the midpoint between city and estuary. Both wore androgenous thermal wetsuits and life jackets, their hands gloved against the chill autumn air. Only the woman's hair, streaming out from her pony-tail like a queen's banner, properly distinguished one from the other. Late November, as light slips from the sky, might not be the wisest time to sail, but he'd been born on the Thames (literally), and she swam like a fish.

The water was smooth and still, the wind fresh and steady, and the boat was handling superbly; Joesbury judged they were push-ing ten knots.

'Charles Frost and Jack Brine were charged this morning.' He raised his voice to be heard above the wind. 'Your friend Gus was released without charge.'

'I really don't think he knew anything about it,' Lacey called back from her perch on the edge of the trapeze.

'Probably not,' Joesbury admitted. He would, if he were honest, be feeling a whole lot better if Fergus Lord were facing a few years behind bars, but that wasn't something he was ever going to say out loud.

In the hours since Theo Cox had fallen to his death from Beachy Head, and while Joesbury was still being held at Charing

Cross police station, the commissioner herself had taken charge of the investigation. Frost and Brine had been arrested that same night. With enough evidence to prove Brine had been behind the shadow, illegal website, the bloke had cracked and admitted everything. Both he and Frost were claiming to have known nothing about the murders at the massage parlour, Emma's kidnap, the acid attack at the leisure centre or the abduction of the baby, but as the commissioner had told Joesbury that morning, the Crown Prosecution Service were confident of building a strong enough case.

Joesbury himself had been released an hour before midnight on International Men's Day, following the work Archie and Georgie had done to prove his innocence. If Theo Cox, Jack Brine and Charlie Frost were good, Archie Leech, it turned out, was better. He'd found the malware tucked away on Joesbury's computer, planted in minutes, that allowed posts in AryanBoy's name to be made remotely, but which to all intents and purposes would look as though they'd been made from Joesbury's office computer. Theo had only needed to sneak into Joesbury's office and access his system once. Joesbury was facing a disciplinary charge himself, albeit a minor one, for not paying due care and attention to information security.

It was a fair cop.

'Ready about,' he announced, pulling in the mainsheet and swinging himself over to the port gunwale. Without being reminded, Lacey released the jib sheet, moving gracefully to join him on the port side before winding the sail in again. Only her first time out in a Laser and she was a natural. The boat sped back across the river towards the south bank.

Joesbury leaned down to check the surrounding water. This side of the barrier, pleasure craft were rare, but you had to watch out for commercial traffic, even so late in the day.

'Nice view of the back of Morrison's,' Lacey called.

Thamesmead on one bank, Dagenham on the other; it wasn't the most scenic stretch of the river. Not far from the estuary, the river was wide, the surrounding land low level, urban, filled with nondescript commercial and industrial properties.

He knew what he was doing.

A rogue wave burst over the bow. The wind dropped, the boat lost speed and its heel lessened.

'They stood to gain over thirty million from the charity heist alone.' Joesbury took advantage of the momentary calm. 'Brine had plans to leave the country, but they could have kept the money streams coming in from the various other channels for some time. With me out of the way, Theo would have continued to be a trusted member of the Met for as long as he chose.'

'He wouldn't have lasted long,' Lacey said, without meeting his eyes. 'There was something off about him. I think, unlike the other two, he was a real incel.'

She might have a point, at that. With the commissioner's backing, his team had pushed further at Goldman Sachs and learned that Theo had left the bank under a cloud, had been firmly encouraged to resign. While undeniably excellent at his job, several of his female colleagues had been reluctant to work with him, citing inappropriate comments, or just a feeling of uneasiness in his presence. It had been something other than the misogynist banter still all too common in some city firms, the head of HR had explained to Joesbury; something about Theo around women didn't feel right.

According to Jack Brine, who was still squealing like a stuck pig, getting Theo into a key post at Scotland Yard had been a crucial part of the group's plan; a way of ensuring the MenMatter movement always stayed one step ahead of those charged with tracking them down.

Joesbury turned the boat again, adjusting the main sail to accommodate the bend in the river. They sailed on, in silence, for a while.

'So how did you persuade Dana and Helen to get the baby out of the city?' he asked, when they were almost in sight of the Woolwich Ferry.

'Dana didn't need any persuasion. Once I told her what Theo wanted me to do, she was practically packing his bags.'

'You're going to be asked, you know, why Theo thought there was even a chance of you doing it. People will be wanting to know what he had on you.'

She wasn't looking at him when she replied. 'I'm going to say I don't think he ever expected me to. It was part of their smoke and mirrors campaign, to throw us off course.'

He thought for a moment. 'Yeah, they'll probably buy that.'

'Do you?' she asked.

He didn't. He knew Theo had had something on her, that there was still a hell of a lot she wasn't telling him. He told himself to focus on the important.

'Did he fall?' he asked.

The setting sun was just out of sight, but streaks of reflected gold, like fire across the water, were creeping out around the bend in the river.

Several seconds slipped by and she still hadn't replied.

'It stays between us,' he said. 'I won't blame you, I'd have pushed him over myself. But I need to know.'

'This again?'

Joesbury steered the Laser round the bend in the river and London unfolded before them against a backdrop of gold. The sky behind Canary Wharf and its surrounding towers was the colour of a ripe tangerine, and the lights of the Millennium Dome rose upwards like the crown of a great king. The beaten copper shells of the barrier piers, beautiful in any sunlight, were at their best at sundown, they gleamed an orange that seemed not quite of this world, sending streams of light across the water like bright carpets welcoming them home.

Lacey let her face break into a lazy smile and he knew exactly what she was thinking. There had been a time, shortly after they'd met, when he'd been convinced the woman he was falling in love with was really Victoria Llewellyn, prime suspect in the worst killings the capital had seen in decades. He'd even gone so far as arresting her in that name. She'd proven him wrong.

Or had she?

'I'm Lacey Flint,' she said, looking directly at him. 'And Lacey Flint isn't a killer.'

She turned away with an air of finality. It was all he was going to get. Then she turned back, surprising him again.

'Besides,' she said, 'we have more important things to worry about right now.'

'Do we. And what's that?'

She smiled again. 'I'm pregnant.'

Acknowledgements

Writing about the cyber world pushed me way out of my comfort zone, so I'm hugely grateful for the brilliance and patience of my young friend, Archie Licudi. All the clever stuff is down to him; the mistakes are mine. Thanks, also, to my brother-in-law, Gareth Cooper; the crane scene was his idea and his technical know-how helped to bring it about. Belinda Bauer was my go-to expert on creepy crawlies and Christina Anderson named my vigilante group – the Mama Bears.

My lovely editor Sam Eades went on maternity leave halfway through my writing of *The Dark*, but a talented trio of Sarah Benton, Rachel Neely and Fran Pathak stepped in to pull the book together.

My agent, Anne Marie Doulton, has excelled herself this year. Huge thanks to her and to the wonderful Buckman family too.

Who's Who in the Lacey Flint Series

Lacey Flint

Lacey was a promising young detective with the Metropolitan Police before one bad case too many prompted her to return to uniform policing and join the Met's marine unit. Now, living and working on the river, she's trying to put her turbulent past behind her. But Lacey is guarding many secrets, some of which, if they come to light, could blow her life apart. We first meet Lacey in the serial killer thriller, *Now You See Me* (Lacey Flint 1).

Mark Joesbury

Carving out a successful, if unconventional, career in the Met's covert operations unit, this newly promoted DCI was deeply suspicious of Lacey when they first met (*Now You See Me*). Well, she was covered in another woman's blood! Although soon drawn under her spell, Joesbury has never, quite, put aside his suspicions. He doesn't confess his feelings until the end of *Dead Scared* (Lacey Flint 2) when, for neither the first nor the last time, both their lives are on the line.

Huck Joesbury

Mark's twelve-year-old son, who likes to play cupid and is remarkably good at it. Huck was abducted in *Like This, For Ever* (Lacey Flint 3), but proved himself every bit as tough as his dad.

Dana Tulloch
A super bright but emotionally fragile detective inspector, best friend to Joesbury and recently married to the love of her life, Helen. The arrival of her infant son, Inigo, has threatened Dana's courage like nothing before or since. Years before she met Lacey, Dana hunted shadowy killers in Sharon's debut novel, *Sacrifice*, when she unwittingly became embroiled in a sinister cult. She still carries the scars. Literally.

Helen Rowley
Dana's life partner (who also appears in *Sacrifice*) and another senior police officer. Helen's pragmatism proves an essential counter to Dana's fragility, especially when the stakes are high. (As they so often are.)

Victoria Llewelyn
The beautiful but terrifying serial killer serving a whole life sentence in Durham prison for the murder of four women (*Now You See Me*). The world believes that Victoria and Lacey were friends in their late teens, when both were living rough on the streets of London, and that a long-standing loyalty drives Lacey's monthly visits to Durham. This is not true.

Cathy Llewelyn
Victoria's younger sister and fellow victim of the violent rape inflicted on both teenage girls, a crime that led, ultimately, to Victoria's reign of terror. The world believes that Cathy died in a riverboat accident, an event that pushed her unstable sister over the edge. This is not quite true.

Emma Boston

A smart, talented journalist who was drawn into the Ripper killings in *Now You See Me*. Two years down the line, she and Lacey are learning to trust each other and have started to call themselves friends.

David Cook

The superintendent in charge of the Marine Unit, fiercely protective of the tidal river Thames and standing for no nonsense. Except, it seems, where Lacey is concerned. We first meet Superintendent Cook in *A Dark and Twisted Tide* (Lacey Flint 4).

Credits

Orion Fiction would like to thank everyone at Orion who worked on the publication of *The Dark*.

Agent
Anne-Marie Doulton

Editor
Francesca Pathak
Rachel Neely
Sam Eades

Editorial Management
Georgia Goodall
Lucy Brem
Jane Hughes
Charlie Panayiotou
Tamara Morriss
Claire Boyle

Audio
Paul Stark
Jake Alderson
Georgina Cutler

Contracts
Anne Goddard
Ellie Bowker
Humayra Ahmed

Copy-editor
Francine Brody

Proofreader
Melissa Smith

Design
Nick Shah
Charlotte Abrams-Simpson
Joanna Ridley
Helen Ewing

Finance
Nick Gibson
Jasdip Nandra

Elizabeth Beaumont
Ibukun Ademefun
Afeera Ahmed
Sue Baker
Tom Costello

Inventory
Jo Jacobs
Dan Stevens

Marketing
Lucy Cameron

Production
Ruth Sharvell
Fiona McIntosh

Publicity
Alex Layt

Sales
Jen Wilson
Victoria Laws
Esther Waters
Frances Doyle
Ben Goddard
Jack Hallam
Anna Egelstaff
Inês Figueira

Barbara Ronan
Andrew Hally
Dominic Smith
Deborah Deyong
Lauren Buck
Maggy Park
Linda McGregor
Sinead White
Jemimah James
Rachael Jones
Jack Dennison
Nigel Andrews
Ian Williamson
Julia Benson
Declan Kyle
Robert Mackenzie
Megan Smith
Charlotte Clay
Rebecca Cobbold

Operations
Sharon Willis

Rights
Susan Howe
Krystyna Kujawinska
Jessica Purdue
Ayesha Kinley
Louise Henderson

About the Author

Sharon Bolton grew up in a cotton-mill town in Lancashire and had an eclectic early career in marketing and public relations. She gave it up in 2000 to become a mother and a writer.

Her first novel, *Sacrifice*, was voted Best New Read by Amazon. uk, while her second, *Awakening*, won the 2010 Mary Higgins Clark Award (part of the prestigious Edgars) in the US. She has been shortlisted for the CWA Gold Dagger, the Theakston's Prize for Best Thriller, the International Thriller Writers' Best First Novel Award, the Prix Du Polar in France and the Martin Beck Award in Sweden.

SHE'LL NEVER STOP RUNNING.

BUT HE'LL NEVER STOP LOOKING.

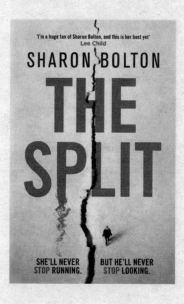

A year ago Felicity Lloyd fled England to South Georgia, one of the most remote islands in the world, escaping her past and the man she once loved. Can she keep running her whole life?

Freddie Lloyd has served time for murder – and now he wants her back. Wherever she is, he won't stop until he finds her. Will he be able to track her to the ends of the earth?

Together they'll find themselves trapped on the ice and in danger.

Who will survive?

THEY MADE A PROMISE, HER LIFE FOR THEIRS.

NOW, IT'S PAYBACK TIME.

A golden summer, and six talented friends are looking forward to the brightest of futures –
until a daredevil game goes horribly wrong, and a woman and two children are killed.

18-year-old Megan takes the blame, leaving the others free to get on with their lives. In
return, they each agree to a 'favour', payable on her release from prison.

Twenty years later Megan is free.
Let the games begin . . .

Have you read all the thrillers in the Lacey Flint series?

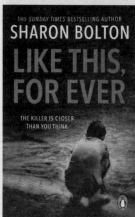